A SHADE OF MYSELF

A HUMOROUS PARANORMAL WOMEN'S FICTION

DEBORAH WILDE

te
da — te da media inc.
vancouver

1

PHONE CALLS AT 3AM MEANT ONLY ONE THING: someone was dead.

The caller was Tatiana, so clearly the dead person wasn't her, even though my boss was in her eighties. My adrenaline rush blunted my grogginess while I quickly sorted through which of my friends or loved ones had bit the dust. It made for an interesting cocktail of super wired and slow on the uptake, and by the time I'd understood that Tatiana was phoning about a quick job, I was halfway to my car, keys in hand, hospital bound.

Yawning and knocking on the wood and glass front door of the client's mansion on swanky Point Grey Road, I wished that I'd worn more than a light sweater over my pajamas. When no one answered, I double-checked the address, though with the electronica on full blast inside that sent vibrations up through my feet out here on the stoop, that was hardly surprising. I tentatively pushed the door open, following the music down a hallway past an Ansel Adams photograph on the wall. Unlike the identical one that I'd hung in my dorm room, this wasn't a mass reproduction.

"Hello?" I called out. "Tatiana sent me."

I'd been working for the elderly artist as her archivist and magic fixer minion for almost two months now, and it had its ups and downs. Tonight's job promised to be a quick in and done, though the last time I'd assumed the assignment would be simple, I'd ended up with a human heart on my passenger seat, vaulting me into one of the top spots as the murder suspect.

The slap of my shoes on the intricate mosaic tile made me suspicious that—yup, I was wearing slippers. They were green and fuzzy with a fake fur trim that clashed with my orange pajamas, although given how much the place stank of weed, our client, Davide Forino, probably wouldn't notice my lapse in professional attire. Tatiana had warned me he was a snowboarding celeb and rumored to be constantly stoned.

I put my hand over my mouth and nose to minimize the chances of getting a contact high. I had no problem with pot, especially not now that marijuana was legal, but I had to drive home. Unfortunately, that left only one hand free to plug my ears against the pounding bass and its sassy conga line in my back molars. With my right hand over my mouth and my left in my ear, I felt like I was playing a children's game.

I stopped on the threshold to the airy living room and bellowed out, "Could you please turn that down?"

A pause, and then the music was lowered to barely tolerable levels, but my ears still rung.

"What?" a man drawled in a dazed voice.

I snorted.

He was sitting, back toward me, in a chair shaped like a scorpion spine that probably cost as much as a new car and resembled a Delia Deetz creation from *Beetlejuice*. Presumably the sitter was staring out the floor-to-ceiling windows at the gently rippling waves with crests of foamy white, which met the inky darkness of an endless night sky.

Oh, to have a view like that. Give me this guy's decorating

budget and I'd have installed long bookcases and comfortable seating in decadent fabrics, not this ridiculously shaped bull-shit that no one could lounge on. Other than a pizza box tossed on the ground, the all-white room was spotless, which meant he had a cleaning service, because he sure as hell wasn't applying that elbow grease.

I hated him a little more.

"I'm Miriam." I stepped over the pizza box and entered the room. "You texted Tatiana Cassin about sensitive material that you needed magically disposed?"

"I did?" Davide spun the chair around, looking like Shaggy after a bender. Which, come to think of it, was what Shaggy always looked like. Except Davide was also scratched up. He took a drag off a joint, ashes dropping onto a ratty plaid bathrobe that fell almost to his knees. At least it was tied tightly, sparing me the sight of dark, thick chest hair covering his torso like a pelt. Or worse.

I took a very long, very slow breath. "Yes. You did."

Davide darted a wary look behind his sofa at—I tried to follow his gaze—his laptop sitting on a bookshelf crowded with snowboarding trophies? Was there a file he wanted scrubbed? My hacker skills only went as far as emptying the trash.

"If it's something electronic—" I said.

"It's not." He exhaled hard then stood up with a grim expression. With the joint clamped in the corner of his mouth, he scratched his belly, picking the bathrobe out of his ass with his other hand. Who said men couldn't multitask? "Over here, dude."

I gave a wide berth to the mangy French bulldog on the large white carpet, snoring and drooling on a chipped statue of a reclining leopard. "Is the dog friendly?"

Davide shrugged and blew out a stream of skunk-scented air. "No clue. Never seen him before tonight."

3

I dug my nails into my palms. He was getting on my last mom nerve.

He opened the sliding doors, letting in a stiff breeze from the water. It ruffled my hair, making me shiver, though I appreciated the fresh air coming in as the stench from his joint vented outside.

I crossed my arms over my very cold nipples, which were now pokey enough to press elevator call buttons, stumbling to a stop behind the sofa when I saw the material in question. I swallowed and backed up, my foot falling out of one slipper as I retreated. The shoe lay on its side, the last thing between me and something red and glistening that no longer made sense.

The fresh air had dissipated the smell of weed enough that the acrid copper tang of blood filled my nostrils. Gagging, I pressed the back of my hand against my nose.

Behind me, the bulldog snorted in its sleep, and I flinched at the startling noise. Letting out a controlled breath, I carefully toed my slipper back onto my foot, wanting as much of a barrier between me and what lay before me as possible.

Limbs, part human, part shifter, were scattered between the back of the sofa and the window like a meaty IKEA bookcase awaiting assembly. Conscious of Davide's scrutiny, I bit down hard on my lip, the pain grounding me enough to continue my examination. How could he just stand there, expecting me to deal with this?

Judging by the human arm, the victim was a Caucasian male. There wasn't much in the way of unique identifiers beyond a small, silly French mustache tattoo on one side of his index finger.

Did the deceased like to cheer people up by springing it on them? Affect a pretentious pose and ridiculous accent? It was goofy and funny and so human, unlike the state of this corpse.

Clenching my fists, I gathered the shreds of my professionalism together. Here was a murdered Ohrist and my prime suspect had phoned it in as a material disposal case. Was Davide some psycho with no remorse looking to avoid a murder charge or was he in shock?

Either way, I had to get to the truth of the matter. I put on my scariest mom voice. "Care to tell me how this body got here?"

"Cool." The snowboarder nodded, sounding relieved. "You see him too."

Ohmigod. My mind went blank, but instinct kicked in and my magically animated shadow, Delilah, jumped up protectively.

Davide made no move in my direction, however. He stared at the corpse, his brows furrowed.

Everything took on a surreal cast and I dug my heels into the ground to center myself. This was so far out of my realm of experience. Was I supposed to secure the crime scene? Arrest him? Davide obviously wasn't of sound mind. Was I in danger?

Pro: if he was high enough to forget going all *Texas Chainsaw Massacre* on someone, I could probably move faster than he could. Con: I was alone in a house with an Ohrist possessing unknown magic who was unsure if he was hallucinating dead bodies.

I pulled my phone out of my pocket, backing up into a nice, dark corner where I could easily access the Kefitzat Haderech. "I should call the Lonestars."

"Should you though?" Stubbing the joint out on a wall and stuffing the remainder of it in his bathrobe pocket, he crouched down by the human torso covered in an explosion of dark feathers and twisted the bird's head toward me. "This dude was a turkey, dude."

Who handled a corpse like that, like it was a joke? I bit down a shiver. All that weird shit aside, Davide had a point. The shifter's red bobbly beard was a sad, wizened thing and the long tailfeathers protruding from his ass were ragged. If there were majestic turkey shifters out there, the deceased had not been one of them.

"Let's restrain ourselves to one 'dude' per sentence." I massaged my temples. If I phoned the magic cops, would Davide try to stop me? My phone didn't work in the Kefitzat Haderech, so I couldn't call from there, and I wasn't sure if leaving the scene of the crime would come back to haunt me.

Or if Davide would let me out of here in one piece.

Focus, Miriam. Keeping one eye on the client, who'd sat down resting against the sliding door, I tried to glean what had transpired from the body parts.

If the victim's right human arm under the ottoman was indicative of how scrawny he'd been, he couldn't have physically taken on Davide, a renowned athlete. Then there was the discarded baseball cap with a pizza restaurant logo on it. If anything said "lured in and murdered," that was it.

I poked the shifter's beak and the spurs on both turkey legs—note to self to change the Thanksgiving menu—confirming they were sharp enough to cause the scratches on Davide's hands, face, and one calf. "What happened?"

"Self-defense."

I quirked an eyebrow and tried not to sound too snarky. "Really."

Davide slung his thumbs into his robe pockets. "I know my crimes."

"A minute ago you weren't even sure this man was real, now you're an expert in law and order?" It came out sounding mean, but I meant it. Something about this didn't track. Davide wasn't acting the way he had less than a minute ago. Something was off.

He smirked. "That was then, this is now."

What was that supposed to mean? The shock had cleared away his high enough for him to think clearly?

"He showed up with pizza and went ballistic." Davide

pointed to a particularly ugly gash on his cheek. "That dude was not a nice person."

"You have an Ohrist turkey leg on your floor in a pool of congealed blood. You're not winning any Good Samaritan awards yourself."

Davide laughed. "You're funny. Wanna get a breakfast wrap after this?"

"God, no." I wanted to wrap this up and get away from the killer showing absolutely no signs of remorse. I liked him better when he'd been high as a kite. Self-defense or not, he'd taken a man's life. Getting a confession was important, right? "So, he attacked and then?"

I heard the coherent sentences coming out of my mouth as if from a distance because the scream in my head was pretty loud. How could he sit there so coldly?

"You what?" I prompted. "Killed and dismembered him?"

Please let it have been in that order. Wait. Was that leading the suspect? Entrapment? Did I even have rules I had to abide by other than telling the Lonestars?

"He had some kind of seizure and dropped dead," Davide insisted. "That wasn't on me."

I put my hands on my hips. "Seriously? Because a seizure doesn't equal slices of human, *dude*. What, did you chop him into pieces instead of calling 911?"

Davide grinned sheepishly, momentarily morphing his right forearm into a single long blade made of bone. "He's a turkey. I'm a knife. I mean, circumstances just don't align like that every day."

Why had I answered my phone? Look at that, no need to pause for breath with a scream heard only in your head. It didn't require a good set of lungs. A good set of frontal lobes, perhaps? Okay, I was losing it.

I clasped my hands in front of my chest, praying for patience. "Your text to Tatiana stated that you had sensitive material to dispose of. This isn't sensitive material, it's a

7

shifter." I applauded myself for staying on topic. And for muscling down the sour bile that surged up every time I looked at the deceased.

"Turkey shifters are crazy sensitive." Davide tapped his head. "Not all there either. Good thing that magic doesn't show up often, right?"

Yeah, a true blessing. I examined the body from different angles, because the pieces weren't adding up to a coherent picture, until I figured out the issue. "Why aren't you covered in blood? Does your magic cauterize it?"

"No..." Davide got a distant look, his brows drawing together. He peeked under his bathrobe, barely making it into another deformed chair before his legs gave out. "Fuck. Fuck. Fuck."

The robe gaped open enough to reveal blood matted into his chest hair. I shuddered, sorry to have called it. Bears had less fur than this guy.

He held his hands up in front of his face like they didn't belong to him. "I think I washed these."

How stoned did a person have to be to forget this? Or had he gotten this wasted precisely for that reason? And more importantly, why had he gone from making jokes about the murder to being freaked out and spaced out once more?

For some reason, the more anxious Davide became, the steadier I felt, giving me a better shot at figuring all this out. Mom composure: staying calm in playgrounds, supermarkets, and murder scenes everywhere.

"You claim he went ballistic," I said. "Out of nowhere?"

At Davide's nod, I left Delilah guarding him while I crouched by the shifter's torso. I didn't glean anything from it, but when I turned over his human arm, my heart skipped a beat at the telltale red streaks on the skin that looked a lot like blood poisoning, but weren't.

The turkey shifter had been dybbuk-possessed. And now he was dead.

That meant…

I looked at Davide, expelling a hard breath. Shit. No wonder his personality seemed to flip. When the turkey shifter, a possessed host, died, the dybbuk jumped into the closest magic body with lowered inhibitions.

Davide.

Enthralled hosts struggled with the dybbuk for control of their body for the first week. Based on Davide's behavior, I'd bet he was attacked first, then once he became enthralled, he'd sliced and diced.

At some point tonight, the real Davide had gained the upper hand, which was when he texted Tatiana for help. He'd been his regular self when I'd first arrived, cycled to the dybbuk being in charge when he so callously discussed the crime, and was now back to himself.

Sighing, I scrubbed a hand over my face. Did that change things as far as calling in the magic police? I walked over to the snowboarder, probing his shadow until my skin itched at the sense of an abomination that needed to be destroyed. Well, I guess it was better that he was enthralled than straight up psychotic. "One moment. I have to confer with my boss."

Davide shot me a panicked look.

"Everything's going to be okay. Don't worry."

He nodded, toking up once more with trembling hands.

I dialed Tatiana, putting her on speaker when she answered. "Hey. I'm here with Davide."

"Yo," he said.

"Yo?" Tatiana sniffed primly. "Is there a problem with the disposal?"

"Potentially," I said. "Given that the object to be disposed of is a dismembered turkey shifter."

"What?" Tatiana snapped. "Davide!"

I smirked. She wouldn't have let me walk into this blind had she known the true situation.

9

"Yeah?" His eyes dropped to his feet like a little kid who knew he was in a ton of trouble.

I placed the phone on the cushion next to him and, recalling Delilah, casually moved behind our client.

"You didn't mention this was piece work in your text," my boss chided. "Are you trying to stiff me out of my proper fee?"

My smirk disappeared, the dark shadow that had swirled down my left arm in a half-formed scythe, now paused. "That's your concern?" I said. "We've got a shit show here. The corpse was dybbuk-possessed. *Was*. Capisce?"

"Yes, Miriam. I get it. And?" Tatiana said with her regular laissez-faire.

"Do we call the Lonestars in? Because I refuse to have more threats of Deadman's Island held over me. Once was more than en—" My sentence ended in a high-pitched shriek as I was forced backward against the wall with Davide's arm blade pressed against my throat.

Minus the rest of him.

It was detachable? Fuck me. My magic fell apart as I panicked, trying to get free.

"Here's how this is going to go down, dude." Davide didn't even quit smoking up while intimidating me, his right sleeve dangling limply without its forearm. That was impressive—no wait.

I attempted to worm a hand between his blade and my very nice, undamaged throat and got my skull conked against the wall for my troubles.

"Your little worker bee's going to do the job she came over for and keep her mouth shut." Davide blew pot smoke in my direction and winked.

"Not without my agreed-upon fee, you drawling hippie." Tatiana tsked him from her side of the phone call. "Enunciate like a normal person."

Now was not the time for the woman who sounded like a Wiseguy to school the enthralled turkey carver on his diction.

He pressed the magic blade harder against me and I swallowed.

"Please. Let me go."

"Fine." Davide snapped his fingers, recalling the bone blade. It slipped up his sleeve to seamlessly fit to his upper arm, becoming a human appendage once more. "But the clock's ticking. Got it?"

My pulse drummed against the thin skin under my jaw, beating faster with my rush of anger. You messed with the wrong worker bee.

Dude.

"No," Tatiana said, unfortunately still on the call. "She doesn't 'got it.' Not until we negotiate my fee."

Delilah puffed up and punched the stoner in the head, momentarily disorienting him.

I sprinted closer, Delilah meeting me to transform into a swirl of dark magic that settled into my scythe, and I smashed it into the floor, severing Davide's shade from his body.

"Is anyone listening to me?" Tatiana said.

Davide's eyes rolled back to show the whites and he hit the ground.

That was good. The furious crimson and sickly gray mass of a dybbuk that spat out of him and attacked me, not so great.

Gripping the weapon securely in my left hand, I cried, "Mut!"

"Miriam." My boss sounded annoyed. "You better not be complying with that man before I have come to a satisfactory working arrangement with him."

The second that the Hebrew letters for "death" appeared on the blade, I cleaved the little ghost bastard into oblivion, dropped to my knees next to Davide, and began CPR. This side-effect of saving enthralleds from dybbuk inhabitation had become commonplace enough that I'd recently redone a first aid course.

"I'm going to count to three," Tatiana warned, "and then I expect an answer."

"A little busy," I said, doing chest compressions.

She humphed. "Call me back."

Upon regaining consciousness, Davide took one look at the mutilated turkey shifter and bolted out of the room, white as a ghost.

Since I didn't want to stay with the corpse by myself, I walked out onto the large balcony, resting against the railing and letting the ocean and salt-tinged breeze calm me before I called Tatiana back. What a senseless tragedy. I hoped Davide wouldn't be held culpable for his actions by either the Lonestars or the dead man's family once he was identified and his loved ones told the terrible news.

3AM phone calls really were harbingers of death.

Clouds rolled in, hiding all trace of the full moon. That's right, tonight was the last night. I stared at the water, my breath easing into rhythm with the caress of the waves, wondering where Laurent was. We'd barely spoken since we'd hooked up almost a month ago. In our last conversation, he'd mentioned having bought condoms and I'd been in a worked-up state of anticipation ever since.

Also, frustration because first he'd been away on a job, and then his mother had suffered a heart attack and he'd flown back to Paris. I'd left messages asking how she was but hadn't gotten a response. Laurent had put an ocean between himself and his family, plus from what little I'd gleaned, there were issues with his father, so for him to drop everything and go, he must have really been worried about her.

He wasn't due back for another week, and I didn't relish telling him what had happened tonight, though he'd be happy to hear that Davide had been saved.

I think.

Had his silence really been because of his mom or was he feeling excluded since he couldn't help the enthralled? I shook my head. No, that was silly. He'd pushed so hard for me to figure out how to save them. He wouldn't get sulky about it. But if it wasn't that, had he had second thoughts about another hookup? Were that the case, we'd deal with it like mature adults and discuss it. My desire to keep our friendship was stronger than the one to get naked with him.

As strong.

It was strong.

I glanced back into the living room. Davide hadn't returned but it wasn't right to put off getting Tatiana's permission to bring in the magic cops, even if that did land our client in trouble. However, before I could head inside, a cough floated up to me from the dark beach below. I peered over the railing.

A figure in all black stood on the sand, mostly hidden by the balcony. "You're not a blank after all," a man said. "I didn't believe that someone could hide their magic for that long, but look at you go."

I tried and failed to see his face. Everything about him was indistinct, including his generic North American voice, so there was nothing to latch on to to help identify him. As I was unable to manifest my scythe, he wasn't a dybbuk or a demon, and it was too dark to summon Delilah and see if he was a vampire.

That still left plenty of unpleasant possibilities.

"Don't be shy," I said. "Introduce yourself properly."

"Maybe next time."

The promise of future encounters. Oh goody. I gripped the railing, rising onto tiptoe to lean farther over and get a better glimpse of the intruder. "What do you want?"

"Call me curious." He moved farther into the shadows.

"Are you a baby shark or are you planning to finish what your parents started?"

My mind reeled. A children's song, threats about my past —hold on, my past?

"Did you know my parents?"

Did you kill them?

It was too far to jump down to the sand, and I didn't want to lose him in the time it would take to get through the house and out to the beach.

"I never met them, but I like to follow whispers." He chuckled. "The faintest ones often prove most interesting."

"What are you talking about?"

There was only the white noise of the waves and the pounding of my heart in answer. He was gone.

I dropped my head into my hands. What were Mom and Dad up to and why did this stranger care about my magic? I hadn't even used my powers in a couple of weeks, spending most of my time recently working on archiving documents for Tatiana's memoirs. Had this other weirdo been stalking me and I didn't notice?

That was a frightening thought. Maybe Eli could give me tips on detecting a tail.

Needing something concrete to do, I found a sheet in a linen closet and draped it over the grisly remains of the turkey shifter.

Davide returned, looking pale and shaky. His hair was wet, and he'd changed into clean jeans and a bright hoodie. He carried a bowl of water in one hand and a package of deli meat in the other.

"Did you call the Lonestars? Am I going to be taken to Deadman's Island?" he said in a dull voice. He sat down on the carpet next to the collarless bulldog, who snuffled awake. Davide placed the bowl beside the animal and dropped a couple slices of bologna on the carpet.

The dog tore into the food with wet smacking noises that made me inadvertently glance at the corpse and shudder.

"Not yet, but I doubt you'll be arrested," I said, "especially if an investigation proves this man died from something other than your attack, like you claim. You were enthralled. I'll testify to that, and it should mitigate you being held accountable for your actions." I narrowed my eyes. "You *were* enthralled when you...got up close and personal, right?"

He nodded, doling out more food and looking miserable enough that I believed him.

"Do you have your phone on you?" I said.

"Yeah, why?"

"Can I see the text you sent Tatiana?" I was grasping at straws but maybe Davide had included something that could help me find the stranger since I didn't have a name or physical description.

He unlocked the phone and tossed it over to me. "Dude, I was so far gone I don't even remember sending her anything."

I scrolled through his texts with a sinking heart, checking once, then twice for the message. Nothing. No text requesting Tatiana's assistance, none providing Davide's address, not even her number saved under another name.

I handed him back the phone and exhaled. "That's because you didn't."

Davide showed the empty deli meat bag to the dog, then frowned at me. "I don't understand," he said as the dog licked the dirty bag. "Who would want to hurt me like this?"

"No one." I clenched the phone in my hand, looking outside. Whether or not the stranger had been following me, he hadn't lucked into a display of my magic tonight. "This attack was never aimed at you. It was a test. For me."

2

———

THAT ASSHOLE ON THE BEACH HAD SET ME UP. NOW one man was dead, another was scarred for life, and I had yet more vague bullshit attached to me. Sharks? Whispers? What did the stranger think I would finish?

Mom, Dad, what did you start?

The blare of my phone ringing jolted me out of my thoughts. It was "Poor Unfortunate Souls" from *The Little Mermaid*, which had amused me to no end when I'd programmed it as Tatiana's ringtone, but now felt uncomfortably prophetic.

I moved into Davide's hallway to have the conversation in private.

My boss demanded a very detailed walk-through of events. She was furious that this job might be a ruse devised to confirm my magic. Not for my sake, mind you, but because she wouldn't get paid.

"This was a perfectly nice case of two dybbuks canceling each other out," she snapped.

The phone beeped at me. In my incredulity, I'd hit a button with my chin. "In what world is a dead and dismembered corpse a perfectly nice case?"

"You know what I mean. This is the second job of mine where the Lonestars are getting involved because of you. It better not become a habit."

"For the record, I'm not exactly thrilled by this turn of events." I paced the corridor. "Some psycho might have staged all this because he's curious if I'm going to finish what my parents started. What does that even mean?"

"How should I know?"

"I want to find out. Lonestars have the resources to find him. I don't."

Tatiana cackled.

"What's so funny?"

"Not one word about justice and closure for the poor dead victim? Maybe you won't give me an ulcer after all."

"Silly me for thinking justice was always a given." I touched the scratch on my neck from Davide's arm blade.

"Methinks she doth protest too much. Don't worry, I'll call the Lonestars." In typical fashion, Tatiana disconnected without saying goodbye.

Davide and I moved to the front stoop to wait for the magic cops. He didn't question me further or get mad at how he'd been used, which made me feel both awful and relieved. I'm not sure what I would have said to make it better.

I rested my head on my knees, my lids heavy, while Davide made us both steaming cups of coffee that neither of us had the heart to actually drink.

Ryann Esposito showed up when the first golden rays streaked the summer sky, accompanied by a morose man in a rumpled shirt bearing the same six-pointed gold star tattoo on his wrist as Ryann.

Vancouver's head Lonestar normally looked like a time-traveling escapee from Woodstock, so the sight of her in dark jeans and a black sweater sent a chill through me. Her hair was still dyed a jewel color—teal now—and shaved on the sides, but it was pulled back in a no-nonsense stubby pony-tail with nary a glittery barrette in sight.

I stuffed my trembling hands under my butt. "That's a different look for you," I said carefully.

"Where's the body?" There was no small talk, no flaki-ness, just a curt impatience.

"Inside." Davide half rose but she shook her head.

"Stay here. I'll examine it and then come speak with you both." She strode inside, followed by the second Lonestar.

Davide and I exchanged nervous looks and I pressed my lips together. Which was the real Ryann? If her hippie chick persona was just a mask she wore to conceal her inner stone-cold killer, could she please put that fake happy self back on?

I'd gnawed three fingernails ragged, run through six different monologues about how I hadn't done anything wrong, and played two disastrous games of *Tetris* on my phone before Ryann returned.

She stood in the doorway, forcing us to twist around to talk to her. I felt like a child in front of the principal. The scary principal with debilitating magic who did not look in the mood for anything we had to say.

Ryann listened to both of our versions of events with an impassive expression and very little in the way of questions or comments.

My nerves grew into a full-blown stomachache, and I hunched over, one arm wrapped around my middle.

"Is there security camera footage to corroborate who attacked whom first, the enthrallment, or this unfamiliar man?" Ryann said.

"No," Davide said. He looked at me like a drowning victim hoping I'd throw out a lifeline, but it wasn't my house, and I shrugged helplessly.

"It's all true," I said. "And it happened exactly as we said. This was a setup."

"Okay," she said.

18

"No, it really—wait. What?"

Ryann yawned and rubbed her eyes. "I believe you."

I stood up and jabbed a finger at her clothes. "Then what's with the bad cop outfit?"

"I haven't had a chance to do laundry, and after the call woke me up, I grabbed the nearest clean clothing." She crossed her arms, scuffing at the ground with the toe of her shoe. "You don't need to be mean about it."

An incredulous laugh burst out of me. Laundry. "Do you know how badly you scared me?" I stomped my foot.

The Lonestar looked down at her outfit and quirked her lips.

"Are you going to arrest me?" Davide stood up as well, wringing his hands.

"No," she said. "The deceased was definitely dybbuk-possessed."

He sagged against the wall. "Thank you."

"Don't thank me yet," she said. "This is now an official investigation. I made a few calls. Wallace Edwards, the vic?" She checked a note on her phone. "He really did work for that pizza company, but he hadn't been seen in almost three days. Missed a few shifts. Then tonight he showed up, stole a pizza from the kitchen, and bolted."

"Wallace must have flipped from enthralled to fully possessed over the weekend," I said. "But even so, this wasn't some hastily assembled plan."

"No," Ryann agreed. "If the man on the beach whom you spoke with is behind this, he needed time to get all his dominos in a row."

A shiver ran through me at the analogy, given both a prophecy about me being the first domino played in some game and a literal domino I'd been awarded by the Kefitzat Haderech.

I set that aside to ponder later. "He had to find the best

candidates to carry out this test. That takes detailed research and planning."

"Gerald, my colleague, is running a few more tests." Ryann gestured inside. "But Wallace appears to have died from a brain aneurysm before Davide attacked, brought on by extreme exertion from using his magic. If the stranger from the beach was culpable in Wallace becoming enthralled, then we can get him for murder. And in the unlikely event that Wallace became inhabited on his own, we can still get this other guy for your attempted murder, Davide." She handed him an ivory card with her name and number printed on it. "You'll need to be prepared to answer questions that may lead to finding that man, like why he chose you."

"Wallace was a pizza delivery guy and I'm pretty public about smoking weed. My late-night habits are well-known. I'd be high and confused." Davide's self-awareness was surprising. He threw me a wan smile as if reading my thoughts. "I mean, it's my lifestyle. I don't have an issue with it, dude. I just know myself well enough to know my blindspots," he said, crumbling Ryann's card in his hand. Realizing what he'd done, he smoothed it out as best he could. "I was an easy target. And now I have to live with the fact that I murdered this du—Wallace."

"I'm so sorry you were dragged into this," I said. Although it was a miracle Davide hadn't been enthralled before now, given how much pot he smoked.

Davide was quiet for a long moment as if wrestling with his next words, and I readied myself for an angry outburst, but when he shook his head, he looked more resigned than anything. "You have to live with this too," he said. "He wanted to get a rise out of you, and he was prepared to use me to get to you. I don't know why he's targeting you, but I guarantee if he's willing to kill someone to get this far, there's going to be more to come. Shit rolls downhill, and lady, you're standing at the bottom of an avalanche." With that, he went inside.

Ryann clasped my shoulder. "He's not wrong. How's your security?"

"At home? Fine. The ward is strong." Thanks to Vancouver's master vampire, the entire duplex that I co-owned with my ex-husband, Eli Chu, was protected by a powerful ward. Even demons couldn't get inside.

"This isn't Zev's style," Ryann said.

"No, and he knows the extent of my powers." I rubbed my bleary eyes. "You want a ride home or back to HQ?"

"That's okay, I grabbed a co-op car." She paused. "I'm surprised you're not insisting on finding this man yourself."

"Would you let me?"

"Not in any reality."

"That's what I figured, so I'm leaving that to you."

Ryann stilled as if she'd expected a fight, then she gave a tiny smile. "All right, then." She walked me to my car. "While you do what?"

"Find out what job my parents were on when they were killed. I have the same magic as them, so if someone has taken an interest in me now, I want to know why." I beeped my fob at my sedan.

"You sure you want to dig that up?" She stepped off the dew-laden grass onto the sidewalk.

"I need to know the truth. Besides, it's got to be better than all the scenarios I've come up with over the years."

"When you looked into McMurtry you ended up with a demon parasite coming through your wall," she said.

"And can you believe there are no exterminators in the area that cover those things?" I tsked and shook my head. "Anyway, more seriously, my home is fortified against anything dangerous. Well, anything that isn't Zev."

"Unless the danger is the truth," Ryann said.

"I can handle the truth."

"That's what they all say before an unkind reality smacks them in the face." She sighed and patted my shoulder. "I think you're pretty self-aware. Hopefully whatever you find doesn't hurt you too much." Ryann headed for a black hatchback then stopped. She looked at me, her brow furrowed, then straightened her shoulders. "Miri?"

"Yeah?"

"A word of warning." The gravity of her tone made my stomach hurt. "I know you started working for Tatiana because she could protect you, but she was not happy about phoning me. She's never had anyone demand that she cooperate with us on a regular basis before."

I laughed, because Ryann had called this one all wrong. "Demand? If Tatiana hadn't wanted to call the Lonestars, then she wouldn't have. I certainly don't have the power to force her to go against her wishes. She's pissed off because she isn't getting paid and because she enjoys holding her cards close to her chest. Trust me, if calling you threatened any self-interest of hers, it wouldn't have happened."

"Perhaps." Ryann pursed her lips. "But what happens when your interests conflict with Tatiana's?"

My boss was powerful and ruthless. I still didn't fully trust her, and I'd never underestimate her, but even if I was of no use to her *and* was getting in her way, she wouldn't risk her relationship with her nephew, Laurent, by harming me.

Would she?

I shook my head. This was all hypothetical anyway because I wasn't going to do anything that turned her into my enemy. "She'd fire me. That's it."

Ryann took a long, tired look at the white clouds drifting over the houses. "Tatiana is one of the most dangerous people I have ever met in my life. I hope you aren't on the receiving end when you find out why."

3

ONE PERSON'S FITNESS PARADISE WAS ANOTHER'S hell on earth—and with every step I took on this ungodly early Tuesday morning, I became more convinced that this nightmare had been conceived by an actual demon.

Billed as a "hike," the Grouse Grind was more of a cluster-fuck of makeshift stairs mixed with steep rocks and dirt slopes that wound up the side of Grouse Mountain in North Vancouver. There was nothing to look at along the way except trees, soil, and the backs of all the people passing me. The joggers were the worst. How dare they flaunt their strong quads and working hearts?

Monsters, all of them. But none more so than my two "friends" Jude Rachefsky and Ava Lewis, who'd harped on me that as a Vancouverite I had to do the Grind at least once in my life.

"Fuck it," I wheezed, almost tripping over yet another uneven rock stair. "These people brought it on themselves. Let the dybbuks take them."

The two women chuckled, their laughter as light as the sheen of sweat on their brows, versus my red-faced mess.

Even their peer pressure wouldn't have been enough to

convince me had there not been a bigger danger. I'd managed to get a few hours of sleep on Monday after I got home from Davide's place before being woken up by Emmett with a call about a potentially enthralled Ohrist.

Two more calls came in that day and the one thing they all had in common? Each of the Ohrists had done the Grouse Grind recently—and not during the Danger Zone. It would have been worrisome enough if dybbuks were hanging out on the trail during the twenty-four hours from sunset Friday to sunset Saturday when they were given time off from their torture in Gehenna to come to earth and find an unwitting magic user to possess, but all the hikers had done the Grind outside of that period.

They all swore they hadn't gotten drunk or high during the Danger Zone, and had they not all had this one thing in common, I'd have believed they were lying.

Better safe than sorry, which was why I'd decided to check it out today—for the sake of the poor magic people humping their way up the mountain. However, I seemed to be the lone humpee in a sea of disgustingly hale fitness freaks.

"You want to be stuck saving enthralled hikers every weekend?" Ava said, nimbly hopping stairs like a goat. "Because you know that's what's going to happen. It'll become a local Ohrist ritual. Grind, Miri, brunch."

"Tatiana was right." I dragged myself up with the help of the wooden railing. "No good deed goes unpunished."

Truthfully, Tatiana had been thrilled about this new development, visions of dollar signs dancing in her eyes. I, on the other hand, was regretting my insistence on setting up a hotline to report enthralleds. The possibility of asshole Ohrists using me as a magic morning-after pill was high.

"That was the longest section." From the top of the staircase, Jude flashed me a thumbs-up, looking daisy-fresh in a white sports bra and cute purple sweatpants. Even her short curly pigtails were obscenely perky.

Ava frowned, sunlight catching the bling on the corner of her cat-eye glasses and the glittery flower design on the head-band in her short afro.

"What's with the frown?" I panted, not having enough energy to point at her. I'd tied my sweater around my waist, and since I'd been using it to wipe off my sweat, it was gross and wet. My T-shirt was streaked with dirt, my lank ponytail was matted to my skull, and none of my attire matched.

"Nothing." Ava tied her hoodie around her shoulders. "You're doing great. See?" She pointed at the sign congratu-lating us for making it a quarter of the way up.

I braced my hands on my thighs, my legs burning. "That's a typo, right? They mean three-quarters of the way." Gasping for air, I read the rest of the sign and swore. "That was the *easy* section? That's it, I'm going back down."

"Don't quit now," Ava said.

"No, even the sign advises it. There's a checklist."

Jude ripped my water bottle out of my hand and shook it. "You still have Gatorade, so that's one of three items you're good on."

I pointed at the next item. "I'm exhausted."

"Are you dizzy? Light-headed?" she challenged.

"No, but you will be when I push you off this mountain for forcing me into this."

"Ouch," Ava said.

Jude nodded. "Yeah, she's a bitch when she exercises. Don't ever go cross-country skiing with her."

"Hey, I'm a delight in Zumba class," I said. "This isn't exercise. It's masochism."

An old lady coming up at a steady clip behind us used her cane to nudge me aside on the uneven path. "If I can do it, you can do it," she said, tramping up the narrow switchback trail without hesitation.

Fairly certain that wasn't true, I imagined ripping that cane from her hand to nudge her off the mountain.

Jude shrugged. "You're right. This is too hard for you. Go back down."

Ava clamped her lips together but not before I saw her smirk.

I swiped my water bottle back and took a small sip from my precious, dwindling stash. Even the simple act of drinking was turned into a torturous mental game of rationing out swallows like I was lost in the desert. "I hate both of you."

"You'll love me when I buy you a beer at the top." Jude slung an arm around my shoulder, which I shrugged off with a glare.

Like I wanted more hot weight on my body. I swear, if my boobs were detachable, I'd have flung them into the forest. No, wait. Those were keepers. My belly. Damn my love of carbs.

"Come on," Jude said. "We'll sing. Take your mind off it. You choose first."

I picked my way over the logs stuck in dirt that delineated stairs in this part of the trail, since, apparently, the fancy rock stairs were a thing of the past. "You think?" Pant. "I have. Air?" Pant, pant. "To sing?"

"We'll provide the soundtrack," Ava said.

Thus commenced a five-minute debate between the two to pick a song they both knew the lyrics to, before defaulting to "Bohemian Rhapsody." It was an apt choice, as I too faced no escape from reality and was considering killing someone.

I figured being overtaken by the spry senior was a new low in my life, but when I found myself basically crawling over rocks up an almost vertical incline with my heart pounding so hard that I felt it in my head, I reassessed that decision.

Even Ava and Jude stopped singing. Sadly, it wasn't because they were too tired, but because they opted to return to an earlier topic of speculating about what my parents had been up to since I'd told them that I was going to look into it.

"Make a list of possibilities," Ava said.

Jude rolled her eyes. "You're as bad as Miri."

"Lists are important to stave off chaos," Ava retorted and we fist-bumped. She uncapped her water bottle and took a swig before offering it to me, since mine was empty.

I exercised massive amounts of self-control and had only one small mouthful before handing the bottle back.

Their guesses were wild—bank robbers, treasure hunters, killers for hire—but I couldn't discount any of them either.

Except for Jude's idea that they were stealing exotic animals.

Once the rocks were behind us and we had a nice short stretch of level ground, I caught my breath enough to speak. "Why would my parents do that?"

"The stranger called you a baby shark, right?"

"So, *I'm* the exotic animal in this scenario?" I chuckled, shaking my head. "My parents weren't trafficking kids, Jude."

She looked abashed as she tightened one pigtail. "Yeah, I didn't think that through."

A man jostled her aside in his haste to pass her.

"Watch it," she snapped. "The top of the mountain isn't going anywhere."

I wiped sweat off my neck with my sweater. "Enough of me. Ava, did Romi finish the socks for her nephew?"

Ava's wife had been knitting a frenzy of baby clothes for her pregnant younger sister in Haifa.

"I'm not finished with this topic yet," Jude said. "Will you be involving Emmett in your search?"

"I wasn't planning on it," I said. "Why?"

"Living with Tatiana is no longer new and exciting." She sighed sadly. "He's bored."

Ava pressed her hands together. "It's sweet how much you care about him."

"Bless your heart," Jude drawled in her Savannah accent. "You see the good in everyone."

Ava snorted her laughter and Jude winked.

"I just don't want him living with me again," my best friend said.

I wagged a finger. "Liar. You loooove your baby."

Jude arched an eyebrow. "You want to go down this road?"

Hell no. "Stop nattering. I'm trying to spot rogue dybbuks." Head high, I marched up the trail to the sound of the women's laughter.

Shockingly, the hike got worse. I'm not sure why I was surprised since it was called the Grouse Grind and not the Grouse Scenic Stroll. Not only was the trail dybbuk-free thus far, I was so sweat-soaked in the cool mountain air that my teeth chattered like one of those wind-up novelty pairs. Whimpering may have been involved.

I even stopped counting people going faster than me as a means of distraction because I'd run out of oxygen to spare for math. Okay, fine. After a woman with a toddler strapped to her back overtook me, I got too depressed, contemplating curling into the fetal position and waiting until I was eaten by bears.

I'd just taken another break to scarf down my last protein bar when nausea slapped me hard, a tremor racking me from head to toe. For a split second, I thought my body was giving out for good and exploding from the inside, but then my magic came awake like a lion from a nap in the sun, sniffing prey.

Calling out for Jude and Ava up ahead to wait, I carefully checked for dybbuks, but there were none in sight. I did, however, smell rotting onions—a putrid, eye-watering intensity that clogged my nostrils.

Gehenna's signature perfume.

"Problem?" Ava cautiously approached, Jude right behind her.

The disgusting stench grew stronger and I plugged my nose. "You don't smell that?"

My friends shook their heads.

I didn't see anything odd, but my magic tingled insistently, so I let Delilah loose. The second my shadow animated, I slid into her green overlay vision of the world.

A dinner plate–sized circle at eye level shimmered as if rippling off hot concrete even though the day was overcast.

The closer I got to it, the more my stomach roiled, the hairs on the back of my neck lifting and my skin prickling at the sense of an abomination I had to destroy. I couldn't get within five feet of it without wanting to scratch my skin off.

"This must be how they're coming through." I backed up. "Either of you ever heard of, I don't know, a thin spot or tear or something?" It would have been nice to have Laurent here with me to confer on this.

"I don't know about a thin spot," Jude said, "but dybbuks are drawn to crowded places. That's why small towns or villages don't tend to have a problem with them." She glanced up and down the trail. "This place is busy, but comparatively speaking, it's hardly downtown Tokyo."

"Vancouver isn't either." Ava gave a wry smile. "I heard once there are..." She snapped her fingers, searching for the thought. "Imagine that dybbuks get from Gehenna to earth via different doors. For some reason, these doors open in certain places more often, because of a phenomenon similar to ley lines, but not exactly."

"Vancouver is a Hellmouth? Great." I made a frustrated noise and walked around the circle, starting at another belch of rotting onion, which preceded the circle ripping open.

Three pulsing crimson shapes flecked with a sickly gray color shot out of the tear on a plume of jagged fog.

I gasped, my shadow scythe instantly in my hand, and jumped in front of my friends. "Mut!"

My friends couldn't see dybbuks, but they saw my

weapon. Ava screamed and ducked, but Jude froze, drained of all color.

The dybbuks ping-ponged off a party of hikers traipsing past. Luckily, they were Sapiens and therefore safe from enthrallment, but Ava and Jude weren't.

"What's happening?" Jude said in a tremulous voice.

I left Delilah to cover them, since she only wielded the scythe when vamps were involved.

"Stay back." Leaping up the stairs, I pushed past my burning hamstrings and swung the weapon. I nailed two of the dybbuks, killing them, but the third one veered off back down the trail. Weapon aloft, I ran after it, rounding a corner in time to spy the dybbuk flying into a young man. I sprinted for him and slammed the scythe into his shadow, spraying dirt.

He pushed me back a few steps and removed an earbud. "Hey, lady. No hiking back down the trail."

It registered that he didn't seem perturbed by my weapon, but I was focused on the angry ghost that had sprung out of the man again. Narrowing my eyes, I impaled the crimson phantom, cleaving it in half. It drained of all color and imploded, dead.

The man heaved a sigh. "You shouldn't do the Grind when high. Whatever you're on might be fun, but take it to the dance floor, not the mountain."

My mouth fell open. "Huh?"

He mimicked my so-called "dance moves"—aka my deadly weapon handling—muttered a rude comment about idiots, tax dollars, and rescue parties, and strode past me, fitting the earbud back in.

Oh shit. He couldn't see my magic because of the Sapien perception filter. But he wasn't truly Sapien either because that dybbuk had fully inhabited him for a second. The man had to have a very weak Ohrist gene, which meant that he had no idea about keeping himself safe during the Danger

Zone.

The only good thing about this situation was that I'd dispatched the dybbuk inside him so fast that the man hadn't collapsed when I severed his shadow.

I headed back to my friends. "We have a problem."

Ava's head was bent close to Jude's. I couldn't make out her words, but she was speaking to my friend in a low, insistent voice.

Jude glanced at me, twisting a finger into one of her curls so tightly that it was starting to become knotted up.

Sighing, I shut down my magic. I'd rescued Jude when she was taken captive several weeks ago and saved her from her enthralled state. While she was working through her trauma with an Ohrist therapist, clearly seeing my magic in action was triggering memories of how close she'd come to being fully possessed, since she'd been fine on the hike until now.

"Jude—"

"I want to keep up my heart rate." She pressed two fingers to her wrist. "How about Ava keeps you company and I keep going on my own?"

My best friend couldn't meet my eyes as she spoke.

"Nah." I toed at a root sticking out of the ground. "You two go ahead. I need to talk to Tatiana about what we're going to do with this thin spot, so I'll take the KH down to the parking lot later."

"You sure?" Ava darted an anxious glance between me and Jude, as if checking to see who needed her most.

"Totally." I smiled with a confidence I did not feel. "I've had about enough of the Grind for one day, though if anyone asks, I did the whole thing like a boss."

Jude said a "bye" that was as fake as my smile and left.

Ava readjusted her headband. "She'll be okay. And you?"

"I'll be fine. Talk later?"

She nodded and hurried after Jude.

They disappeared around a bend almost immediately.

I sat down on a tree log just off the path, kicking at the dirt with my heel. Jude knew I was dybbuk hunting today. What did she think was going to happen? Obviously, I'd have to use magic. She needed time to get over her ordeal; I understood that and could be as patient as she needed. What was frustrating was her total denial that this was even a problem. She should have been honest with herself—and me—and not accompanied us.

Even if hiding my magic around her solved this, I refused to. It was on Jude to work through her issues because if she couldn't separate my magic from her kidnapping, I didn't see a way forward.

I'd even tried to make a to-do list but had failed to come up with a plan to fix this. I rubbed my hand over the back of my neck. Since I could do something about the dybbuk here on the Grind, I pulled out my phone.

Voices drifted up from lower down the trail. "Did you hear he went subthirty?" one man said.

"I can't get my time to under forty-five minutes," a woman griped.

"Let's make it forty-four," the man said.

The two hikers came into view, sprinting up the trail.

I gaped at them. Forty-five minutes to hike the Grind? I'd be lucky to climb it in two and a half hours. And someone had done it in less than thirty? No way that person was a Sapien. They either had magic or they'd made a deal with the devil.

Shaking my head, I called Tatiana, sharing my findings about the circle.

"It's unusual but not unheard of." She made a *hmmm* sound. "Move it back, Emmett."

There was a loud thump from her end of the phone.

"Move it yourself," the golem groused in the background. "You're killing my back. Besides, I didn't sign on to rearrange your furniture."

There were sounds of a tussle and then he spoke into the phone. "Come get me, partner. I'm boooorrrrrred and she's mean."

"Yes, get him out of my hair. For good." Tatiana had taken possession of the cell again.

Smiling at a couple of young female hikers, I held the phone away, making "blah blah blah" motions with my hand.

They laughed and wished me good luck.

I'd heard some version of this bitching on a regular basis since Emmett moved in with Tatiana on temporary bodyguard duty. Everyone expected her to send him back to live with Laurent when the danger had passed, but she'd kept him and the two had settled in like an old, disgruntled married couple.

"Tell Emmett he can come to my place tomorrow, but it's too crowded on the trail to keep him under the radar." I poked in the dirt with a skinny stick. "What do we do? I'm not sitting here bounty hunting rogue escapees for the rest of my life."

Tatiana clapped her hands and I tensed. "What?" I said.

"Bounty hunter. Brilliant idea, bubeleh. That's your new official title. We can charge a bundle for that service."

"While you're counting your piles of money, Scrooge McDuck, how do we fix this?" I clapped my hand over my mouth at my outburst, ready to grovel and blame fatigue and lack of food and liquids, but Tatiana laughed, amused by my insult. The woman was entirely unpredictable.

"I'm not sure. The only thing I can think of is... Wait there." She hung up before I could press for details or warn her not to try to come herself.

If she was faster than I'd been, I was flinging myself off the nearest cliff.

4

Making myself as comfortable as possible on the ground next to the trail, I prepared a story about how my ankle was lightly sprained and I was waiting for my husband to come back and assist me the rest of the way. I could have saved my energy, because not a single person asked if I was all right, all of them determined to reach the view at the top in record time. Or, more likely, the beer and food.

It was nearing noon and the hot August sun had driven all but the insanely determined—and me—away. I did my best to follow the shifting shade, my stomach growling loudly and my throat thick and sticky from lack of water. The only upside was that I'd sweated everything out and didn't have to pee, since there were no outhouses on the Grind.

Had another dybbuk burst onto the scene, I'm not sure I would have had the energy to deal with it, but luckily, the situation didn't arise.

Dappled sunlight filtered down through the tree canopy, the birdsong a soothing music, and the air rich with the scents of mulch, cedar, and pine. Rich with my body odor too, but I was mostly nose blind on that one by now. It was peaceful and lovely being here by myself, and I fell into a meditative state, my normally whirring brain quiet for once. This was not due to some zen achievement on my part, but because I no longer had the energy to think or move.

Even the thrum of anxiety that I'd lived with since meeting the man on the beach was muted. I hadn't heard from Ryann that they'd caught him, but I doubted he'd followed me up here without me noticing.

A cracking twig startled me out of my trance, and I nervously glanced over my shoulder, in case the universe had taken my earlier request seriously and sent a bear to eat me.

It was so much worse.

I blinked at the sight. Rubbed my eyes and shook my head to clear it of the hallucination, because there could not be a white wolf prowling out of the forest.

There was no way it was Laurent because he was in France, except that left the alternative being a real wolf or a strange shifter. I grabbed a fallen tree branch and jabbed it at the beast. "Don't come any closer."

Flicking his tail, the wolf shot me a "seriously?" look, annoyance clear in a pair of very familiar emerald eyes.

I shot up onto my feet, simultaneously smoothing my hair and cleaning dirt off myself. This could not be happening. If Laurent was having second thoughts about the two of us sleeping together then seeing me looking less appealing than a Dickensian urchin did not bode well for my sexual satisfaction.

I was going to kill Tatiana for not mentioning that he was back.

Right after I finished committing lupicide.

Was a heads-up text too much to ask for? Perhaps from the bottom of the mountain before he just trotted up here in a ridiculously short amount of time not even winded? I chucked a pebble at him. "Shoo."

Deftly avoiding it, Laurent marched around the circle of

shimmering air. He sniffed it; he pawed at it. He even growled at it.

Nothing happened.

I flashed him a thumbs-up. "Doing great there, Huff 'n' Puff."

The wolf scampered about ten feet down the trail from me, turning back to flick his tail again.

I crossed my arms. "What? You just show up, snarl at the air, do nothing, and I'm supposed to run along and let more hikers get eaten?"

If wolves could frown, I'd swear that's what he was doing, but when I didn't react, he growled softly.

"Got it. You're the big hero. I'm just the grunt who climbed the mountain and found the problem in a gazillion acres of forest. Knock yourself out. Fix it." I flicked a leaf off my arm. I may have been hungry, filthy, and dehydrated, but I'd tapped into a well of anger and I was drinking deep. It was refreshing in a toxic sort of way.

He raced back up and butted me in the hip with his snout.

"If you have something to say, then shift, because a hiker could appear at any time."

He shot me a "duh" look.

"Oh." I rocked back on my heels. "Is that what you wanted? For me to keep anyone from coming up?"

The wolf huffed. Animals shouldn't have the ability to convey irritation so clearly.

"Jeez. Shoot me for not being fluent in wolf." I stomped back down the trail to the nearest bend and planted myself in such a way that I could see both oncoming hikers and Laurent.

Golden light spread from the wolf's back paws, blossoming up his legs and across his torso.

At the sound of cheerful whistling, I spun away from the hypnotic sight. "Sorry," I said to the hiker. "There's been an accident. Search and Rescue is dealing with it, but you need

36

to hang on a moment." I glanced over my shoulder, spying a flash of blinding white that made me quickly look away, and pointed to a spot several feet away where the wolf could not be seen. "Wait there, please."

I forced myself to watch the hiker and not Laurent, though I strained to hear what was happening. Had a dybbuk appeared? Was that why he'd drawn upon his Banim Shovavim magic?

A desolate howl echoed through the woods and the hiker jumped, wide-eyed.

"What was that?" he said.

"Coyote?" I dropped my arms because I'd hugged myself at the sound. I'd never get used to how much it hurt Laurent to use his acquired magic. It consumed him, turning his eyes black as pitch and his fur into a blinding expanse of white.

"You think?" The hiker craned his neck, walking closer to try to see for himself.

I darted a look up the trail. The wolf had bolted, nor was there any sign of a dybbuk. "All clear," I said. "But be on guard for wildlife." Or dybbuks.

I kept an eye on him in case he was attacked, but he bypassed the spot where I'd seen the shimmering circle without incident, and when I went to investigate, it too was gone.

While I killed dybbuks, Laurent's powers only allowed him to dispatch them back to Gehenna. Since he ripped open a portal to send them back, could one happen naturally, allowing dybbuks to slip through? And if so, had he sealed it?

"Laurent?" I peered into the trees, rubbing the back of my neck and assuring myself that the wolf could take care of himself, even as his tortured cry still rang in my ears.

My phone rang.

"All gone?" Tatiana said without preamble.

Whether she meant the wolf or the circle, the answer was the same. "Yes. Why didn't you tell me Laurent was back?"

"He wasn't." There was a crash of glass on her end. "Emmett, you klutz!"

"That was definitely him. Hello? Hello?" I smacked my hand against a tree trunk because she'd hung up.

My churning thoughts, extreme irritation, and several rounds of "I Will Survive" carried me up the large steps of the final steep quarter. Panting, I crested the top and slowed to a stop with a sigh. Vancouver stretched out before me, the breathtaking view going all the way past the city across the sparkling blue water to Mt. Baker in Washington State. But my sigh was because that horrible climb was finally done.

A fellow hiker snapped a photo with their phone. "All the toil and pain are worth it for this one moment."

"Totally," I said. Yeah, right. I could have taken the damn gondola up and seen the same thing. The only way you'd ever get me up this trail again was if they installed an escalator to the top.

"Stretch or you'll cramp up," Laurent grumbled from my other side.

I'd become a damn Pavlovian dog, lighting up when I heard him. Frowning so I didn't grin stupidly at the sound of his crochety French-accented English, I turned to look at him with a suitable neutral expression.

Screw the city view, this was way better. Sunlight kissed the olive skin on his lithe body, his shaggy curls falling over dazzling green eyes that I vividly remembered fogged with lust. His T-shirt was tucked into the waist of his baggy shorts, showcasing the tapering line from his shoulders to his waist and his tight six-pack. I imagined licking my way over those ridges and my nipples tightened.

"Is that for me?" I'm almost certain I meant the bottle of Gatorade and paper tray of fries that he held, but if he chose to interpret it in a different way, I wouldn't argue.

"I haven't decided." I'm almost certain he meant the food and drink, but if not, I might very well argue. "Do you generally greet returning travelers with such charm?" He sat down on a bench and popped a fry in his mouth. Setting the drink down next to him, he lazily draped an arm along the back of the bench.

My mouth watered, but I had my pride, so I stretched out my leg muscles as if I didn't care one way or the other. Then my stupid calf cramped up and I gave a strangled scream that was followed by a loud stomach rumble.

Laurent dragged a fry through the puddle of ketchup in the corner of the container with a teasing slowness before eating it.

"Do I smell vinegar?" I said nonchalantly, crossing one leg behind the other and bending to the side for a quick IT band stretch.

"Yup." He crammed four more fries in his mouth.

I stretched out the other leg. Whatever. I had my own money. I didn't need his charity potatoes. "How's your mother?"

"Better." He paused, looking down at his fries as though they were surprisingly good. "Thanks for asking."

I'd asked several times already via text, but he hadn't seen fit to answer. Balancing on my left leg, I grabbed my right foot and pulled it behind me to get at my hip flexors. A quick debrief and then I'd collapse somewhere privately and stuff my face. "How did you deal with the problem back there?"

"Reopening and closing the rip sealed it up again."

My hypothesis was correct. "You've seen this before?"

"No, but history has recorded infrequent cases of it. No one has figured out why it happens, but most things in life can be solved by rebooting them so I figured"—he shrugged —"might as well."

"You rebooted it." I gaped at him. "And that worked?"

"Yeah." Laurent cracked the Gatorade and held it out to me.

"No, thank you," I said evenly. The two of us still needed

to discuss how we intended to proceed—as friends, friends plus benefits, or what—but standing in a tourist-thronged crowd when I was starving wasn't the place to do it. I did, however, have to satisfy my curiosity about one thing. "Why did Tatiana say you weren't back?"

"Because I wasn't. She called me after she spoke with you and asked that I get my friend Cam to do me a favor."

"Who's Cam?"

Laurent looked around to make sure we weren't overheard, and still lowered his voice. "You know the woman who mentored me?"

I nodded and switched legs for what would hopefully be my final stretch. Laurent had had a mentor who taught him how to use Banim Shovavim magic as an Ohrist. She'd also taught him everything he knew about killing dybbuks.

"Cameron's her kid."

"Okay, but how did this favor get you here? You can't use the Kefitzat Haderech and Banim Shovavim can't transport without it."

"Cam's Ohrist. Uses light to travel. It's a rare ability but it gets you from one place to another in the blink of an eye. Something with photons and light particles traveling superfast. One minute I was at my parents' apartment, the next Cam showed up and got us to the mountain. From there I shifted and found you."

I grabbed the armrest of the bench for support because I was more wobbly standing on this foot. "I'm surprised Tatiana hasn't recruited him."

Laurent's brows drew together.

"Cameron," I clarified. "Seems like a prize catch for Team Tatiana."

"Thanks for the kind words, and believe me, she tried." A blonde in her early thirties with a light sheen of sweat on her face and a runner's wiry body draped her arms over Laurent's neck from behind, resting her head on his shoulder. "I didn't want to be tied down." The woman grinned, her expression radiant. She struck me as the kind of person who enjoyed life to the fullest. "You must be Miriam. I'm Cam. Isn't the Grind the best? What a great hike."

My foot hit the ground and I came out of my stretch in the most ungainly way. "There's nothing like it."

"Thirty-eight minutes." Cam held up her hand for Laurent to high-five, and when he didn't, lifted his hand and slapped hers against him.

He rolled his eyes, but his lips quirked.

I lunged around the bench like this was a normal cool-down routine for me after climbing a mountain.

There was a lot to unpack here: that Laurent had not used a single gendered pronoun when describing Cam, that she had climbed the trail in just over half an hour, or that the shifter with personal boundary issues sat there letting her hug him.

No, wait. Now he was letting her help herself to his fries. The ones that I'd been denied. A drop of sweat fell into my eye and I blinked it out rapidly, my face scrunched up.

Laurent swore at Cam in French, and she chuckled, keeping a death clamp on the container.

My legs screamed in pain but I couldn't stop my lunges because I'd been possessed by the Energizer Bunny from Hell in my compulsion to show how fit I was.

"Mad respect," Cam said. "After that hike, I just want to flake out and stuff my face."

"I can go for hours." My eyes were blurry with tears because my left leg had seized up and I was stuck in the lunge.

"Do you need help?" Laurent said.

"Nope." I twisted my torso from one side to the other as though this was all part of my plan. Welp, it had been a good life. And hey, in several hours when I still couldn't move, I could watch the sunset from this lovely vantage point and

41

enjoy nightfall all by myself on an empty mountain, until at some point in the wee hours, I fell over and died, finally to be eaten by bears. Maybe they'd even commission a statue of me: *The Overzealous Hiker*, bronze.

"Want some?" Cam held the fries out to me.

Not if my life depended on it. I wouldn't give Laurent the satisfaction.

"No, thanks. After all the fresh air of the Grind, I'm craving a salad." Potato salad. Pasta salad. Chocolate shaped like salad.

Laurent's eyebrows drew together. "You eat salad?"

"Jesus!" Cam elbowed him hard.

"Only when I run out of bacon grease to spoon directly into my mouth." Using my hands, I wrenched myself out of the stupid lunge, more relieved to be standing upright than I had been to finish the Grind.

Cam shook her head. "Sorry, Miriam. He has no tact."

I stretched my arms over my head, the stitch in my side having spread to include my entire chest, making it tough to get a proper breath. "I wouldn't know. We're just sort of work colleagues."

A muscle ticked in Laurent's cheek and my smile broadened, though my happy rush quickly faded as I kicked off a clump of dirt stuck to my dingy white sports sock. My shirt was soaked with sweat stains, I was filthy, my hair was a damp mess, and hunger and humiliation were about to make me extremely bitchy. Exit, stage left even. *Now*.

"Thanks for helping out," I said, "but I've got to run. Nice meeting you, Cam."

"You too."

I really wanted to dislike her, but she was so damn cheerful. And it wasn't her fault that Laurent had given me the best orgasm I'd had in years and then reappeared with a younger woman in tow. Maybe she really was just here because Tatiana had requested her help.

Right. And maybe I craved a salad.

Laurent untangled himself from his friend. "Cam is taking me back to Paris to get my things, but I'm coming home tomorrow."

"I'm surprised you lasted as long as you did with Jacques there," Cam said through a mouthful of fries. "You're a softie where Leila's concerned."

I liked a woman who didn't let small things like talking distract from her enjoyment of fried foods. However, I liked her first-name basis with Laurent's parents somewhat less. "Don't let me keep you from your plans."

Laurent shrugged into his T-shirt. "Mitzi."

I gave them a firm wave. "Bye."

While my stride was relaxed, my jaw was tight enough to shatter teeth. Whether or not Laurent and Cam were more than friends, it didn't change the fact that he shouldn't have ghosted me. Or dumped an introduction with his gorgeous younger friend on me at this particular moment.

My indignation grew while I nursed a Pilsner and devoured a plate of onion rings. I couldn't even sit on the patio with the other patrons to enjoy the fresh air and people-watch because the way my luck was going, I'd spy the two people I didn't want to watch.

I nursed my wounds seated in a dark corner of the pub, checking in with Ava about Jude, and then sending my best friend a quick text to let her know I'd really made it to the top and was going home.

Because that's what friends did, I mused, having a long and necessary pee while waiting for Jude to reply. They communicated with each other, even if one of the parties was going to make her friend's head explode if she didn't quit with all the avoidance.

She finally sent a thumbs-up emoji. I refrained from sending a few emojis of my own, realizing that my mood right now wasn't really because of Jude.

It was about my other useless friend, flaunting this personal life he'd never once mentioned in my face.

I fumed all the way down the gondola ride, wedged into a corner by cutesy couples taking selfies, and drove home white-knuckling the steering wheel.

Sadie was eating her after-work snack of cereal when I entered the kitchen. She hadn't yet changed out of the brightly colored T-shirt with the camp logo where she was a junior theater counselor. "You're filthy. Tatiana got you burying bodies now?"

"Don't give her ideas." I grabbed a jar of Nutella out of the cupboard, got a spoon, and dug in. "I did the Grind."

My child grimaced. "Gross. Why?"

I waved the spoon at her, speaking through a mouthful of gooey chocolate. "Right? Thank you. The one sane person in the wild dybbuk chase I've been on all day. Tatiana had me track down a thin spot where dybbuks were getting out and I've been surrounded by happy exercise people."

"Yikes." She drained the milk in the bowl and took it to the sink. "Do you have to close the mountain or something?"

"No," I said with lethal pleasantness. "Laurent fixed it." I shoved another spoonful in. Take that, charity potatoes.

The bowl clattered loudly into the basin. "I thought he was in France."

I took note of her carefully casual tone. Sadie didn't know that anything had happened between Laurent and me, but she hadn't quite sorted out her feelings about the existence of magic. She adored Emmett and thought Tatiana was great, but there was a reticence around Laurent.

Then again, she'd had the same hesitation about Naveen, Laurent's best friend who her father was interested in, so on second thought, maybe magic wasn't the problem. At least she wasn't a fan of Zev. Their first encounter had put her off vamps, though lucky for BatKian, it hadn't extended to our

Buffy rewatch. I'd have been pissed off if he'd ruined that for us.

"He came home early." I screwed the lid back on the Nutella jar. "What are you up to tonight? Seeing Caleb?"

"No. The kids exhausted me today." She sounded so much like a disgruntled mother that I laughed. "We were making props for 'Under the Sea' and it's like they were all high on sugar. They fingerpainted my arms. It took me ages to clean it."

"Ah. Hence the seaweed." I motioned at one of her two long black braids.

"Little monsters." She plucked a dark green strand out and flicked it into the trash. "I thought I'd caught all that. No wonder I got weird looks on the bus home. Okay, I'm going to nap. Let me know when dinner's ready."

I bobbed a curtsy to her. "Yes, ma'am. Any other needs I can attend to?"

"That will be all for now," she said loftily, yelping when I swatted her butt. "I'll be on cleanup duty."

"You sure will."

Between my kid and a hot shower, my crankiness had dialed down to a simmering three out of ten. I collapsed on the sofa, stuffing an ice pack under each of my hamstrings and the heating pad under my back for twenty minutes of rest and relaxation before making dinner.

My shitty day was over, and I'd negotiated a day off tomorrow. Tonight, I'd veg out with that bottle of Moscato chilling in my fridge, and then sleep in. Take a full day to rest before diving in to investigate whatever job my parents had been working when they were killed.

It was an excellent plan. So of course, it was doomed to go to hell.

5

MY LOVELY, LAZY INTENTION OF SLEEPING LATE ON Wednesday morning was thwarted by a loud pounding on my front door. I jolted awake, decided that being upright was a really bad idea, and flopped back onto my pillow with a groan. Moscato went down a little too easily, especially when it was ice cold, the weather was hot, and I was playing a drinking game where I had a glass for every way that I planned to tell Laurent off.

I am a very creative person.

I forced my eyes open, the light filtering in from the slit in my curtains burrowing into my brain with razor-sharp teeth. The asshole sun was almost as bad as the tenant above me who decided to tap dance. Shit. No, I lived in a house. That was my head.

I pulled the pillow over my face, intending to lie there and moan, but sadly, the person at the front door didn't respect my privacy during this difficult time. Also, it might be Ryann with an update, so I dragged my butt out of bed, raking a hand through my hair to push the tangled mess out of my face.

When I finally made it downstairs and saw who it was, I

sighed, resting my forehead on the door just in time to have my visitor's next burst of knocks slam into my skull like an ice pick.

I threw the door open. "It's my day off."

Emmett's face fell. "You invited me."

It took a moment for his two faces to resolve into one. Back to bed for me.

"You didn't forget, did you?" With the slouchy jumpsuit that matched her huge red glasses and a big floral wreath on her head, Tatiana looked like a pixie. An evil one.

I was about to reschedule but the golem looked so forlorn that I pasted a smile on. "Of course not. I've been looking forward to our visit."

"Awesome." Emmett stepped inside, rubbing his hands. "Today is going to be epic. What's up first?"

My smile dimmed. He expected me to entertain him all day? "We're gonna party like we're 1999," I said.

"You suck at song lyrics. You mean like *it's* 1999," Emmett corrected.

"Do I?"

Tatiana looped her purse strap over her arm. "I'll pick him up tonight after my client meeting."

"I'd like to come to that." I'd been meaning to broach the subject with her for a while.

She crossed her arms, exposing a jangle of thin gold bracelets. "You look like death warmed over."

Emmett was already opening and closing cupboards in the kitchen. He was welcome to whatever he found. I didn't have the energy to corral him.

"Be that as it may." I leaned against the door frame, swallowing to clear the gummy feeling in my mouth. "I'm the one carrying out the jobs and I'd like to get a sense of who's hiring us. My impression of the person could come in handy."

Coffee or cold shower first? My stomach lurched at the thought of anything in it. Shower it was.

Tatiana thought about it, then nodded. "Remember, I have final say on whether we take the assignment or not."

"Sure."

"Bear's Den at seven sharp. And look nice. Vikram enforces a more formal dress code a couple times a month." Tatiana paused, looked me up and down, then jabbed me in the chest. "Better yet, have Sadie pick something out for you."

What were those bony digits of hers made of? Titanium? I rubbed the sore spot, far too hungover for a snappy comeback.

"Don't be late." She tottered back to her behemoth of a car.

I shut the door before I saw her maul the curb in her attempts to back her vehicle out of its spot.

"I'm bored." Emmett wandered back into the foyer.

I rested my head against the door frame again because it was easier than using my muscles. "Let me take a shower and then I have a super fun activity planned for you."

"What?"

"Digging."

"More work?" He turned around, kitchen-bound again. "I'm not a mindless slave."

I tugged him back by his overall shorts. "You're right." He *should* have been a mindless slave like other golems, but sadly he had opinions. Many, many opinions. "Except this isn't work. It's training."

Emmett notched his chin up. "Don't try your Mr. Miyagi justifications. I'm Cobra Kai." He balanced on one foot with his arms up, like Karate Kid Golem was about to launch a crane kick.

I poked him and he stumbled sideways. "What if we need to bury a body? Huh, smart guy? You're stronger than I am so we need to time you and see how long it takes." I grabbed a floppy sunhat from the coat closet. "But if you don't want to be on those kinds of jobs, I can't force you."

He snatched the hat away and slapped it on his bald clay head. "Get me a shovel."

Emmett was like a child in so many ways, bless him. He accepted my explanation that of course he'd have to clear out weeds and roots in a real gravesite and that the tiny arugula and pea plants I'd laid out for him were stand-ins for underbrush in the forest.

"This seems like overkill." He dropped the last bag of fertilizer on the ground.

"You need to brush up on your mobster movies, partner. The plant cover?" I indicated the veggie starter plants. "Makes the ground look undisturbed. We then sprinkle the earth with salt, or in this case fertilizer, to keep animals away since it nulls the scent of putrefaction."

"I knew that," he grumbled.

I made a big production of opening the stopwatch on my phone. "Remember, speedy but not sloppy. Our lives depend on it."

He struck the dirt with the tip of the shovel. "Tell me when."

"Go." I settled on a chaise longue in the shade, applying sunscreen and offering the occasional instructional comment. Confident he had the gist of things, I slid my sunglasses on and stretched out, turning my face to the sky. Between the cold shower, double espresso, and two Tylenol, my head felt much better.

The *tchack* of the shovel provided a steady rhythm to the melody of trilling birds and the faraway drone of a Weedwacker.

"Done!"

I fluttered my eyes open and hit stop. "Forty minutes. Way to go." Should we actually require this service, we were fucked, but I'd gotten a nice nap.

I even felt well enough to check in with Ryann, but there was no progress on tracking down the stranger from the beach. She didn't think he'd gone to ground in Vancouver. I hoped that was true and another encounter between us wasn't likely before he was caught. Although it meant he was out there doing who knew what with the information about my magic.

Ryann promised to keep me looped in on all new developments.

This stranger remained the best and fastest way for me to get answers. The only other person who had been close to my parents who was still alive was my cousin Goldie, and she didn't know they'd had magic.

I drummed my fingers on the arm of the lounger. Where else could I look? I'd gone through the box of birthday cards that my uncle Jake had sent a million times and never come up with anything to explain their murders. Maybe million and one was the charm?

I'd just turned the sprinkler on to wet the newly planted veggies—and for Emmett to run through—when my phone rang. I grabbed it, ready with one of the many impressive speeches I'd come up with last night to serve Laurent with, but it was Military Marsha, the self-appointed head of the book club that I was in.

Shit. Had I forgotten to prepare something for our next meeting? Let's see. Depressing historical tale with an overabundance of navel gazing? Skimmed. Shitty rosé? Purchased. Confident I'd pass any checklist that Marsha threw at me, I caught the call on the last ring. "Hello?"

"It's a nightmare!" Marsha screeched. "Kit and her husband went to Wreck Beach as some sort of spicy date for their thirteenth anniversary. What's wrong with lace? That's traditional."

I rubbed a hand over my jaw. "Is this nightmare because you loathe nude beaches, or do you feel that lace isn't getting its due in the anniversary pantheon?" It was totally the first one.

There was a tick of impatient silence. "Kit is hosting book club this month."

"So?"

"Let's just say she did not sufficiently cover herself with sunscreen."

"Reaallly?" I sat forward. "And what, pray tell, was the body part unprotected from the sun?"

There was a pause. "Her anus."

I barked a laugh. "What a bummer."

Marsha couldn't stop her snort. My jokes never amused her, so I took this as a major victory and did a seated wiggly dance.

"Don't worry," I said. "The rosé will keep until the next one."

"That's not the issue," she said icily to the sound of paper rustling. "The rules—"

"Welcome email," I corrected. There was more rustling from her end. "Wait. Did you print it out? How many pages was it?"

"The *rules* state that should one host be indisposed, book club automatically moves to the next person on the list." Even over the phone, her molar grinding was audible. "You."

The soaking wet golem in my backyard shook water on me before leaping through the sprinkler again.

"Yeah, no. That can't happen." I dabbed my damp face with the hem of my sundress. I didn't have time to clean my house before Sunday so that it glittered like a Mr. Clean commercial, nor was I about to race around buying snacks to fulfill everyone's different dietary needs. There were so many that the last time I'd hosted, I'd requested doctors' notes verifying these were actual medical debilitations and not just because "bread made you bloat."

Besides, what was the point of book club without cheese?

That's right, there wasn't one.

"Rules, Miriam." There was a sharp thwack as if she'd rolled the printed pages up and smacked them against a table.

"For the last time, the email isn't legally binding, no matter how much you wish otherwise."

"You have to host." Her voice cracked.

I frowned. Emotion? From the ice queen? Surely not. But I had to ask. "What's really going on? And don't say rules. Are you okay?"

"Don't be silly. I'm—" A door slammed open on her end, accompanied by a roar of male voices.

I jerked the phone away from my ear. "What was that?"

The sound of a second door closing cut the men off, replaced by the distant sound of cars.

"My husband is having a few frat brothers stay with us for their twentieth reunion. For a whole week. They're having such a good time." Any more brittle and she'd shatter.

I banged my fist against my forehead. "Lovely."

"Last night, they got drunk and had a farting competition in the hot tub. Such jokers, always competing."

"Hey, babe," a deep voice said on Marsha's side. "Had a bit of a grease fire sitch."

"It's out though, right?" Wow. Points to her for sounding calm.

"All good. Also, we need more bacon." There was a loud kissing smack. "You're the best."

Marsha's deep breathing was understandable, but this was the last book club of our "agreed to" year membership. If Kit couldn't host, then I was free, and Marsha couldn't stop me. She could go to a movie or visit a friend if she had to get out of the house.

I was allowed to set boundaries.

Marsha still hadn't spoken. Uh, how long could a person safely breathe deeply before hyperventilating?

I didn't even like book club. Plus, I'd be expected to come

up with conversation guides. "This book is a masturbatory wank. Discuss." wouldn't cut it. I'd tried.

I sighed. "I'll buy more rosé."

"Thank you," Marsha whispered.

Damn it, hosting book club was going to be so much work. But if it kept her from losing her shit, I had to support her. With one caveat. "We're having cheese."

"God, yes," she said viciously. "The lactose intolerant crowd isn't holding my brie hostage this time."

My eyebrows rose. This was a version of Marsha I could get behind. Maybe final book club would be fun after all.

"I'll see you Sunday. And Miriam? Thank you." She hung up, leaving me staring at the phone and wondering what had just happened.

"What's next?" Emmett stood over me, dripping.

I flung a towel at him. "Wanna clean my house for booze?"

"Toots, you said the magic word." Forgoing the towel, he strode inside, dripping water everywhere.

He did such a good job cleaning house for the next three hours that I told him he could go through my closet for something to wear to dinner. He laughed, said "As if I'd be caught dead looking like you," and went upstairs to find Sadie, who'd just gotten home.

I looked down at my sundress. It was cute, wasn't it? It didn't need to be ironed or dry cleaned, which was practical. I wandered into my living room, gazing adoringly at the sofa that I'd bought last month. It was a vision of decadent wine velvet that stood out like a sore thumb in an ocean of beige.

When it was delivered, Sadie had clapped her hands and declared this was more like it.

Even Eli had nodded in approval, reminding me of the old red brocade chair he'd had in his first apartment that I'd always curled up in. "Given how much you loved that chair, your furniture choices always confused me. I understand now you wanted to blend in because of your hidden magic, but I'm glad you're finding that part of yourself again."

I mulled over his words. The sofa was a good first step but tonight was time for my next one. Smiling, I marched into my bedroom for my transformation.

One hour later I was sitting on the edge of my bathtub, draped in midnight-blue silk, while Sadie applied false lashes onto my left lid.

I flinched. "Watch it. You almost took out my eye."

"For the one billionth time, I did not." She held out the tweezers. "Do it yourself. Oh wait, they looked like a second pair of eyebrows when you tried. Guess you're stuck with me."

"Are you this mean to the camp kids?" I checked how tacky the glue was on the second pair of lashes.

"When they bitch as much as you do? Yes."

Emmett laughed, standing at the bathroom counter and testing shades of lipstick on his hand. He'd borrowed a ruffled pirate shirt and black jodhpurs from Sadie's cosplay costumes. The pants were too short and too small, held together with a belt, but the shirt was okay, since it was baggy on Sadie. He looked kind of raffish, especially with the black top hat he'd perched jauntily on his head. "You two are exactly alike," he said.

"Wow," Sadie said.

"Truth hurts, kid." He made a face at a sheer pink gloss, adding it to his discard pile.

"Hey!" I prodded my child. "Show some respect."

She wrapped her arms around me. "I adore you, Mom, and I'm proud to have inherited your mean genes."

I leaned into her embrace. "That's better."

"Now." She straightened up, waving the tweezers menacingly. "Sit still and keep quiet while I make you look beau-uutiful."

Emmett snorted and I kicked his shin.

The pain of kicking someone made of solid, hardened clay was mostly worth the gain.

I admired my smoky eyes with the swipe of green shadow that made my brown eyes look sensual while the false lashes brightened them up. Then I sucked in my cheeks. "Cheekbones, who knew?"

"I could give you a ten-minute daily makeup routine," Sadie said hopefully. "Super easy."

I applied my scarlet lipstick. "That's about eight and a half minutes too long for me, kiddo."

"One day," she muttered darkly and left the bathroom.

It took a few minutes to pry Emmett away from his primping in front of the mirror, but we made it to the parking garage leading to the hidden magic speakeasy with five minutes to spare.

My heels clicked against the concrete, the hem of my fitted spaghetti strap dress swirling around my ankles.

A Mercedes SUV gunned past us out of the lot. This parkade served a lot of office workers so at this hour, it was mostly empty, though I spied Tatiana's gold beast taking up two and a half spots.

Once inside the elevator, which smelled of cigars, Emmett hit the button for the Bear's Den before I could. Only people with magic could see it.

I tapped him on the shoulder. "Did you have to train to reveal hidden spaces?"

"Naw. I'm a natural. Did you?"

"Tiny bit." It had taken weeks to train myself out of a life-long habit of ignoring all signs of magic into being able to see it everywhere, but I'd gotten so proficient that I could even drive into a hidden space without incident.

We stepped out of the elevator into the tiny concrete area

with the broken payphone, and I depressed the switch hook twice. The wall swung away, the funky bass solo from inside bringing a smile to my face and getting my hips swinging.

Vikram, the owner, greeted us, looking sharp in a dark suit. His salt-and-pepper hair was brushed away from his brown skin like a mane, though in reality, he was a bear shifter. "Tatiana is waiting for you at the back."

There was loud applause, and the rest of the house jazz quartet joined the bass for the rest of "It Don't Mean a Thing." The clarinet and piano turned the melody into a soaring, dizzying tune, the bassist adding a deep groove and the percussionist keeping them all in line, pushing them to the limits of the beat.

"With the client," Vikram finished.

"Thank you, my good man." I fluttered my lashes and he grunted.

"You know how much that last visit of yours cost to clean up and repair?" he said, glowering.

There were about seven people involved in that fight, and I'd saved his best customer from certain death. Where was the gratitude? Still, there was no point arguing. I patted my updo of loose curls, secured with a scarlet flower, and launched into my best friend's Southern drawl. "Honey, I'm not about to ruin my look."

Emmett had reached the limit of standing and fidgeting, leaving the foyer for the main part of the speakeasy.

"Make sure he doesn't steal anyone's drink," Vikram admonished.

"Yeah, yeah." I hurried after the golem past round burnished tables hugged up to curved leather banquettes under softly glowing sconce lamps.

A black metal chandelier dripping with crystals over the long bar at the far end of the room threw dozens of prisms on the gold brocade wallpaper. The patrons were dressed to the nines enjoying cocktails in every color, while the scent of roasting meat, freshly baked rolls, and dozens of delicious appetizers made my mouth water.

Emmett slid into a back booth that I'd dubbed "the royal court" because Tatiana liked to conduct her machinations from it, be it entertaining clients, or just drawing like she had at our first meeting, while keeping an eye out for telltale signs of intrigue, secrets, and scandal.

She'd honed her ability over decades of practice to appear immersed in her sketching while not missing a thing that was happening around her, and this booth gave her a clear line of sight into all corners of the speakeasy. The only part she couldn't spy on was the back half of the attached art gallery.

Tatiana set her menu aside and checked her gold watch, ruffling the explosion of silk feathers on her yellow sweater. "Punctual to the dot."

There was no more room on the curved padded bench, so I took the chair that had been pulled up to the table, letting her critical tone wash over me, and stuck out my hand for our prospective client to shake. "Hi. I'm Miriam Feldman."

"Giselle Mueller." The young woman regarded me frankly with wide hazel eyes, unlike the blink of surprise she'd given the golem, a smattering of freckles dotting her porcelain skin. Her light brown hair held in a clasp at the nape of her neck accented the graceful line of her throat, while her handshake was firm, her long, elegant fingers enveloping mine. She reminded me of a swan, glowing with vitality.

"And this is Emmett," Tatiana said.

The golem barely nodded, flagging down a server.

Giselle yawned, then covered her mouth. "Excuse me. Those red-eye flights wipe me out."

"Where were you?" I draped my purse strap over the back of my chair.

"New York. I dance with the Ishikawa Ballet Company in Manhattan."

I wasn't a huge ballet fan, but they'd put on a high-profile production of *Don Quixote* a few years ago and I'd seen some of the clips that had gone viral. "Wow. That's impressive."

The dancer's smile lit up her face. "Thank you. I've worked hard to get here."

"Giselle is the name of a ballet, isn't it?"

She nodded. "My mom had to give up her dream of being a ballerina. Luckily, I loved ballet as much as she did, and her dream became mine."

Giselle sounded pleased that everything had worked out so well, but frankly, that sounded like a nightmare more than a dream. Any parent living vicariously through a child put a ton of pressure on them, especially in fields where parents became rabid in hopes of having their kid make it big. I wasn't about to insult Giselle's mother, however, so I smiled politely.

"Are you ready to order?" Our male server placed a gin and tonic in front of Tatiana and a white wine in front of Giselle.

I hadn't picked up the handwritten menu yet, but Tatiana ordered the salmon with a side salad. Giselle decided she'd have the same, while I hastily scanned the daily specials for something healthy as well.

"I'll have the steak in the butter sauce, medium-well, the pommes frites, and a salad,"

I said. "Oil and vinegar on the side." There. No heavy dressing for me. Pleased, I handed the server my menu.

"And to drink?" He poured me ice water out of a large glass carafe.

I opened my mouth to say I was fine with the water, but only a strangled croak came out as I gawked at the couple who'd just entered.

In all their shining finery, Laurent and Cam.

6

CAM LOOKED BEAUTIFUL IN A SIMPLY CUT BLACK dress, her blond hair brushing her shoulders. She said something animatedly to Laurent, and while he shook his head, his lips quirked up in a half smile. Laugh lines crinkled around his intense green eyes as he led her to the far side of the speakeasy with his hand on the small of her back.

The shifter had donned a suit that clung to his shoulders and hugged his thighs, the deep navy fabric almost iridescent.

They were a gorgeous couple. Or just gorgeous friends.

Like he and I were friends? I twisted my linen napkin into a tourniquet around my fist. I'd had a couple longish relationships since my divorce ten years ago, and while I'd been hurt when those ended, I hadn't felt the betrayal that washed over me now. I hated how pathetic and small I felt, but his obliviousness toward my feelings was cruel.

Someone kicked me under the table, and I blinked, finding Emmett giving me a curious look. "Order already."

"Gin and tonic," I said. "Double."

Laurent and I had fooled around exactly once, minus any penetration. We hadn't made each other promises of monogamy, but there had been future "intentions," for lack of a better word. He'd bought condoms and I'd been masturbating like an adolescent boy while waiting. Of course, he had every right to change his mind about us, but I deserved some common courtesy before he showed up with his new girlfriend.

She was Laurent's girlfriend, right? I'd never had a platonic male friend go out for a fancy dinner with me, but maybe our five-year age difference came with a generational gap? I shook my head. It didn't matter what she was to him because this wasn't about Cam, it was about me, and the basic level of respect I deserved.

After making a big production asking about seventy-two different drinks, Emmett settled on a Whiskey Smash. The waiter didn't ask him if he wanted anything to eat. Did he already know that the golem only drank? How often had Tatiana brought Emmett here? Talk about playing favorites. I'd only ever gotten a single breakfast from her in this place.

Once our server left, I folded my hands on the table. I'd come to the Bear's Den for work and didn't care that Laurent was pulling out Cam's chair when all I ever got from him was grief. However, just like his aunt, he had mastered the art of appearing caught up in something when he was taking in the entire room and committing the details to memory.

I smirked in anticipation of the moment he saw me. No longer the mountain urchin, I looked sophisticated and sexy. Even better, I felt it.

No one was going to make me feel invisible ever again. More importantly, I'd never make myself feel that way.

Emmett slung an arm along the back of the banquette. "Ballet, huh? You got mangled feet?"

Jeez, tact much? I kicked his leg and he made a "what?" face at me.

"Big-time," Giselle said.

He glanced down, then leaned forward, his eyes gleaming. "Can I—ouch!" The golem glared at Tatiana, who smiled sweetly. She had totally pinched him. Wait. His arm was hard clay.

She rubbed the tines of her fork off with her napkin. Wow. Stone cold.

Cam's tinkly laughter floated across the room, accompanied by Vikram's gruff guffaw. The owner had stopped by their table to present them with a bottle of champagne. How cozy.

Good thing I was a professional and didn't let minor aggravations like this get to me.

I yanked my knife out of my sourdough roll. "New York is quite the way to come to engage Tatiana's services," I said. "I guess you wanted the best."

I had no idea if Tatiana was the best or the only magic fixer option, since she hadn't made me the orientation package that I'd requested, but a little flattery was never amiss.

My boss squeezed lime into her drink, giving me an amused look. "I didn't realize you weren't local, Giselle. If I do decide to take on your case, I'll have to make sure I'm not stepping on Kadeem's toes."

I perked up, my fingers twitching in my desire to start a list. So, there were other fixers.

Giselle rubbed her thumb over the wineglass rim. "The thing is," she said with a sigh, "I've already talked to Kadeem about this. He didn't think I had a case."

The server placed our drinks in front of Emmett and me. I immediately sucked half of mine back.

"Was I your second choice or have others refused you?" Tatiana said mildly.

"Oh boy," the golem muttered and took a healthy swig.

I glanced around checking for exploding organic material, like plant life or body parts.

Laurent watched me through narrowed eyes, not even pretending to be studying the menu in front of him. Cam, however, was engrossed in hers, her lips pursed. To be fair, there were a lot of delicious options.

Giselle explained that she'd asked Kadeem for another fixer's name, and he'd given her Tatiana's.

"Wasn't that nice of him?" Tatiana said. The ice in her drink shriveled down to nothing.

Being an expert multitasker, I sussed out the closest emergency exit while jerking my chin at the irritated Frenchman to pay attention to his own business.

Laurent tugged the cuffs of his jacket straight, tiny gold cuff links winking in the light. His neatly pressed suit may have been cut with a tailor's precise eye and made of the finest fabric, but being Laurent, his curls remained untamed, his jaw dusted with stubble.

I wrapped my arms around myself, convinced he was stripping away the filmy material of my dress through eye voodoo, then dropped them. Screw that. *See what you're missing, buddy.* I patted my hair ornament, the movement thrusting out my spectacular boobs, and turned a bright smile on Giselle. "Why don't you tell us your problem and Tatiana will decide for herself."

My boss sniffed, but at my pointed look, said she was all ears.

Giselle looked uncertainly at me, but I nodded encouragingly. "Do you ever get the feeling that you're not living your life correctly?" she said.

I frowned. "Correctly according to who? There are a bunch of different ways to achieve what you want. Do you mean you don't have the right job? Or that you're with someone you thought you wouldn't be?"

Tatiana sipped her gin and tonic. "That's called regret."

The waiter arrived with our meals. We made small talk while he distributed the plates, my mouth watering at the grilled meat.

Get in my belly. I dug right into my steak, dragging the piece through the herbed butter, while Giselle toyed with her salad.

"That's not what I mean. More like a train being switched onto another track."

"I'm afraid I don't quite understand." Tatiana forked a delicate piece of salmon that was laden with capers.

"I don't know how to explain it." Giselle reached for her wine with a defeated expression.

Emmett rolled his eyes, but Giselle had gotten me wondering.

She'd flown to Vancouver from New York to press her case in person after being turned down already, but she couldn't articulate her problem. Could magic be involved and be preventing Giselle from giving the details?

Laurent still watched me, so I forked a huge pile of salad, eating it with a look of bliss like it was the most delicious thing I'd ever tasted.

He shook his head and finally quit staring at me. I immediately crammed another piece of steak into my mouth.

"When did you first feel like that train had been switched to that other track?" I said.

Giselle's eyes shone with gratitude. "It was about a month ago. Shortly after I'd been promoted to coryphée. It's a lead position in the corps de ballet."

I glanced at Tatiana to make sure she was okay with me taking over the questioning, but she nodded. "That sounds great, but did something specific happen?" I said. "Was there jealousy or open animosity from a fellow dancer?"

Giselle ate her fish while thinking over my question. "No. Everyone was really supportive. Then the artistic director announced that we'd be performing *The Sleeping Beauty* next year. Thanks to my acting abilities I was cast as the fairy Candide and a second study for the lead role of Aurora."

"So, what's the problem?" Emmett said gruffly.

"I just…" Giselle's lip trembled, and she hurriedly had a sip of wine.

"What my colleague means to say," I interjected, "is it sounds like your career is on the upswing."

"It is. I was overjoyed about everything, but that's when this feeling that I'd made a mistake started. It began as an itch, but just kept growing and growing. Now it's like a deafening scream that I can't get away from and can't release." Giselle grasped my arm. "Please. You have to help me. I feel like I'm going crazy."

The woman seated across from me seemed gracious and genuinely nice. Could she be experiencing the resurfacing of a repressed memory?

"That's terrible," I said gently. "I'm really sorry you're feeling that way."

Giselle sagged back against the leather booth. "Thank you. When I told Kadeem all this, he said it was stress. He was so dismissive."

"I hear you. I've been there with men."

She picked up her coral clutch and toyed with the clasp. "I didn't tell him this because I felt so defeated by his attitude, but there's something else that might be relevant." Snapping open the purse, she deposited something in my palm.

It was a gold "G" pendant on a slender gold chain.

I held it up to the light but didn't see anything unusual about the necklace. "Why do you think this is part of it?"

Emmett held out his hand for it, but I shook my head. Giselle would never get it back.

"I've had this necklace forever," she said. "My parents gave it to me when I turned thirteen and it's been my good luck charm ever since, but I lost it three years ago."

"Then you should be pleased you've found it again," Tatiana said.

"Of course, but I tore my place apart when it went missing. And don't ask me if I'm sure because I am. It was right

64

after my audition with the company, and I wanted to wear it to celebrate the good news that I'd gotten in, but the necklace was gone. I haven't moved apartments, but around the same time that I was promoted and got my roles in *The Sleeping Beauty*, there it was, in my underwear drawer. There's no way I never saw it there."

"Okay, that's weird." I gave her back the necklace. What if something more nefarious was at play, like magic on the jewelry causing this distress?

"Right?" The relief in Giselle's voice was unmistakeable. "Finally, someone believes me."

I speared a tomato. "What type of powers do you have?"

"A bit of empathy magic. Pretty low level." Her magic wasn't causing the problem.

The *Friends* theme sounded. Giselle dug her phone out of her purse and answered it. "Hey, hang on. It's too loud here." She stood up and got out of the booth. "Sorry. It's my best friend. I asked her to call with anything important from the company meeting today. Is there somewhere quieter to take this?"

"The foyer where you came in," Tatiana said.

Giselle nodded her thanks, gracefully weaving around the tables.

When she was out of earshot, I asked Tatiana what she thought.

"I understand why Kadeem passed." She wiped her mouth with her napkin. "Don't look at me all crestfallen. I've had jewelry I swear I'd lost show up again in a place I'd searched a million times. It means nothing."

"What about this whole deafening scream?" I countered.

"Stress."

I tamped down a stab of disappointment. Tatiana was doing the exact same thing to Giselle as Kadeem had and just writing her off. Maybe that's what fixers did, but I'd expected better from my female boss.

"Giselle has suddenly been promoted, there's more at stake with her career." Tatiana waved a hand in dismissal. "She needs a prescription for antianxiety medication. The macher was right."

"Macher? The big shot? You mean Kadeem?" I used my remaining fries as delivery devices to soak up the last of the butter sauce.

"Macher can mean that, but it also means a fixer. Gender neutral. I'm a macher."

"I've spent two months with you, and you never bothered to tell me this? This is fascinating. What else?"

Emmett picked up his second Whiskey Smash, sloshing the alcohol over the rim. He licked it off his wrist. "Giselle is a tsuris-hound."

"That's my suspicion, yes," Tatiana said.

"What the hell is a tsuris-hound?" I held up my hand when Emmett began explaining the Yiddish definition. "I know what 'tsuris' means. Troubles. Aggravations. What is it in this context?" And why did Emmett have the inside track on fixer slang? Sorry, macher slang. Even if he was living with Tatiana now, I was her main minion. Employee. Emmett was just a subcontractor.

"Think of it like a drama queen." Tatiana held up her empty glass. "Some people don't know how to be happy. They're addicted to misery and strife and if there isn't any, they find some minor incident to blow out of proportion."

Vikram came over with refills for both Tatiana and me.

"Where's mine?" Emmett said.

The bear shifter pointed at the glass that was half-full. "You haven't finished the one you have."

Grumbling that that wasn't the point, Emmett went to fetch himself another drink at the bar.

"Thanks, Vikram," I said. Warmth spread through my chest that I now warranted the same personal attention as my boss.

"The wolf said you looked on edge and I should keep them coming," the owner said.

Giselle was partially visible in the foyer, shaking her head as she paced, still on the call.

But Laurent and Cam had left the building, with only the detritus of their dessert plates and the champagne bottle left as evidence of their tête-à-tête.

I ground the ice cube I was crunching to powdered snow. "Did he now?" I growled.

Vikram's eyebrows shot up. They were very shaggy, yet regal, which made sense for a bear shifter.

"You have very nice eyebrows," I said. I'd decided at our first meeting that Vikram and I would be friends and I meant it. Whatever weirdness Laurent was pulling, I, for one, would behave in a mature fashion. I handed the owner back the refill. "I'm good with water, thanks."

Vikram touched his brows briefly and blushed. "Who compliments eyebrows?" He lumbered away.

"I think there's something going on with Giselle beyond being a drama queen," I said. "But even if that's all it comes down to, why not make her happy, take her money, and look into it? You can always tell her there were no conclusive results."

Tatiana shot me a withering look. "The same reason Kadeem wouldn't take her on as a client. My reputation is everything and I won't have it bandied about that I fail. Tsuris-hounds are the worst for complaining far and wide about their dissatisfaction."

"It's not like you're on Yelp." I paused. "Are you?"

She rolled her eyes, stirring her ice around with her straw.

Like it wasn't a possibility. I smooshed the lemon wedge into my water. "Besides, everyone fails. Lawyers lose cases. Mechanics can't find every car problem. People still use their services."

"Not me."

I pointed a finger at her. "What about Fake Topher's death?" *I'll see your rebuttal and show precedence.*

"That was your failure, not mine," Tatiana said.

I scowled at her.

"In the end," she said, "there were many people who shared the blame for that mishap. None of them me."

Oy vey. How nice to live such an exemplary existence. "You've never failed? Not even once? I refuse to believe that."

She grabbed a sourdough roll from the basket in the middle of the table and buttered it with forceful strokes. "I don't see why you're so invested in this case anyway."

"Giselle wants to know the truth about why she's feeling this way. If something is wrong, then she needs to know what it is and why it happened. I get that. It's part of the reason why I came to work for you. To learn the truth about my parents' murders and get closure."

"The truth isn't always a good thing." She took a small bite.

"Spare me the platitudes. At the very least, I can check out the necklace. Maybe it's been spelled and if I'm right, you can gloat to Kadeem. Or any other magic fixer." I let that dangle there in case Tatiana wanted to pick up what I was putting down and enlighten me.

"Miriam's jealous that I'm your favorite and the only one you've shared things with," Emmett said smugly, returning in time to catch my last words.

Suddenly the golem with the emotional maturity of a child was Mr. Insightful? What's worse was that he was right. Tatiana had shared a softer, more personal side of herself back when a death curse had hung over her head. I thought that had finally blurred the lines between us of employer/minion, but apparently not quite as much as I'd hoped.

And not as much as it had with Emmett, who now lived with her.

I drank my stupid glass of water.

"First, get real," I said. "Second, yes, I would appreciate not operating in the dark. If I'm going to investigate this, I may end up in New York. You wanted to use my ability to travel through the Kefitzat Haderech to expand your business dealings, so at least tell me if I'll be stepping on anyone's toes."

"Enough kvetching already. All you had to do was ask," Tatiana said.

I slammed my glass down and glared at her.

She raised her hands. "Emmett was in the room with me during certain phone calls and he picked up things." She paused, her lips thinning, then sighed. "I'm not used to willingly sharing information, but you're right and I'm sorry."

I brushed crumbs off the napkin in my lap, trying not to preen because receiving an apology from this prickly, guarded woman was as great a victory as having breached a fortress. "Thank you. So, machers?"

"Years ago," she said, "there were only a handful of us in the world."

"Tatiana was the best," Emmett said.

"Suck-up," I said under my breath.

Giselle finished her call and stepped into the main room. Straightening her shoulders, she headed for the bar.

"Kindeleh." Tatiana raised an eyebrow at Emmett and me in mild admonishment. "When Samuel and I moved back to Vancouver, I went into semiretirement. All of us machers were getting older, so we divvied up territories and picked replacements to take over. The major cities in the world each got their own. Paris, Shanghai, Mumbai, Rio, Mexico City, New York, etc."

Emmett's attention had drifted and he people-watched with a bored expression on his face.

"People from smaller centers go to the larger ones for assistance and had I not lived here, Vancouver wouldn't have had its own, but I wanted to keep my hand in the game."

Tatiana fiddled with the large green beads on her necklace. "If you're on a job for me, then no one will bother you. I'd give Kadeem a heads-up, just out of courtesy, if you actually did end up in New York."

"So, the part about having to clear this job with him before you take it was a lie?" I reached for another roll and then decided better of it.

Tatiana picked a candied pecan out of her salad. "Never let anyone know exactly how powerful you are, bubeleh." She paused. "Or how weak. Be careful getting into bed with the Lonestars."

I pressed my toes into the ground as if physically testing my next step. "We share an interest in this potential suspect. I'm not drawing an arrow to my jugular with the sign 'slash here.'"

She smiled indulgently. "May I offer you one more platitude born of my extensive wisdom?"

If you must.

"Please do," I said politely.

"The girl's a lightweight." Emmett nodded at Giselle, who held a mostly full shot glass and was coughing.

Tatiana barely glanced over. "The danger with finding out the truth isn't about whether or not you can handle it, but that it lays you bare for others. And that can force a show of strength in retaliation."

"I want vengeance for my parents' deaths." I shrugged. "That's not news to you."

"I didn't mean just you. Clients always want to know the truth, but when they get it, they can become problematic."

Giselle's case was a puzzle. And in the end, maybe it would be one of those baby ones that consisted only of four large pieces, but my gut said it would take a lot more to make the picture snap into place. "I think solving this for her would be interesting."

"If that's all you want," Tatiana said. "How about a job

handling a delicate negotiation? I was approached by a wealthy businessman in Russia interested in our services. It's time sensitive and I need to get back to him as soon as possible."

"Is 'wealthy businessman' a euphemism for criminal?" I reapplied my lipstick.

"Ours is not to judge," she said reprovingly. "You'd be dealing with two very temperamental and magic-happy groups. It would be dangerous, which you seem to enjoy, and would require tact, out-of-the-box thinking, and a keen sense of character. That's got to be far more interesting than Giselle's problem."

I felt ten feet tall. The thing about Tatiana's blunt nature was that any compliment she gave me, while hard-won, was genuine. I seriously considered accepting the Russia assignment, but even if I had to think on my feet while appeasing thugs, it didn't call to me in the same way.

"I'd like to help the nice woman who flew all this way to speak with us."

Tatiana shook her head. "I have a bad feeling about this job."

"You always have a bad feeling."

"And I'm generally right. You almost landed in Deadman's Island on that murder case."

"I also cleared both my name and Laurent's. I would have been tossed there for sure if I hadn't. Plus, I didn't see this hesitation when it came to getting that death curse on you stopped."

"Of course not. I'm of paramount importance." Tatiana patted her hair coyly.

I dropped my lipstick into my purse. "Can we take Giselle on rather than Boris Badanov?"

Tatiana snickered, then smoothed out her expression. "Stay professional, Miriam. Fine. But if my reputation suffers, I will throw you to the wolves."

I snorted and she glared at me.

"You know what I mean."

"I won't screw up."

She ran a finger through the condensation on her gin and tonic. "I haven't been to Moscow in a while. This might be the perfect time to visit. Dust off the old skills."

"You want to get back in the game firsthand?"

She shrugged. "Not permanently, but your drive to get the most out of every case is contagious. I'd forgotten how fun it could be."

I opened my mouth to protest that I wouldn't call murder, manipulations, and threats by vamps and Lonestars fun, except that wasn't exactly true. "In that case, you're welcome."

"Suck-up," Emmett said under his breath.

My boss glanced up. "Ah. Here comes Giselle. I'll tell her the good news." She got out of the banquette and went to speak with our newest official client.

Tatiana had given me a long leash, but it still was a leash. She could strip away safety measures and alliances I'd built up should she choose, not to mention place roadblocks in my path to find my parents' killer. If Giselle's case was a bust, Tatiana wouldn't shrug and move on. Would she shorten the leash? Or strangle me with it?

Emmett nudged my foot. "Assume the worst, prepare for the worst."

"That's not the saying. It's 'hope for the best but prepare for the worst.'"

"Not the way Tatiana sees things." Emmett saluted me with his drink. "L'chaim."

GISELLE WAS EFFUSIVE IN HER THANKS FOR TAKING her case but sighed when I asked if she had gotten bad news with that call. "It wasn't anything about me personally. Just company politics. Alcohol affects my training," she said, "so I don't drink, but the level of bullshit that went down pushed me over the edge."

I assured her we all had those days.

Over coffee and tiramisu, which I was too full for but ate anyway, she shared stories about life in a ballet company. Some were funny, others just grueling. She was only in her twenties but had already sustained stress fractures in her spine, along with hip and knee problems, not to mention the mangled feet.

I was grateful that Sadie had gone the theater route and wasn't on a first-name basis with a sports physiotherapist by the time she was twelve.

Before she left, yawning incessantly from jet lag, Giselle reluctantly left the necklace in my safekeeping. I promised to get it back to her as soon as I could.

Tatiana picked up the bill for dinner, and then she and Emmett departed. I had to do a bathroom run first, after which I stopped by the bar to speak with Harry, the gargoyle bartender.

Harry acted as a go-between for supernatural parties. Since gargoyles were an endangered species, they occupied these roles in exchange for being left alone, and he'd helped me out on a regular basis arranging meetings with Zev.

"Oi, Miri." He had a bar towel slung over one broad shoulder, his rock-hard (literally) biceps flexing as he grabbed different bottles, expertly mixing up concoctions in highball glasses. The colors of his full-sleeve tattoos winked in the lights.

He'd forgone the manbun tonight, his hair tucked behind his ears and falling to his shoulders, but he wore his trademark long silver chain over his unbuttoned shirt. "How's it going, luv?"

"Still alive. That's my basic metric these days. And you?"

"Cream crackered." He laughed at my confusion. "Knackered. But I'm taking a few days off."

"That's good." I pulled a small package in green tissue wrapping paper out of my purse and slid it toward him. "This is for you."

He set down the blue gin bottle, throwing me a sweet smile. "Really?"

"Yes. Just a little something in appreciation for all your help."

Harry wiped his broad gray hands on the towel and carefully eased the tape off, a look of wonder on his face at this simple action. Had anyone ever given him a gift before? When he saw the woven brown leather cuff inside with small brass rivets, his entire face lit up. He snapped it around his wrist, holding his arm out to admire it. "It's bloody brilliant. Thank you."

"My pleasure. Enjoy your time off."

He nodded, already turning to show his gift off to one of the patrons at the bar.

Smiling, I headed for the foyer, stopping briefly to ask Vikram if anyone was taking over Harry's go-between role while he was away. I required some assistance from the gargoyle with the next step in both Giselle's case and investigating what job my parents were on, but I hadn't wanted him to think the gift was a bribe, so I'd intended on asking him tomorrow.

Vikram told me I could speak with Giulia while Harry was away. I'd met her once before when she'd helped Laurent and me track down my date who'd become dybbuk-possessed. Since I knew where to find the cat gargoyle, I thanked him and headed into the parkade, only to find Laurent sitting on the hood of my sedan.

He leaned back onto his elbows.

My heels tapped against the pavement, my chin up. I was glad we were doing this now. It would save me thinking about it when I tried to fall asleep. I dug my keys out of my purse, refusing to admire the line of his body draped on my car.

"Did you have a nice time this evening?" I said, beeping my fob at the sedan, which unlocked with a soft click.

Two women rounded the corner of this level of the parking garage, laughing over some story. They glanced over at us, assessing the potential threat level, like I always did, but seeing none, continued to their car.

"I like that color on you," Laurent said.

I looked down at my dress. It was a lovely shade of blue, especially with the light playing over the silk. No. He wasn't going to distract me. I crossed my arms. "We're both adults here. I would have appreciated some contact before running into you on the mountain, but—"

He poked the slippery fabric like it fascinated him, and I stepped back, my pulse fluttering. I required physical space to keep a cool head because like it or not, he and I were having this talk.

Dropping my keys back into my bag, I stood tall, shoulders back, but my determination to project a confident modern woman was undermined by my underwear making a break for it, and rolling down my belly, precariously hugging the curve of my ass.

Seriously? Now? The universe had a sick sense of humor. I pressed my thighs together to keep the slippery garment from getting up close and personal with my knees and cleared my throat.

"If you and Cam are together, then the polite thing to do would..." I trailed off, my mouth dry because he'd sat up straight, his eyes practically spitting fire.

"You think I fucked you and then showed up with some other woman?"

"Technically we didn't fuck—" I swallowed.

Laurent slid off the car. The smile on his face may have appeared charming, but there was a touch of wildness in it. "You think I'm that much of a douchebag?"

In his anger, his accent grew heavier and I thrilled at it, not caring at how messed up that was. I wanted to poke and prod him, unleashing the wolf. That would be far more fun than a straightforward conversation between mature adults.

The car with the women in it drove past us and disappeared down the exit ramp. I fanned away the stench of exhaust. Had it suddenly gotten hot in here?

"No. Well... Not exactly." I stomped my foot, using the movement to distract him as I slid my hand behind me and surreptitiously hitched up my underwear. *Stay.* "You confused me, okay? I didn't hear from you after you went back to France and then the first time I saw you, you were all huggy with a woman you were very careful to avoid assigning pronouns to and you let her have free rein on your fries." I tossed my head. "And now I sound hysterical, which, I assure you, I very much am not."

A surprised laugh burst out of him, his rigid shoulders losing their tension.

"Is this funny?" I narrowed my eyes.

"Very." He sat back down on the hood as if he had all the time in the world to be entertained.

Outside the parkade, an ambulance siren grew louder before whizzing past and fading away.

"Keep it up, Huff 'n' Puff. You're inching toward a definite yes on the douchebag front." I sat down next to him only because my underwear had continued its slow slide downward. Have a very fast talk, get him to leave, grab my underwear, and get in the car. That was the plan, and I was sticking to it.

"I will address your many charges." He kissed the tip of my nose. "What was the first one? I got lost with all your words."

I wiped off his kiss, feeling super childish and churlish. "Stop that. I don't even understand what's happening right now."

"Allow me to explain."

"Oh, please. I'd like nothing better."

He grinned and kissed my nose again.

Scowling, I permitted it, but only because it was nice when he leaned in and his cedar and sandalwood scent wove around me.

"You didn't hear from me because my visit was..." He ran a hand through his curls, making them stick up like a little kid's. "It's hard to go home. There was a lot I wanted to tell you, but I didn't have it in me to translate everything into English."

He generally seemed so comfortable and confident in his bilingualism, but of course stress and high emotions would take their toll.

"So, the truth is, it's not all about me?" I said it slowly like this was a foreign concept.

He laughed again and I ducked my head to hide my smile. "Your words, not mine," he said. "As for Cam, she's a child."

"How old is she?"

"Thirty," he said with a dismissive wave of his hand.

"Take the contempt down a notch there, Methuselah. You're thirty-seven and I'm forty-two. Our age difference isn't that much smaller. Unless you're implying that I'm cradle robbing?"

He nodded earnestly. "Oui. I thought that was implicit when I called you a cougar that time."

"Wow."

A security guard rode past on his bike doing his rounds and nodded hello.

"But there is nothing between Cam and me," Laurent said. "We're just friends."

"You and I are friends," I said.

"She's not an 'I've eaten her out' friend."

"Oh my God!" I was cough-laughing. "Don't ever describe me that way."

"Would it help if I added that you tasted delicious?" His smile was piratical.

"What is wrong with you?!" Beet red, I dropped my head into my hands.

He gave an aggrieved sigh. "All right. I won't. As for Cam, there is no attraction. She's too happy." He said it like it was an incurable disease. "And she's one of those touchy people. It's easiest to let her hug me and get it over with, otherwise it's like a game to her."

"Mmm. And Cam? What's her take on you?"

He pressed a hand to his heart. "Are you implying I am other than perfect?"

While further sexual acts would be mindblowing, it was these silly giddy moments that rocked my world beyond anything. He was playful and unguarded and I wanted nothing more than to keep teasing him and draw more of this side out for only me to see.

"Your words, not mine." I said it lightly, but my stomach was aching and not from overeating. I was feeling possessive of him and I didn't have that right. We weren't those people to each other.

"Cam would never date a shifter. She says we are all 'high maintenance.'" He did the quotes.

I made a "yikes" face. "She's not wrong."

"You wound me." He shook his head. "Alors, the reason we were at the Bear's Den is that using her magic really drains her. It's even worse bringing an extra person along. After jumping me here from Paris and then back again, she'll be laid out for a while. I wouldn't have asked but too many Ohrists could have become enthralled on the Grouse Grind by the time I'd gotten back on my own."

"It was a thank-you dinner?"

He nodded. "She loves the Bear's Den. The least I could do was treat her."

"Then I'm glad Vikram also gave her a very nice bottle of champagne."

Laurent snorted. "He pretends it's a gift, then he charges me for it. Do you believe me? About Cam?" He sounded both perversely grumpy and worried.

It was wonderful.

Everything was cleared up. We were fine and now it was time to take my leave because I needed some space to get my head straight. My underwear disaster had fallen to a distant second in terms of things to obsess over. I'd gone through an emotional whirlwind where this guy was concerned in the past couple of days, and I had to sort through my tangled feelings.

"Yes," I said. "I believe you."

Laurent made a pleased little hum at the back of his throat.

Resting my feet on my bumper, I wrapped my arms around my knees. It'd be rude to leave without inquiring further about his trip. I wouldn't do that to my other friends.

"How did you manage on the flights?" I said. Laurent hated flying, feeling like he was trapped in a cage.

"Poorly. And it didn't get better once I landed."

"That bad?"

His side brushed against mine, his body growing more relaxed. "I hate hospitals, so yes. And then there's my father. That's another yes. My mother was the one bright spot and that was with her recovering from her heart attack." He gave a wan smile. "One good thing came out of it. It broke the veneer that we were some happy family. Maman and I even talked about the past. A bit. But still. And I no longer feel the need to speak to my father at all."

That wasn't exactly progress so much as extreme dysfunction, but he'd had a breakthrough with his mother, and I wanted to be supportive. "I'm glad," I said. "Were you there alone? What about Juliette's dad?"

I didn't know the man's name, but Laurent's niece had accused him of avoiding her father during his visit to Vancouver. Sheesh, his family had a lot of bad blood. Hearing the little he was telling me now made it seem like he and Tatiana were thick as thieves. My family was unconventional and intensely irritating at times, but I was grateful for our relationship. We fought, we worked it out. I couldn't imagine not speaking to Eli, Sadie, or my cousin Goldie for any length of time out of anger.

"Gabriel?" He rolled the "r" in his French accent and a delicious shiver slid through me.

Laurent didn't notice, busy frowning at his shoes. He shot me a sideways glance, then after a moment shook his head. "No. He wasn't there."

"That's hard to have dealt with all that on your own."

He shrugged like he was used to it and my heart twisted.

I switched back to a more lighthearted topic before I said anything that would drive him off. "There's still the most serious charge that you have yet to refute. You taunted me with fries."

"True." He tapped a finger against his lip, and I tracked the movement, wanting to suck it into my mouth. "What if I promise to never withhold your beloved salad?"

I punched him but he caught my fist and tucked it against his chest, twisting to face me.

"Hi, Mitzi," he said softly. "I missed you."

I preened like a cat. "Hey, Huff 'n' Puff. I might have spared a thought or two for you."

"Come home with me tonight. We can get technical and fuck." His voice lowered to a growl.

Squirming, I crossed my legs. "This is my week with Sadie." *I am a responsible parent. I will not abandon my child to have sex. Really really good sex. Though she is sixteen and it's not like I would have to spend the night. What am I saying?* I gave myself a mental slap. "I can't."

His eyes darted to the nipples poking up through my dress, the gleam in his eyes sharpening when I licked my lips. He could press me backward against the hood, his body pinning me in place while I gripped his biceps, his mouth devouring mine.

I ran my hands up his arms, while he leaned toward me, his fingers skipping up the inside of my thigh, nudging my legs apart.

My breathing turned shallow. The cool metal hood under my thighs did little against the hot flush spiralling through me. My lids fell half-shut. There was the barest tease of breeze against my thighs, but it was replaced with the heat of his fingers.

I blessed my sliding underwear for making access so much easier and arched my hips.

Laurent flared his nostrils and dipped his head to mine.

A car backfired, and reality crashed down like ice water. I was sitting spread-eagle on a car with my dress halfway up my thighs, out in public where anyone could pass by. I pushed his hands away, smoothing down the fabric.

He stood up with a wry shake of his head. "I should go. Boo needs to be fed."

"Yeah." Holy shit, I needed to go home and get myself off. Although one good pothole on the drive back might do the trick.

"Au revoir." He headed for his truck, and I smiled wistfully, wishing the night didn't have to end so soon.

"Laurent?"

He turned around.

"We were always okay." *I should have trusted that you wouldn't callously screw around, but my insecurities had run rampant at the sight of the two of you and I'd felt impossibly old and unglamorous.* And it didn't matter how many empowerment speeches I gave myself, sometimes I would regress and not have the confidence I should because I'd felt overlooked for so many years, relegated to an ex, a mother, a person-adjacent adjective instead of being first and foremost myself.

Except I didn't voice any of that because my throat was tight, and we weren't those people to each other. We were good friends having a good time.

Laurent's expression softened, as if maybe he understood all of that anyway, and I pressed my lips together, hoping nothing in my expression gave my thoughts away.

Then he threw me a cocky smile. "Of course we were okay."

His superciliousness eased a knot in my chest. He hadn't read anything into my words beyond the obvious.

I opened my car door, almost not catching his final quiet words.

"We had to be."

8

TEN MINUTES OF BEING AWAKE ON THURSDAY AND I was already hot and sticky. It was day one of a five-day heat wave and like many homes in Vancouver, I didn't have air-conditioning, just a couple of fans. My entire house was as muggy as a swamp, complete with its own little monster in the form of my daughter.

Sadie lay a hand against her forehead, wilting dramatically over the counter. "I'm dying. Will you make my lunch?"

"Talk to me when you're having hot flashes on top of everything." I had just stuck my head in the freezer, so my words were kind of muffled, but it did nothing to douse the fire burning within me. A pox upon both perimenopause and sexual frustration. Even though I'd gotten off in about ten seconds last night fantasizing about Laurent, it was hollow and unsatisfying. Hmm. If my daughter went to her dad's right after dinner on Sunday, how soon was too soon to go over to Hotel Terminus for my long-awaited booty call?

Would five minutes later seem desperate? Did I care? Ooh, should we have sausages for dinner? I could defrost them and BBQ.

"Mom!"

"Ack!" I jumped, whacking my head on the freezer door. I rubbed it. "What?"

"I need the mini ice pack to keep my coconut buns from getting too mushy in the heat."

I pulled it out for her, along with the sausages, and shut the door. "Tell me that's not all you're eating."

"And strawberries." She placed the ice pack in her lunch bag.

"Whatever. I'm too hot to care if you die of malnutrition. We'll revisit this in November." I threw the meat in a metal bowl and placed it in the fridge. "Hold up, missy."

Sadie blinked at me, the picture of innocence, about to grab the last sweet roll filled with a delicious coconut paste from the bakery box and add it to her already bulging Ziplock.

"Are you seriously not leaving me a single one?"

"Ah Ma got them for me."

"Guess again. Dad said your grandmother specifically mentioned that I should get at least one." My former mother-in-law had gotten me hooked on these cocktail buns, which originated in Hong Kong, back when Eli and I were still married. While Mae and I didn't have a ton of contact after the divorce, and even less so now that Sadie could make her own arrangements to see her grandmother, she still made sure that I got my occasional fix.

It was very kind of her, even if her reasoning was that whitey here couldn't be trusted to trek out to the neighboring city of Richmond where the (in Mae's opinion) best Chinese bakery was, rather than just go to the closest place that sold them. She wasn't wrong.

And since she wouldn't have her precious granddaughter eating subpar gai mei bao, it was a big win with zero effort on my part.

I motioned for Sadie to hand one over, which she did after

pretending to lick it first. "Like that would stop me," I said, biting into it.

"Gross." Sadie checked her backpack, naming off each item under her breath to make sure she had everything for work. "Let's go for ice cream tonight at Casa Gelato."

"Good idea." I swallowed another bite. "We can ask Jude." And I could get a more honest response than an emoji.

"It's a date." She pecked my cheek. "Bye, Mom."

"Bye, kiddo. Have a good day."

With one child accounted for, I finished the coconut bun, washed my hands, and went to check on my other baby. "Hi, sweetheart." I stroked a hand over the wine-colored velvet sofa. "You doing okay in this heat? Do you need a fan?"

I'd spent more on this couch than any other single item of furniture that I owned. For the first three days, I'd banned people from sitting on her, but then I'd relented and thrown a transparent tarp over top. That way everyone could still admire her beauty, but not grubby her up. It was a very sensible idea, even if a little voice in the back of my head whispered this was the first step to wrapping my entire house in plastic and buying a lifetime supply of air freshener.

However, after a week of Jude calling me Bubbe Miriam and dropping off the most hideous chachkas she could find from second-hand stores, along with doilies to put underneath them, I relented and declared my sofa open for use.

Satisfied that my precious was holding up all right in this heat, I went outside to water the newly planted arugula and pea plants along with the rest of my garden. There was a water ban on lawns, which meant mine would be brown in no time, but we were allowed to hand-water fruit and vegetable plants early in the morning and later in the evening.

Some people found gardening a soothing activity. I was not one of those people. Eli planted most of my garden and I reluctantly watered it, soaking each section up to a count of sixty. I had no idea if that was long enough, but I hadn't dried anything out yet with this system.

Truth be told, I did love the smell of wet, rich earth.

After I'd rolled the hose back up in its holder, I headed upstairs and got dressed in the thinnest sundress I owned, an orange and white Hawaiian print–inspired ankle-length maxi. I threw my hair in a ponytail, swiping on some light shadow, mascara, and tinted gloss. I'd have foregone makeup entirely because I was shvitzing so hard, but Giulia was the kind of creature one made an effort for.

After opening all the windows in my car to cool it down to the sixth level of Hell, I drove downtown to the condo complex where she resided. It was a good thing I remembered where to go because my phone was totally dead. I'd plugged my cell in to charge but it didn't even have enough juice to turn on yet, and I couldn't call Laurent for directions.

While I found the building no problem, I wasn't sure how to get Giulia's attention. She didn't respond to my whistles, and I'd left my phone in the car, so I paced back and forth in front of the gates to the inner courtyard, occasionally touching my ear like I had a Bluetooth unit on. I repeated her name loudly throughout this fake call, pretending I couldn't believe what she was saying and hoping she'd hear me.

"You know you are not actually speaking with me, ragazza, sì?" said a honey-rich female voice.

I spun around, my hand on my heart.

The cat gargoyle lay on her belly, just outside the front door of the main entrance. I hadn't even heard her jump down from the rooftop. She propped her head on her front paws, blinking languorously with eyes that glittered like fathomless beads under a heavy brow. While she had no tail, she gave the impression that she'd be flicking it slowly if she did.

"Ciao, Giulia," I said.

"No Laurent?" Her wide mouth pouted.

"Not today." Was that a mistake? "Nice collar."

She stroked the wide mosaiced band in blues and purples that popped against the mottled black "fur" texturing her body. "It was a gift from Cam," she said. "You know this one?"

"We met recently." Great. Now I looked like a dick for not bringing a gift.

She scoffed and tossed her head. "She thinks to buy my favor. Ma quella ragazza é completamente pazza." She flicked her claws out of her three long toes, dragging them slowly across the pavement. They were so sharp and she was so strong that cracks spiderwebbed in the concrete. "Laurent is mine. We women know when another is moving in on their territory, yes?"

"Yup." I tried to scratch the spot between my shoulder blades that had suddenly gotten very prickly. "Only a fool would try to get between you and him."

Giulia sat up abruptly and I took a large step backward. The gargoyle's head came to about chest height on me, her wide cat ears adding another couple of inches. She nodded earnestly, making expressive jabbing motions with her front paws. "Exactly. You will protect him from her?"

This temperamental Italian would eviscerate me if she ever found out what I'd done with "her Laurent." My mind flooded with very explicit memories of going down on him while he fingered me and I flushed, fanning out the front of my sundress.

"What is with that look on your face?" Her nostrils twitched.

"N-nothing," I stammered. "It's hot. But you don't have to worry about Cam. Laurent doesn't think of her that way."

"Good." She jutted her chin up pertly. "You will make sure no others get their paws on him either."

"Happy to." It wasn't as if there was any possibility of a future between Giulia and Laurent, but I still felt like I was breaking some sisterhood code. "Enough of him. I heard you're filling in for Harry and I hoped you could help me."

"Mommy." A little boy pointed at me. "That woman is talking to the cat."

"Don't point, Jacob." His mother gave me a strained smile but hurried him past like I was contagious.

The kid glanced over his shoulder and Giulia hissed at him, her fur standing on edge. He broke into tears, but in the second it took for the mother to look back, the cat was once more a statue, and I was the one who got glared at.

"Kids are delightful," Giulia purred. "Their perception filter is so weak." She paused. "Just like they are."

I shivered. She didn't eat children, did she?

"Now, what do you need?" she said.

Inanimate gargoyles' original function was to ward off evil. The few who gained sentience and had wings did this by flying over the city and seeing what evil lurked. Those without wings, like Giulia, did it by gaining sight through the sightless, such as statues or ornamental faces on façades of buildings. She let them be her eyes, or as Laurent had more poetically put it, she "saw through the eyes of those who blindly watch."

However, if she was filling in for Harry, then she had to know the supernatural who's who. I hoped that gargoyles' knowledge of the magical community worked like my cousin Goldie and her friends being able to name every single vaguely famous Jew in the past hundred years.

"Two things," I said. "Do you know of any gargoyle living up north in British Columbia about thirty years ago who'd have been plugged into any supernatural goings-on?"

Tatiana's advice about being careful who I showed my weaknesses to weighed on me, but I'd figured asking Giulia about any other gargoyle who might have intel on my parents was a safe bet as gargoyles were neutral parties.

Giulia scratched under her chin. "That would have been

Fernanda, but she died years ago." Damn. "Mi dispiace, I can't help you with that. What is the other thing?"

"A demon with the ability to read magic off objects."

Tatiana had told me back at the speakeasy that while sensing magic wasn't an Ohrist ability, some demons had this power. Whether a Banim Shovavim could also do this was another question, but as the only person I could ask was one of the Wise Brothers, that was a hard pass.

I'd suggested calling Nav, but my boss had ordered me to use him only as a last resort, reminding me that the last time he was called in to help, he'd almost destroyed an item in Zev's possession and sent that dangerous vampire on a rampage.

That was true, but Nav had also sheltered Eli and Sadie during the Great Ward Mishap. That bought him some points from me if not from Tatiana. However, I had this other way to track a demon down, and I acceded to her wishes.

Giulia grimaced. "Demons are dirty and nasty. You do not want to tangle with them, bella."

"I'm afraid I have to."

"It could be dangerous. Will you be taking Laurent with you?" She said it very casually, but her eyes narrowed.

"Wasn't planning on it."

She brightened. "Va bene." She rattled off an address. Good to know I was expendable.

Two young male tourists with German flag patches sewn onto their backpacks approached, asking me to take a photo of them with the gargoyle.

Behind their backs, Giulia bared her canines and licked her lips.

All the color drained from my face. "I'm not sure that's such a good idea."

The tourists gave me an odd look, and one pressed his phone into my hand. "Here. Please." They swung their packs off, setting them to either side of the gargoyle.

My heart almost stopped when one placed his hand on Giulia's head, but at least I'd have a camera to document the carnage for when the Lonestars showed up to remove the mutilated corpses. My definition of silver linings had changed substantially since reclaiming my magic.

The two guys threw peace signs, and I snapped a few pix, shocked when Giulia didn't move.

The tourists grabbed their stuff and thanked me, heading off for their next photo opp. They didn't notice the newly formed slits in the bottoms of their packs slowly leaking items. Better their physical property than their intestines.

Giulia smirked. "The look on your face. I wouldn't hurt them." She paused, a crafty expression sliding over her features. "While they could see it coming."

I was so dead if she found out about me and Laurent. "Heh."

"Okay, ragazza." She rubbed her head against my chest. "Watch over Laurent."

"I will."

"But not too closely. Ciao." She knocked her stone head into my boobs before leaping back up to her rooftop perch.

I rubbed my poor girls, glad of my escape from one temperamental supernatural. Now on to the next. An Elmer Fudd voice in my head said, *Be vewy vewy quiet. We're going on a demon hunt.* Let's hope this ended better than his attempts with that wascally wabbit.

9

ACCORDING TO GIULIA'S INTEL, THE DEMON LIVED just over the bridge on the North Shore in a trailer park. The residences were older but well-maintained, with personal touches like flowerpots, patio furniture, and cute gnomes and mushrooms adorning their lawns.

My eyes widened when I pulled up in front of the address I'd been given. It was like the demon's memo on blending in consisted of one word: "flamingos." Dozens of the pink plastic birds circled the place. Black beaks, black and yellow beaks, with sunglasses and without, hooked to a hose and spouting water, lying down, on one leg or two, the one trait they shared was watching me with vacuous eyes while heat shimmied up from the asphalt pad I'd parked on.

Shuddering, I walked up the front stairs, avoiding the railing that was one sneeze away from collapsing, but no one answered when I knocked.

"You looking for Kirby?" The pot-bellied neighbor watering his tomato plants spat a glob of phlegm into the dirt. "Try the playground. Likes to jog there." He jerked his chin at a narrow road that wound through the trailer park. Sure. Exercise. That's why the demon hung out there.

My stomach in knots, I thanked him and hurried back to my car. Finding my phone still dead due to a wonky connector cable, I cursed, unable to alert anyone that this fiend was cruising the playground like it was an all-you-could-eat buffet. I forced myself to obey the signs reminding drivers to slow down, while itching to slam my foot on the gas.

When I arrived at the playground, I wrenched the car into park, relieved to find the place empty. Then I took a second glance and almost broke into hives. The long metal slide would burn kids' legs in the relentless August sun, the swing set listed precariously to the left, and the partially rusted merry-go-round was, quite frankly, a death trap.

It was the land that time forgot, a 1970s throwback, all sharp edges and splintering wood. The demon could just sit back and let kids tenderize themselves.

"Get back here!"

At the sound of the growly woman's voice, I ran into the forest to my right, making eye contact with the demon for one moment.

It was glamoured as a young goth of Asian descent, with dyed black hair cut in a severe bob with short bangs. Black tattoos with intricate shading blossomed up her left arm and across her collarbone, clearly visible under her black tank top. She had a metal barbell piercing in one eyebrow, a ring through her septum, and studs in both cheeks where her dimples would be, as well as in the Cupid's bow dip above her full purple lips.

She was quite striking and more in line with what a glamoured demon should look like, in my opinion, than the dapper Chester, former owner of a curio shop, had been.

There was a snap of twigs from up ahead, and I caught a flash of a boy with red hair. The demon slashed a hand across her throat at me and took off after the child, crunching dry leaves under her thick-soled knee-high boots with their heavy silver buckles.

"Stop!" My magic scythe slammed into my hand and I sprinted after the pair, trying not to trip over roots or lose my footing on the uneven ground as we ran in a wide circle back to the playground.

Even though my sides were burning, I wasn't as fast as them and could only watch helplessly as the demon grabbed the child and shoved the struggling youngster into a black van, which peeled out.

"Fuck!" I took off after them, weaving through traffic, not bothering to try to be subtle about following. My dead phone was as useful as a brick. I was on my own with this kid's life in my hands.

That poor boy. From his height I guessed he was about nine or ten. Was he Sapien? Ohrist? Could he fight back? Did he understand exactly how much danger he was in? Leaning on my horn, I swerved into the left lane, running through the light as it changed from yellow to red. I couldn't let that van get away.

We crossed back into Vancouver over the Lion's Gate Bridge, and I frowned as the demon-mobile turned into Stanley Park. Why would a demon take an abducted child there? The Sapien park was jammed with tourists and families while the Ohrist version was the Lonestar headquarters. I honked repeatedly at a truck that cut me off, making me momentarily lose sight of the van.

I rammed my sedan into a space barely bigger than it was between two cars, earning me the finger from the driver behind me. My heart was pounding because I never drove this aggressively, and my hands shook with adrenaline and the thought of failure. I shot into the exit lane, catching sight of the van's brake lights as it took a curve up ahead, but by the time I rounded the treelined street to the long, straight stretch ahead, it was gone.

I pulled over. It must have gone into the Park. But how? I knew of only one entrance to access the Lonestar grounds, and it was clear on the other side. I'd never find the van if I took the long way round because Stanley Park was larger than Central Park in New York.

It would be great if I could access hidden spaces via the Kefitzat Haderech, but it didn't work that way. Magically created destinations were a no-fly zone, unfortunately.

I eased my car back onto the road, driving slowly and scanning for a way into the hidden space.

There. A gap in the trees revealed a glimpse of the seawall, a path that curved in a ten-kilometer loop around part of Stanley Park, with the Burrard Inlet beyond. Superimposed over the opening, like a hazy phantom, was another version with towering cypress and pine and no concrete, joggers, or cyclists. I swallowed. Was I really supposed to drive toward it? If I was wrong, best-case scenario, I'd hit a tree. Worst case, I'd kill people on the seawall and then fly into the water.

A car behind me honked and I motioned for it to pass me. Gripping the wheel with clammy hands, I jerked my car toward the gap, stepping on the gas. The vehicle flew forward and I screamed, positive I was making a horrible mistake, but the sedan bounced out into the magic Park, hitting the narrow dirt road gently.

The black van was parked to the side.

I pulled up behind it and cut the ignition, bolting outside only to find that the van was locked. I peered in through the windows, but finding it empty, spun around, scanning the forest. The demon could be anywhere with the boy by now. Where in the real park did this correspond to? Everything was trees and more trees, except next to the van was a dirt trail leading down a slope to the water where a wooden dock had been built.

The blistering sun beat down, plastering my sundress to my back.

Stanley Park didn't have a dock. Throwing a hand up to shield my eyes, I squinted at an outcropping far offshore. It kind of looked like Siwash Rock, but that made no sense. In the real park, Siwash Rock was this natural rock formation that was about fifty feet high, boasting these distinctive twisted Douglas firs on top. But it sat maybe thirty feet off the seawall in the water, whereas this one was quite some distance out.

A black boat that seemed to suck all light from the space around it, a nightmare version of Vancouver's small rainbow-colored open-air ferries known as Aquabuses, sailed toward the rock. Except the Aquabus didn't operate in the water around Stanley Park. It made stops along False Creek at popular destinations like Granville Island, Science World, Olympic Village, and the west end.

Was the demon taking the child to its lair? Demons did create homes in hidden spaces for themselves here on earth, but one could conceivably make use of an existing hidden space like the Park. I shook my head. That still left a lot of questions, like why the Lonestars allowed it, and how the demon had access to ferry service.

I carefully started down the trail, dirt and loose pebbles skidding out from underneath me. Fred McMurtry had been possessed by a demon parasite. Could other Lonestars be in league with demons? Or if not in league, then turning a blind eye to certain activities in exchange for...what?

About halfway down, I froze. An unkindness of ravens had landed on the pier, dozens of beady eyes and sharp beaks marking my approach and blocking my way. Goosebumps broke out over my skin, my hand drifting to the pocket containing Giselle's necklace.

Slowly, I took a few more steps, but when I was less than five feet away, the largest one puffed up, flapping its wings and screeching a caw. I stumbled back and the others joined in, their cries a warning siren.

"You seek to go where you should not," a voice rasped.

Feathers tickled the back of my throat. "Poe." I coughed their name.

The androgenous bird shifter sat on one corner of the pier on the wooden planking, garbed in a ruffled black shirt and trousers, and looking cool despite the searing heat. Their long hair remained the same deep still blue as a pool at night, while shrewd dark eyes regarded me above a beaky nose. They pulled out a deck of cards, turning them over in their gnarled hands.

A cloud rolled across the sky and a gust of cold wind blew across my skin. I shivered, but not from the weather. Our last card game had shown me scenes from my life—and death—in an alternate version of an assault I'd suffered. Part of me feared that Poe had shown me the truth of what should have happened and that embracing my shadow magic thereby thwarting my demise came with a price I had yet to pay.

When the cards had gone crazy, flipping between visions of darkness and light, I'd forcefully aborted the game by stabbing a card face with a knife. Poe had been furious, pressing me to keep playing and reveal more until I smashed a glass into the side of their head, and Tatiana showed up to move them along.

It wasn't chance that led to this meeting. I'd bet Poe had been stalking me for the right opportunity.

Too bad because I'd vowed to never play games with them again.

I pointed to the rocky outcropping. "Is that where the demon went?"

Poe nodded.

"How do I get there?"

"You don't."

"A child's life is at stake. Even you can't be indifferent to that." I stormed closer. Or tried to.

The second I stepped onto the pier, the ravens blocking my way flapped their wings and the dock rocked violently against sloshing waves.

I grabbed the railing for balance. "You didn't just randomly show up. You know a way across, and if you don't tell me, I swear I'll make your life a living hell."

"You need this." Very slowly and deliberately, they pulled a silver disc the size of a dollar coin out of a pocket, holding it up so I could see the engraving of the ouroboros on it. "There is no way to cross without it."

I eyed the ravens. Rushing Poe for that token was impossible. Nor could I use the KH to bypass the water. There had to be some way that didn't involve a game. Was it close enough to swim?

There was a large splash and I caught the end of an enormous serpent-like tail disappearing into the water.

"You wouldn't die if you dived in," Poe said. "Though you might wish otherwise."

"Did I ask?" I crossed my arms. "Didn't think so."

Poe smiled, a slash of tea-stained teeth dividing their face. "It was obvious you were wondering."

"What'll it cost me to get that token?" A muscle ticked in my jaw.

"One round of blackjack." Poe resembled an evil guard, determining who got through and who didn't. It didn't surprise me that they had dealings with a demon.

My brain screamed at me to turn around. "Do I have a choice?"

"You always have a choice," Poe said.

The clouds blew away, the sun back in full force, like Mother Nature herself beamed down her approval of this option.

I snorted.

Tangle with whatever was in the water or play cards with a master manipulator. I was blessed with choice. I could walk away, but what if there were other kids there? There was still a chance to save that boy. There had to be. The demon could have killed him back at the playground, but she'd taken the trouble to bring him out here. Did she need him for some other reason? Did she prefer to feast slowly, draw out his pain?

I tapped my foot impatiently, conscious of the clock ticking to save that boy. "What are the terms?"

"Just play. Win or lose you get passage." The token disappeared, replaced in a sleight of hand by a deck of cards, which Poe shuffled, the cards flying from one hand to the other.

Great. That meant this wasn't about high score wins; Poe sought something else from me. Had they come to collect on a debt I owed the universe for staying alive?

The ravens still blocked my path to Poe.

"Move your little posse and be quick about it," I said.

Poe whistled and the birds flew up to circle us, their gazes boring into me. Like that was so much better.

I walked over to Poe and motioned for my two cards. The dealer laid them on the planks, so I crouched down to check my hand, careful not to let Poe see.

A ten of hearts and a nine of...ravens? The illustrated black birds standing in for either spades or clubs were freaky enough, but the hearts were beating. I wiped my fingers off on my sundress.

"Hit or stand?" Poe tilted their head at me, their hair falling to one side like a curtain blowing in the wind. The dealer's face-up card was a five of clubs so at best they had sixteen and would have to take another card.

"Stand."

Poe flipped a three over for themself. "I call."

Ignoring the click in my right knee from squatting for

more than thirty seconds, I turned mine over. "Ninete—ow!" I sucked my finger into my mouth.

One of the ravens on the card face winked. The little fucker had bit me.

A drop of blood fell on the card.

I watched in horror as the illustrated ravens shook their feathers out, resettling themselves to create a new space that was filled by a new raven formed from the blood.

The number on the card face changed from a nine to a ten.

The boards of the pier seemed to melt underneath me, and I grabbed on to the edge, convinced I was falling into quicksand.

Poe blinked impassively at me, the dock still intact. The shift I'd felt, whatever it was, hadn't been wholly external. Something was different in the world itself, but also in how I felt.

"What did you do?" I jabbed my injured finger at Poe. "Why is there another raven?"

"A new player," they murmured. "You are surrounded by so many magicians. Now there is one more than there was when we first began to play this game." They nodded their head. "And an unexpected one at that."

A brilliant light engulfed the entirety of the ten of hearts card while the now-ten of ravens became blanketed in darkness.

"Perhaps in another universe you would have fared better without them," Poe said, "but that is not the way of this universe anymore."

"Who is it?" I demanded. "Are they evil? What's with the light and dark?"

Poe calmly gathered up their cards. "You'll find out in due time."

"Answer me, damn you. You did something to me, didn't you? Is the ultimate game to make me paranoid and doubt myself? Tell me the truth!" I grabbed the shifter by their shirtfront.

The real ravens sped down from the sky like a tornado, engulfing me, their wings thwapping against my body. I swatted them away, but by the time I'd dispersed the last one, Poe was gone, leaving only a silver token on the pristine pier to show they'd been there at all.

10

THE SMALL FERRY BUMPED TO A STOP AGAINST THE dock, and I grabbed the token, running my finger over the ouroboros, the smooth disc warm to the touch. I pushed my unease over Poe aside, a different anxiety taking over when the small gate swung open on its own.

I nervously stepped on board, the token held aloft. "Hello? Is there a ferryman I'm supposed to pay? Or ferrywoman?"

No one appeared.

"Ferry nonbinary individual?" I babbled. "I'm happy with whomever, I just want someone or something to accept payment from me because I really need to get to my destination."

The gate clanged shut behind me and I jumped.

"Is that a thumbs-up that we're good to go or am I stuck here like when bus drivers take a coffee break? Because if it's the second, there's a kid's life at stake, so maybe they could get their beverage to go?" I sat down on the plastic bench running the circumference of the ferry, with enough room to seat perhaps two dozen people. The windows were nothing more than glassless square holes, the roof a hard canopy.

In the middle of the ferry there was a post with a large captain's wheel attached. It turned itself to the left, and with another bump against the pier, the ferry pulled away.

The boat was silent, the ride glass-smooth despite the speed.

I sighed, relieved to be back on the demon's trail, but with time to kill during the crossing to the rock, my thoughts wandered back to the game. It wasn't productive to speculate on Poe's motives, especially when I had to be in top form for whatever lay at the end of this journey.

Facts, then.

The one concrete detail from this round of blackjack was that of a new player. But on which of the many gameboards I played?

Ironic that for a person who prided herself on her love of facts and trivia, I'd found myself in a world constantly scrambling for the merest crumb. Everyone hoarded information: Poe, Tatiana, the Wise Brothers, even Laurent played things close to his chest at times.

Facts—truth—were hard won in the magical community. I guess that wasn't so different from the Sapien world, where murders went unsolved and money buried all manner of truths, but there were still processes in place there, admittedly flawed, to seek justice and get answers.

Everything in the magical community was games and secrets and tricks, even for the simplest of matters. I laughed bitterly. Who was I kidding? Nothing in this world was simple.

Take this mission. My straightforward attempt to find a demon who could read a magic signature on Giselle's necklace had landed me on a ghost ship about to sneak onto a mysterious rock and rescue a child.

I held my hair, whipping around in the breeze, out of my face. "Hey, Ferry, are you going to wait for me because I'll need a ride back? Tell me children ride free."

Come to think of it, Poe had said only that I'd be able to cross. Not cross *back*.

A hot, tight sensation sparked in my belly, sweeping through me like lit rocket fuel left unchecked. It blazed and incinerated, feeding off my fury at everyone seeking to dupe me. At myself for being duped.

"Listen up," I said peevishly. "I am a woman with zero patience, zero tolerance for bullshit, and zero hesitation to bust you into splinters with my scythe. So, give me some assurance that I'll get passage back this instant."

I tried to summon my weapon to underline my threat, but as I was alone with no demons, vamps, or dybbuks on board, I failed. Anxious about what lay ahead and how I'd return to reality with a young boy's life at stake, I hung out at the prow, watching the rock loom closer.

It wasn't much larger than the real one back in Stanley Park, and I didn't spy any signs of life, like demon hoards armed with quivers of burning pitch. I tapped the token against the window frame. Poe was many things, but I trusted their word that the demon was there somewhere. Hopefully Goth Girl didn't have a nest in the trees up on top because my rock-climbing abilities made my trail-hiking skills seem positively Olympian.

Every so often, that huge tail slipped out of the water, keeping pace and close enough to be freaky but not near enough to afford me a view of what the rest of the creature looked like.

I gripped the window frame, leaning forward as if that could make the ferry go faster.

We finally made it to the rock, part of its face sliding away to allow the boat to glide inside. I drew my magic cloaking over me, my eyes needing a moment to adjust to the dimmer light inside the rock.

The stone wall closed, trapping me wherever I was, and,

summoning up my courage, I scrambled over the gate and dropped onto the metal dock.

The air was a lot cooler in here, permeated with the strong odors of salt water and fish. Patches of lacy lichen fanned out over damp stone walls.

A steeply curved metal staircase with rubber grips on the treads and railing led from the dock down through a hewn-out space to a narrow high corridor lit by two strips of buzzing bulbs.

I stuck to the shadows as much as possible, skirting the pools of light, super paranoid, even with my invisibility mesh. The first door I came to was open. A man and a woman sat with their backs to me monitoring a wall of screens playing different CCTV footage. There were schoolyards and playgrounds, dark alleys and nightclubs, thousands of different places all teeming with life.

Every so often one of the pair would hit a button to freeze one of the screens and type something into their laptop. Was this an evil Batcave where demons monitored humans, seeking the weak to prey upon?

I continued down the hallway to where it ended in a T-junction. A group of people stood outside a door to my right chatting quietly. I couldn't hear them, but there were both men and women of different ethnicities and ages ranging from about midtwenties to maybe sixty. None of them wore any kind of uniform, but they shared a certain flinty-eyed hardness.

Turning away from them to my left, I hurried toward the sole door at the end of the corridor, glanced over my shoulder to ensure no one was watching, and slipped inside. I gasped, the sound landing like a train rushing past in the unnatural silence.

The room was filled with humans in cages barely big enough for the people to stand in and maybe an arm's length across. Was this a nightmarish petting zoo or were these poor individuals like unwanted pets to be put down?

The cages that were occupied glowed brightly, the enclosures made not of metal but magic, while the empty ones were shadowy impressions of bars. I ran over to the closest cage and dropped the cloaking in front of my face so the imprisoned woman could see me. I didn't want to become totally visible in case this room was monitored.

"Don't be scared. I'm here to help," I said. "How long have you been here?"

The elderly woman stared at me with glazed blue eyes under a fluff of white permed hair, trying to communicate with me, but there was a sound barrier on the cages, and I couldn't hear her.

All the prisoners were relatively clean but there was no sign of bedding or food. My shadow scythe half formed in my hand under the cloaking but I forced the magic down. I had to be smart and conserve my energy for when I needed it most if I was to help everyone.

Unfortunately, there weren't any locks on the cages and without knowing what kind of magic they were made of, I wasn't about to touch the bars.

Yet again, I cursed the fact that I couldn't just take them through the Kefitzat Haderech, but even if the KH led to hidden spaces, any Ohrists in the bunch would be killed by the phantom skeleton there. I wasn't sure it would be all that welcoming to Sapiens either.

I ran through the row of prisoners searching for the child. In a cage in the far corner sat a short man with red hair, wearing the clothes I'd attributed to the boy. He was alert and furious, smacking the bars and yelling, even though no sound came out. Every time he touched the bars he was shocked backward. The air stank with electricity from the charges.

I felt marginally better that the demon had kidnapped a short man and not a child, but the fact was I had to get out of here and alert Nav and his people about what was happening because I had no way to free them myself.

How could the Lonestars allow this abomination to happen in their territory?

When I felt in my pocket for the token to get back on the ferry and across to the Park for help, I found Giselle's necklace. Swearing softly, I put it away. If I coerced Goth Girl into checking it for magic, I'd give up any chance of rescuing these people, but I'd also taken on this job and promised Giselle answers. She deserved to know the truth about her situation. Everyone did.

I shook my head. My priority was to rescue these people and then find another demon to examine the necklace.

"I'll be back," I promised the short man, unsure if he could hear me.

He doubled over, coughing. Other prisoners were doing the same, some trying to cover their faces.

A faint smell of rotten eggs wafted out of the vents. I bolted for the exit, the room swimming and the door growing farther and farther out of reach. I reached for the knob, my arm elongated and weaving like a python. Whoa. I pressed a hand to my forehead, sweating and clammy at the same time. My steps became wobbly and slow, but I pressed on until my legs buckled and I hit the concrete on my knees, my magic falling away.

I dimly registered the sharp pain of impact through the foggy haze blanketing my brain and the stream of tears blurring my vision. Swaying, I crashed onto my side, a pair of thick-soled, knee-high boots with heavy silver buckles coming into view a split second before my eyes rolled back into my head.

"Demon," I slurred and blacked out.

I came to cuffed to a table in an interrogation room. My head was still woozy from whatever drug or gas they'd pumped into the air when I passed out.

"Let me out!" My words were fuzzy and my lips and tongue felt too fat.

"You're not in a position to demand anything." Goth Girl entered, slamming the door behind her.

"You messed with the wrong person." The words were slightly gargled but she got the gist.

The demon dropped into the chair across from me, entirely unconcerned. "Do tell."

"Harm me and there won't be a corner of the earth you can run and hide in."

"Got a regular cavalry coming to help, do you?"

"Yeah." I leaned over the table as far as my constraints allowed. "Lonestars, vamps, shifters, *demon hunters*. You've messed with the wrong woman. Now let me out." Better. I sounded mostly normal.

She stared at me a moment, then shook her head, her eyes glinting dangerously. "Did you assume I'm a demon based on my tattoos and piercings?"

"No, I assumed it because you abducted an innocent person." And partially because of the other stuff.

Goth Girl grabbed me by my shirtfront. "It's not enough that I had to put up with Satan worshipping cracks for years, you think I'm an actual demon?"

I twirled my hand for my magic to twine around my arm and solidify into my scythe to prove my point about her nonhuman status, but nothing happened.

For me, that is.

To me, however, was an entirely different story. She hauled me up above her head, the cuffs straining and yanking painfully on my arm. I begged her to stop, but it was like she hadn't heard me.

"I mean, you'd think that a Banim Shovavim would know better than to make horrible assumptions but apparently not." She dropped me hard onto the chair, the impact shuddering through my tailbone like a sharp spike.

How did this demon know what I was? And why threaten me at the playground and put humans in cages? Ohhhh. Damn. The critical piece of this puzzle snapped into place in my groggy brain.

I rubbed a cuffed wrist. "This is the supersecret demon-hunting organization that Naveen Kumar is part of, isn't it?"

The organization that he'd said he could tell me about but then he'd have to kill me.

Goth Girl slow-clapped me.

For someone as precariously on the fringes of the magical community as I was, confusing a person for a demon was a tough screwup to amend. With this particular Ohrist, because I realized that with my luck there was only one person she could be, my mistake meant I was fucked.

Just like Mara, the executive assistant to one of the partners at my old law firm, had held true power in our company, I was far more worried about crossing this woman than anyone else in this organization.

I mustered up a weak smile. "You're Clea, aren't you? Nav's—"

Her eyes narrowed and I swallowed the word "assistant."

"Indispensable colleague. The preeminent organizer and person who keeps him on track. Keeps them all on track," I added, wondering how much of my foot was still in my mouth.

She crossed her arms, leaning back in her chair so the front two legs lifted off the ground. "I'm the second-in-command."

"That's great! Girl power for the win, am I right?" I held up a fist to bump but at her flat stare, dropped it. There had to be a way to dig myself out of this hole. "I'm very sorry for my extremely wrong assumptions," I said. "I take all the responsibility for us getting off on the wrong foot. But we share a common goal."

Her chair thudded back down, and she leaned in with a

scary look. "We have nothing in common. I've devoted my life to ridding the world of evil. You're Tatiana's minion who'll jump, fetch, carry, and run through hoops for the person with the deepest pockets. Or am I wrong that you let BatKian keep the Torquemada Gloves?"

I repositioned the cuff so it didn't bite into my skin. "They weren't a demon artifact. They had no magic."

"You didn't know that when you refused to hand them over on Torres's island, did you?"

"That wasn't about money," I said tightly, narrowing my eyes. "I was keeping my family safe."

"Wow, you aren't only motivated by a paycheck but by your entitlement to special treatment." She gave me a snarky smile and flashed a thumbs-up. "Way to go."

Sometimes Delilah brushed against me like a purring cat, but right now my magic felt like claws digging into my back. I longed to turn the pain outward and slap that look off Clea's face.

I clasped my hand around Giselle's necklace, letting it dig into my flesh until I'd gotten a handle on my temper. "I need to speak with the demon who can check for magic on this necklace. Please. For a poor Ohrist." I pulled it out of my pocket and held it up. "The woman who owns it is going slowly mad. If I can rule this necklace out as a cause for foul play, it would mean a lot. And if it is demonic, you'd be instrumental in thwarting an evil artifact."

Clea pursed her lips, so I kept talking, detailing Giselle's distress. I might have embellished it, but it was for a good cause.

The door opened and Nav entered, a lock of platinum-blond hair falling over one brown eye. "Give me the necklace and I'll deal with it. You wait here."

There went my hopes that he was off on some job and we wouldn't cross paths. "You can't sideline me," I protested.

"Can't I?" He looked at Clea. "I'm fairly certain I can."

"Oh, you totally can," she said. "Miriam broke about a hundred rules with her trespassing."

I tugged on the cuffs. "I thought I was saving some kid from a—"

"Watch it," Clea growled.

I changed tactics. "I didn't trespass." I showed them the token. "Look. I had this."

Nav spared it a brief glance. "Bully for you. This coin doesn't grant passage. You shouldn't have been able to get on the—" He clamped his lips shut.

"The what?" If there were consequences to riding that ferry, then Nav was damn well going to pony up about them.

"You must have come through the Kefitzat Haderech. That's trespassing," Clea said.

"And yet I didn't." I turned back to Nav. "Does the water taxi of doom have a name? Let me guess. Matt Demon? Hades Christensen? Chris Hellsworth? *Hell*-en Mirren?"

"How droll." Nav looked up at a knock on the door. "Yeah?"

A woman stuck her head in. "I need Clea."

"I got this," he said to Clea. "Go."

"Nice meeting you." I waved as she left. She didn't return the sentiment. Eh. I'd win her over. "Now, where were we? Oh yes, the name of that lovely transport system. Tell me or I'll go into extreme detail about what Eli did when I was breastfeeding to help unblock my mammary glands, thereby scarring you and making it impossible to ever get it on with him."

All he'd done was provide me with hot compresses, but given Nav's look of sheer horror, I could imagine how he'd taken it.

Exactly as I'd intended.

"The Succubus," Nav said reluctantly.

"You mean like the Aquabus but sexier? Wait. Did I ride

some weird succubus boat shifter? Succubus Prime?" I frowned. "No, that's not funny."

"None of this is funny," he snapped. "Do you have any idea how much trouble you're in?"

"Why?" I widened my eyes theatrically. "Will I get an STI? A succubus-transmitted infection? Get it? We both know you aren't going to hurt me, Nav."

"Because of Eli? Guess again," he said.

"Because Laurent will eviscerate you, if Daya doesn't first."

"Assuming they ever found out."

I sighed. "Fun as needling you is, cut the crap already and tell me."

Moving as slowly as possible, Nav unlocked the handcuffs and I rubbed my wrists. "The Succubus shouldn't have completed its journey across the water. Not without this." He rolled up his sleeve and I squinted at the mark in the crook of his elbow.

It wasn't a tattoo. The design had been branded onto his flesh, the raised pattern starkly visible against his brown skin. The hamsa, a five-fingered hand with an eye in the center believed to ward off demonic spirits, was less than an inch high.

My cousin Goldie had a hamsa amulet hanging in our kitchen when I was growing up, each of the five fingers and the area around the eye adorned with swirls. Nav's was a simple outline though it clearly conveyed the image.

I sighed. Was Clea this organization's equivalent of former Lonestar Oliver Anderson? Not about the Banim Shovavim prejudices but an extreme belief in the rightness of her actions due to the exalted nature of her position?

I tapped the inside of my elbow. "Since I don't have my own hamsa, should the boat have fed me to the giant tail thing?"

"Only your desiccated husk after it sucked out your soul. Succu-bus." He smiled evilly.

"Then why did it bring me all the way across? Are you sure Poe's token didn't work as advertised?"

"You got it from the ravens?" Nav stuffed the tiny hand-cuff key in his pocket "Now I'm one hundred and fifty percent positive it's a dud. The Succubus is irrevocably tied to the hamsa."

Poe, you bastard. You scammed me for info and then assumed I'd die. Well, revenge was a dish best served cold. And yours would be icy.

"I don't know why the Succubus allowed you passage," Nav said, "and I don't like it."

"Trust me, I'm not loving this mystery either." I followed him back to the room with the cages. "What do you people call yourselves?" When he didn't answer, I elbowed him. "Come on. Who am I going to tell since I bet Tatiana and Laurent already know?"

"Carpe Demon."

"Yeah, right. What is it really?"

Nav held the door to the cage room open for me.

"Carpe Demon it is. So, what's your favorite part of a demon to seize, Mr. Kumar?"

"You are a royal pain in my arse."

"Back at you." My expression turned somber seeing the cages again. "All these humans, they're really demons?" Most of the creatures had assumed nonthreatening forms.

Nav nodded and pressed his hand to a scanner on the wall.

The cages vibrated and I clapped my hands over my ears at the sudden cacophony of growls, whines, snarls, cries, and words screamed in languages I'd never heard and wasn't sure I could reproduce.

The human glamours dissipated, revealing demons of every shape and size: reptilian, humanoid, mammalian, serpent-like. Some had skin like lizards, others were bumpy or had hard exoskeletons. Two horns, six horns, no horns, antennae. Geez. Too many eyes, not enough eyes, limbs, claws, fangs, fur, feathers, hair, the unglamoured demons came in every color of the toxic waste palette.

All of them wore slender collars around their necks.

Nav summoned his light staff and led me to Kirby, the demon that Clea had captured from the trailer park. He stuck the staff through the bars and prodded the demon, who was a red hairless rat about the size of a German shepherd.

The demon snarled at him, his flesh blackening from the weapon's touch.

"Cooperate and I won't do that again." Nav motioned for the necklace and I dropped it into his hand. The cage bars disappeared and he handed it to the demon. "Is there magic on this?"

Kirby touched it briefly. "No. It's just a necklace." He sounded like a broken dentist's drill.

"That's it?" I shook my head. "Check again."

The demon turned his back on me, the bars on the cage once more appearing.

"If he says there's no magic, there's no magic." Nav handed me back the pendant. "Come on, I'll walk you out."

All that for nothing?

Nav insisted on taking the Succubus back across the water with me to my car to ensure that I was well and truly gone. What a prince.

"At least I've got ice cream to look forward to," I muttered, unlocking my sedan. "You don't have to watch me go."

Nav smiled infuriatingly and crossed his arms, not budging.

My irritation grew all the way home, along with my worries about why the Succubus had taken me across the water instead of killing me. I forced a smile when Sadie greeted me at our front door saying she'd already called Jude and to hurry because she'd been waiting forever.

We parked at Casa Gelato, the giant pink warehouse that was our favorite ice cream place, and Sadie hopped out of the car.

"Wait," I said. "Grab my bag."

She retrieved my purse from the passenger side mat and handed it over, then ran across the street to the entrance, her black hair flying.

When she was halfway across the road, she turned back. "I'm getting a double!" She held up the wallet that she'd pilfered.

"Try it, you little thief." I laughed.

Then a car whipped around the corner.

"Sadie!"

My daughter registered a split second of confusion, her slim body flying onto the hood and cracking the windshield before she bounced off and rolled onto the concrete like a ragdoll. Her head was twisted away from me and her crumpled body was still.

Sadie was never still. Even at night she twitched and turned, bunching up her covers, and often ending up lying sideways on the mattress. I waited for her to jump up with a laugh that she was kidding, using those acting skills of hers to con me into buying her a whole gallon of gelato to take home.

Please, God, be acting. I dropped to my knees, the concrete scraping my skin. I felt its warmth the same way I felt Sadie's when I pressed three fingers to her wrist. If she was dead, she'd be cold, right?

There wasn't a pulse, but I could never find my own on the wrist. I always had to check under my jaw. I was sure it was the same for finding Sadie's.

The driver had gotten out, babbling and frantically calling 911, her words a buzzing in my head.

I kept searching for Sadie's pulse, careful not to move her head in case of injury and scared to lean over to check if her eyes were open or closed. Maybe pulses were harder to find if a person was unconscious?

"Get up, sweetheart." I slipped the runner that had fallen off back onto her foot. "You can have a double scoop. A triple. Just wake up, okay?" Her chest didn't rise and fall.

I clamped my lips together against the scream building in my head, because if I released it, it would have no end.

Someone tried to pull me off her, but I swung out at them and gathered my baby into my arms.

Her lifeless eyes stared up at me and I had to look away, focusing through tears on a bird sitting in one of the cherry trees in the shaded area provided for people to enjoy their ice creams. How dare the world look normal? A crack splintered my reality, my grief pulling me into the chasm where madness lived. The impossible truth that my child was gone burrowed into my skull like a splinter that I'd never be able to dislodge.

I smoothed Sadie's silky black hair back from her face, intending to kiss the tiny scar at her hairline from when she'd fallen off her bike years ago.

The scar was gone. I stilled.

I checked all along her forehead, but it wasn't there. My brain stuttered. A missing scar, my scream that could never be fully released.

This wasn't right.

A man knelt down next to me. "I know this is hard, but you have to let her go."

"No." I closed my eyes, took a deep breath, and screamed.

11

WHEN I OPENED THEM AGAIN, I WAS ON MY KNEES in the dirt next to my sedan, my cheeks stained with tears.

Nav stood over me, his eyes clouded with worry and a hand outstretched to me. Beyond him, the tiny ferry bumped against the dock, while ancient trees stretched tall and proud to the sky.

It took me a second to process that I was back in the Park. Sadie wasn't dead, and the illusion that convinced me otherwise was broken.

"What did you do?" I scrambled to my feet and lunged at Nav.

He grabbed me, twisting my arm behind my back. Not hurting me but keeping me in place. "Calm down. You said something about ice cream, and then you hit the ground, crying, like you were in a trance. I couldn't get you to respond."

A kernel of logic burrowed up through my fury. Nav didn't have illusion magic, and even if he did, he'd never mess with me that way.

"Someone made me think my daughter was dead." I was breathing heavily, white-knuckling my keys for the bite of pain to convince myself that the nightmare was over. "Did Kirby lie about the necklace? Is there really magic on it that screwed with my head?"

"He can't lie. None of the demons can," Nav said. "Not with those collars on. The necklace is harmless." His jaw tightened and he assessed the woods with a wary look. "Someone was here and cast that illusion on you." He phoned Clea asking for trackers to be sent over.

I rested my back against the car, waiting until he'd wrapped up the call. "I'm staying."

"No, you're not."

"Make me go, then." I laughed, bitterness spewing out of me. I wanted to destroy whoever or whatever had made me feel that way. If Nav and his people thought they could stop me, then I'd love to see them try.

Especially, I smirked as I drew my cloaking over myself, if they couldn't even see where I was.

Nav swore, his eyes darting over my vanishing form, then stomped his staff against the ground. A blinding light shot out to envelop me and he screamed in pain, tendons in his neck straining as his magic hooked into me.

"I cultivated a new ability just for you, poppet," he rasped, and tore my cloaking away.

The black mesh hung in tattered shreds, binding my arms and legs together. I couldn't free myself.

Nav dumped me in my car like a trussed-up turkey while I called him every name in the book.

"I'll free you the second you promise to go home."

"Naveen, you bastard!"

"Miriam." I reluctantly looked up at his sharp tone. "Let my people find whoever did this. Go be with Sadie and shake off what you just experienced."

The fight drained out of me, my mama-bear urge to protect my cub stronger than my need for vengeance. I sighed. "You win. Will you text me if you find anyone?"

"I promise."

I ignored the speed limit in my dash home to see my daughter for myself and ensure this wasn't yet another illusion. A much worse one, giving me a brief, shining joy before plunging me back into the darkness.

After the world's worst parking job, I ran inside, calling Sadie's name. My heart stopped for what felt like an eternity until she poked her head out of the kitchen.

"Finally," she said, pulling out her phone. "I'll text Jude to meet us at—oomph!"

I crushed her in a hug, breathing in the scent of strawberry lip gloss. She was real. This was real. *But her death felt real, too.*

I grabbed her by the shoulders. "What was the name of the made-up language you spoke as a kid?"

"Why?"

"Answer me!"

"Zzz language," she said warily.

"How many imaginary children did you have?"

"Twenty-seven girls and one boy." She pulled free. "You're scaring me."

I scrubbed a hand over my face. "Sorry. Bad day at work." Whoever had cast that illusion had built it around what I'd said about going for ice cream. I had to trust they couldn't dig into my memories.

Trust that this was reality and Sadie was safe.

"Can we go for ice cream another day?" I said. "Or somewhere else?"

"No." My daughter shoved her feet into flip-flops, and I let out a breath that they weren't her runners.

She shot me weird looks all the way over to Casa Gelato but didn't protest when I insisted on holding her hand crossing the street from the parking lot to the building, having checked six times in both directions first.

Jude waited for us outside, peeling herself away from the

building's pink wall at our approach. "This is a new and interesting regression," she said in her Southern accent.

Sadie pulled her hand free. "Mom got freaked out at work. And now she's going to buy me a double scoop for treating me like a child."

I shoved a bunch of bills at her. "Whatever you want. Get tickets for Jude and me too."

Sadie's eyebrows shot up, but she snatched the money and raced inside.

Jude twirled a finger around my face. "You don't look so good."

I took her hand in mine. "Are we okay? Up on the Grind—"

"Sug, you're as white as my silky linen drawers. Stop worrying about us," she insisted, "and tell me what upset you."

I suppressed a sigh. Leaving out the details of Carpe Demon, I told her that I was tricked into believing Sadie was killed by a car here.

Sadie stuck her head out of the door, holding the tickets up. "Come choose your flavors."

Jude looped her arm through mine. "Let's put some fat and sugar into you. I don't know how to fix this, but I do know that food is always a good place to start."

The gelato place was bustling. Colorful chalk murals of the Seven Wonders of the World adorned the walls, and servers busily handed out samples of their over two hundred flavors, ranging from the more esoteric like durian or wasabi to bubble gum and lemon sorbetto.

I ordered my favorite coffee chocolate chip in a waffle cone without bothering to try any samples. I was still jittery and just wanted Sadie and Jude to order their chocolate raspberry gelato and pink champagne sorbetto so we could cross that nightmare street and sit safely in the outdoor courtyard.

Sadie refused to let me hold her hand this time, so I sandwiched her between myself and Jude, walking across the street with my hands up and halting cars like I was a traffic cop.

My daughter covered her face, begging the ground to open up and swallow her.

"I'm not sitting with you." She beelined for a broad leafy tree at the back of the cobblestoned seating area.

Jude and I sat on a bench against one of the walls enclosing the area.

"How's it going with Dr. Takimoto?" I said.

"Great," she insisted. "What about you all?"

My family had started seeing her therapist and I didn't mind talking about our sessions in general terms, but I was peeved that she'd brushed off my question. "As good as can be. We've only had two and it's taken Eli and Sadie this long to get comfortable, but I noticed a difference at the last one at how much they were willing to discuss." I changed the subject to one she'd answer honestly. "Hey, did you hear back from that European importer? Do they want to carry your new line?"

Jude sighed. "Yes, but there are some problems with distribution in eastern Europe. At the very least, I'll be in the western countries and probably the Czech Republic."

"That's amazing. Mazel tov."

"Thanks. It's an important step toward world domination." She gazed up at the sky, a thoughtful look on her face. "Every time my art ends up in a new place, I think about the journey from my head to their homes. All these strangers who may not share my language share my vision of beauty and they want to incorporate it into their lives. It's like they're taking part of my life's blood, my spark, and keeping it alive."

"That's a beautiful sentiment."

Sadie squealed and I tensed glancing over, but she broke into laughter, reading something on her phone.

Jude nudged my leg. "She's fine." I waited for her to share some more with me because we hadn't connected in a meaningful way for a while, but the mood was broken.

I licked a trickle of gelato off my cone, then held it up. "Check it out. Looks like a penis head."

"I wish dick tasted this good," Jude said.

"And jizzed chocolate chips."

We broke into snorts of laughter, causing a dour old lady sitting nearby to frown at us.

"Did you really finish the Grind?" Jude said.

"Yes, I did, you doubter, and I'm never doing it again."

"The rift got handled?"

"You're safe to continue your masochistic hikes." I bit into the cone. "Still no leads on what my parents were up to."

Jude ate her sorbetto, chewing thoughtfully. "Did they find the man from the beach?"

"Not yet."

She squeezed my hand in sympathy. "What about your uncle Jake?"

"What about him?"

"He must have had thoughts on the matter."

"If he did," I said, wiping a drip off my hand, "he didn't share them with me. I meant to go through all his birthday cards again, but things got crazy. I doubt I'll find anything new though."

"He never sent a letter with those cards?"

"No, he was very careful to keep things anonymous. Fifty in cash, no return address, and he didn't even call me by name. It was always 'Dear Sam.'" I smiled wistfully.

"Why Sam?"

"Because when I was little, I pronounced my name Mir-I-Am. So Jake called me Sam-I-Am or Sam after the Dr. Seuss character." I laughed. "Jake loved puns and he'd send messages like 'You're getting older, roll with it' and my birthday cash would be wrapped in toilet paper. Or the one with 'Have a toad-ally amazing birthday' had a toad sticker in the card. You get the idea."

"Groanworthy, but you're right. They don't sound like secret messages."

"They were horrible," I said fondly, recalling some of the other terrible puns he'd come up with." I frowned. "On the last card he ever sent, for my fortieth, he wrote 'Happy 40th. May you have all the keys to your happiness.' And he included a key. I never thought much about it, but what if the key actually opened something?"

Jude swallowed the last of her cone. "Do you still have it?"

"Yeah. I kept the cards in a memento box." My next bite sat like a stone in my stomach, so I threw out the rest of the gelato. "Jude, that was the last card. What if he discovered something he shouldn't have and was killed for it?"

"You said he died of cancer."

"That's what his obit in the paper said." I rubbed a splash of gelato off my hand. "Who knows if it's true?"

"There's one way to find out," she said.

"Have the old people finished their desserts yet?" Sadie said, standing out of swatting reach.

"Eh?" Jude pressed her hand to her ear. "Speak up, youngster."

"Don't take us back to the home," I said in a warbly voice.

"Sorry. You've had your outside time for the day." Sadie clapped her hands. "Now come along or I'll get Nurse Ratched to medicate you."

Jude tossed her napkin in the trash. "That's what you get for not censoring her reading."

"Don't blame me." I fished my car keys out of my purse. "That's on Advanced Lit."

We said goodbye to Jude and made our way home, Sadie's leg bouncing for the entire ride. Even with the windows down, the car was boiling, the warm air doing nothing to cool things down.

"Why so anxious?" I flicked on my turn signal to take us onto East Broadway.

"No reason." She glanced at her phone.

"Oh good. Then you can vacuum and dust the inside of the car when we get home."

"Shouldn't I stay safely in my room so you don't worry?"

"Nope. I'm over it." That wasn't entirely true, but she'd flip out if I kept hovering. And teasing her like this helped restore my sense that all was well. "Vacuum the inside and do the windows as well. Unless you want to make dinner in this broiling weather."

She sighed. "I'll wash the car."

"Great. Tell Caleb you'll speak with him later." Her mouth fell open and I laughed. "Old people for the win."

I got the better end of that deal because all I had to do was throw the sausages on the BBQ, while Sadie gave me the stink eye for forcing her into child labor.

Later that evening, she locked herself in her room to call her boyfriend and I pulled out my phone having found a working cable to finally charge it. I wasn't sleepy and I didn't want to be alone, but who should I call? I'd just seen Jude, Daya had mentioned the other day that she had a crazy number of C-sections to perform, and Ava was working tonight.

Even though Ryann was going to phone me when they found the stranger, I left a message asking her to call.

I hovered my finger over Laurent's contact. He'd become a close friend. I could call him if I wanted to, but before I could, I got a text from Military Marsha inquiring about my book club preparations. I screamed into a sofa cushion because I'd forgotten it was on Sunday. As in the day I was supposed to finally get it on with Laurent.

I was never getting laid. My Hanukkah bush would

become a withered shrub, a mass of dead foliage, a desolate no-man's-land. I'd wander around with it for forty years and then I'd die. I stabbed out a reply to Marsha that I had the preparations well in hand (versus what I really wanted in my hand or my mouth or really any part of me at this point), then texted Laurent that I wouldn't be able to see him on Sunday because I'd be too exhausted from hosting book club.

He didn't respond and I figured, whatever, one more person blowing me off. I went to sleep in a huff and didn't even touch my book.

The last thing I expected was to be woken up ridiculously early by the wolf shifter knocking at my front door.

He hadn't shaved yet, his dark stubble as scruffy as his curls. He wore basketball shorts that ended just above his well-defined calves and the faded "Bite Me" T-shirt that I'd first seen him in.

Never had I wanted to follow orders so badly. Yawning, I leaned against the door frame. "What are you doing here?"

"Training," he barked.

"You woke me up to watch you work out?" I squinted at him, debating the merits of the idea. On the one hand, sleep. On the other, watching his muscles flex and clench, sweat rivulets rolling down the hard line of his body. Ooh, maybe I could provide him with a water bottle to douse over his head, necessitating the removal of his shirt.

"Not my training. Yours."

Talk about bitter disappointment. "I think not."

Yawning, Sadie trundled down the stairs in her penguin pj's, strands of hair escaping her braids. "Who comes over at 6AM?"

"No one reasonable," I said. "And definitely not anyone expecting me to exercise."

"Your mother has to learn to protect herself," Laurent said.

"Whatever," my kid mumbled. "I'll start the coffee since

you've deprived me of my last hour of precious sleep. I'm sure exhaustion won't affect my brain development or anything."

"Not any more than the caffeine will," I said. "One shot of espresso only."

"Just because it's early doesn't mean you have to be a monster," she said without heat.

"It's too early for this much chatter." Laurent sounded pained.

"Whose fault is that?" I planted my hands on my hips.

"Seriously," Sadie muttered.

Laurent pointed at my daughter. "It wouldn't hurt you to train either."

She stopped, brightening. "Like punching? Can I bring Phoebe?"

"Who's Phoebe?" He frowned.

"My mini flamethrower," Sadie said in a "duh" voice.

He pinched the bridge of his nose. "You let your child play with fire?"

I crossed my arms, aware that I wasn't wearing a bra and the T-shirt I'd slept in was very thin. "It was only supposed to be a prop."

"No weapons, no punching," he said. "Not yet. First you run."

"Get real." Sadie laughed and shuffled into the kitchen.

I yawned again. "What she said. Come back in two hours. Or preferably never with that offer."

"I heard all about your adventures yesterday." Laurent spoke softly, an edge to his voice.

I pretended to knight him. "I now dub thee Town Square." "Quoi?"

"You and Nav are the worst gossips ever."

"What are you going to do the next time you can't access your magic and someone or something wants to hurt you?"

"Try and get away. I've taken self-defense classes, thanks."

"How far can you go before you become winded? How fast are you? You are going to build up your stamina and speed until I deem them acceptable. Then you'll learn fight moves."

Good thing I hadn't told him about that stranger and my magic test. He'd probably make me do a ropes course or something. "Why can't I punch you now?" I said sweetly.

He braced a hand against the door frame and leaned in, his eyes glinting. "Because I can't touch you platonically. Alors, we are both going to run until the only thing we want is a cold shower."

Did someone have blue balls? All because of little ol' me? "Well, when you put it that way..."

I shut and locked the door on him.

"Mitzi," he purred from the other side. "Do you need me to drag you out?"

Tamping down a grin, I placed a hand against the door as if physically connecting with him. "Try it," I said and went into the kitchen. Like hell I was running at the ass-crack of dawn.

Sadie set the espresso pot on the hissing gas burner. "What happened to the wolf?"

"His name is Laurent." I scrounged in the fridge for the milk and a package of banana chocolate chip muffins.

"Emmett calls him the wolf." She got mugs out of the cupboard.

"Emmett is not a role model. Use your manners." I poured us both milk, heating it in the microwave.

"Even when Laurent wakes us up at 6AM?"

"Yes. Even then."

"Says the woman who shut the door in his face."

The microwave binged and I removed the mugs. "That was in the interest of self-preservation."

"I beg to differ," Laurent said, strolling into my kitchen. "That was very rude. Though I agree that the golem is not a suitable role model."

Shrieking, I almost dropped the cups. "Did you just break into my house?"

"No." He gave me an innocent smile. "I took you up on your offer to drag you out."

"Cool." Sadie moved the burbling Moka pot off the burner and shut off the gas. "I'm still not running but I'll trade you caffeine for lock-picking tips."

Suddenly she liked him? I shot her a pointed glare and she shrugged.

"I didn't break in. Your mother's bedroom window was open. And you are running. You're also going to learn the tell of an Ohrist's magic and how to hide because they need line of sight to use their powers on you."

That was a very important lesson for Sadie, but instead of voicing my agreement, I spoke the thought I was preoccupied with. I looked up at the ceiling. "That's on the second floor." He looked confused so I clarified. "You climbed up my house into my window, then came down the stairs all without me hearing you?"

"Yes," he said. "But I made sure my runners were clean, so I didn't track dirt anywhere. Can I have a muffin?"

"No."

"Help yourself," Sadie said. "The coffee offer is still open if you know how to pick locks."

He took the muffin with the most chocolate chips visible in the top. I'd wanted that one. "Come running with us so I can assess your fitness level," he said. "I'll teach you that and fighting." His first bite took out half the muffin.

Sadie pursed her lips like she was considering his offer.

This conversation was getting away from me.

"No one is doing anything without my permission. You." I handed Sadie the mugs. "Pour. You. With me." I pushed Laurent out of the kitchen.

When we were in the living room and safely out of Sadie's earshot, I placed my hands on my hips. "I appreciate that you may be frustrated at the delay in our...next meeting..."

Laurent watched me, his lips pressed together and his shoulders shaking.

"Am I amusing you?"

He gave me a slow grin and my stomach did a flip-flop. "The cold shower part was true. But it's also true that you took forever climbing the Grind."

"How would you know?" I pressed a hand against my flushed cheek. Of all people, why did Laurent have to hear my fitness wasn't exactly top of game?

"I asked Jude." He sat down on my precious sofa, bouncing up and down to test it.

That traitor. See if I ever fed Jude again.

I smacked Laurent on the shoulder. "Stop that. You'll wear out her springs. First of all, I'm never doing the Grind again so it's irrelevant, and second, I could have been Usain Bolt and that wouldn't have helped me escape Carpe Demon."

"But together with fight techniques, it might have. I've already spoken to Tatiana—"

"You what?"

"And she agrees. You can't just rely on magic in this line of work so I'm going to train you." He nodded decisively. "This is a very nice sofa. It reminds me of wildflowers."

No, my heart was not going to melt at that reference to the mural in my bedroom that Laurent had said was the one thing in my house that matched my personality. Fine. I melted a bit, but I was still resentful.

"Here I thought you were being altruistic," I said. "Is she paying you?"

"Yes."

His admission was bittersweet because while Tatiana investing her precious cash in my health was a huge step in our relationship, I wanted Laurent to be here because he couldn't stand to stay away. Even if it was totally fair that he be paid for this.

That made me a bit pissy when I asked my next question. "Your job doesn't extend to training my daughter, so what's that about?"

He walked over to the window and looked out at the back-yard. "Kids in my pack." He took a breath, addressing the window. "We trained them starting at a young age, especially the ones without magic."

Laurent had never spoken to me about his old life. I had dozens of questions I wanted to ask, but I was scared I'd push him away if I did. "This isn't the same thing," I said. "Sadie isn't pack."

He turned to face me. "Eli is a trained cop who can handle himself in both worlds, even without magic. Now Sadie must as well." He strode into the foyer. "I'll ask Juliette to work with her if you don't feel comfortable with me doing it."

"Laurent, no. Wait."

He opened the front door. "Figure out a training schedule with Tatiana and she'll fill me in."

I threw myself against it to stop him from leaving. "Would you hang on one second, you idiot? Of course I don't have a problem with you training her, it's just the idea of my baby doing that means accepting that she isn't safe." I ran my hand through my hair. "I'd hoped it was enough to make Zev promise to leave her alone, but it's not."

"Even Sapien females learn to defend themselves," he said.

"I know. It's a smart idea and I appreciate the offer. I'll pay you for your time with her." I held out my hand to shake but he pushed it away.

"I don't want your money," he said gruffly. "Meet me outside. Bring Sadie. We'll go for half an hour today." With that, he walked out, shutting the front door behind him.

"I think you insulted him." Sadie stood in the kitchen doorway holding both our mugs.

I took that bracing first sip of the day, almost burning my mouth. "Me too. You okay with this?"

"Running before camp? No. But if it gets me to the good stuff, I'll do it."

I glanced at the front door. *So would I.*

12

After a nice, easy warm-up, which gave me hope that we'd ease into this torture session, Laurent broke into what he deemed a slow jog. His pace seemed all right at first, but after ten minutes, I was wheezing. Sadie wasn't even winded, happily carrying on a detailed monologue about the different musical theater roles she'd love to play, starting with her A-list.

Laurent looked shell-shocked that any one person could speak for that long without ceasing, which brought me great joy.

I fell farther and farther behind until they rounded a corner, at which point I slowed to a walk. A brisk walk. Ish. Why hadn't I brought water? Even at 7AM this heat wave was kicking my ass.

When I turned the corner, Laurent and Sadie were sitting on someone's lawn waiting for me. Sadie was still talking, gesturing excitedly as she explained the difference between two of her third-tier choices.

Laurent's eyes were glazed, but he managed weak nods every so often. Ha.

Sadie bounded to her feet. "Sprints now, right?"

"Please, God, no," I said.

She ignored me. "Where do you want us to run to?"

"Sprint to that brick apartment building and back," Laurent said, pointing. "I'll time you."

"That's like ten blocks," I protested.

"It's three blocks away. Don't be a baby, Mom." Sadie crouched down in a sprinter's start. "Me first."

"By all means," I said.

Laurent pulled out his phone and started the stopwatch. "Go."

She bolted.

He watched her complete the first block. "Good form. Fast. She's a natural. Is her father a runner?"

"Yeah. Eli ran track in high school and university while I specialized in coffee shop sitting. Luckily, she takes after him in this regard."

"She's like you in more ways than one."

I fanned myself, moving under a tree to seek out some shade. "Her ability to talk nonstop?"

"That too." Laurent checked the stopwatch. "She had lists of different musical theater success scenarios, but she also told me about her university plans because it's smart to have a plan B. And she isn't deterred by the odds of achieving her goals. Like you."

Sadie tagged the front walk of the apartment building with her foot and turned around.

"I'll take that as a compliment," I said.

"It is. But just like you, under all the lists and smart backup plans is the pure rush of living on the edge," he said. "You buried it for a long time, but you're addicted to that feeling now, compounded by a noble cause. It's why I do what I do. Same with your ex, Nav, and Tatiana."

My daughter raced toward us with a flat-out pedal-to-the-metal enthusiasm.

"Yeah, well, Sadie isn't fighting evil. And since when are you Mr. Chatty? Remember how wonderfully grumpy and untalkative you used to be?"

"You made it too easy to talk to you. That's on you." Laurent grinned and I made a snarky face in return. "As for Sadie, she wants to entertain people. That's its own noble cause." He shook his head. "That belief coupled with the desire to do whatever it takes and the thrill of living an exciting life leads people to engage in more extreme actions to achieve their goals." Laurent paused, dropping his eyes to the stopwatch. "To feel alive."

With one block left, Sadie was starting to slow. I was about to point out that like me, she was levelheaded enough to make smart choices, when she amped up her speed, pumping her arms and legs as fast as she could, her braids flying out behind her. She ran across the residential street and jumped the curb, but her foot caught, and she crashed to the pavement.

"Sadie!" I bolted for her, my heart in my throat at her stillness, but she jumped up, blood trickling down her leg.

"All good!" she cried and resumed her run.

I returned to Laurent, one hand on my chest as I took deep breaths to come down from the rush of adrenaline.

Ignoring the nasty gash and bleeding, Sadie finished her circuit, a determined look on her face. She was panting, her face beet red. "Nailed it, right?"

Laurent shot me a pointed look before replying, "You're a natural."

I ended the training session, not because it was my turn, but because my kid needed to wash gravel and blood off her leg and get some Polysporin on it. Laurent didn't argue, though I could tell from the stubborn set of his chin that I wasn't getting out of it altogether.

When we got back, I gave Sadie the keys and told her I'd be inside momentarily.

"Sorry you didn't get your cold shower run," I said to Laurent. "And next time let's skip the pop psychology of me and my kid, shall we?"

"Not wanting to hear it doesn't make it any less true," he said. "Trust me, I know. See you, Mitzi." He pivoted around, falling into a loping stride that looked casual and relaxed but was incredibly fast.

I snorted. He even ran like a wolf.

I headed inside to make sure Sadie tended to her cut properly. And to possibly hug her three or seven more times than her injuries required to the point where she pushed me away in annoyance with a huffed "I'm fine. Geez," then stomped out of the bathroom.

If she was that exasperated, she was okay. I put the first aid kit away and washed my hands.

Laurent had me thinking, not about Sadie, but about Giselle. I'd ruled out magic on the necklace, which left my hypothesis that some past trauma was trying to make its way to the forefront of her consciousness.

I said bye to my kid as she left for work, then hopped in a hot shower, lathering up with my foamy shampoo.

If the discomfort that Giselle was experiencing was tied to memories trying to resurface, could there be more than psychology at play? Had she'd gone so far as to have someone magically block out something that had happened to her? Call them Person Y. Giselle had empathy magic, so she hadn't done this to herself, though her powers might be part of why she was tapping into the sensation that something was wrong.

I wrung the water from my hair before massaging conditioner in.

Could Person Y have slapped me with the illusion of Sadie's death to try to clue me in to what was going on? Were they trying to help Giselle?

I soaped up my legs, running my razor over them.

I'd broken through that false reality easily enough, but maybe without a hard push, she wouldn't be able to. In which case she'd never be able to heal from what had happened.

This hypothesis had a ton of what-ifs, but I'd ruled out the easiest possibility, which was magic on the necklace. Giselle was upset enough to have sought Tatiana out even after being turned down by Kadeem, so I refused to discount what she was experiencing. Either magic, her subconscious, or both were trying to force her to face the truth.

Person Y hadn't shown themselves to me, and Nav hadn't texted, which meant his trackers hadn't found anyone. Whomever this illusionist was, they didn't want to be found. What was Person Y's stake in all this and why couldn't they approach me directly? There weren't a ton of Ohrists with that ability, but tracking everyone down who was capable of casting illusions would still take time.

I rinsed off and stepped into my steamy bathroom to dry myself. Giselle was no help, but if I could speak with a close friend of hers, maybe I could get answers.

But first, back in the realm of my personal life, I had to find out what Uncle Jake's key opened if anything. After I'd gotten dressed and quickly scarfed another muffin, I grabbed the memento box stored at the back of my closet shelf and dumped the contents onto my bed, searching for the last birthday card he'd sent.

It was buried halfway down the pile. I flipped the card open, nodding in relief that the key was still taped to the inside. It was too large to open a safety deposit box. Jake had died a year and a half ago and his house had been sold so if it was directing me to something on his property, I'd have to break into a stranger's home.

Following a hunch, I looked up self-storage businesses in

my old hometown up north. There was only one. It was doubtful that he'd paid past his death for a unit, but easy enough to eliminate that place as a possibility. I pocketed the key in my capris.

Right before I stepped into the KH, there was a knock on the door.

Ryann was there, her expression especially grim when compared to her rainbow-colored skirt and bright purple shirt. Guess she'd done laundry.

"What's wrong?" I motioned for her to come in, but she shook her head.

"We identified the man from the beach." She stifled a yawn, sipping from a travel mug.

"That's great. Who is he?"

"James Learsdon."

"And?" I pressed my fingertips against my throbbing temples, my anxiety flaring up.

"Still no sign of him." She popped the lid back on the cup with a firm thwack. "We'll find him. We've verified that he's too young to have killed your parents and he only has low-level healing magic, so he didn't murder Fred McMurtry either."

"That's something, I guess."

"It's the bare minimum," Ryann said. "The victim at Davide's house? Wallace? He was majoring in French and German and delivered pizzas because his partial scholarship didn't cut it. Learsdon got that poor kid possessed and sent him after Davide to lure you out. I know it in my bones and I want him taken down." Her eyes flashed. Ryann looked so much like an anime character at the best of times that I expected a spurt of fire to blast out of the top of her head now.

"You'll find him. How's Davide?"

"A mess. How are you holding up?"

I shrugged. "As good as I can be knowing James is still on the loose."

"I could get a Lonestar to watch you. Just in case."

I considered it, then shook my head. "Thanks, but no. He got what he wanted from me. Now it's my turn."

"Call me if you reconsider. Meantime, stay vigilant." She waved and left.

I leaned against the door frame. Should I be glad that I could eliminate James as my parents' killer? Frustrated that I hadn't learned anything about sharks or whispers or what James believed that my parents had started and I would finish?

I'd initially left finding him to the Lonestars because they had more resources, and having done my duty and handed the case over to them, I didn't want to get in their way, or more importantly, get on their bad side. Especially since Ryann had explicitly warned me against going after him.

The Lonestars wanted Learsdon for murder; I wanted him for answers. That didn't mean I had to hunt him down like they were. I'd been a librarian; give me access to his home, or possibly workplace depending on what he did, and I might unearth a treasure trove of information without ever stepping on the Lonestars' toes.

Keeping that in my back pocket for later, I pressed the key to my lips. "Please let Uncle Jake deliver one final gift to me."

I stepped through the shadows into the Kefitzat Haderech. The warm, dimly lit cave's scent of fabric softener was particularly eye-watering today. "Morning, sunshine," I called out over the drone of a vacuum cleaner.

Pyotr, the gargoyle host with the most, was cleaning the chute that dispensed single socks with a long suction hose and didn't hear me.

I tapped him on the shoulder, and he jumped, whacking his head on the vent.

The Russian gargoyle rubbed his stone head, his bug-like

eyes and downturned lips more mournful than usual, and turned off the small cannister with his foot. "You sneak like cat."

A shower of lint rained from the chute onto his head and ears, and he sighed like this indignation was exactly what he expected from the universe.

"Here. Let me help." I brushed him clean, jerking my chin at the large rock slab that usually contained the lone socks. "You gave them all away? That's great."

"Not great. Socks stopped falling. Chute is blocked. No travel until have sock."

"We both know that's not true. You just tell people that to get rid of the things."

"Rules are rules." The gargoyle hit the power button again, aiming the hose up the chute.

"Can't you make an exception?" I yelled. "I need to get somewhere quickly."

Pyotr shoved the hose at me. "Then you clean."

That's how I found myself shoved halfway up a laundry chute, courtesy of the gargoyle's cold hands on my butt, while I wielded the hard plastic wand extension like a hammer to chip through the block of lint.

"This is some kind of special bullshit." I coughed at the burst of dust that fell into my mouth. "You could have given me a face shield or something. And quit pinching my ass."

"You think this is good time for me?" He huffed, ramming his shoulder against my butt for more leverage. "I could have been dentist. But no. Make a difference, Petrusha. Mouths are dirty, Petrusha."

I blinked a drop of sweat out of my eye, chiseling away more of the blockage. "There's dentist school for gargoyles?"

"School?" He sounded perplexed. "What school? Find bad tooth and pull."

I shifted, trying to get a better angle, and my flip-flop slid into his mouth. Something wet swiped across my toes and I shrieked, jerking upright. The hose broke through the lint and the entire impediment bounced off my head and Pyotr's chest, cracking into pieces on the ground like a dry hay bale.

The gargoyle had been knocked askew and he spun with me still sitting in his hands above his head, weaving like a flag in a hurricane. I dropped the cannister hose trying to keep my balance.

Pyotr did a little hopping dance to avoid the vacuum. A surge of hope shot through me that I'd be deposited safely but a barrage of socks exploded out of the cleared chute, knocking me off the gargoyle and onto a lumpy pile of fabric.

Getting my bearings, I smacked Pyotr with the hose, which splintered and broke. "Did you lick my toes?"

He cowered, covering his head. "I thought you wanted me to!"

"Not ever." I shuddered. The kinkiest action I'd had in recent memory, and it had been with a depressed gargoyle wearing brown plaid. How was this my actual life? I smoothed a hand over my hair and clothes, seeking any semblance of dignity, then grabbed a bright blue sock adorned with tiny Pokémon. "Open the door."

A narrow green door appeared in the rock face on the far side of the cave.

Pyotr glanced down at the ground. "Are you mad at me?"

"Not really." I held up a hand. "So long as it doesn't happen again. Okay?"

He shuffled his feet, wringing his hands in front of him. "Will you still bring me movies?"

Like I'd say no to that woebegone face even if I was mad? "Of course."

"Thank you," he whispered.

Aww. Did he even have any other friends or was he stuck in this joyless void serving the Kefitzat Haderech with no company except the neon sign? A foul-mouthed golem, a grumpy wolf, the Loki of the hip replacement set, and stone

Eeyore here; I was really racking up the charmers in my inner circle. I used to work with very nice people. Normal people.

And how dull had that been?

I hugged Pyotr, and he patted my back with a large hand and very gentle touch. "Don't lick without consent," I said.

The advice that moms had to dispense, I tell you.

13

With the address of the self-storage place firmly fixed in my head, it took only a couple of minutes' travel along the poorly lit rocky path until another door led me out to the parking lot alongside the building.

It was raining, but after the high temperatures in Vancouver, the cool, wet air felt delicious. I cloaked myself, hopping puddles across the gravel driveway to the large awning. My hair and feet were soaked, but the rain masked the sound of my approach to the couple opening the front door. I grabbed it just before it locked and slipped inside.

Stealthily I moved from one storage unit to the next, testing out Jake's key. After the twenty-seventh locker, I figured it was a bust, but to my amazement, I unlocked the next heavy padlock.

Rolling the orange corrugated metal door up, I slipped inside, recalling my magic as I turned on the light. An entire living room had been re-created inside. A faded brocade armchair sat on a threadbare Persian rug next to an old standing lamp. Photos of kids and grandkids lined the upper shelves of metal bookcases. Super weird. Especially since Jake didn't have kids.

I hauled one of the Rubbermaids from a lower shelf, which was filled with children's artwork. Another container held old Halloween costumes while the third one I checked was filled with cracked Christmas ornaments. I picked up one of the books stacked on the rickety antique table. It was a baby book for some kid called Tiffany. This definitely wasn't Jake's unit.

"Tiffany! You've come home." A hundred pounds of tiny grandma rushed into the storage locker from the hallway and knocked me into the armchair with her cane.

"There's been a mistake," I said.

"The only mistake was you staying away for so long." Her eyes misted up and her cane wobbled. "Two years? Why didn't you come home?"

I jumped up. "Maybe you should sit down."

"You were always such a good girl." She eased herself into the seat, her legs not even touching the ground. "Tell me what's been happening with Nathan." She tapped the container with the Halloween costumes, motioning for me to sit down.

Staying here would be a waste of my time, but she seemed so eager for company. What could it hurt to answer a few questions and make her feel better? I'd take fifteen minutes to do a mitzvah and then go check out Jake's old house.

"Nathan's still a scamp," I said.

"I thought he'd settle down in his teen years."

"I wish." The first few lies about Nathan's troubles at school were clumsy, but then I really found my rhythm, expanding to include the joyous news of Aunt Elma's daughter who had triplets and cousin Jody's new puppy. "Sadly, this is a short visit, but I'll come back, okay? Did you come to get something from the locker? Do you need help to your car?"

"Yes, dear. If you could reach that box of photo albums over there?"

I obliged, stretching onto tiptoe to grab it—and froze in that position.

What the hell?

My eyes moved back to the old woman, who was no longer smiling. Instead, her cane jabbed my hip, her Ohrist magic coursing through it and paralyzing me in place. "Now, you little hussy. Why did you break into my locker?"

"I'm Tiffany," I protested, struggling to free myself. My magic felt like it was trapped under glass. I still had my powers, I just couldn't access them.

The lady jabbed me again. "If you were the real Tiffany, you'd know that Nathan is a horse."

Were regular horse updates a thing? Because she'd sounded very invested in catching up on his life.

The woman's frown deepened and I chose my words with care.

"All right. You caught me. But I wasn't trying to steal from you. My uncle Jake left me this key and it opened your locker. I thought his stuff was here."

"Jake didn't have a niece."

My Achilles tendons burned from holding this position and my arms were getting heavy. "It was honorary. Could you release me?"

She forced me even higher onto my toes and I winced. "Last chance before I call the Lonestars."

"No! Please. My name's…" I was going to say Miriam and then a gut instinct had me change it. "Sam."

Another jab. "Bully for you. What was Jake's favorite color?"

"I have no idea."

"Favorite food?"

"Steamed broccoli."

"Hummus." She tapped her cane across the floor and popped a lid off a Rubbermaid. "You don't know him at all."

"I do. Hummus was my favorite food. Not his."

"You sure about that?" Her magic fell off me and I dropped down onto my heels.

Had I remembered things wrong?

The old woman held a manila envelope in her hand. I stepped forward and a corner of it began to smolder.

"Jake set protections on this. He was worried about who might come around. If I flick my wrist, this envelope is toast. Understood?"

I nodded, vibrating with the strain of keeping myself in place. I couldn't get to her fast enough to grab it and if I used my magic, she'd burn it.

"I'll give you one more chance to prove you knew him."

"I was a kid when I saw him. These stupid questions prove nothing. People's favorite colors and foods can change."

"Then I'll give you an easy one. Did Jake have any siblings?"

Not by blood, but he did have one by choice. "A brother," I said softly. "Noah."

"Wrong again." She flicked her wrist and the envelope burst into flame.

"No!"

She dropped it to the concrete floor, and I ran over to stomp out the flames but she poked me back with her cane. The fire blazed high and bright for a moment and then winked out.

The envelope was untouched.

I gaped at it, and she chuckled, sliding it over to me with her cane.

"Oh, just a little song and dance there, dear. I hardly ever get to put those parlor tricks to use. I hope you don't mind. But no, you take it." She smiled up at me. "You gave the answers Jake said you would."

I snatched up the envelope, which wasn't even hot. "His favorite food *was* steamed broccoli?"

"No. But you hated it, so he ate your share. It was hummus, but he let you hog it."

"Of course he did." I clutched the envelope to my chest, my eyes damp. "Do you know what's inside?"

"A letter, though I have no idea what it says."

"How was he when he wrote it?"

"Heavily medicated at the time. I'm not sure what you're hoping to find, but it may just be gibberish."

"He really died of cancer, then?" A knot in my chest eased when she nodded. As shitty a way to die as that was, it was better than him being murdered. "Were there people with him when he passed?"

"Yes, dear. You can rest easy on that. You'd have been there if you could."

"He told you about me?" My words were sharp, but he might have put her in danger.

"You don't remember me, Miriam, but I was acquainted with your parents. And I know that only the most extreme circumstances would have made Jake send you away."

All these years, I'd felt so alone, forced to tell that awful lie about Mom and Dad dying in a house fire. Even if I couldn't share the truth now, just learning that this woman had known them and didn't believe the story made me feel reconnected to my hometown in a way I hadn't since that tragic night. I wish that she'd been closer to Mom and Dad because they wouldn't have shared their professional dealings with a casual acquaintance.

"Thank you for hanging on to this," I said. "I don't know your name. Sorry."

"Rhonda. Jake was a good boy and a good friend. And it was nice of you to humor a senile old lady with those stories." She winked and I blushed.

I paused. "Uh, if it's not too rude, why does your storage unit look like a living room?"

"My daughter and her kids moved in with me," Rhonda

said. "I adore them, but a lady needs some peace and quiet now and then."

"I hear you."

Letter in hand, I said my goodbyes. The elderly woman was lovely but I hoped I didn't have to go back. It was too hard revisiting the past.

I could have taken the KH straight home, but I wasn't able to face whatever Jake had written on my own, so instead I went to Jude's studio.

Tatiana was wrong about truth forcing a more extreme action. My encounter with Rhonda had brought a much-needed closure to Uncle Jake's death and all I felt was gratitude knowing he hadn't died alone.

Jude answered my knock with a look of surprise, wiping her hands on her clay-stained white apron. "I didn't expect to see you here."

"Yeah, do you have a moment?"

She paused.

"Bad time?" I said neutrally.

"I mean, I'm kind of busy, but what's up?"

"Jake left me a letter."

"Oh. Well, damn, come in." She motioned me inside her studio, which smelled damp, like moist dirt from the clay.

She thought I wanted to talk about us. Or her. We would, but I let it go for now, just needing my friend to talk this new development through with.

I followed her to the sink at the far end, skirting several buckets. Water from wheel work couldn't be directly dumped down the drain so Jude let it sit in buckets until the clay had settled to the bottom and the clearer water could be disposed of. "What are you working on?"

The last time I'd been here, her studio had been trashed, but there were no signs of that now. While the kiln and pottery wheel were currently unused, the containers of glaze were stacked neatly on shelving units alongside plastic-wrapped packages of clay and the brushes and sculpting tools in the holder on the long table were neatly cleaned.

"I've got some pieces to fire later." Jude pointed at the shelving unit holding unpainted plates of various sizes. "But first I'm reclaiming clay. Got to stay on top of it." She lifted a slab of clay out of a shallow basin inserted in the large stainless-steel sink. Freeing it from the cloth it had been resting in, she dumped it onto a smooth board lying on the countertop.

"Is this the loud thing you do?" I'd learned enough over the years to have an okay grasp of the basic process.

"Yup, but not for a minute. Talk to me." She cut the clay into slices with a taut piece of wire that she held by two small wooden handles. "Are you nervous to see what's inside?

I fiddled with the edge of the envelope flap that had come unglued. "Yes and no. Mostly I'm angry that I never thought to find out if there was more to Jake's birthday cards than good wishes. He sent this two years ago. What if I've blown my shot to pursue whatever he learned? If he learned anything at all."

"That's fair." Jude fit the slices back together and cut the entire thing in half. "Getting loud now." She grabbed one square piece and slammed it down against the counter where it reverberated with a thwack. The next square was slammed down on top of the first one, perpendicular to it.

I worked my fingernail under the loose flap and tore the envelope open, while Jude pounded everything into a single large square and then made a number of horizontal slices to break it up again.

"How do your hands stay clean?" I said.

"Because the clay isn't too wet. Here, feel."

I poked it, then examined my fingertip. "How many more times are you going to do this?" I said loudly since she'd resumed thwacking the pieces together again.

She shrugged. "Might be as many as nine or ten times. I

need to get all the color variations and bubbles out of it. Want me to stop while you pull out the contents?"

I shook my head, wanting a moment to sit with my feelings, both about what I might find and that Jake had loved me so much that he'd eaten my reject food instead of what he really liked. It was so unfair that I'd lost him too, after losing my parents.

By the time Jude moved on to rolling the clay into a ball of dough to get ready to use on the wheel, tiny wisps of her red curly hair stuck to her forehead.

"Good arm workout."

She flexed for me. Her biceps were rocks. "I am one toned muthafuckah." She paused. "You don't have to do this now if you're not ready." The clay made a sucking noise as Jude worked it into a ball.

"No. I sought this out and I'm as ready as I'll ever be." I pulled out the first sheet of loose-leaf paper, squinting at the illegible printing.

The message was brief. One sentence brief.

"'It wasn't an...'" I shook my head. His writing was a garbled mess.

Jude looked at the paper. "Accident." She pinched the balls of clay together with her thumbs.

"Their murders? He knew that from the house fire." I flinched as Jude slammed the smushed clay together again.

"Sorry," she murmured. "Last bit."

I flipped the page over, hoping for something else, but that was it. "Maybe this really just was his drugged-up last ramblings." I shook my head. "Let's see what else we've got."

"Hang on. Let me just finish this." She placed the glossy, smooth clay that she'd shaped into a Yule log in a bag that she rolled tight around the clay to press out any air. She twisted the end and wrote the date on it in black marker. "Done. Show me."

Setting aside the letter, I pulled out the rest of the papers and almost dropped them. Jake had drawn pages and pages of stars along with the words "the Ascendant."

Jude took them from my trembling hands. "Does this star mean something to you? It's not a Magen David. Those have six points."

The Jewish symbol consisted of two triangles forming an equilateral six-pointed star. The Lonestars' tattoo also had six points though it was more stylized, like a starburst, or a spur, which was apt.

Jake's drawings all had five points, but regardless of that, why did I keep coming up against stars?

Was learning the truth behind my parents' murders my mazel, my destiny?

I shook my head. I wasn't following any predetermined plan. I made choices born of free will and circumstance. Anyone in my position would be determined to find out why their parents were killed.

"I have no clue what the star means," I said. "And why ascendent? Like an ascendant star? An astrology thing?"

The air-conditioning kicked in, blowing my hair into my face. I held the strands clear with one hand, flushing despite the breeze.

Jude tapped the paper. "Ascendent meaning gaining power? A star as in a celebrity and ascendant meaning they're an influencer? Ooh. Or literal star power as in nuclear fusion."

"What?"

"Remember when I was toying around with a line based on the night sky?" She moved the basin out of the sink and washed her hands.

"Yeah."

Jude tossed the paper towel she'd dried them on into a trash can. "I got really into astronomy for a while. Stars shine because of nuclear fusion."

"I can't see my parents being tied to either famous influencers or nuclear fusion."

"True. That doesn't seem likely. Did he write anything else?"

"That was it." I stuffed the pages back in the envelope.

"What now?"

"Now I convince a certain golem to tap into his faulty divination magic."

"Well, you handled lawyers for long enough," Jude said. "This ought to be a piece of cake."

"From your mouth to God's ears," I said in an exaggerated Yiddish accent and we both burst out laughing.

14

Since I had to speak to both Emmett and my boss, I drove over to her house. Much as I didn't want to face Tatiana, this conversation was best handled in person. And on a full stomach because I was hangry enough to throw someone off a bridge. I stopped at a great Italian deli on the way for a grilled panini loaded with salami, bocconcini, and eggplant, eating it at the tiny outdoor patio area and washing it down with an icy-cold limonata San Pellegrino.

The golem wasn't home when I got to my destination, but Tatiana's assistant Marjorie led me to the artist's bedroom.

"How are you getting on with Emmett?" I admired the colorful abstracts hung in the hallway and signed with Tatiana's broad scrawl.

Marjorie blushed. "He's really nice."

Oh geez. Emmett was nowhere near self-aware enough to handle a crush with tact. I made a note to speak to him about being kind to her.

Tatiana's room looked like a bomb had gone off with colorful clothing draped over every surface. The doors to the walk-in closet were open and Tatiana was inside, on tiptoe, reaching for a hat box.

"You need help with that?" I said, hurrying over.

"I've got it." She retrieved it safely. "Marjorie, get me more compression bags."

"Okay." Her assistant scuttled off.

Tatiana opened the lid, set a black and gray fur hat on her head, and struck a pose. "What do you think?"

"Very *Doctor Zhivago*, but it's still August, even if you're going to Moscow."

She tossed the hat on her bed. "I hate when seasons interfere with my fashion choices."

"I bet you do. Where's Emmett?"

"Out collecting fees." She smiled. "He was very excited to take that job on."

I rolled my eyes, picturing him dressed like some Mafia goon and threatening to break heads if people didn't pay up.

"I heard you showed the necklace to Carpe Demon," she said.

"That's not really their name, is it?"

Tatiana shrugged. "It's the only one we're given."

"Well, it was a last resort. Is that a problem?"

"Not so long as you email me a detailed description of everything you saw. Those people are very tight-lipped about their organization."

I perched on the edge of a chair, careful not to crush any clothing. "And they probably have penalties for people who blab."

"Did they say it was a secret? Make you sign an NDA? Swear you to silence with a blood oath?"

I thought through my interactions with Carpe Demon. "No."

"Then that's their problem." She opened a drawer in her large dresser and frowned at the contents. "So? Was there any magic on the necklace?"

I shook my head.

"I hate to say I told you so." She opened another drawer.

"Oh no. Wait. I delight in it." Her eyes sparkled and I got the sense that there weren't many people in her life she got to tease.

"Before you lecture me about a blemish on your reputation again—"

"Tell me you don't wear cotton undergarments." She scooped out an armful of silky lingerie and tossed it into one of the suitcases.

I averted my eyes from the crimson thong dangling off the corner of the suitcase. "What's wrong with cotton?"

"Everything. I see I'll have to take you lingerie shopping. Raymond!" she bellowed. "Where's my calendar?"

I ran to the door. "All good, Raymond! Never mind." The last thing I needed was her having Raymond pencil in a time to choose new underwear for me. That was an excursion I could happily die without taking. "We'll figure it out when you get back," I said. "Meantime, I was right that something odd is going on." I filled her in on the illusion that I'd suffered. "I believe that Giselle has repressed a memory and someone is attempting to bring that to my attention."

Tatiana studied the two dresses on hangers that she held, then put both on top of the lingerie. She fixed me with a steely blue gaze. "Why do you persist in seeing good in the world?"

"As if. I'm super cynical and suspicious."

"As if," she mocked. "Since you reclaimed your magic, your best friend was kidnapped, an assignment turned into a murder case, and I was threatened with a death curse."

"Your point?"

"After all those experiences, a cynical and suspicious person would see the illusion for what it was: a warning to back off."

Loath as I was to admit it, that was a fair assumption. "Regardless, I've come this far, and I plan to see it through."

Shaking her head, she picked up a beaded ivory sandal,

walking around with it held out like a dowsing rod. "I'll allow it, only because if someone is going to the trouble of scaring you off, then Kadeem was wrong not to take the case. And I can charge Giselle danger pay." She shook the sandal. "Where are you?"

I got onto my knees and looked under the bed. "It's here." I handed the sandal over, shaking off the dust buffalo attached to it. "Speaking of Kadeem, can you let him know I'm going to New York now to speak with Giselle's friend? Do I need to check in with him?"

I wasn't exactly hiding my Banim Shovavim status, but I didn't need other machers looking too closely at me either.

"I'll clear it. You don't need to see him."

"Thanks." I paused. "They still haven't found the guy who was testing my magic."

"That's unfortunate." Immersed in her packing, she failed to add anything else.

Unfortunate? Was she preoccupied with her trip or just didn't care that James might be sharing my magic with people or creatures who might want to exploit it?

Peeved, I decided to show myself out.

In typical Tatiana fashion, she waited for me to get to the bedroom door before speaking. "You've gotten some excellent results in our previous jobs, continue that level of achievement with the rest of Giselle's case."

I rocked onto the outsides of my feet, warmed by her praise. "I will. When do you leave?"

"Sunday night. And I want that email before I go." She glanced into the hallway. "Marjorie! Did you fall down a well?!"

"I'm here." Marjorie manifested a pallet made of light and dropped the stack of compression bags onto it.

Tatiana raised an eyebrow. "You've been practicing."

Her assistant blushed and nodded, sailing the pallet to her boss. It was wobbly, practically tipping over a couple of times in the short distance, and she almost dropped it on Tatiana's foot when she lowered it to the carpet, but both Tatiana and I praised her, nonetheless.

Marjorie bounced on her toes happy and flushed—right as a crescent of light popped up next to her.

Tatiana cried out, her hand outstretched, but I was on it. I flung my mesh cloaking over the young woman. *Not today, ohr.* The supernatural energy that these magic people drew from demanded payment in the form of an Ohrist's life at some random point when they used magic. But as a Banim Shovavim, I could stop that.

When the light vanished and I recalled my magic, Marjorie was ghost-white and swaying on her feet. I muscled my shoulder under her arm and led her to the bed.

She kept apologizing even though I assured her there was nothing to be sorry for.

"Enough nonsense," Tatiana barked. "You're fine. This is our burden as Ohrists." Her fierce scowl was betrayed by the trembling hand she laid on Marjorie's shoulder.

"The chances of it ever happening again are minuscule," I said gently.

Marjorie nodded, but from the way she twisted her fingers together, her eyes downcast, I had the sense she might not ever use her magic again.

I crouched down so she'd look at me. "Do you want a glass of water?"

Hovering protectively over her charge, Tatiana helped her assistant up. "We'll have tea. I'll make it. Come, Marjorie."

"You want me to stay?" I said.

"No. I want you to get me information on Carpe Demon as I requested." Tatiana's expression softened and she nodded. "Thank you, Miriam."

"Of course."

I drove home feeling grateful that I wasn't an Ohrist, even though we Banim Shovavim had our own price to pay for magic use. If any of my kind believed the story that the angels had laid down about us being evil, and judged themselves accordingly, they'd damn themselves to eternal torment in the Kefitzat Haderech. Exactly like the woman I'd met on my first visit there had done.

But if they solved the riddle the neon sign gave, like I had, understanding that it was the angels' prejudices and we weren't inherently wicked, that fate would be avoided.

Ohrists, on the other hand, had this axe hanging over them. The ohr might never show up in generations of a family or the tiniest magic act could set it off. It was a hell of a thing to live with.

After I dutifully sent my boss the few details of Carpe Demon's layout that I had, I took the rest of the evening off. Sadie was out with Caleb for another hour, so I sat in my backyard with a book, losing myself in the latest Tana French mystery.

Well, I tried to, but I kept circling back to James Learsdon and my parents, so I gave up on the chapter and started typing out facts.

My parents were murdered almost thirty years ago, and their deaths were covered up by the Lonestar in charge of Northern British Columbia: Fred McMurtry.

In exchange for his cooperation, he was brought into the demon realm and infected with a parasite that cured his cancer but also piloted him or something until he was murdered in the same way with the same cover-up a couple months ago at his home.

This parasite was capable of transporting Ohrists from one place to another, through walls, which was why Eli and I now had a ward around our property.

Early Monday morning, I'd been called to Davide Forino's house, supposedly to dispose of some sensitive material. Instead, I'd found a crime scene. Wallace Edwards had been dybbuk-possessed, using a pizza delivery to gain access to

Davide, a well-known stoner. He'd then attacked the snow-boarder, died from excessive magic use, at which point the dybbuk had enthralled Davide.

The text that Tatiana had received from Davide asking for her services hadn't been sent by him.

James Learsdon, the stranger on the beach, hadn't admitted to setting up the crime to verify my powers, but he'd been surprised that I'd hidden them all those years and hadn't been a blank. He'd asked if I was a baby shark or if I was planning to finish what my parents had started and said he followed faint whispers. About what?

I googled him, sorting through results until I'd narrowed it down to three likely candidates, since I didn't know what he looked like. After a bit more digging, I eliminated two of them. One man was in Wyoming for a rodeo competition and the other had posted on social media about his brother's wedding that night.

The last one was an archeology professor. I noted that down, along with his age, thirty-five. Ryann had already told me he had healing magic, so I added that fact as well.

Shaking out the cramp in my hand, I resumed jotting down my thoughts.

Two years ago, Uncle Jake had disguised a key to a storage locker in one of his pun-laden birthday cards, leading to an envelope held by a woman called Rhonda who'd known my parents and didn't believe the house fire story either.

I had to pass a test to get the letter because Jake was worried someone would come after it, but all that was inside was the sentence "It wasn't an accident" and pages of stars with the words "the Ascendant."

Despite the many facts, I barely had any grasp of what I was dealing with. The best thing to do would be to go to sleep, let it percolate in my brain and see what popped loose.

Sadly, there were no new epiphanies on Saturday morning, but I had to put aside further questions about my parents in favor of my paying assignment. After I let Giselle know that I was coming to New York and got her permission to speak with her best friend, I stepped into a shadowy corner in my hallway.

Transitioning into the KH felt like stepping into a warm, shallow pond, the shadows rippling outward and a sponginess beneath my feet. In the single, slow blink that it took to cross over, I was certain that the only thing carrying me through was Wile E. Coyote logic, and if I so much as glanced down, gravity would kick in and I'd plummet into a bottomless chasm.

Coming out on the other side came with the same small tug as when I exited gentle waves onto a beach, the shadows falling off me like droplets.

Pyotr wasn't there. A sign on his table read "Back in 15. Help yourself to a sock." Le gasp. He was permitted a break? It wasn't exactly union standards, but good for him. I grabbed a fuzzy pink ankle sock as it floated out of the chute and headed through the narrow green door.

The path between doors was generally a pulsing strip of light, giving me about ten feet of vision before becoming an all-consuming darkness that felt like the empty void into which we were born and in which we'd die. Today, however, the lights were out. I backed up against the rock wall feeling behind me for the door I'd stepped through, but it was gone.

"Hello?" My voice echoed off the walls in a distorted echo. I couldn't animate Delilah or summon my scythe and my cloaking was pointless. "Yo!" I snapped my fingers. "This does not conform to work safe standards."

I'd have given anything for the neon sign to light up with some smartass comeback, but there was simply silence and darkness. I'd gotten used to traveling through the Kefitzat Haderech without getting the heebie-jeebies, but this was another level of creepy entirely. I inched forward, one hand on the rock wall, unable to stop myself from making a list of every single horror movie cliché.

The cold metallic bite that usually permeated the air felt more pronounced, as if it was a hungry predator with teeth. That sensation of being hunted amplified when the opening strains of Bach's Toccata and Fugue on a pipe organ started up. My heart leapt into my throat, my fight or flight instincts kicking in, and I ran blindly through the darkness, my arms outstretched in front of me, until a hand grabbed my shoulder.

If I was going down, I was going down fighting.

15

Screaming at the top of my lungs, I broke into a flurry of kicks and punches, wishing I'd gotten a little further along in my training, because I was hitting empty air.

A brilliant white glow filled my vision.

"No! I won't go into the light!" I lashed out to break the Grim Reaper's hold and heard a grunt and a "sorry" said in a Russian accent.

The regular path light sputtered on and off before settling into its usual dim glow.

Pyotr peered at me with wide, concerned eyes. He wore a headlamp, now switched off, while an old tape player on the ground at his feet played Bach.

The neon sign winked on, displaying a montage of my horrified expressions like it was one of those cameras on a roller coaster capturing the rider at the pinnacle of their terror.

"Laugh it up," I snarled.

It morphed into its face, silently chuckling.

I clutched my chest. "Were you trying to kill me?"

"Vampires get in. Worse than mice. Caused trouble.

Kefitzat Haderech short-circuited." Pyotr kicked the pile of ash at his feet, then patted my head. "All fixed now."

I flashed him a thumbs-up and gratefully stepped through the door that appeared into the late afternoon sun in Manhattan.

The Ishikawa Ballet Company had its studio in Tribeca, just off Church Street. Ambulance sirens wailed accompanied by the steady pound of jackhammering. The air was thick with exhaust and the heat radiated off the concrete. I was glad to arrive at my air-conditioned destination.

I headed up the narrow flight of stairs to a reception area, texting Giselle that I'd arrived and checking in with the woman behind the desk as the sign above her head requested. She said I was expected and sent me up another flight.

Muted piano music came out of the first studio. I peered through the glass at a male and female duo practicing a series of turns accompanied by a live pianist. Giselle popped her head out from the next door, her hair in a bun. She wore a pink leotard with pink tights, her feet bare.

"Danika will be here in a sec," she said.

Inside the room, I was assaulted by a hot steaminess, a generation of sweat baked into the walls and sprung floor. It reeked as bad as a men's hockey changing room, which I was familiar with thanks to Eli.

I returned her necklace. "There isn't any magic on it."

"Thank you." She put it on, then moved a dog-eared notebook off her chair so I could sit down.

I caught a glimpse of the cramped notes and scribbles in the book before she'd closed it.

"Ballet dancers are chronic note takers," she said. "We're expected to write down all the corrections we've been given after every class from about age eleven." Her fingers tightened on the notebook. "Did you learn anything else?"

"I may have, but if it's all right, I'd like to speak with your friend first." My very vague understanding of repressed memories was that they were delicate and tricky. I didn't want to confuse the issue by possibly implanting a false remembrance.

Giselle was hesitant, but finally nodded, just as an upbeat Black woman rushed into the studio, her black leotard and blue leopard-print tights soaked with sweat.

"Oh my God, today has been nuts." Dropping her toe shoes on the ground, the woman sat next to them, her legs outstretched. "I've got five minutes so talk."

Giselle made the introductions. "Miriam, Danika. Danika, Miriam."

The other dancer nodded at me, slipping what looked like padded cups over her toes.

"Is Hans in a mood?" Giselle said, fingering her necklace.

Danika laughed. "Be prepared to nail your barre work or suffer."

Giselle winced. "I'll leave you to it."

Once she was gone and the studio door was closed, I jumped right in. "Has Giselle had any bad relationships?"

"Relationships? What are those?" Danika covered her feet with her tights, which were cut to bunch up into footless stockings or pull over the toes for full coverage. "We spend all our time here. She's dated casually but the guys were nice enough."

"What about her family relationships? Problems with parents or siblings?"

She adjusted the tights over her other foot. "She's an only child. Kind of distant from her parents, but I get the sense that was to get away from all the pressure."

"Has Giselle ever confided in you about a bad situation she was in?"

"No more so than regular shit dancers put up with. But not like you're thinking." Danika stood up, pointe shoes in hand. "Like I said, we're always here and everyone is up in each other's business. If anything had happened to her, I'd know. Anything else? I gotta bolt."

"One more question. Did Giselle ever hurt any other dancer? Behave in a way that maybe ruined their shot at a role or something?" Maybe Tatiana was right, and I'd empathized so much with Giselle's desire to know the truth that I'd tempered my natural suspicions.

Giselle's distress might be due to guilt. The dance world was incredibly competitive. Had she sabotaged another dancer and blocked it out, possibly by magical means, only to have it gnawing at her subconscious now given all her good fortune?

Danika's eyes narrowed. "No way. She's too bighearted for her own good. Are we done?"

"Yeah. Thank you."

She tore out of the room, clearly annoyed that I'd disparaged her friend, but I was pleased that my assessment of Giselle's character was spot-on. She was a good person.

I sought another angle. Dance people were like theater people. Sadie often hung out backstage with friends even when not rehearsing because that's where they escaped to, and I knew from other moms over the years with competitive dance kids how much time they spent at the studio.

I had one more shot to confirm whether I was right about Giselle repressing something and that was by going to her old dance school and questioning her former instructors.

I texted Giselle after my chat with Danika and she provided the name of her old studio. Since she'd grown up in Riverdale in the Bronx, I consulted the handy subway map and hopped the number one bound for Van Cortlandt Park.

It was fun sightseeing as the train rattled along aboveground after Dyckman Street station. When I had a moment to myself, I was coming back to spend some time in NYC. It wasn't so much the shopping that appealed to me, though I'd try to catch a show, but walking around various neighborhoods in big cities was one of my favorite parts of traveling.

The subway whooshed into the station at Van Cortlandt Park & 242nd Street in Riverdale, slowing to a stop with a high-pitched screech of brakes. There was barely anyone on the platform, so I didn't have to fight my way to the exit, and I descended the long, covered stairway quickly, pleasantly surprised to see so much green space.

The studio wasn't too far away, but I quickly wove my way through pedestrians worried that it would close before I got there. At one point, I heard a trumpet, and spun around certain that it was already sundown and that this was the angel Dumah blowing his horn to recall dybbuks to Gehenna, but it was just a busker.

I'd heard that trumpet only once, that first Saturday at dusk when I'd reclaimed my magic. However, even without the audible reminder, I was more attuned to the end of the Jewish Sabbath since then.

The sounds of traffic and honking fell away in the quiet foyer of the studio where I was greeted by a wall of photos showing dancers performing competitive numbers from jazz to contemporary and ballet. Some of the group production numbers looked to have budgets rivalling any off-Broadway staging. Just past the photos and before the office was a huge glass case filled with trophies. These kids were winners, excelling in solos, duos, and group numbers.

There were numerous first place trophies for G. Mueller in various ballet competitions, but what was more surprising to me were the occasional first and second place wins for an R. Mueller, in what appeared to be a lower level. Mueller wasn't that common a surname. Did she have a cousin at this studio?

I knocked on the office door and the woman on the phone held up a finger for me to wait. She was surrounded by papers, while the ancient printer behind her slowly spit out more forms. Dust motes danced lazily through beams of sunlight.

After a heated argument about some student's placement, she hung up. "Sorry, we're registering for next year and parents are breathing down my neck."

I gave her a rueful smile. "Hopefully I can change your mind on parent behavior. I'm new to the area and looking around for a good dance school for my daughter. Yours was recommended to me by Giselle Mueller."

"Gigi is such a beautiful dancer." The administrator handed me an application form that looked more detailed than the one I'd filled out for my mortgage. "She's one of our biggest success stories."

"I noticed another dancer with the last name Mueller, but I wasn't aware that Giselle had a sibling."

"Yes, her sister, Rory."

I tightened my grip on the application. Sister? This had to be what Giselle's subconscious was trying to remember. But why and how had she forgotten Rory in the first place? The woman was looking at me curiously, so I said the first thing that popped into my head. "She didn't win as often."

"No, but she worked very hard at her craft." That wasn't exactly the ringing endorsement that Giselle had gotten, but then the woman sighed. "That's not fair. Rory had a ton of potential, but she was never given the chance to realize it as fully as Giselle was."

"Why not?"

"Some kids are natural performers. Their talent just hits you from day one. Others have to grow into it, but if they're encouraged and supported properly, they can end up becoming just as beautiful dancers."

"I'm guessing Giselle was the former and Rory the latter. Why?"

"The mother in large part. Also, it's easier to teach dancers like Giselle. She was identified right away as the one to throw effort behind and Rory just sort of slipped through the cracks. I'd like to say that if I'd been more than a junior instructor back then that I'd have stepped up and steered Rory down a different path but..." She shrugged. "There's always politics."

"That's really sad," I said. If Rory's abilities had been nurtured, would we be at this point today with a missing sibling and a potential demon illusion? "Did the girls ever get to dance together? I didn't see any trophies with both their names on them."

"No. Rory generally trained at the level below Giselle."

"But the girls got along?"

"As far as I remember." She excused herself to answer the phone.

I tucked the application form into my purse and, thanking her, headed directly back to the ballet company. Wondering if there was a good way to break the news to Giselle that she had a younger sister, I called her on the subway ride back to Manhattan, asking if she had a few minutes to speak in person.

She agreed, arranging to meet at a sushi restaurant across the street from the ballet company because she'd finished for the day and was starving.

I did a cursory search on the train ride back. A few different Rory Muellers popped up online, but they were either men or the wrong age. None were a potential match.

I slumped against the seat, the train car rattling over the tracks. Was the illusion I'd experienced a warning, as Tatiana believed, or someone trying to alert me to the truth? I easily came up with pros and cons for both scenarios.

By the time I joined Giselle at the sushi place, there were several small, delicately crafted plates on her table, but she'd polished off the food.

I ordered a green tea and some vegetable gyoza, and sat

back, considering my client. "Do you know anyone called Rory?"

The piece of fish Giselle had just picked up slid off her chopsticks and onto her plate. She frowned, needing a couple of attempts to successfully grasp hold of it, then shook her head. "Should I?"

Both Giselle and her best friend were certain that Giselle was an only child. I'd broken the illusion of Sadie's death in no time, so why hadn't Giselle remembered Rory yet? Had they been estranged before this happened?

The server brought my food and, thanking her, I poured sauce over the steamed dumplings and drank some tea to buy me time while I sorted through my thoughts, but there was no easy way to break it to her. "She's your sister."

Giselle started coughing, hurriedly reaching for her water glass and gulping down half the contents. "That's impossible."

I pulled up some photos that I'd taken of the dance trophies and showed them to her. "I confirmed it with someone at your old dance school. Rory Mueller is your younger sister."

Giselle covered her mouth with a trembling hand. "But why can't I remember her? Who would do such a thing to me?"

"I don't know." I swallowed a dumpling and while it was light and delicious, it sat in my stomach like a stone. Giselle would have mentioned if someone claiming to be a sister who she had no memory of had contacted her, so where was Rory? Was her silence by choice or something more nefarious? I lay my chopsticks down on the plate.

Giselle had said she felt like her life switched tracks a month ago. Was that when this Rory incident happened or was that simply when Giselle's subconscious had started pushing her to remember Rory and she'd forgotten about her sister for longer than that?

"Danika didn't know you had any siblings either," I said. "Have you been friends the entire time you've been with the company?"

"Does that mean I forgot Rory for three years? That can't be right." The young woman's eyes filled with tears, and I bowed my head hoping she hadn't made the connection to the next logical conclusion. "I don't believe I'm the kind of person who wouldn't talk to her own sister for three years. So why haven't I heard from her? Where is she?" She was twisting her napkin so hard that her fingers had gone white.

I grasped at the only straw I had. "You should speak with your parents. If they remember her, she might be perfectly fine, but someone is keeping the two of you apart."

"I can't," she said softly. "I had an eating disorder for years. It's not unusual in my world but my mom didn't exactly discourage it. It takes grit to make it as a dancer and she pushed me to be the best but..." She shrugged, her eyes downcast. "I had to separate myself from her when I went pro."

I reached over and squeezed her hand, and she gave me a grateful smile. "What about your dad?"

"He always went along with whatever Mom wanted."

"What if I spoke with them? I could say I was doing a PR piece and wanted some background info. That way I could find out if they remember Rory."

"Would you?"

"Of course."

"Thank you, Miriam." Giselle touched her "G" necklace, tugging the pendant along the chain until her hand rested over her heart. "I can't believe I have a sister. This is the best news ever. Maybe even more than getting into the company." She laughed. "For sure as good as. You'll reunite us, right?"

"I promise." In my head, I heard Tatiana groan, but Giselle's eyes sparkled, and she looked at me with such hope. What else could I say? I was furious at whomever was behind this and I'd do anything I could. Giselle wouldn't have to live with unanswered questions like I had. She might be heart-broken now, but I'd find her sister, no matter what. Besides, even if all I found was Rory's grave, then technically, I'd still be reuniting them.

I snorted. And my boss said I wasn't cynical.

16

IT WAS ALMOST 9PM WHEN I GOT HOME. I DRAGGED myself inside and kicked off my shoes next to a pile of teenagers' runners and flip-flops. So much for my hopes of a quiet night in. Sighing, I walked into the living room. "Greetings and salutations, youngsters."

"Hi, Miri." Sadie's boyfriend Caleb dumped chips into a bowl. I nodded in approval at today's T-shirt offering of Calvin and Hobbes. His parents had raised him well. "Sparky, your mom's home!"

My niece Nessa peeled herself off the couch where she'd been watching the twins, Aiden and Olivia, shoot zombies. Eli must have loaned us his game console. "Auntie Em," Nessa said, using the nickname she'd given me after I first showed her and Sadie *Wizard of Oz* when they were little. She preened like a cat, showing off her new pixie cut. "What do you think?"

Cutting off six inches of black hair gave the seventeen-year-old a fresher and more mature look that made those Chu cheekbones pop. Poor Sadie had missed those genes, getting stuck with my rounder cheeks. "Love it."

"Now to convince Mom to let me get a nose piercing." Nessa crossed her fingers.

"Good luck with that."

She rolled her eyes. "Too true."

Sadie wandered out of the kitchen, her arms filled with pop cans that she deposited on the coffee table.

"Green or purple?" Her friend Kai held up two nail polish bottles.

"Definitely purple," my daughter said.

"Told you," Kai said to their other friend Emily, a lanky blonde.

"Fine." The girl placed her hands flat on the table for him to do her nails. "But you didn't have to be so bossy about it."

I snapped my fingers. "Hands off that bottle, Kai. You're a menace."

"Come on, Miri. I was twelve when I spilled the pink polish. And besides." He raised an imperious eyebrow. "The floors you got after looked way better than that ugly carpeting. Really, I did you a favor."

"Spill a drop and you'll end up like Sadie's sister."

He waved me off with a flick of his black-painted nails.

"Child?" I tugged on Sadie's elbow. "A moment?"

I pulled her into the kitchen and stopped short. "Nadi, why are you making grilled cheese?"

The petite girl in a bright green headscarf flipped one of the sandwiches browning on the stove. "Because you were out of peanut butter."

Not what I meant, but this was what happened when you spent years encouraging your daughter's friends to make themselves at home. "Just put everything back in the fridge when you're done."

"Will do."

I motioned for Sadie to follow me onto the back porch, shutting the door for privacy. "You know I don't mind you having friends over, but you're supposed to give me a heads-up."

"Text and voice mail." She crossed her arms. "What's the point of you having a pricey cell plan, young lady, if you aren't going to check your notifications?"

"Very funny." I checked my phone to find two unread texts and one voice mail from her. "All right, my bad. Just keep everyone downstairs and out by eleven, okay?"

"Deal." She skipped off back to her friends.

I stole one of Nadi's sandwiches, which was delicious because she'd put in a squirt of mustard, and trudged upstairs.

Once my belly was full, I sank into a steaming-hot bath filled with Epsom salts, submerging myself up to my eyeballs. The grime of the day, both literal and emotional, washed away while I did my best to keep my thoughts clear of missing siblings and the Ascendant. I kept adding more hot water with my big toe until the tank was cold and my skin was pruney. Then I emptied the tub and threw on pj's, crawling under my cool sheets with my fan pointed directly at me.

I was drowsing in a lovely half-asleep state when I remembered book club. Shit. I grabbed my phone and made a shopping list. My house had remained mostly clean after Emmett had swabbed the decks, so I'd put Sadie setting to rights any mess made by her gang. Still, preparations were going to take up most of the day, especially since I had some business to take care of with my friendly neighborhood golem.

My child was less than enthusiastic about being pressed into cleaning duty on Sunday morning, but after flicking on her light and opening her curtains, I only hung around to hear the moaning long enough to ensure she was out of bed and processing the list I'd left her, before heading over to my employer's house, having confirmed Emmett was home.

I caught Tatiana coming out her front door on the way to a friend's house to borrow a carry-on bag and updated her about my findings.

"Missing sibling, huh? Well, it's not a vampire doing it. This is bigger than their compulsion abilities are capable of." She rooted around in her enormous purse for her car keys.

"Could it be a demon?"

"Hard to say." She frowned at the reading glasses with one broken arm that she'd pulled out, then tossed them back in. "I don't know enough about demon magic."

"What about any Ohrists with illusion magic?"

"Don't know any personally but I can ask around." She cackled. "Kadeem isn't going to be happy he missed out on this." She jingled the keys. "Must run. Carry on."

"Wait! I won't see you before you leave tonight. Be nice to the criminals." I hugged her.

She resisted for a moment, then hugged me back tightly. "Now." She stepped back. "Don't drop the ball while I'm away. Even though I'll only be gone a few days." She sighed, her body sagging. "I'm really too old to be flying halfway around the world only to practically turn right around again."

"Can't you stay longer?"

"I could, but in my experience, you don't want to hang around after doing jobs like this."

"Well, safe travels." I saluted her and headed inside.

Emmett was running bills through a cash counter machine in the kitchen, wearing pinstriped trousers with a toothpick wedged into the corner of his mouth.

Jazz streamed from the phone plugged into the small docking station. Combined with the checkerboard floor, red vintage furniture, and mint green cabinets and appliances, I felt like I'd stepped back in time.

I sat down across from the golem. "Are you running an illicit gambling operation or just plain old counterfeiting?"

"Tatiana prefers that her clients pay cash." He slotted another stack of bills into the small machine. They filed through with a *thwwwwft* sound, beeping when the stack was sorted.

"Since when do you listen to jazz?" I moved aside some cash to place my purse on the table.

"It's a special playlist that Tatiana made for me. She loves this music." He shrugged. "It's growing on me. Like a fungus."

Tatiana hadn't made me a playlist, but instead of feeling jealous, I was happy for Emmett. After my scare with that illusion of Sadie's death, I'd felt a renewed appreciation and gratitude for my family. If Emmett and Tatiana were bonding that way, I didn't begrudge that. The golem hadn't had it easy in terms of feeling loved or wanted, and despite all of Tatiana's success, friends, and acquaintances, she spent a lot of time at home with no one except her two assistants. Sure, she had her art, but she didn't have family of any sort other than Laurent. And that relationship was complicated at the best of times.

"Speaking of Tatiana." Emmett switched his toothpick from one side of his mouth to the other. "She bitch to you about going through security at the airport?"

"No, why?"

"Apparently, her hips have so much metal in them that guards keep trying to strip-search her for weapons."

"Poor guards," I said, grimacing. "I hope they die with no regrets."

He chortled. "I told her to film it."

"I didn't know Tatiana had a hip replacement."

He shrugged. "She's part Terminator or something."

Sure, Emmett. I fell into the sound of sorting bills and the wail of a clarinet. Was Tatiana the reason Laurent loved jazz so much? The image of Tatiana and a young Laurent bonding over old jazz albums gave me a fuzzy feeling.

Emmett secured a bundle with an elastic band. "You here to hang out?"

"No." I wrapped an elastic around another bundle. "Have you ever had feelings for anyone?"

"Like wanting to kill the wolf?" The golem ran the last of the cash through the counter. "Often."

"Less murder, more romance."

"I have yet to meet my match."

"But if you did, you'd want that individual to be kind about your feelings, right?"

He sucked on the toothpick, a grim expression on his clay face, like he was about to go into a sure-death battle or unclog a toilet. "Listen, toots. You're like a sister to me. A much, much older sister, but—"

"Not me! Marjorie." I stacked the secured bundles in a neat pile.

His eyebrows shot up. "Say what?"

"She likes you and…" My eyes narrowed because I hadn't realized that someone made of red clay could blush. "Emmett, do you like her?"

"I mean she's okay," he mumbled, but he wouldn't meet my eyes.

"That's wonderful. And you don't have to do anything right now other than get to know each other better." It elated me that Emmett had someone he really liked.

"And then what?" He motioned to his groin. "I don't have the equipment to do anything else."

Never in my wildest dreams had I imagined having "the talk" with a golem. "If the two of you get to the point where you want to be intimate, there are a lot of options available for pleasuring each other, both with and without toys." I kept an encouraging smile on my face, hoping he didn't sense how awkward I felt.

He slammed his hands over his ears. "This is weird. Stop."

We sat there in silence for a few moments listening to Billie Holiday singing "The Very Thought of You."

Emmett scratched his head. "Maybe you could send me some articles?"

"I can do that. Segueing to a different topic, look at these." I handed him Jake's letter and he flipped through the pages.

"This is some creepy shit." The golem cracked his knuckles. "You want me to handle this psycho?"

"No. I want you to use your divination magic and see if you get any deeper meaning out of it."

He handed me back the pages. "My magic doesn't work on command. You know that."

I pulled the flask of whiskey that I'd taken from my personal stash out of my bag and set it on the table between us. Emmett reliably accessed his magic when he was either drunk or scared.

He unscrewed the cap. "Give me ten minutes."

Did I feel guilty for encouraging his drinking habits? Only mildly. The golem didn't seem to metabolize alcohol like humans, and while I'd seen him pound back the booze, he'd never gotten blackout drunk or passed out.

Once half the bottle was consumed, he belched, his eyelids heavy. "Oh yeah. That's the good stuff. 'Kay, gimme."

I pushed the pages back to him and he held them up to his face, squinting bleary-eyed at them. He sat that way for so long that I thought this was a bust, but just as I reached for the papers, a starburst zipped across one eye.

"The shark seeks the star, the flowers seek the shark," he crooned.

I hurriedly typed out his dreamy words on my phone. Another shark? Or did it mean me, since James had asked if I was a baby shark?

Cosmic swirls and stars danced in his eyes. "You seek the flowers and the star seeks you."

Did that mean the Ascendant? Could something that sounded like a mystical force be actively looking for me? I shivered. This was a little too close to the Eye of Sauron. Props to Eli for making Sadie and me sit through all the *Lord of the Rings* movies so that disturbing thought could be stuck in my head now.

"Anything else?" I prodded the golem's shoulder, but he didn't answer. "Emmett?" He usually snapped right out of these trances. My brow wrinkling, I lightly slapped his cheek. "Hey, buddy. Come back to me."

His expression remained slack and dreamy, my friend lost to the universe dancing across his gaze. An asteroid flitted from one eye to the other before flaring brightly and disappearing.

"Emmett," I said sharply.

He blinked back to his senses and reached for the flask. "Huh?"

I heaved a sigh of relief. Then I asked him about five times if he was okay, which made him extremely snippy. I dropped it for now, switching topics to his divination.

Emmett didn't have the ability to interpret his prophecies, which sucked, but he might springboard off something I said, so I showed him the prophecy because he didn't tend to remember them once he was out of his trance. "Let's start with the easy part. Flowers have to refer to my parents, Noah and Adele Blum"—pronounced Bloom—"because that's who I'm looking for. Or at least, I'm looking into what happened to them."

"Why would your parents look for a shark, when that's more dangerous than they are as flowers?"

"Because they knew they were in danger from one? If the shark is their killer..." I shook my head. "If that were the case, why would James ask if I was a baby shark? And what's the star? Is it the Ascendant?"

"Could be an actual thing," Emmett said.

"How could a physical item seek me?" I typed a series of question marks. "Say you're right. Suppose the shark was seeking a treasure of some sort, this star, and my parents were looking for that shark. Did they hope to stop them from getting the treasure?"

"Or to steal the treasure for themselves," Emmett said.

"Maybe." I could intellectually admit that my parents were the type of people to steal treasure, I just wasn't ready to fully accept it. "Or this star is another person." And the Ascendant could be its handle.

I stilled. Could they be the new player that Poe showed me in the cards? I was drowning in possibilities and variables and I had to narrow them down. I folded the pages and put them back in my purse. "I have a lot more avenues to pursue than I did before. Emmett, I could kiss you."

"Ew, don't."

"It's just a figure of speech. I'll find you those articles I promised." I spent the next few moments looking up appropriate reading material for him, and forwarded some articles about sexuality and intimacy but told him to start with the links on relationships and making connections.

When I left, Emmett was hunched over his phone, diving into the research and humming along to jazz.

It was a nice change to see him happy.

As for me, I had to get ready for book club. I hit up the first stop on my list: the bakery that sold both the gluten-free and cranberry crisp crackers necessary for book club. Unfortunately, the young man with the pencil mustache behind the counter was more intimidating than any demon.

"Hi," I said. "I'm looking for some gluten-free crackers for my book club."

"Which type of flour are you interested in?" he asked in a bored voice.

Being a smart woman, I knew that "the gluten-free kind" wasn't the answer he was looking for. "Rice?"

He made a face like I'd tracked dog shit into his store. "Then I recommend you go to Whole Foods."

Okay, buddy, tone it down. "What would you recommend?"

"Today we are featuring arrowroot, sorghum, and teff." These were recited in a snooty tone along with a mean glint in his eyes like he was waiting for stupid follow-up questions he could condescendingly answer.

Arrowroot in my experience was a cookie fed to teething babies, which, admittedly, I'd bought more than once for myself because they were yummy with tea. I couldn't begin to guess what teff flour was, but sorghum sounded like a badass ancient warrior. "Sorghum," I said confidently.

"With or without ajwine?"

For the first time in many years, I felt the stomach-churning nervousness of being called upon in class, and, having no idea which answer was correct, choosing whichever felt best.

I swallowed hard and prayed. "With?"

"Excellent choice." He wrapped the crackers beautifully in a beeswax food container and presented it to me with more flourish than the unveiling of the Eiffel Tower. "And for those guests who cannot absorb the whole grains of the sorghum?"

Really? You couldn't mention that little drawback to me before I'd ordered the crackers that were probably going to cost as much as my sofa? "Teff."

"A bold move, considering many guests have diabetes." He inhaled as though it pained him. "But very well."

I rubbed a hand over the back of my now-sweaty neck. "I meant arrowroot."

The man nodded slowly like he'd finally drawn the correct

answer out of the dim-witted lump before him. "That would be best."

I paid the extortionist prices and left, but not before Delilah stole behind the counter, unscrewed a jar of edible glitter, and knocked it off the shelf all over him. *Take that, you condescending jerk.*

Since I'd promised Marsha, and who was I to break a promise, I loaded up on cheese products: stout-infused cheddar, cave-aged gruyere, and oh baby, a double-cream wheel of brie. At last, having fought traffic all over town, my shopping was done. I pulled up to my house, hot, cranky, and starving. Noon had come and gone a couple hours ago and I had to stuff something into my mouth before hurriedly getting ready for book club at three.

I opened my trunk and pulled out a reusable shopping bag bulging with goods, only to be slammed up against my car so hard that the breath was knocked from my lungs. The bag slipped from my hands and a slow-motion "Noooooo" tore from my lips as the package of teff crackers bounced to the ground, rolled down the lane, and stopped, completely intact.

Not only were they unbroken, the pool of organic lemonade from the now-shattered jug ran downhill from them. Holy miracle, Batman. I had another jug in the trunk but I wouldn't have had time to go buy more crackers and Marsha would have freaked the fuck out if any little detail of book club had been missed. The universe loved me today.

Then a hairy hoof stomped on the crackers, grinding them to dust.

A stocky Tasmanian Devil–looking demon stood in the middle of the road snorting and growling. Like its animated counterpart, its mouth was full of oversize pointed teeth and its red eyes contained a hint of madness.

"I'd get away from the dog if I were you." My neighbor Luka stood on his porch, a glass of iced tea in hand. "Looks rabid." Rather than being his usual grumpy self, he sounded almost pleased that there was a feral animal wandering his neighborhood. The worst of his expectations had been confirmed.

I backed up. Dog, huh? "What breed do you think it is?"

"That big? Probably a mastiff, but it looks like it's got some shepherd in it."

The demon made a constipated noise, its tongue hanging out, and flexed its massive hands. Perception filters were quite the marvel if Luka couldn't see it stood upright.

Or, you know, was a demon.

"I'll phone the SPCA," I said. "Have someone come and get it."

His wife, Dora, called for him and Luka reluctantly went inside.

I unleashed my scythe, black shadows slithering over my skin. "Did you make me believe my child was dead?"

The demon extended his claws and spun toward me like a tornado, kicking up enough dirt to blind me.

My eyes watering, I jumped out of the way, the backs of my knees hitting my bumper as I slashed at it, nailing the fiend in its shoulder.

It yowled and snapped my scythe from my hands, tossing it onto the road where it vanished.

The demon grabbed me in a headlock, its teeth grazing the hollow of my neck.

Feeling blindly behind me, I grabbed one of the bottles of rosé from my trunk and bashed that fucker like I was launching a ship. Glass and booze sprayed out in an arc, but my attacker didn't even flinch.

Its chokehold intensified. Black dots danced at the edge of my vision, and I clawed at it, my lungs burning. When that failed, I animated Delilah to tear the demon off me, gulping down one huge breath of air before the demon slashed her.

I screamed, bile surging up at the bloody torn flesh on my forearm.

The demon was on me again in a flash, but before I could catch my breath through the pain or solidify my magic into another weapon, there was a deafening wail. Through my glazed eyes, I spied Military Marsha by her open car door, her face drained of all color.

I croaked a warning noise. The demon glanced back, then it threw me into the street like trash. The impact rattled my teeth and sent a fresh wave of burning agony through my still-bleeding arm.

Marsha just stood there.

"Get in your car!" I yelled. "That dog is rabid."

Marsha stopped screaming and shot me a confused look.

I couldn't get to my feet fast enough, so I sent Delilah shooting out after the demon, which was less than ten feet away from Marsha. If it got its claws into my shadow, I was done for, but I had to protect the woman.

"Mar—" My cry cut off with a sputter because she flicked her fingers at the demon.

Its feet became twisted wrinkled lumps and it teetered, unbalanced.

"You!" Marsha hit it again with her magic and the rest of it began to rapidly age. "Are not!" The demon bent double, barely able to hobble away slowly. "Ruining!" She kicked it, and the now-feeble creature that was mostly a hump and wrinkles fell over. "Book club!"

Panting, she continued kicking it, a crazed glint in her eyes.

She'd lost it. A past version of myself would have taken joy in seeing her so undone, but right now I was just horrified. Whatever thin barrier on her sanity book club had been shoring up, it was gone now and she was putting herself in danger.

I pulled her off him, scared she'd hurt herself. The pain was making me woozy and I couldn't get my scythe to solidify. We had to get behind the wards.

The demon grabbed my ankle with a gnarled hand.

"Get on the lawn!" With a jolt of adrenaline that made all colors sharper, I shoved Marsha away, my weapon snapping into place.

"Let go of my mom!" Sadie yelled, sprinting toward me.

Terror seized my heart. No. Not like this. "Sadie, stop!" I shrieked.

The demon jumped up, shaking off its weird fast-aging, and spun toward my daughter.

Everything slowed down. It was disorienting. Was this real or just another illusion? I didn't know, I couldn't figure it out, and I couldn't take the risk.

I ran toward Sadie, my weapon raised in my good hand, but it was like slogging through thick mud. My legs didn't work properly. There was no way for me to get her to safety before the monster grabbed her off the front walk.

The demon hit the property line at the same time as Sadie. He reached for her and bounced off the invisible magic with an electric crack.

Marsha grabbed Sadie by her collar and hauled her back a few precious inches.

I may have peed a little in relief that we had wards. In the seconds it took the demon to throw off the electric shock, I hacked off its head, kicking it into the gutter.

The demon's lifeless eyes stared back at me.

With a whoosh, its headless corpse burst into flames, burning high and bright for a fraction of a second before winking out, leaving only an oily stain on the ground.

Confused, I looked over at Marsha, who stared at Sadie, now by my side.

My daughter clutched her mini flamethrower, Phoebe, her chest rising and falling raggedly.

I looked from the demon's head to the surprised Ohrist to my child and made my magic vanish. "At least we saved the fancy cheese."

17

SMALL MERCIES, BOOK CLUB WAS CANCELED.

I'd voiced my decision to Marsha while she cleaned, stitched, and bound my wound, as she'd been a nurse before becoming a nurse educator. She agreed, albeit reluctantly, that that was probably for the best.

"I have to say, you're being remarkably calm about everything," I said.

Marsha finished treating me. "Not everything is within our control. How does that feel? Too tight?"

"No." I moved my arm and winced. It throbbed like a mother, but the binding was comfortable and there wasn't any blood seeping through. "Sit down. You've dealt with enough. I'll inform the others."

I popped a couple of painkillers and made the call.

Marsha's love of rules and protocols meant that we had a phone tree in place should an emergency (as defined by section 13 subsections D–G of the "rules") occur. No, a demon attack wasn't on the list, but as Marsha had snapped out of whatever sense of calm had possessed her during crisis mode and was currently drinking rosé straight from the bottle and laughing maniacally, I took it upon myself to dub this subsection H, "Unforeseen Arcane Crisis," and carry on appropriately.

Once that was set in motion, I texted Nav a picture of the demon's head sitting on a towel that had the words "Resting Beach Face" printed on it.

I thought it brought a much-needed levity to the situation.

Sadie, thank goodness, was fine. Better than fine. She was the one who added sunglasses and a bottle of sunscreen to the tableau.

My heart swelled with the knowledge that whatever the magic community threw at her, she'd handle it. And if not, I'd keep her behind those lovely protective wards forever.

All joking aside, charbroiling the demon had given my daughter's confidence an enormous boost. She was so excited about how she'd helped, that she ran next door to tell her dad all about it.

About a minute later I heard an explosive "YOU DID WHAT?" through the wall connecting our townhomes and opened my front door.

Eli stormed in holding an electric razor, with only half his head shaved down to the scalp.

"Good look," I said calmly and offered him a cracker with a smear of brie. "Fromage?"

I wasn't being cavalier about what had happened, but the only one dead was the demon and book club was canceled. This was the best of all possible outcomes in this new normal. Sometimes I had to live in the moment.

My ex stared at me incredulously, but before the tomato-red flush hit the top of his head, Sadie was tugging on his arm to come see the demon head in the kitchen.

I followed behind them enjoying the outstanding brie. His loss.

"Ta-da!" Sadie did jazz hands while I helped myself to another cracker with cheese.

Eli crossed his arms, his brows drawing deeper and deeper together, and his lips pressed together like he was trying to hold in a fart.

"Let it out, baby." I licked brie off my finger.

He snorted a laugh. "This is so inappropriate."

"Ah, but laughter is cheaper than drinking," I said.

Sadie had done a good job cleaning up, allowing the head to really shine as a showpiece in the spotless kitchen.

"Our kid is torching demons now?" he said with a pained grimace. "Really?"

"Really," Sadie said. "And I'm standing right here."

He raised his eyes to the ceiling, away from the head. "I hate everything about this. All of it. In its entirety."

"Poor Dad. Team Feldman-Chu for the win, right?" She put her hand out flat.

"Right." I placed mine on top of it.

It took Eli a second, but he added his. "Right." He gestured at my injured arm. "Are you okay?"

"Yeah."

Eli dropped his voice to a whisper. "What's with the crazy lady in the living room?"

"That's Marsha," I said. "She stitched me up." I ran a finger over the bandage. The painkillers had kicked in. "Did a good job."

"Military Marsha? Did she see the demon?"

"Big-time. It turns out she's an Ohrist. Today is full of surprises."

Sadie bounced on her toes. "Her magic was insane. She ages things superfast. Like she melts them through time. It's bonkers. I wish I had powers like that. Guess I'll stick with Laurent training me."

"Laurent?" Eli's left eye twitched and he slammed the electric razor on the counter.

Sadie cast an anxious glance between me and her dad.

I shut the razor off.

Eli shot our kid a thumbs-up. "Training is good." It was a tad forced but better than nothing.

I poured a glass of water, which I handed to Sadie. "Here. Make Marsha hydrate."

She dragged her feet leaving the kitchen, but at my encouraging nod, left.

"Training implies she's going to be doing more fighting," Eli said disapprovingly.

"She might." I held up a hand. "I'm not necessarily talking about supernaturals." He knew better than anyone the depraved depths that Sapiens were capable of. "Laurent already checked her running abilities since he'd rather have her get away than fight. Physical moves come next."

"And flamethrowers?"

"I didn't realize she knew where I'd hidden it. If you like, I'll put you in charge of that. You can teach her weapons safety, same as if it was a gun." My ex still didn't look happy. "What's the real issue here? Laurent?"

"I don't like that he thought of it first." That was a huge admission from him.

Laurent might be insulted if I took Sadie's training away from him, but Eli was her father. "Do you want to train her?"

It was a testament to how far Eli had come in accepting the existence of magic and all the new dangers that came with it, as well as to the few therapy sessions we'd had with Dr. Takimoto that he thought it through carefully. "I do. At least in the basics. Laurent could take over for more specific moves to stay safe from anyone or anything with magic."

Sadie returned with the empty glass. "She's calmed down, but I think you better go check on her, Mom."

"Okay."

Someone knocked on the front door.

"I hope that isn't one of the book club people," I said.

"I'll get it." Sadie left and a moment later we heard "Hi, Nav."

Eli's eyes widened and he grabbed for the electric razor, his hand darting to his half-shaved head as footsteps drew closer.

I fell over the counter, laughing.

"Stop it," he hissed and ran out the back door, the razor cord trailing behind him like a tail. He disappeared down the stairs just as Sadie and Nav entered the room.

"Where'd Dad go?"

Nav perked up.

"He had to run." I wiped tears from my eyes, my chuckles dying down.

Nav did a pretty good job transferring his interest to the demon, circling the head.

"I torched it." Sadie gestured with her hands. "It went all whoosh and huge and then it was gone and man, did it reek. Wanna see the gross oil stain it left on the road?"

"No, thanks." He placed his hands on her shoulders. "Listen to me very carefully. You were brilliant, but don't ever do that again. You could have been seriously injured or worse."

"I won't," she said. "Not until Laurent trains me."

Nav glanced at me with an assessing look.

"You're actually going to start training with your father," I said. "Laurent will take over later."

"Really? Dad wants to train me?" Sadie looked so happy that I made a mental note to tell Eli. Even though she spent every other week with him, it wasn't the same as having a father-daughter activity. "He's always been so reluctant to discuss his cases with me or what he faces at work."

"I didn't realize you were curious about that." This was a big deal, especially given Sadie's anxiety, and I wish she'd been able to mention it before. However, I didn't want to make an issue of her only bringing it up now.

"Duh. He's dealing with murderers. It's like how Jude said the more I knew about magic, the less scary it would all seem. You're willing to talk about it, which is cool, but Dad? Forget it."

Nav asked for a chopstick, using it to poke and prod the head. "I'd planned to do the same as your dad with Evani, when she was old enough to ask questions about my work. But you've got me rethinking that."

"Totally," Sadie said. "It's much better to be open with her and tell her the truth because kids can make up some really scary shit. Especially around losing their parental figures."

"You should tell your dad that," I said.

"Yeah, maybe I should. Do you think he would train Nessa, too? I mean, it's good for girls to learn to defend themselves. He doesn't have to say anything about magic."

"That's something to discuss with him."

"'Kay. I'm going to run next door and ask."

She ran out the still-open back door, slamming it behind her.

I flinched. That kid would master wrestling vampires before she learned how to close a door softly.

Nav continued examining the demon head.

Sadie's statement about her father had brought up a lot of emotions for me. I felt smug that for all of Eli's bitching about magic, his Sapien job induced just as much anxiety in her as mine did. Sad, that she'd never felt able to talk to either of us about her fears regarding his job, and mad that my parents didn't treat me the way I treated Sadie, and shared more about what they were involved in. Or, if they couldn't do that, told me I might be in danger and asked my opinion on how I felt about that, like I did with my daughter.

When Sadie was born, I'd been overwhelmed by the advice in parenting books and had resolved to try to be the kind of mom to her that mine had been to me. But, looking back, I'd done the opposite, because while I had a lot of fun and happy memories from my childhood, I didn't remember having any deep conversations. Not even when my magic first showed up. I shook my head. It's funny, I'd never realized that.

"How'd you browbeat our friend into agreeing to train Sadie?"

I blinked at Nav and shook off my musings. "Laurent? He offered. Said they trained kids in his pack at a young age."

That earned me a startled look. "He doesn't talk about his pack." There was a pause and then Nav tapped the demon's head with the chopstick. "This is a kargh thurt demon."

"Is it the one who cast the illusion on me?"

"No. Kargh thurts are dumb goons. Relatively easy to summon, bind, and force to do your bidding, even by Ohrists."

"Hired muscle. Then who or what cast the illusion?"

"We're still investigating. You planning on telling me the full story?"

"Client confidentiality, so sorry."

"Says the woman who breached my headquarters."

"That's on you. Hypothetically, if a demon casts an illusion, are there limits on it, or is it widespread? And how does it differ from an Ohrist with illusion magic?"

Nav wrapped the head up in the towel, tying a knot in the top to keep it from rolling out. "Both have limitations, but demons can hold illusions for much longer. Months, even years, versus weeks."

So, depending on when Giselle forgot about Rory, I still couldn't narrow it down. "But illusions can be broken, right? I did."

He picked the bundle up and slung it over his shoulder. "True, but I don't know if that was a Banim Shovavim thing or because as Sadie's mother, you wholeheartedly rejected any reality in which she was dead."

Giselle had mentioned feeling like her life had switched tracks. A growing itch that something was wrong. "Could someone with illusion magic not make it stick all the way?

Make the victim feel like there was a splinter in their brain, an itch they couldn't scratch?"

"For sure. It's a great way to drive someone crazy."

"That's sadistic."

"If it's a demon, poppet? That's what they do." He shrugged and headed for the front door. "If I learn anything else, I'll call."

I shut the door behind him, then winced. Marsha. I ran into the living room. "How are you doing?"

She sat in a chair rolling the peeled-off wine label between her fingers, but when her eyes met mine, they were clear. "You know how sometimes you really need a good orgasm?"

"Yeah." *Please don't get TMI with me.* I was far too sober for that.

"I needed that." She flexed her fingers. "Not necessarily the demon part but using my magic."

"You've been hiding it?"

"Sort of? I didn't think of it that way, but my husband is a Sapien so I put my powers away."

"For how long?"

"Ten years."

"I hid mine for almost thirty."

"Whoa. Want a drink?" She picked up the half-empty bottle, then immediately set it down with a grimace. "I wouldn't recommend this."

"I'm good." What were the odds of Marsha and me having magic-hiding of all things in common? No wonder she was so anal and controlling. She'd had to keep a tight hold on her powers for a decade.

She hiccuped then covered her mouth with her hand. "What's your magic?"

Book club was over, so if she was prejudiced against my kind, what would it matter? I'd never have to see her again.

"I'm Banim Shovavim."

Her eyebrows shot up. "That explains a lot."

"Right," I said tightly.

She laughed and nudged my shoulder with hers. "Kidding. I couldn't give a shit. I'm just glad to have one less person to hide this from."

"My ex-husband is Sapien. So's my daughter."

"You got through their perception filters?"

"I had help. You think your husband—"

Marsha shook her head firmly. "No. Richard's a great guy, but this would break him." She stood up. "Speaking of which, I'll call him to give me a ride home. I've imposed on you long enough."

This was it. The graceful uncoupling I'd been longing for. Marsha would drive off into the sunset and I'd never have to think about her and her myriad of rules again.

Except she'd looked so damn sad sitting by herself on my sofa, drinking shitty rosé alone.

"Don't leave yet. We haven't even had book club." Well, I'd said it, now I had to stick by my words.

She crossed her arms. "You said it was canceled."

"Old book club was." I rapped on the coffee table. "I hereby call the inaugural meeting of the Magic Babe Book Club. There are two rules. One, we always have cheese. And two, we only read books that we want to, not because we feel we have to out of some stupid sense of self-improvement." I held out my hand. "You in?"

"What the hell." She shook. "So, are we the only members?"

I smiled. "Of course not."

Forty-five minutes later, Jude, Daya, Ava, and her wife, Romi, sat with Marsha and me in our backyard around a table laden with crackers, tons of cheese, grapes, and several bottles of wine.

Ava and Romi had brought Romi's seventeen-year-old niece, Tovah, who was staying with them for the weekend. Tovah and Sadie were a bit shy upon meeting, but they had

Evani with them upstairs and I had no doubt that the ice would be broken soon enough.

I couldn't say the same about this group. Awkward silence reigned. Romi made stilted conversation with Daya about imported grapes, while Ava's question about whether Marsha enjoyed bowling fell flat.

Jude crammed yet another cracker with cheddar into her mouth and rolled her eyes at me.

I poured myself a glass of cold Riesling. I didn't like it half as much as the Moscato, but I was scared if I cracked open the bottle in my fridge, I down half of it out of nerves at how badly my idea was bombing. All these women were great and social. What had gone so wrong putting them all together? "Why don't we throw out ideas for our first book?"

Marsha said something so quietly that I had to ask her to repeat it. "There's this historical romance I've wanted to read."

I almost dropped my glass. Her rules and discussion questions were one thing but forcing me to read pretentious novel after pretentious novel when I could have been luxuriating in more enjoyable books was an unforgiveable crime. "Is there now," I said flatly.

"Is it an Eloisa James book?" Daya said.

"Who?" I said.

"She writes a lot of witty historicals." Daya sliced off some gruyere. "I like her."

"Me too," Romi said, "but I'm more Julia Quinn person."

"Regé-Jean Page." Ava sighed dreamily.

"Even I wouldn't kick him out of bed," Romi said, nodding.

I was totally lost but the other women were now bonding over this person, firing opinions about his best scene as the duke.

Jude handed me her phone with a photo pulled up on it.

"Regé-Jean Page. He was the lead in Julia Quinn's *Bridgerton* series that was adapted for Netflix."

"Oh." Those eyes. That cocky, sexy smile. "Okay, I get it."

"You don't," Marsha said, helping herself to grapes. "Not until you've heard his British accent. It takes him to a whole other level."

"She's right," Daya said.

"Fine." I brushed cracker crumbs off my lap. "I'll watch it, but we're discussing book choices now. Is that the one you wanted to read, Marsha?"

"It was a Tessa Dare book, but—"

"Oh!" Daya clapped her hands. "Colin and Minerva's book?"

Marsha nodded.

"*A Week to Be Wicked*," Romi said.

"We are so reading that one," Ava said. "Smart wallflowers are the best."

This was more like it. "We're agreed, then?" Off their nods, I smiled. "Then it's settled. Eat and drink up, ladies, and we can figure out when the next meeting should be."

The talk around the table became more relaxed and friendly. Relieved, I had a sip of wine.

Jude flashed me a thumbs-up. I had a new and better book club, we'd survived a demon, and Eli and Sadie had something to bond over. Now to find Rory, figure out who the shark was, what this Ascendant was, and get hot and heavy with Laurent. Oh yeah, most definitely that last part.

18

New book club didn't drain me like the original one would have, and Marsha even hugged me stiffly at the end, which was odd but not unpleasant.

Before Jude left, I spoke to her about Emmett taking longer to snap out of it when he gave me the prophecy. Unfortunately, she couldn't tell me why that had happened, but she said she'd look into it and report back. For all that she complained about the golem, she looked as worried as I felt about this unwanted development.

Neither my hostess duties nor my fears about the golem explained why I didn't go visit Laurent that night. It was because Sadie and I had our *Buffy* rewatch. We were deep in season six with "Normal Again," the episode where Buffy believes she's in an insane asylum.

After Sadie moved next door for the week, I watered the plants, wondering if there was a takeaway from the show to be applied to Giselle's case. Buffy had been hit by the demon's illusion magic when she'd gone after the Trio because they summoned it.

What if someone had sicced this demon on Giselle in retaliation for something? But what? Her best friend had described her as bighearted, which was my impression of her as well. Or worse, what if Giselle was caught in an illusion that had been placed on *Rory*? I had to learn more about her sister.

Bright and early Monday morning, I returned to the Bronx to visit the Muellers. They lived in a large older apartment off a busy street. I introduced myself as a PR person from the ballet company who'd come to get some quotes for a spotlight piece we were doing on our website about Giselle.

Mrs. Mueller was delighted and led me through a large living room filled with plants and into a kitchen that was immaculate save for the line of white powder running along the wall. "Damn cockroaches," she said. "It doesn't matter how much I clean, poison is the only way to stay on top of them." She filled the kettle and placed it on the stove, then sat down at a small table with me.

She possessed the same willowy beauty as her daughter, dressed in jeans and a soft scoop-neck shirt in the exact light pink as a ballet leotard. I started the conversation asking about any funny anecdotes from when Giselle was a child.

Her mom laughed, recounting the time when Giselle was three and insisted on wearing a crinoline in a half-tutu shape that was supposed to be tied around her waist. Giselle tied it under her chin and wouldn't take it off, insisting everyone call her Princess Giselle Hedgehog.

While we drank Darjeeling, she told me a couple other funny stories, none of which mentioned a sibling. There hadn't been any family photos hanging in the living room to check out. One of my concerns with asking directly about Rory if her mother was stuck in this illusion as well was that I'd trigger that same kind of deafening scream that Giselle was suffering from. I didn't want to induce any trauma, so I decided to tackle the issue obliquely.

Mrs. Mueller placed a hand against the teapot. "I could make more hot water if you like."

"I'm good, thanks. You must be so proud of all your daughter's success."

"Overjoyed. I always knew she'd make it. Some kids just have the spark and drive and the talent. Giselle was one of them. Becoming coryphée and now Candide? All our dreams are coming true." Interesting that she was still so fixated on Giselle's career when her daughter was estranged from her.

It was a timely reminder that this woman hadn't gotten help for her child's eating disorder, placing body shape over the well-being of her own daughter. If she'd behaved that way toward the favored child, how had she treated Rory, who hadn't been as talented?

Could that be at the heart of this? Could Rory have chosen to erase herself from a family that didn't appreciate her or her talent? Even Giselle had distanced herself from her parents, so what might Rory have been driven to do to escape the scars of her past?

Was it possible that Rory had illusion magic and she'd come after me as a warning to leave this alone? Nav had said kargh thurt were easy to summon and bind.

"Giselle is also the second understudy for Aurora," I said, continuing the conversation. "She's being asked to take on more responsibility, which is great."

Mrs. Mueller flinched like I'd hit her. "Giselle would never be Aurora. She's so much better." She said it with such vehemence that I leaned back in my chair, worried she was going to attack me.

"I beg your pardon?" I said carefully. "She *is* understudying the role in *The Sleeping Beauty*."

"Of course she is," the woman said calmly, taking a sip. "She's good enough to be the first understudy."

The back of my neck prickled. We all believed that I'd broken the illusion of Sadie's death because I refused to accept that reality, but hadn't something specific twigged me to the fact that it didn't feel right? I grasped for the memory, hazy as a faded bad dream.

Sadie's scar. She didn't have it in the illusion. It was a broken seam in an otherwise flawless presentation.

Was Rory's real name Aurora? I gripped the table. That had to be it. Rory was a nickname, a shortened version of the name Aurora. No wonder this all became churned up for Giselle a month ago when she got the understudy part in *The Sleeping Beauty*. She had her sister's name being shoved in her face constantly.

"Is Rory still dancing?"

Mrs. Mueller blinked at me. "Who?"

I checked the notebook that I'd been jotting things down in. "Her dance studio mentioned a girl called Rory that Giselle was close with?"

Mrs. Mueller frowned, gathering up the mugs and putting them in the sink. "I knew all the dancers in Giselle's class since I carpooled them all at one point or another to different competitions. They were a close group, but there wasn't any Rory."

"I must have heard it wrong." I closed the notebook and thanked her for her time, promising to send her the link when the article went up.

Finding Aurora Mueller had shot to the top of my to-do list.

However, that was easier said than done. I stopped in a café for lunch and did some cursory searches, but they didn't yield any useful results. Setting my phone aside, I forked a piece of mediocre quiche into my mouth.

Fact: an illusion had removed all memory of Aurora Mueller from the minds of her sister and parents, but not the people at the dance studio. Was it targeted only to those closest to her? Or only sustainable on family members?

If Rory had orchestrated all this herself, either through her own magic or with the help of someone else's, I'd have to tread carefully and respect her desire to remove herself from her family. Once I found Rory and ascertained she wasn't in any danger, then we could have a discussion about how to handle Giselle's awareness that something was wrong.

The obvious move now was to ask the Lonestars to search for any record of Rory's death. That avenue was also a no-go, since once I opened that door, the magic cops would insist on taking over the search, regardless of whether Rory was an Ohrist like her sister. A person in an Ohrist family was missing; that would be enough justification for them. Nor would they appreciate the potential delicacy of the situation. They would farm the case out to their colleagues in whichever city Rory was last seen.

I couldn't ask for this favor and then expect to see the investigation through.

And Tatiana wouldn't appreciate her case being taken away. I ran through my options, remembering the US Social Security Death Index that our lawyers used on occasion. It was quite reliable for Americans who'd died after 1972.

Once I returned home, I headed into my backyard because it was day four of our five-day heat wave and my house was muggy as shit. I dragged my lounge chair into the shade and scanned the SSDI database on my phone. No one by the name of Aurora Mueller had died in the last five years. There was no point going farther back than that because that's when Rory had won her last dance trophy.

She might have died as a Jane Doe, but I preferred to work on the assumption that she was alive. I could ask Eli to check for credit card activity, but I didn't want to burn a favor on such a long shot. Someone had gone to extreme lengths to make sure Rory wasn't remembered. They wouldn't pull a stupid move like having her use credit cards in her own name, and if Rory was the one with illusion magic, then she'd be careful to cover her tracks.

I tapped a finger against the phone case.

How could I find a woman who could be anywhere in the world? No Lonestars, no getting any Sapien police involved. If a demon had orchestrated all of this, I could go to Nav's people, but I was reluctant to for the same reasons as the Lonestars.

There was one party without any vested interest who might be able to find the young woman. While Tatiana might not object to me speaking to Zev, what would it cost me? At the moment, my slate with him was clean, but this would put me back in his debt. It wouldn't matter that successfully solving this case ultimately benefitted Tatiana, a woman who Zev had some personal history with and fondness for. Ultimately, I'd be the one on the hook.

Was it worth it?

Going with the "better to be safe than sorry" line, I phoned Tatiana in Moscow to confirm she didn't have a problem with me speaking to the vampire. She sounded jetlagged and our connection was patchy, so the conversation was brief, but I got permission.

I realized that I should have asked her about the Ascendant because if it was a thing that someone was looking for, she might have come across it in her line of work, but when I tried her again, the call went to voice mail. I didn't bother to leave a message.

However, there was someone else I could turn to who owed me for playing me, then sending me off to my death.

Poe.

Vampire first, then the bird shifter. Ravens did like shiny things after all, so perhaps Poe would know what the star was and if it was called the Ascendant. Given Jake's crazy drawings, it felt like the thing to prioritize in terms of tracking down.

Plus, the idea of this star seeking me out was creepy.

Harry was still out of town, which left Giulia to arrange any meeting with Zev. I rubbed the back of my neck, not up to her next interrogation about all things Laurent. Let's see. Zev and I hadn't crossed paths since he'd shared his memory of his wife. Did that confession buy me leeway to show up at Blood Alley and request an audience? I wasn't so audacious as to just knock on his office door unannounced, but I could send my appeal through another vampire.

Zev didn't sleep much during the day because he was so old. I had my suspicions that Yoshi was at least as ancient, but I'd wait until dusk to head down there, since I had plenty of other work from Tatiana to catch up on.

She'd given me decades' worth of love letters from her late husband, Samuel, to catalogue. I'd barely dug into them, but I'd already fallen in love with the man's wit and adoration of his wife. I was also really hoping they didn't get racy, because I did not need those images in my head, however, I was only in the courting stage of their relationship and thus far, the letters were quite chaste.

A while back, I'd thrown out the idea to Tatiana that instead of writing her memoirs, she should publish a coffee table book that went beyond her art to act as a scrapbook. She'd pick the appropriate paintings or sketches to illustrate various periods of her life that were further documented by clippings and photos and these love letters. Pulling out the elements for Tatiana to approve would mean a lot more work on my part, but the more I got to know her, the more I was convinced that a typical prose memoir wouldn't do her life justice.

She'd loved the suggestion but hadn't had much time to work on it. Her assistant Raymond had dropped off this memento box with the letters about a week ago and that had been the last time we'd touched base about this project.

While catching up on my reading about Samuel and Tatiana's first meeting and the dance she led him on until she'd agreed to date him, the time until my next appointment passed quickly. I freshened up, putting on an electric-blue wrap dress, fluffing up my curls, and applying my basic glam up routine of gold eyeshadow and red lipstick.

My heels clacked on the cobblestones as I stepped from Gastown to Blood Alley, striding confidently under the metal sign with its gargoyle statue sentinels. Even on a Monday night, the popular Ohrist tourist attraction was buzzing.

A large group was splitting up, the men wearing T-shirts with "Groom's Crew" printed on the front. The poor groom had been dressed in a gaudy sundress with a coconut bra. The bridesmaids (wearing sashes denoting that status) all wore short shorts and crop tops, while the lucky lady had been poured into a hot pink prom dress, all crinoline and cheap satin that had crawled out of some 1980s nightmare. Both she and her fiancé had sashes that said "Last Night of Freedom" on them.

The couple kissed each other with much laughter and good-natured teasing about what each one was allowed to do.

There was a flurry of high-fives between the two groups and off they each went. I skirted around the women, wondering how many bad decisions would be made tonight. Blood Alley had temptations that made Vegas look like Disneyland. Good luck to them.

Most of the red lightbulbs above the black doors were already lit up, and I had no interest in the ones that were currently open to patrons, heading straight for a private room at the top of one of the narrow, crooked streets.

Stopping in front of the door to the private sake bar, I ran a hand nervously over my attire. I was mostly certain my presence here would be tolerated, but there was always the element of unpredictability. Gathering my courage, I squared my shoulders and knocked confidently.

After a moment, Yoshi opened the door and raised his eyebrows. His black hair had been buzzed close to his scalp, accenting his sharp cheekbones. I'd always suspected Yoshi was ancient, despite looking like he was in his early twenties, but with his head shorn, his skin now looked drawn tight over his skull, aging him.

"Can I help you?" he said.

"I'd like to speak to Mr. BatKian, please."

"Ah." He opened the door wider. "Come in."

The bar was so small that I noted in a single glance that Zev wasn't here.

The door clanged shut behind me and a bolt was turned. Slowly, I faced Yoshi, careful to show nothing more than a pleasant smile. There was nothing I could do about my hammering heart, but one way or another, I was walking safely out this door.

19

"Is Mr. BatKian around?" I said.

"No. He's out of town until Saturday. Sit down, Miriam." Yoshi moved behind the glossy bar without his usual fluidity. His motions were often too fast to perceive and yet incredibly graceful, but today he moved slower, almost carefully. Were vampires subject to aches and pains when they grew old, like the rest of us?

I slid onto a barstool across from him.

Yoshi considered the wall of sake bottles, each one spotlit in its own display cube, before reaching under the counter and pulling out a bottle of red wine. "How do you feel about Malbec?"

"Kindly."

Chuckling, he produced two wineglasses. "I picked up this bottle when I was in Argentina and have been looking for the right opportunity to open it."

Why were we having sharing time? I set my purse on the bar.

The wine glowed like the heart of a ruby as the vampire poured it through a small glass aerator, holding the items with strong, elegant fingers. He held up his glass and I clinked mine to it.

"Cheers," he said.

"L'chaim." I tried very hard not to think of blood when I took that first small sip. The Malbec was earthy with dark fruity notes and of a much better caliber than I was used to. "It's delicious."

Yoshi tasted his wine, making a small noise of satisfaction. "If I couldn't detect your heartbeat," he said conversationally, "I'd never know you were nervous. You put up a good front."

"You locked me in and served me wine. Makes me wonder if I'm being braised for better flavor."

The warmly lit walls took on the menace of a jaguar's den penning me in.

He laughed, a lethal feline enjoying my presence. "I see why Zev likes you."

I kept my eyes on the vampire, my magic at the ready should he make the slightest move out of the ordinary. The beast was playful now, but the fangs could come out in an instant. "'Like' might be a stretch."

"Perhaps it is. I heard you riled up the Carpe Demon kids. You have a knack for leaving lasting impressions."

I tilted my head, studying him, but his expression didn't hint at anything other than amusement. "With all due respect, Yoshi, is there a point to this?"

"Would you like to know why you were able to cross the water to their little hideout?"

This felt like a test.

"Not if it's going to cost me," I said. "It's not that interesting a mystery."

He grinned. "Come on. Humor me. No strings attached. Besides, I heard your breath catch when I offered."

No point denying it. "Okay, why could I cross when I didn't have the required hamsa branded on me?"

Yoshi leaned in conspiratorially. "Because it's not about the hamsa. People put far too much stock in symbols."

Was that a message of some sort about my curiosity about stars and dominos? But how would he even know about that? "What's it about, then?"

"I could brand that hamsa all over my body and I couldn't get across the water." He had some more wine. "The ferry's magic discerned that you were on the same side as the demon hunters and allowed you entry."

"Sides?" I slowly spun my glass, torn between relief that it wasn't anything more sinister than that and disappointment that I wasn't some special exception, able to go anywhere.

Wards worked on the basic principle of detecting intent and keeping those planning on causing harm out, but Nav was very sure that the hamsa was necessary for access. Had he been lied to?

Even if the hamsa was irrelevant, I wasn't on Carpe Demon's side. In fact, I'd butted heads with them repeatedly. Plus, if whatever cosmic force had allowed my crossing had based its decision on me wanting to stop an alleged demon who turned out to be human, then Carpe Demon needed better security.

"Then just because the Succubus determined I was on the 'right' side that once, it doesn't mean that will happen again."

"Exactly."

"Regardless," I said, "sides seem like a simplistic reduction."

"Is it?" He hit a button on a sleek remote control. You could have knocked me over with a feather when the distinctive rumble of Johnny Cash came on. "Did you expect traditional Japanese music?"

I waved a finger around his lightweight charcoal pants and asymmetrical white linen shirt, the sleeves rolled up to expose his tanned forearms. It was simply but elegantly made from quality fabrics. "That would be a simplistic reduction.

Based on evidence, I'd guess something minimalist like Philip Glass."

"I do like his music." Yoshi surveyed me lazily, furthering the impression of a deadly jungle cat about to swipe at me with a paw. "Why did you want to see Zev? Maybe I can help you."

"I need help tracking down a missing Ohrist. It's for Tatiana's client." I drank some more wine.

"You think a vampire is behind it?" There was an edge under the silky tone.

"No. Someone or something has cast an illusion to make a family forget one of the daughters. It's either an Ohrist, possibly the missing woman herself, or a demon. Hence why I'm asking you."

Yoshi held up the wine bottle, but I shook my head. "I'll do it," he said, "but you'll have to do something in exchange."

"I figured. What?" My magic coiled into a hard pulsing knot deep in my gut, and I curled my hands around the wineglass.

He flexed the hand that had held the bottle, a tight wince flashing over his face. Was he injured? "Kill Topher."

I jerked, sloshing alcohol onto the bar top.

The vamp's calm expression didn't change as he wiped it up, but he took his eyes off me, giving me a brief respite in having to keep up appearances.

"Absolutely not," I said.

"Why not?" He glanced up, but I had my pleasantly interested expression firmly in place. "You killed Lindsey."

My first vampire death. I didn't regret it exactly, since it had been her or me, but I wasn't jonesing to make it a regular occurrence. Besides, after all I'd done to save Topher Sharma, I wasn't about to hasten his demise.

If I said no outright, Yoshi could refuse to help me. Let's see. Tatiana's last employee, Max, had been killed by a vampire named Kirk whom Yoshi had been sent to hunt down. That gave me an idea.

"No problem," I said. "I'll just follow the example you set with Kirk."

Yoshi shot me a puzzled look.

"I'll wait, like you did with Max. You remember him, right? The man you stood there and let Kirk murder instead of intervening seconds earlier to kill Kirk and save Max's life? Hmm." I drummed my fingertips on the bar. "Waiting fifty years sounds good. Do we have a deal?"

Yoshi slapped a hand down on the bar with a delighted expression. "The kitten finally shows her claws. And if I stipulated it had to be done immediately?"

"Forget it."

"Convincing the Sharmas to let Topher be turned wasn't a way of earning their gratitude, was it? And you won't sacrifice him now to gain something more valuable." He pursed his lips thoughtfully.

"Unlike some," I said icily, "who don't care who they kill or who condone murder when they could have prevented it, I don't take murder lightly."

"Now that's a simplistic reduction," he said.

"I can't wait to hear how." I propped my elbow on the bar.

"It all comes back to sides and how choosing one isn't as simple as you make it out to be." I must not have looked impressed enough at his explanation because his lips quirked. "Think of it like this then. It's about how your truth affects things around you and whether it aligns."

"Even though I was mistaken about who the demon was, the Succubus allowed me to cross because the truth of my actual goal, to help an Ohrist, aligned with Carpe Demon's mission statement?"

Yoshi held up his glass in cheers. "The missing woman? I can find her. Or whatever of her there is to be found, but if you're on Topher's side, then I won't. And that means going to the Lonestars or Carpe Demon. You've been hired to do a job and Tatiana prizes her professional reputational above all else. So, tell me, Miriam, which side takes priority? Which truth? The one that values life, even Topher's? Or the one that doesn't conflict with Tatiana and your duty to this case?"

"What's your problem with Topher? He can't be such a pain in the ass that you want him dead."

"His presence is stirring up other vampires. Giving them ideas about who they can and can't turn."

If they started turning Ohrists, the Lonestars would come down hard. No wonder Yoshi wasn't happy. "That's on Mr. BatKian. He sanctioned this and let his Ohrist granddaughter be made into a vamp."

I raised the wine bottle with an inquiring look, but Yoshi refused a top-up.

"Just because something is true for one," he said, "does not make it true for all."

"You made your point." I slid off the barstool. "But I'm not killing Topher. I'll figure it out."

"Your call." He took his time finishing his wine, leaving me waiting for his last words. "Remember, with every choice, you pick a side. And unless someone is in your head, it's impossible to always understand those choices." He worked the cork back into the bottle. "Don't make the mistake of reducing people to simplistic character qualities of good or evil and assuming you can predict their behavior, because as I said, knowing what side someone is on in any given situation is a complex judgment call. Just a bit of friendly advice."

"Why?" I crossed my arms. "We're hardly friends."

"Things have been a bit dull around here. You've livened them up."

"I don't believe you." I backed up toward the door, refusing to take my eyes off him until I was safely outside.

"Smart woman. Don't ever believe anyone. Not completely."

"Because of sides," I said flatly.

He tapped his nose. "Now you get it. However, regarding the missing Ohrist, I'm on your side. If a demon did this, then those self-righteous hunters will get their panties in a twist that you bypassed their jurisdiction and you won't be winning any points with the Lonestars, either."

"Basically, me making enemies amuses you."

He shrugged.

A week ago, I'd been so insistent on calling the Lonestars at Davide's house and ensuring I couldn't be threatened with Deadman's Island. But this case didn't involve murder as far as I knew, and I had every right to investigate on behalf of my client. Should Rory no longer be alive, I could reassess my options then, but for now, the side of me that wanted to unearth the truth for Giselle and keep Tatiana happy had taken over from the side that worried about burning bridges with the Lonestars.

I'd never realized how situational it all was, and it made me uneasy to think about what that implied about other people in my life whom I assumed would always be there for me.

I bumped into the door, feeling behind me for the handle. "Are we done?"

"If Topher is off the table..." Yoshi placed his glass in the sink, again making me wait for his next words.

I ground my teeth together.

"Let me feed off you." The suggestion was as blandly made as if he'd offered to get the door for me.

Delilah leapt up, scythe in hand.

Yoshi gave an exaggerated sigh. "Zev has already told me that you can't be compelled and I'm not going to turn you."

"Based on your say-so?"

"Based on my promise not to. A promise is a bond."

Behind my back, my hand tightened on the door handle. "Then what's the attraction of feeding off me?"

Delilah remained alert but lowered the weapon.

"Someone my age doesn't have to feed very often," Yoshi said, "but I've never tasted a Banim Shovavim and I expect that you'd satisfy me for quite some time."

Satisfy him or work like an energy booster to get him moving normally again? He moved vigorously—for a human. For Yoshi, his actions were almost sluggish.

"I knew you were braising me for better flavor," I said. "And the downside for me? Since I'm not compellable and won't swoon in delight at the experience?"

Yoshi pressed a hand to his heart. "So suspicious."

"There's always strings."

"The string is that this is a one-time proposition. Walk out that door and you'll have to bring someone else in to help you because you won't find Aurora Mueller."

There it was. He already knew the missing woman's name. I let go of the handle, rubbing the back of my neck. I was sick and tired of everyone being up in my business.

The undead asshole had the gall to smirk.

Giselle deserved to know what had happened to her sister and why her family had been fractured that way. She'd already been dismissed by both Kadeem and Tatiana, and who's to say that anyone else would prioritize her over their own agenda? I was the only one firmly in her corner and all I had to do was give up some blood.

"Promise me that you won't unmute yourself to get me all hot and bothered and I'll agree."

"I promise," he said.

Recalling Delilah, I sat back down on a barstool, fiddling with my sleeve. "So how do you want me?" I winced. "I mean, wrist or neck or do we insert an IV drip and you suck it out like a Slurpee?"

"I prefer the neck. Old habits."

I sat up, stiff as a board. "Have at 'er."

Yoshi pushed my hair off my shoulder and tilted my head to the side. "Relax."

I slowly inhaled and exhaled. "Will it hurt less if I do?"

"No, since I can't compel you to enjoy it. But if you're tense, your blood will taste bitter."

"Horrors."

He flashed his fangs and I jerked.

"I didn't even touch you," he protested, his eyes warming in amusement.

"Sorry," I mumbled, but it hadn't been fear that had made me jump. *The shark seeks the star.* Yoshi's fangs reminded me of shark teeth. Great white sharks could live more than seventy years, well beyond most animals' life spans, in the same way that vamps outlived humans.

What if the shark in Emmett's prophecy was a vampire? I couldn't ask Yoshi or Zev. I didn't dare. Even if it did reference a vampire, that didn't explain why I would be a baby shark.

Yoshi caressed my neck with his finger, jolting me from my thoughts, his breath whispering against my skin.

I smelled the wine he'd just drunk and a hint of musky cologne.

The tip of his fangs grazed the side of my throat, and I twisted my hands in my lap. *Relax.* Rolling back my shoulders, I let out a deep breath, and nodded.

Yoshi cupped the back of my head like a lover's embrace then sank his teeth in.

I swallowed the tiny gasp of pain but was immediately flooded by a rush of calm. There was nothing lustful or sexy about it and that eased any remaining tension. I was looser and more pliant than after the few yoga classes I'd taken, all aches and pains fading away. This wasn't so bad. My head fell back and my lids fluttered shut.

The vampire snaked his arm around my waist, basically propping me up as he fed.

...Dad running alongside my wobbly bike yelling encouragement...

...skinny-dipping with Eli in the moonlight...

An icy tendril snaked down my spine. I'd agreed to give the vamp my blood, not my memories. I fought against his hold, but he kept feeding, kept tainting these snapshots like mold blighting a plant. "Let go!"

...the one time I spanked Sadie, the penicillin that she'd flung off the spoon a pink splatter on my shirt...

...The shark sees the star, the flowers seek the shark, you seek the flowers, and the star seeks you...

Delilah pressed the scythe against Yoshi's neck.

The vampire withdrew his fangs, holding himself still until my shadow stepped back, though she kept the weapon raised.

I placed a hand on my chest, feeling my ragged breathing. "I should kill you for that."

He held up his hands. "I didn't know that would happen. I swear. It doesn't with Ohrists and you're the first Banim Shovavim I've tasted."

"You should have stopped when I first told you to." I touched my finger to the sensitive spot on my neck, but the puncture wounds had already closed. Other than my deep sense of violation, it was as if it had never happened. "How long will it take to find her?" I said in a cold voice.

"A day, maybe two?"

"Contact me the second you have."

"You have my word."

Uncertain about whether I'd come out ahead on this transaction, I glanced back at the vampire sheathed in shadow with the eeriest sense that my life had just switched tracks.

20

THE LAST THING I WANTED TO DO WAS GO FROM that encounter to finding Poe. The frying pan to the fire? Even if it was climbing out of the fire back into the nice toasty pan, I wasn't up to it. My quota on head trips was full.

I took Tuesday off to catch up on totally boring and banal things like grocery shopping and laundry.

Laurent texted me about going on a run, which would have gotten the anxiety out of my system, but that required too much energy, so I promised I'd go tomorrow.

Jude showed up in the late afternoon while I was mopping. Flushed, I wiped a strand of hair out of my eyes with my arm. "Come in, but careful. The floor is wet." I eyed her clothes and hands, which were free of any clay residue. A rare occasion for her. "Why so fancy today, lady?" I teased.

She slipped off her shoes. "Got a minute to talk?"

I raised my eyebrows. "Sure, while I finish mopping the kitchen."

We were years beyond guest status at each other's homes. Jude helped herself to a cold drink and then took a seat while I dumped the dirty water from the bucket into the sink.

Were we finally going to discuss how she felt about my

magic? For all my griping, was I ready to hear what she had to say?

"I got some answers about what happened with Emmett," she said somberly.

Oh. I rinsed the bucket a few times before refilling it with hot water and bleach. It couldn't be great given her serious mood, but I kept my voice light, hoping for the best. "What'd you learn?"

"Before I took on Zev's commission to make Emmett, I consulted another Ohrist who I tracked down living in Rome." Jude turned her glass slowly in her hands. "He'd made a few golems in his time, but after going through radiation and chemo, his magic had become unreliable, so he retired. At the time, I was only interested in the process, but I reached out to him now."

Water sloshed over the edge of the bucket when I set it on the floor. "Is Emmett in danger from this magic?"

"Possibly. In the same way that Ohrists draw upon ohr to fuel their magic, Banim Shovavim necromancers draw upon the dead."

I paused, the mop half-wrung out. "So, you mean Emmett could be consumed by spirits?"

"No." She fanned a hand in front of her face. For all the chemicals she dealt with in her pottery, she couldn't stand the smell of bleach. "Let me finish. These necromancers don't consult individual ghosts who see the future. They tap into the spirits' collective stream."

She looked up at the ceiling, gathering her thoughts, while I swept the mop over the floor with a swishing noise, mentally urging her to drop the bomb already.

"Think of these divinations like a river that Emmett steps into," Jude said. "Necromancers can withstand the current, but Emmett wasn't born with that magic. It was infused into him." Her lips twisted wryly when she said that, and I gave her a sympathetic smile, but it was automatic because my body felt tight with anger. She should have checked the repercussions before she set that magic in him. "Most of the time he can withstand the current," she said, "but if it's too strong he runs the risk of being swept away."

"What would happen to him?"

"He'd remain his divination self forever, half here and half not." Her voice was heavy with sorrow.

I practically stabbed the baseboard with the mop. There was no way of telling what type of prophecy would carry him away for good. While divination was a useful tool, it wasn't worth the risk. Said the woman who'd used him multiple times for her own gain. And wasn't that a bitter pill to swallow? I'd accidentally been dragging my friend closer to death. I gentled my motions, doing my best to remain even-keeled while we sorted this problem.

"I'm happy to never ask Emmett for a divination again," I said, "but he does it randomly too. How do we stop that?"

"We can't. It's part of how he was created." Jude finished her drink, then clutched the glass tightly, her eyes on her lap.

The water turned cloudy when I dunked the mop in the bucket and I wrung it out with more force than necessary. "Too bad you didn't ask the Banim Shovavim necromancer before he died."

Jude looked up sharply, her eyes flashing. "There it is."

"There what is?"

"You've been dancing around me ever since you saved me from the dybbuk," she snapped. "You blame me for all of it, don't you?"

"Me?" I slapped the mop against the floor. "You're the one who flinches if you see my shadow. Hell, half the time you do it if I get too close to you. You feel all torn up about Emmett, but you're treating me like a monster."

"You think I don't know that?" She raked her hands through her curls. "I should feel grateful but—"

"I don't want your gratitude," I said stiffly. "I just want you to be normal with me."

"I know." The heat had gone out of her tone. "I'm trying, but every time I see you, you remind me of death."

The mop clattered to the floor. I looked down at my body, half convinced that I was only a shadow like Delilah because surely if I was flesh and blood, my best friend couldn't have stabbed me in the heart. I wasn't the Grim Reaper. I'd saved her life and yet she couldn't see me as anything more than my scythe? I tasted my pulse at the back of my throat.

"I didn't mean it like that," she said quietly.

"Right." Numb, I bent to retrieve the mop, latching on to the previous thread of our discussion as a way to make it through the rest of this visit. "Maybe if Emmett's aware of the danger, he can do something to prevent himself from falling into that trance state."

Jude's chair scraped back and she stood in front of me. "I never wanted kids because my art was my baby. We joked about world domination, but I had this vision of my creations finding homes in every corner of the globe. And after years of work, it was finally happening." She licked her lips nervously. "Then I was kidnapped and enthralled."

There was a long, heavy pause that I didn't fill because I was scared to open my mouth and say something I couldn't take back. I fiddled with the mop, my attention on a nonexistent spot.

I felt her eyes on me, heard her tiny sigh. "I spent the time I was chained up preparing to be fully possessed and die, but you saved me. I'd been granted amnesty. Maybe the first Ohrist ever to have been gifted that."

"You could have just sent a fruit basket," I snarked.

She clenched her fists, two red spots hitting her cheeks, and unclenched them with visible effort. "I was alive, but I couldn't create."

"You don't use your magic in your art." I picked up the

bucket and dumped the water down the drain. "The fact that you were stymied is not on me."

"I know that."

"Then why do I remind you of death? Explain it to me, Jude, because I don't understand. You say I gave you this gift and it's not about losing your magic, then why am I still the bad guy?" Swearing under my breath, I stashed the mop and the bucket next to the BBQ on the back porch, slamming the door on my way in.

"Why were you okay using Emmett for his prophecies when you were so angry that a Banim Shovavim had died for that?" Jude said. "That should have been the last thing you ever did, but you used him because it helped you. I did the same. The woman who did this to me had her memories erased so it's not like I could lash out at her. It's shitty and I'm sorry. But it's not like I'm the only one at fault here."

I hopped up on my counter, watching the moisture on the floor slowly disappear. I'd wanted Jude to be honest with me and now that she was, I wanted her to take it back. There was comfort in not knowing. I wish I didn't know that I'd pushed Emmett that much closer to magic Never Never Land, albeit accidentally. But if I could forgive myself for that, couldn't I forgive Jude for what she'd said? She wasn't acting from a place of malice, she was doing what she thought was best, same as my interactions with Emmett.

Truth sucked, but I'd still rather that than silence, lies, and secrets.

"Well." I blew a strand of hair out of my face. "Seems like Dr. Takimoto is going to get a few more sessions out of us both."

Jude nodded. She didn't ask if we were okay. Our friendship was the scraped-up raw version of itself and it needed time to heal. But the outburst had helped.

"That was a lot of truth bomb for a Tuesday afternoon. Got anything else to share?"

"Uh, yeah?" She leaned back against the island.

I raised my eyebrows. "I was kidding."

"This is important though. The Wise Brothers collect information that they hand over if you successfully play their game. And you said they always reply truthfully to your questions if they know the answer."

"That's right." I wasn't sure where she was going with this, but my curiosity had been sparked. "Laurent and I paid a real shitty price to learn about Frances Rothstein, the Banim Shovavim who'd placed the death curse on Tatiana, but at least we knew the information was reliable."

Jude rummaged around in a cupboard, pulling out the remaining bar in my chocolate stash. "Calling Emmett's magic a prophecy is misleading because it's only a partial prophecy. He can only build upon facts that already exist. Think about it," she added at my frown.

Joining her at the table, I cracked open the package, biting into a large piece of dark chocolate and almonds. During the Topher Sharma case, Emmett had offered up the twinkle twinkle little star prophecy. Most of it was already fact, put into motion by Oliver. Only the final bit about the star being snuffed out had yet to transpire. Even now, with the shark and flowers, that part had happened decades ago with my parents.

"The Wise Brothers deal in certainty," I said. "Their facts are clearly laid out, whereas some of what Emmett says has happened, but I have to interpret it all for any of it to be useful." I finished up my first piece and broke off another. "That's interesting, but I fail to see what you're so worried about. Other than the possible harm to Emmett, of course."

"Got a pen and paper?"

I retrieved the items for her glad that my floor was mostly dry. House and clothes all clean, groceries bought, I was a domestic powerhouse.

"I thought that the Wise Brothers and Emmett existed at

opposite ends of a spectrum, but I was wrong. My Ohrist contact filled in some important information." Jude drew a triangle. "This top point is the Wise Brothers. Their information is neutral in the sense that it already exists, be it a person's name, their location, or whatever. It's fact. That's part one. The second part is that there's no cost to them for the information extraction, only to you." Beside the top of the triangle, she scribbled "Wise Brothers. Info neutral. Cost to player not dealer."

Information and games, I had a hunch where this was going. "Emmett's prophecies aren't a game," I said slowly, goosebumps breaking out along my arms.

"They're puzzles and puzzles are games." Jude tapped the lower left corner with her pen. "This is Emmett's magic." She wrote "Partially neutral. Cost to dealer."

I dropped the rest of my chocolate piece, the rich flavor turning to sawdust. "The final corner is Poe, isn't it?"

"Not specifically Poe, but all raven shifters, yeah." Jude squeezed my hand. "Don't be scared. When you played them that time, you aborted the consequences by stabbing the card face before the game could finish. Thank God," she added.

Something in my stomach twinged.

I bit my lip. "I didn't just play them once. There was a second time."

Jude's face drained of all color. "Fuck me." Her reassuring squeeze turned into a death grip on my poor hand. "What happened? Very specifically?"

I pulled free, turning my engagement ring around hard enough to leave grooves. "Poe took advantage of an urgent situation. They handed over a phony token, believing they were sending me to my death via sea monster and there wouldn't be repercussions, but I'm alive and well." I turned hopeful eyes on her. "So, I don't have to worry about that game either, right? And I won't ever tangle with them again."

In my head, I crossed Poe off my list as the one to ask

about the Ascendant. It wasn't ideal, but I'd have to find someone else.

Jude gnawed on the end of the ballpoint. "The sea monster wasn't their end goal, Mir."

"Then what was?" I licked chocolate off my finger. "When Tatiana told me not to get involved with Poe, she didn't say why. I figured it was a general warning, like stay away from vamps. If there was something specific, why wasn't I told?"

"According to my Ohrist connection, people have forgotten the reason why you don't play games with raven shifters, but they're tricksters who live to introduce chaos and conflict in a person's life."

"Obviously. Poe always makes me feel crappy playing a game with them. But what's the catch?"

"Their shifter abilities come from ohr, but they don't care about that. They care about these games. I don't know where those powers stem from and neither did the Ohrist, but like ohr, the source has to be fed."

"That's their problem. Cost to dealer," I said.

Shaking her head, Jude drew a circle around the final point on the triangle. "First of all, their information isn't neutral, and it isn't like Emmett's prophecies where the future aspect of it only comes into play if you do something with it. Remember how mad Poe was when the game of memory got interrupted?"

"Yeah."

"It's because they didn't get any concrete information out of you."

"Cry me a river," I said.

"Did they this time?"

I touched the finger that had been bitten when I played blackjack. "Yeah, one of the suits on their cards used ravens. A bird came to life and bit me, then another raven joined the others, changing the card from a nine to a ten. That's when Poe announced there was a new player, but there's always a new player. What makes this person or thing a bigger deal?"

"The game brings the information into being," Jude said. "This person wouldn't exist otherwise. Though," she added, "it doesn't mean they're your enemy. We don't know what side they're on, only that they are tangled up in something that involves you."

I'd wondered what Poe got out of these encounters, and damn, that was quite the answer. "So, this is my fault? Fucking awesome. Who are they? Where are they?"

"Hey." Jude's eyes flashed in irritation. "Don't shoot the messenger."

I held up my hands. Note to self: we were still both touchier than usual. "Sorry."

"As for who? It's hard to say. They might already have been put on the gameboard or they may be yet to be unveiled. The only certainty is that either now or in the future they will be a part of this because of that game with Poe."

"If shifters pay the price for failing to bring new information into being, then I hope Poe suffered huge torments when I stopped our first game," I said viciously.

"Every time someone turns them down, the raven shifters suffer," Jude said. "It's why they manipulate people into engaging with them."

"My new mission is to spread the word far and wide about the exact danger of raven shifters," I said with steely determination.

"Like how people spread the word about the dangers of Banim Shovavim?"

I narrowed my eyes. "It's not the same thing."

Jude shrugged. "If you say so. You got room for another target on your back?"

"I'll make room for this one." I tapped my fist on the table. "I appreciate you finding this out before I brought something else into being."

I walked Jude to the front door. There was an awkward moment where we would have normally hugged but we stood there. Then she moved in one way, and I moved in the other and we banged foreheads.

Jude rubbed her head. "Agree to just put this disaster of a day behind us?"

"Agreed."

"I'll visit Emmett tomorrow," she said. "See if there's any way to keep him safe..."

"You got this." We fist bumped.

I shut the door behind her, leaning against it with a hard exhalation.

This visit had destroyed all post-Yoshi calm that I'd built up from my mundane chores. If I stayed home, I'd obsess over what I'd called into being, and how soon I could expect it to fuck up my life. I needed to do something to seize some measure of power back.

I smiled. I had just the thing.

After a quick dart through the KH, I stepped out onto the grounds at the college in Maine where James Learsdon taught. With the time difference between Vancouver and the east coast, the sun was already going down, bathing the sky in vibrant gold. It was a smaller campus, marked by tree-lined walkways and ivy-covered stone buildings with front pillars that were reminiscent of the Parthenon. I'd gotten the location of the archeology department online before I came, and it took me only a few minutes to track it down.

The cool, dim hallways were deserted this late in the evening. I counted off numbers on doors until I reached Professor Learsdon's office. Even though a small sign taped to the door announced he was away for a couple weeks until the start of fall term, I sent Delilah under the crack at the bottom of the door frame.

Suddenly, a scythe appeared in Delilah's hand.

Without thinking, I drew my cloaking over myself because

that could mean only one thing. My quick instincts saved me because barely a second later, heavy footsteps echoed down the corridor, and two brawny vamps rounded the corner.

I pressed myself flat against the wall, surreptitiously calling Delilah back to me as one of them heaved his brick-like shoulder into Learsdon's door. The frame gave way with a loud crack and the two stepped inside, while I peered in from the hall.

The professor's doctorate was hung in a place of honor over his desk. On either side were photos of him on various archeological digs, his face lit up with an expression I recognized as the thrill of the hunt. Yet there was nothing to cement that this was the same person who'd come after me. I was trusting Ryann's identification and my own deductions that an archeology professor would be interested in my magic.

Was his quest for the Ascendant not about what it could do, or even the physical object itself, but the same scholarly love of puzzles that had driven me to figure out what the Torquemada Gloves really were?

"This is a pointless idea," said the vamp who hadn't broken down the door, pronouncing "idea" as "idear." He shook his head. "Learsdon isn't stupid enough to leave hints about where he's hiding and Dagmar's kidding herself if she thinks he kept the real elixir formula from her. It didn't work. That's it."

"You wanna tell Dagmar that?" This vamp dropped his "r" making it an "ah" sound.

Their New England accents calmed my fears that the two had followed me from Vancouver as did the fact that this had nothing to do with my past. But it made me think I was right about this Learsdon. What were the chances of there being some other person with that name sketchy enough to set up a magic trap where someone died and also have bloodsuckers after them?

The vamp I dubbed Mr. Ah yanked the top desk drawer out and upended the contents onto the floor, while Mr. R pulled file after file from the cabinet, raining paper down like a snowfall.

I skirted around the edges of the room examining documents as the vamps threw them out, mildly curious about this elixir they wanted, but the files were all student related. The destruction turned personal with the travel photos smashed to the ground and stomped underfoot. When the vamps started in on the books, shaking them out for hidden papers before dumping them on the floor and carelessly leaving footprints on covers, I saw red.

I held my magic in through sheer force of will, almost vibrating with the effort to remain silently hidden in plain sight.

Once they were satisfied with the carnage, they left, bitching about what they'd do to Learsdon if Dagmar took her anger out on them for this failed venture.

The vamps hadn't exactly been quiet about this breaking and entering and campus security could show up at any time, but I couldn't leave yet. Keeping one ear cocked for footsteps or voices, I rifled through indexes for any mention in Learsdon's books about the Ascendant. I'd gone through a good dozen of the most promising titles with no luck when I heard the staccato of a walkie-talkie and booked it out through the KH. Home safely, but no wiser.

21

THE FIRST THING I DID WEDNESDAY MORNING WAS touch base with Ryann that vamps were after Learsdon and while they didn't know where he was, she might want to track down a bloodsucker called Dagmar. If Dagmar got to Learsdon before the Lonestars, not only would I be denied answers, I'd never know if he'd blabbed about my magic and someone else would come after me to pick up where he'd left off.

That's when Laurent showed up to make me keep my promise about the run. I was so antsy that I didn't even try to weasel out of it.

After a quick warm-up, we jogged in silence, which was good because I could either run or talk. But once we hit his predetermined halfway point and turned back, he spoke up. "I haven't had a chance to find out everything that's been going on with you since I've been away."

I used some of my precious energy to squint at him, because this was unheard of. "You willingly want to hear me discuss my life?"

"Maman remarked that my social skills had improved," he said with a curmudgeonly expression. "She made me promise to keep it up."

I heaved a sigh. "I'm just a means to an end."

"Yes, so keep your monologue to five minutes or less."

I elbowed him, but laughing, he dodged me. Jogging and speaking. Right. I could do this.

Two minutes later, I decided I couldn't and slowed to a walk. "It's time for the cool-down portion. Very important to prevent cramping."

Laurent raised an eyebrow but let me get away with it.

The fur and claws came out when he learned about James. Laurent seemed as upset about the events at Davide's house being a test for me as the fact that two people were inhabited by dybbuks and one was now dead.

"I will kill him." Laurent's words were muddy because he spoke through elongated teeth.

I stopped in my tracks, spinning him around so that I faced the street and he faced a row of hedges. "No. You have to swear not to go after Learsdon." I stroked his arm. "Let the Lonestars deal with him. There are already vamps hunting the man and I know you can handle it, but I don't want you to put yourself in danger over this."

His wolf characteristics grew more extreme before he wrestled them under control. Once he was fully human again, he nodded and sighed. "D'accord."

I didn't discuss Giselle's case because of client confidentiality, but I did tell him about Uncle Jake's letter and the Ascendant. I didn't mention Emmett's prophecy, nor did I share Jude's insights on the Wise Brothers, the golem, and raven shifters. Given Laurent's reaction to James, he'd go full wolf on me hearing about the rest. Not a great situation to handle in broad daylight.

He listened to the rest of my story without comment, only interrupting a couple of times for clarification, and by the time I finished, we were back at my place.

We didn't even have sweaty shower sex when the training

session was done. Rude. He escorted me up the stairs, laughed when I collapsed in my foyer, then with a reminder to stretch, sprinted off to run six times around the city or whatever.

He and I were going to have a talk about motivation. Running for survival's sake was theoretically a good reason but, in reality, was rather lackluster. I did best with immediate gratification.

I was that kid who lived for getting gold stars. I'd moved past that as an adult, but would an orgasm for every successful kilometer I ran be so remiss? I'd even take a kiss. Or a brownie. I was amenable to many different options.

By the time I got out of the shower, Yoshi had come through with a text containing an address in Venice and the words "Cocktail attire. Now."

I threw on the silky blue dress I'd worn to the speakeasy dinner with Giselle, wrangled my hair and makeup into something vaguely glam, and hit the Kefitzat Haderech. I'd find Aurora and if I got to kill an illusion-happy demon along the way? My day would be perfect.

After a quick hello to Pyotr, I took a sock, stuffing it in my clutch. I'd add it to my ever-growing collection of lost socks in my bedroom closet, which I really needed to clean out. Minutes later, I stepped out to a beautiful summer night in the shadows of an Italian boutique hotel made of pale pink stone with a bright white arched portico. It was 1AM here and the streets were alive with people spilling out of restaurants and bars.

I winked at a drunk couple that I'd startled, then strolled into the lobby dazzled by the intricate pattern of the marble floor and the enormous crystal chandelier, both of which managed to stay on the right side of good taste. Faint piano music echoed through the space from deeper in the building, so I followed it to open glass doors at the back.

Where I was promptly stopped by two enormous men dressed in black with earpieces who spoke to me in Italian.

"English?" I said.

"Do you have an invitation?" The man held one of those handheld metal detectors. What kind of event had this level of security?

"Is this a private party?" I looked between the two, but the second guy remained stone-faced.

The first one finally gave a brusque nod. Thanks for the stunning amount of information.

"Sorry." I spun around and walked back into the lobby. My shoulders prickled like they were watching me, which I confirmed was the case when I glanced back. I didn't slow down until I turned down the short corridor to the restrooms, at which point I cloaked myself and walked back in, deftly avoiding the guards.

Hundreds of tiny white lights had been strung up along the pillars and under the canopy of the long patio along the edge of the Grand Canal. Water lapped gently at the deck's pilings, mingling with the sounds of rapid-fire conversations in a half dozen languages and the pianist in one corner striking up a lively tune.

Look at me up past midnight. Sure, it was still afternoon in Vancouver, but I was here and that's what counted.

The patio was packed so I unobtrusively planted myself off to the side, remaining hidden. Initially, the different groups of people seemed like any you'd find at a party, but there were far more men than women. The men dominated the floor with the women relegated to one side, like at a middle school dance.

I couldn't see anyone who resembled Giselle, but since I had only glimpses of the women from where I stood, I made my way over to their area careful not to bump into anyone.

A pattern emerged among the men's groups. For every two or three men who were engaged in conversation, there were four more flanking them—no, covering them like backup. No one's smiles reached their eyes.

They reminded me of sharks. Were these people vampires? They certainly had that same lethal predator vibe.

I discarded that idea because waiters circulated with hors d'oeuvres, which were being eaten by most of the crowd. Also, there was a disproportionate number of men either openly wearing crosses or with them tattooed on their forearms. Especially the men speaking either Italian or Slavic languages.

One man to my left, wearing a pinkie ring with a diamond that almost blinded me, raised a glass. "A la famiglia!"

A corpulent man with a cigar clamped in his mouth clinked his highball glass and toasted back in Russian.

Family?

I gasped, slapping my hand over my mouth. These were mafioso. My shock deepened when I saw Giselle.

Our client stood in profile chatting with two older women drenched in gold jewelry, but there was no mistaking her light brown hair, lithe dancer's body, or perfect posture. Had Yoshi been unable to find Aurora and mistakenly gotten Giselle instead? What was she doing in Italy with this crowd?

Checking thoroughly that no one was paying any attention to me, I dropped my cloaking and intercepted her on the way to the bar. "Giselle?"

She turned with a brittle smile. "I think you have me confused with someone else."

I rocked back on my heels, my mouth hanging open. Aurora and Giselle weren't just sisters, they were identical twins. Almost identical. This woman was Giselle's doppelganger, except she had a tiny birthmark on her right cheek. A handy visual to tell them apart.

"Aurora?" I said.

The woman shook her head. "That's not me." Her velvet

off-the-shoulder dress and chignon were elegant, but her fingers were bitten to the quick and her eyes looked haunted.

I put out a hand to keep her from leaving. "Listen to me, please. I realize this sounds crazy, but your real name is Aurora Mueller."

She gave a tiny head shake and took a step back. "You have the wrong person."

"No, I don't. Look, if you would just come with me for five minutes. Just to the lobby. I can explain."

"My fiancé, Edvin, is waiting."

"But—"

A security guard appeared at her side. "Signorina Lotta, are you okay?"

Lotta?

"I'm fine, Antonio," she said, "but I'd like Edvin to take me home."

"Certamente. I'll have the boat brought round." Wow. Okay.

The guard placed a hand under my elbow but there was nothing courtly about it.

Practically hauled off, I glanced back in frustration.

Lotta joined a blond man, whose back was to me. While she spoke to him with flustered gestures, he rubbed between her shoulders as if to calm her.

The guard kept his hold on me until we reached the lobby. "Leave Signorina Lotta alone."

"Got it." Rubbing my arm, I found a quiet corner in the lobby and sat down.

Despite what she'd said, this woman had to be Aurora. Was Edvin another mafioso? Had he placed the illusion on Rory?

On the slight chance that I was wrong, and this woman really was Lotta, I called the dance studio in the Bronx, once again pretending to be the mom who'd been referred by Giselle. "A friend of mine has twins like Giselle and Aurora." I paused but she didn't correct me. Good. One thing confirmed. "She's wondering if they could start in different streams? Put one in modern and the other in ballet because they don't work well together."

The woman assured me that wouldn't be an issue.

I flashed back to the studio's trophy case. Poor Rory, not being good enough to compete at the same level as her twin. That must have burned.

"These girls aren't identical like Giselle and Aurora though," I said.

The woman on the phone laughed. "If it hadn't been for Gigi's birthmark, we'd never have been able to tell them apart."

Dread skittered up my spine. "You mean Aurora's birthmark."

"No. Gigi's."

I almost dropped the phone. If Giselle was the woman here at the cocktail party, then my client was really Aurora? And she'd taken over Giselle's identity? Willingly?

Realizing the woman was waiting for me to say something, I laughed, hoping it didn't sound too fake. "Right. Sorry. That's what I meant. It's been one of those days. Hey, do you have a photo of the Mueller twins together? My friend was hoping to show her daughters twins actually cooperating."

The admin said she was sure she could find something and would email it over.

I think I managed to thank her and say goodbye like a normal person, but I wouldn't have bet my house on it, because I remained in shock.

Our client was really Aurora but believed herself to be Giselle, while the real Giselle had no idea who she was.

"You surprised me," a man said.

I stiffened, one hand on my racing heart and the other holding my scythe.

A buff blond man who was one of those prime Nordic specimens sat across from me, his legs crossed and a snifter of amber liquid dangling carelessly in one hand. He looked like the kind of guy who enjoyed a hot sauna followed by a dip in an icy river and probably had a shelf full of Olympic medals for Alpine skiing. In comparison to the flashy, posturing mafioso, he was understated in a simple charcoal suit, but he also gave the impression that he didn't need to act tough because he was well aware of his limitations—none —and acted accordingly.

He'd also been the one comforting the real Giselle at the bar in the Mafia party.

This individual was handsome and affable and made me want to smile to keep his attention; he wasn't an Ohrist if I had my weapon. When I probed deeper, he wasn't dybbuk-possessed either. He also wasn't a vampire because otherwise Delilah would have held the scythe.

"Edvin, I presume. You're a demon," I said flatly. The discrepancy between his charming demeanor that was pure sunshine and his true nature of evil sent shivers up my spine.

He shrugged, flashing me a toothpaste-ad smile. "Guilty as charged." The demon nudged the edge of the blade with the toe of his highly polished leather shoe. "Put it away."

I lowered the scythe down the side of the chair where it wouldn't attract attention from any passing Ohrist, but I wasn't about to relinquish it. "I owe you for the kargh thurt you sent. And that charming illusion you hit me with."

It was an educated guess that he'd been the one to send that thug demon and make me believe that Sadie was dead, but the demon nodded matter-of-factly.

"That was the surprising part I mentioned." He sipped his alcohol. "You shouldn't have survived my kargh thurt." I didn't enlighten him that without Marsha's help he'd have gotten his wish. "Ah well," he said. "But the illusion of your daughter dying? Most people don't see through my weavings so easily. Then again," he reflected, "most don't want to."

He changed the arrangement of roses on the table next to him to appear to be sunflowers. No one here in the grandiose hotel lobby blinked.

"Right," I said, "blame the victim. What did you do to the Mueller twins?"

"Only what I was asked to." He calmly sipped his alcohol. "Aurora wanted her sister's life, and I didn't even need to expend any magic to enhance her dancing skills to pull off the ruse. Besides, who was I to deny such an impassioned plea?"

I shook my head. This was crazy. "Even if Rory did say she wanted Giselle's life, she didn't mean it literally."

"How do you know?" Apparently, the light above our heads was not to his liking either, because the demon switched the inset pot lights for a metal chandelier with real candles.

"Stop that," I said.

A huge fluffy rug appeared under a group of tourists coming back to the hotel for the night.

"Just having some fun." He pulled a mulish face like I was being unreasonable. "If I was serious, you wouldn't have known it was an illusion either. Now, answer my question. How do you know she didn't mean it literally?"

"Because—" Aurora had always lived in the shadow of her twin, but even so, she wasn't capable of something this heinous. Was she? "When did you cast the illusion on them?"

"Three years ago." He paused, smiling like a prosecuting attorney about to slam-dunk a case. "Right after the actual Giselle was accepted into the Ishikawa Ballet Company."

Oh my God. Rory had stolen Giselle's dream and co-opted it for herself. I clenched the scythe even tighter, gripped by a hot rush of anger. If Mrs. Mueller had believed in Rory as much as her sister, or if even one teacher had intervened and placed the twins on the same dance path, this tragedy could have been avoided.

He held out his glass. "Do you need a drink? You seem rather agitated."

I pushed it away because there was one thing that didn't jibe with his explanation. "If Giselle, I mean my client, the real Aurora, did that, she wouldn't have hired me to find out why she felt so unsettled. She wouldn't have begged me to find her sister if this was what she wanted to begin with."

His eyes twinkled as he swished the liquor in his glass around, the ice cubes softly clinking together. "You're assuming I intended my illusion to remain seamless when driving them mad is such a fun side effect."

The handle of my scythe bit into my skin and I loosened my grip. "Them? You're pulling this 'side effect'"—I did the quotes—"on both women?"

"I couldn't simply switch them. That would have been too complicated for even my illusion magic to sustain. Aurora became Giselle, so I had to put Giselle into a new life, extracting her from her old one. That comes with certain side effects."

Her bitten nails, her fragile state. "What does she think is going on?"

"That she's a beautiful woman with an adoring, wealthy fiancé who keeps her grounded when she has her little episodes where she believes she's a ballet dancer." He tapped his head. "Mental health is so important."

"Thanks for so conveniently laying all of it out," I said sarcastically.

"Why should I deny it? It's not like you can rectify the situation, and I'm rather proud of my work. There were a lot of pieces to manage on this one." Everyone in the lobby suddenly had a horse head, be they in hotel uniforms or fancy dress.

This was all a big joke to him.

I swung my scythe, then yelped and threw the hissing snake I held across the room.

A heartbeat later, there was no snake, no scythe, just me standing in the middle of the lobby being frowned at by people with normal human features.

"A for effort," the demon said.

I sat down, seething. There had to be a way to get the jump on him.

"I learned something very important from our last encounter," the demon said.

"Yeah, what was that?"

"Your weakness. The only reason you broke my spell that fast was because of your strong bond with your child. Interfere in my affairs and your daughter's quick death will be a mercy you beg for." He stood up. "And I don't mean an illusion. Salut." Raising his glass in cheers, he strolled back to the party.

22

I UNCLENCHED MY FISTS, TAKING DEEP BREATHS until the vice around my chest loosened and I could analyze the situation logically. If Edvin died, his spell on the twins would break, but was that the only way?

What about Giselle—the real Aurora? I shook my head. Thinking of them this way was going to get confusing fast. I'd continue to refer to my client as Giselle and use the nickname Gigi for her twin until their real identities were restored.

Despite what Edvin had said, I didn't believe Giselle knew what she was getting into when she said she wanted her sister's life. It was one thing to envy a sibling and quite another to erase them from your reality. The odds were good that Giselle hadn't known she was dealing with a demon. Given she now wanted to be reunited with her sister, perhaps she could undo this.

I pictured Gigi's gnawed fingernails, how vulnerable she'd seemed, and Edvin's glee at her "mental health" struggles with her true ballerina identity. I couldn't bear to leave her with him a second longer than I had to, not to mention that my own client was heartbroken that she'd forgotten her sister.

This had gotten too big to handle on my own. I'd been lucky to break the demon's illusion and I'd had Marsha's magic to help me when the kargh thurt showed up. There was no way I'd test my luck when Edvin had made a direct threat against Sadie.

I needed Carpe Demon, especially since Edvin would still have to be taken out. He'd come after my daughter if the illusion was broken any other way than through his death.

As soon as I got home, spying through Eli's window to make sure he and Sadie were safely behind the wards for the evening, I made myself comfortable in my living room with all the lights on and Delilah for company, and called Nav.

"Any way to break a demon illusion without killing the demon?" I stretched out on my divine divan, with my shadow lounging at my feet.

"You owe me five dollars," Nav said.

"For what?"

There was the crack of pool balls. "Not you," he said. "Laurent. Cocky bastard thought he could make a trick shot."

"Say hi." I was a petty, petty human being for wishing he was at home pining for me.

"What am I? Your girlfriend passing notes?" He paused. "Yes, Laurent, it's Mitzi." Another pause. "There's this incredible new technology called a phone. Use it."

I stroked the top curve of my velvet sofa like it was a cat. So pretty. "You're more delightful than usual this fine evening, Naveen. Who pissed in your cornflakes?"

"I was all set to cuddle up with an expensive bottle of whiskey but this one dragged me out to go smash balls. And not even in the good way."

A loud roar came through the phone and someone yelled, "Rematch!"

I winced, holding the cell away from my ear. "There's a good way to smash balls?"

"Oh, innocent child." Nav sighed. Ice tinkled. "I can make anything good."

"Aaand back to the demon."

"Hang on. This pool hall has been inundated by cretins." The noise became muffled for a moment and then I heard the chirp of a pedestrian crossing and traffic. "All right. My answer is that it depends. Who's the demon?"

I stared at the ceiling, debating my answer. "If I tell you, do you promise not to do anything without my go-ahead?"

"So long as your go-ahead doesn't take long. I've been very patient with you but there's a demon on the loose and I don't like when that happens."

"I don't either, but I want the best possible outcome. His name is Edvin."

"Don't know that alias," Nav said. "Describe him."

I did, adding where I'd met him. And with whom.

"Lovely," the Brit said in a flat voice. "Is this illusion on more than one person?"

"Yes."

"That makes it harder. We have to identify each individual caught in it and bring them in to HQ to be deprogrammed one at a time. Depending on how deeply it's taken root, the process can be extremely painful."

Delilah was crowding me off the sofa, so I shut her down. "Would the demon know as soon as it was broken for the first person?"

"Not sure. We've only attempted this a couple other times and the demon was already locked up, so we didn't check when they became aware that their magic was disrupted."

I might get away with freeing Giselle before Edvin caught on, but there was no way to help Gigi without him finding out. "The demon threatened Sadie if I messed with his business."

"Stop crowding me," Nav said. "I heard her."

Laurent said something I didn't catch, but Nav told him to take his wolf hearing and wait inside his truck.

I curled up against the corner throw pillows. The more people looking out for my daughter the better, but it was also confusing when technically Laurent and I were just friends with benefits. "Did he leave?"

"No, because Hell didn't freeze over. When will you give me your answer on how to proceed?"

"I'll speak to my client tomorrow. It's her life and she needs to be involved in this decision. I also need to clear this with Tatiana."

"Bloody hell. She's going to run me through the wringer negotiating her fees again. You're lucky Sadie is a sweetheart because you, poppet, are a pain in the arse."

"So you've said. But seeing as Daya would skin you alive if you didn't help Sades and you're trying to get in good with my baby daddy, I'm confident in my leeway to expand the pain well beyond the arse region." I smiled beatifically from my end of the phone.

"You mean the man who bolted when I got to your house?" Nav said with a sniff.

"Awwww. Want me to pass a note for you?"

On the other side of the phone, Laurent laughed.

"Shut it," Nav muttered.

"Me or him?" I said.

"Yes."

I smirked. "I'll touch base when plans are firmed up more."

"What am I supposed to do with the wolf breathing down my neck? Our pool game is clearly ruined. Take him off my hands," he ordered imperiously.

"Good night, Nav. Night, Huff 'n' Puff." I hung up with a smile, which quickly disappeared upon realizing that I'd have to bring Eli and Sadie into this conversation. My desire to free the twins from the demon's magic didn't give me the right to unilaterally make a decision that painted a target on my daughter's back.

I headed next door before I could chicken out and laid out the entire case for them. Surprisingly, they listened calmly.

Sadie, sitting on the floor, shook a bottle of blue polish. "I can't just hide behind the wards. I have work and a life."

"I know," I said. "Ideally, Nav will assign people to tail you. They're good and you wouldn't even know they're there. But if either of you are uncomfortable with this idea, we don't proceed."

"Then those women are stuck." She uncapped the bottle and applied the first layer to her toes.

"Not necessarily. We could kill the demon instead of undoing his illusion first. It might take a bit longer to target him instead of removing the women to safety, but eventually, they'd be free."

My daughter wiped polish off her little toe with a cotton ball. "Eventually could be years."

"Or days," Eli pointed out. He perched on the sofa doing biceps curls with a ten-pound weight. "My vote is the second plan."

"No." Dipping the applicator into the bottle, Sadie redid the blue on her small toe. "I don't want them to wait. Between Nav and Dad protecting me, I feel okay about this. You can rescue them while the demon is being hunted down."

"You should probably touch base with Naveen about this," I said to Eli. "Purely professionally, of course."

"We've been speaking," Eli said.

"My mistake. I thought given the way you ran out of my kitchen like an embarrassed teenager that there was drama."

Eli shot me the finger.

I stood up and kissed Sadie on the top of her head. "I'll keep you all posted on each step, but now I'm off to bed. Good night, fam."

"Night," they chorused.

No wonder so many books and shows featured single people fighting evil. It was much easier to go out there with magic blazing when you only had to think of yourself.

I'd intended to go to bed, but the road to Hell and all that, so I made a quick call.

"Hey, Nav," I said. "Still want me to take Laurent off your hands?"

He told me that Laurent had gone home. I almost provided an excuse about needing to speak with Laurent about the case, but I didn't. I had nothing to be embarrassed about.

Thanking him, I hung up, heading directly for my car. Time to go into the forest and visit the big bad wolf.

Low lights gleamed through the dirty frosted windows of Hotel Terminus when I parked at the curb, now a bundle of nerves. I took a moment to fix my hair in the small mirror on the visor, my leg bouncing. What if sex between us was terrible? Like if we couldn't find our rhythm and just humped limply along, my dry desert Hanukkah bush failing to become a lush wet oasis? What if he was a two-minute wonder and I had to fake my enthusiasm?

What if I gave him carpal tunnel from trying to get me off for too long?

Argh! I wrenched the key out of the ignition, slammed the door, and marched up to the side door, rapping on it briskly.

"Attends," Laurent called from inside. A moment later a bolt clicked free. He slouched against the door jamb, clad only in jeans, his dark curls messed up like he'd run a hand through them. "Come for another run?"

I shook my head.

He raked a very slow gaze over me and I gave a giddy little bounce.

"Hmmm." His brow furrowed. "To discuss a case?" He

scratched his chest, those strong fingers rasping over the dusting of hair on his sculpted pecs.

I bit my bottom lip. "Nope."

He tilted his head, one eyebrow quirked. "Are you here to fix our technical oversight and fuck?"

I curled a strand of hair around my finger, my body lit up with nerves and anticipation. "What if I was?"

23

LAURENT HELD OUT HIS HAND, HIS EYES DANCING, and I placed my palm in his. He pressed a kiss to the inside of my wrist, his teeth grazing over the sensitive skin, his eyes two luminous green orbs locked on mine.

Between the faint rasp on my wrist and the intensity of his look like nothing short of the apocalypse was going to stop this from happening, my nipples hardened. I nudged the door closed with my hip and he unfurled a lazy grin.

Threading his fingers through mine, he tugged me through his living room toward the back hallway. Breathless, I lost my sandals in the journey.

Boo scampered over to greet me, but when I stopped to scratch the kitten behind her ears, because this had all gotten very real, Laurent gave a frustrated growl that made me laugh, the last of my nerves blowing away.

He led me into his bedroom, lit by the lamp on his bedside table, and stopped.

I glanced around, wondering if there was a mess he wanted to hurriedly clean up, but the room was sparse, devoid of anything personal including strewn clothing.

Happily, it smelled like cedar because I'd grown to love that scent.

Laurent ran his thumb over the back of my hand. "It's nothing special, I know." He paused, lowering his voice to almost a murmur. "I haven't done this in a while."

I lay my free hand on his cheek, charmed by his shy admission. "Neither have I." He nuzzled into my hand, and I was swamped with a wave of tenderness.

"Bien. We shall stumble through together. Come." He crawled onto his dusky blue sheets and patted the bed.

I stretched out next to Laurent on my side, watching his lids fall closed. He brushed my face with his nose, inhaling then sighing contentedly. My stomach tightened and I closed my eyes as well, skimming my lips over his. Part of me wanted him to shove me up against a wall so I could climb him like a freaking monkey, but there was something delicious in these hesitant, light kisses, as delicate as butterfly wings.

Laurent kissed across the top of my cheek and I squirmed. "What are you doing?"

"Your freckles are darker now." He gazed at them in fascination.

"Because they're my sun freckles." I tilted my face up to allow his continued kisses, twisting his curls around my fingers and gently releasing them. He hadn't even touched me yet and I was melting, becoming a limbless puddle of molasses.

"Nope. They're your star freckles."

I repressed a shudder. "That's incredibly sweet but I'm not sure stars and I have the best relationship," I said in a testier voice than I intended.

"You're wrong. Cygnus." He pressed his mouth to one high on my cheekbone. "Lyra." He dragged his lips to the next one.

"Are you naming my freckles after constellations?"

"Oui." He pressed his lips to a freckle on the bridge of my nose then grinned. "Because you're made of stars, Miriam. Summer starlight after a cold, dark winter."

And just like that he'd made me breathless again. The thumping of my heart was a warning that our "just sex" had become far more dangerous, but if I was made of stars, this self-destructive, grumpy, French wolf shifter was the moon that I wanted to soar around.

Did Laurent feel like there was more here than friends enjoying each other? I was torn between wanting to ask and not wanting to hear the answer, whatever it was, because any reply would have ramifications that I wasn't sure I could deal with.

"You charmer." I half-assed it, waiting to see if he'd grow serious or brush off his words as teasing.

He laughed. "I am French."

Right. I shoved away the hollow disappointment that jolted through me. I'd walked into tonight with my eyes wide open, so I could suck up the fact that this was exactly what it appeared to be and nothing more.

I forced myself to keep my tone light. "You owe me a name for that last freckle you kissed."

He held up his fingers over my nose like he was framing a picture and narrowed his eyes. "Cassiopeia." He dragged the word out, his low voice shivering through me.

I fluttered a hand in front of my face. "You have the best dirty talk, Huff 'n' Puff."

"Book learned, remember?" He peered at me delightedly, resting his hand on my hip, and flexed his bare foot against mine.

That tiny intimate action of his toes pressing into the sole of my foot sent a jolt of desire spiraling through me. I leaned closer, framing his face in my hands, and kissed him.

Laurent flexed his fingers, the motion bunching the fabric of my dress. He changed the angle of our mouths, his tongue finding mine, and I clasped the back of his neck, throwing my leg over his hip and falling pliant against him.

In response, he wedged his knee between my legs, pressing his firm body close, and I moaned, rocking against his hard cock. I was dizzy with wanting him, keeping one hand on his shoulder to anchor myself. He slid his hand along my thigh and pushed my underwear to the side, sliding a finger inside me.

My head fell back, and I saw white behind my closed eyelids as sparks crackled in my blood.

Feeling how wet I'd become at his touch, he chuckled softly and sucked on the skin under my jaw for just long enough that pleasure almost crossed the line into pain, but he pulled back just in time, laving the spot with his tongue. I relished the burn his mark had left and the heat and press of his long frame.

Teasingly, achingly slowly he stroked me, his mouth making up for it in hungry kisses. He came up for air long enough to roll me on top of him. Eyes hazy, he parted his dark, wet lips. "J'ai envie de toi," he said in a husky voice and crashed his lips back to mine.

He could have just said he'd forgotten to pay his phone bill. Didn't matter. Just say it in French. I mapped the planes of his chest with my hands, drifting lower and lower until I flicked open the snap of his jeans.

He kicked his pants and underwear off while fumbling at my dress.

"It unties," I said, helping him.

"Next time wear something that slips off."

"Uh-huh," I squeaked, because he'd sucked one breast into his mouth, kneading the other one with very talented fingers.

If I could drown in an inch of water, could I drown in sensation? What would that look like?

"Stop thinking," he growled, lightly tapping my head.

I gave him a saucy smile. "Make me."

Laurent flipped me onto my back, pushing my dress off my shoulders while reaching under me to unclasp my bra, which he flung away. He straddled my legs, totally nude, his erection jutting out, and surveyed my body with a greedy look.

Feeling powerful and beautiful, I braced myself up on my elbows and sucked him into my mouth.

A groan tore from his lips, his eyes laser beams watching me. I grabbed his ass cheek, which flexed, and pulled him deeper.

Laurent allowed it for a few moments, his strong fingers threaded into my hair, then withdrew with a shake of his head. "I won't last." He leaned over and removed a condom from the bedside table but paused before ripping it open. "Keep touching yourself." He placed my hand on my clit, starting the motion.

My cheeks flamed but I no longer knew if it was embarrassment or because I was burning up from the inside. My chest rose and fell in ragged breaths as I stroked myself, watching Laurent rip off the foil and roll the condom on.

He stretched out on top of me, my soft curves fitting to his hard ridges, pinned my free hand to the mattress above my head, and thrust inside, going still as if to absorb the moment.

I sucked in a breath.

His eyes, when they found mine, were clouded by a thread of concern. "Yes? Good?"

"Only if you fuck me right now," I said through gritted teeth. I teetered on the brink of losing myself and I wanted desperately to fall.

He smirked.

"That's not the correct response." I bucked underneath him a couple of times. "Have you forgotten how it's done?"

His eyes flashed, which sent me closer to exploding all the

coiled desire inside me. "Are you taunting me?" he asked in a dangerous voice.

I scraped my teeth up his neck, before biting down on his earlobe. "Yes," I whispered.

He snapped his hips, the force of his movement smacking the headboard against the wall. "Is this how you like it?" he purred. "Me fucking you into the mattress?"

I scrabbled at his shoulders, feeling my pulse everywhere our bodies connected. "Yes."

Laurent lapsed into French and that sent me flying. My orgasm tore through me, Laurent following a moment later.

We lay there, his body still on top of mine and our foreheads pressed together. The hot air was heavy with the musky, salty smells of sex and sweat. He carefully got off me and headed into his bathroom where the water turned on.

I flung my arm over my eyes, unable to move, and quaking with aftershocks that I wasn't certain were all physical, but before I could think too hard about that, a fan hummed on, cool air sweeping the room in waves. I scooted over on the bed to catch more of the breeze.

The bed depressed with Laurent's weight. "Do you want to clean up in the bathroom?"

Was that a hint? I opened my eyes. He didn't look especially impatient, but he was slipping on a fresh pair of boxer shorts. "Sure," I said with a brightness I didn't feel.

"I set out a towel for you."

Nodding, I headed into the bathroom, and gave myself a quick wipe down. My hair was a mess of snarled curls and my mascara had slipped into raccoon mode. Wonderful. I fixed both the best I could with water and my fingers.

I didn't care if he wanted me to go since I hadn't intended to stay over, but I was scared that if we kept having sex his gravitational pull would be too strong to resist, and I'd be consumed. The smart thing would be to stop this now before I got in too deep.

Decision made, I reached for the doorknob.

Delilah jumped up to block me, her arms crossed, almost scaring the shit out of me.

"Oh no," I said quietly, so Laurent didn't hear me talking to myself. "You are *not* becoming some manifestation of my deepest desires. Move."

She cocked her hip. Seriously? I willed her to disappear. This should have been simple since I was the one in charge.

In theory.

She fought me. Or one side of me fought another side.

I stepped back, scrubbing a hand over my face. *Damn you and your analogies, Yoshi.*

How badly would I scare Laurent if I asked for more? Even if more was a simple date?

"Give me time," I whispered.

After a long moment, she fell back into being a normal shadow once more.

I threw open the bathroom door and strode back into his bedroom.

Laurent lay on his side, one arm stretched out under his pillow. He gave me a sleepy smile that disappeared as I picked up my clothes. "You're leaving?"

"Yeah. I need to go." I turned away, but he caught my hand.

"Stay and talk to me. Tell me about your day." His voice was warm and low, infused with intimacy.

I blinked rapidly, then pressed my hand against his forehead. "You want an update on the few hours since I last saw you? Do you need a healer? Is this a deathbed thing? Shit, am I going to have to find someone else to have sex—" I yelped, laughing and tumbling onto the other side of Laurent because he'd yanked me down.

I smacked him with the pillow, but he hauled me into the crook of his arm.

His fingers ghosted along the back of my neck, making

every tiny hair stand up.

I brushed his curls out of his eyes so he could see me stick out my tongue. Not because I wanted to watch his dark lashes sweep against his olive skin as his lids fell closed, making him look much younger.

Boo raced in and jumped up on top of Laurent, settling against his hip.

"No claws," he admonished with a wince. But he didn't move her.

Soothing as it was to lie here, there wasn't much to tell him since I couldn't talk about Giselle. Even if I could, it was much nicer to quietly snuggle, listening to his breathing deepen and slow, than discuss demons.

I did, however, have one question before Laurent fell totally asleep. "Can you think of anyone to ask about the Ascendant?"

"Just Tatiana," he murmured.

"I don't want to wait until she gets back. I'd been thinking Poe because ravens and shiny things. They might have heard of the Ascendant, but it's not an option."

"Why not?" He yawned.

I shrugged and he nudged me, his eyes still closed. Learning about raven shifters bringing things into existence was going to undo all his lovely relaxation, plus I really didn't want to tell him. But he nudged me again, so I mumbled what Jude had told me, hoping he was half-asleep and didn't really hear me.

His eyes snapped open, clear and fully awake. "Are you fucking kidding me?"

Boo jumped off Laurent and crawled onto the pillow above my head. I reached up to scratch her, flopping onto my back.

"Spare me the 'I told you so.'"

I turned my head to find a hurt expression on his face. "I wasn't going to say that."

"Please," I scoffed. "It's your new favorite pastime."

"Second-favorite," he said with a wolfish grin.

"Not the time for jokes," I snapped, sitting up.

"Miriam," he said gravely, "you're not the only one who's gotten mixed up in one of their games. I didn't know about the consequences until now, and I'm certainly not going to condemn you for something I, myself, was foolish enough to partake in. We'll find someone else to ask. If you want me involved," he added.

Dealing with McMurtry, revealing the job my parents had been on, the investigations into my past, they all felt like something I should do on my own. Or maybe I was simply scared to tangle this last piece of my life up with him before our status was clarified. If he wasn't interested in taking things further, then I had to start pulling back. I shrugged sulkily.

"Ask Harry." There was no judgment in his voice about me not agreeing to his participation.

"Harry's out of town. Giulia's filling in." I gnawed on the inside of my cheek. It would be smart to have Laurent by my side for any return visit to the temperamental cat gargoyle. "Would you come with me to see her?"

He yawned, a tiny crease appearing between his brows. "Now?"

"No time like the present." I slid off the bed and stepped into my underwear. I'd been getting too cozy and I should have gone home immediately. This wasn't a sleepover relationship. But once I was on the bed, it would have been weird to bolt. This was the perfect way out.

We dressed in silence. Laurent still looked sleepy, but he was accompanying me. I slipped into my wrap dress. For all his protests and belief that his priority was killing dybbuks, Laurent was always there for the few people he gave a damn about. This wasn't special behavior just for me.

I fastened the ties on the dress. By his own admission,

Laurent hadn't had sex with anyone in a while. I was thrilled that he'd broken that dry streak with me, but did the fact that he'd gotten physically intimate with me mean he was open to something beyond sex?

The only relationship that had ever mattered was the one with Eli. When I met Ben, I thought he had the most potential since my divorce, but dybbuk possession and dating didn't mesh, and that dream died a swift death. However, the thought of being with Ben was like strolling through a beautiful garden on a sunny day. It would be lovely and cheery and orderly.

A relationship with Laurent would be like learning I could safely hold fire. That I'd been given the gift of cradling this mesmerizing wild element. If anyone else tried it, the flames would devour them, but I kept its destructive nature in check.

The thought was exciting and exhausting in equal measure. Had I been in my twenties, I'd have gone for it without a second thought, but as much as I wanted to broach the topic with him, I'd want to take things slow. The gentle flicker of a candle, not the roar of a bonfire. And slow wasn't exactly his favorite speed.

Laurent didn't say much as we headed out, though he scowled when I insisted on taking my car.

"Please?" I batted my lashes. Given the thoughts in my head, I wanted to be in control of something, even if it was as small as driving during this information quest.

He rolled his eyes but got into the car without comment. However, just before I released the emergency brake, he hauled me against him, kissing me for one bright, ferocious moment before releasing me mindwhacked and tempted to climb back into bed with him.

"Allons-y," he said with an innocent smile and closed his eyes.

"Bastard," I muttered to his low chuckle, and off we went into the night, following a star.

24

GIULIA MAY HAVE HAD A CAT FORM, BUT SHE WAS A gargoyle, and they weren't exactly known for their acute sense of smell. How was I supposed to know she had super powerful feline scenting abilities that would immediately detect that Laurent and I had just had sex?

I, pinned underneath her, felt this was very unfair.

Saliva dripped off her canines and onto my dress as she strained against Laurent's chokehold, attempting to rip out my throat.

Her attack had taken me so by surprise that I hadn't had time to cloak. One second Laurent had whistled for her to jump down from the condo tower roof and join us on the sidewalk, the next she had me on my back, her claws tearing into my limbs.

Cloaking at this point was pointless and my weapon couldn't be manifested for a gargoyle. I'd have summoned Delilah, but honestly, shock and sheer terror had immobilized me as much as the cat.

I had a boulder with teeth on top of me trying to kill me.

"Giulia, stop!" Laurent said.

"You're mine!" she howled and headbutted the love of her life.

I gasped, hearing the thud.

Laurent swore but didn't let go, still wrestling her off me, despite the blood trickling down from his eyebrow.

"Hey, rocks for brains." I counterattacked as best I could, but she didn't budge. "You could have killed him. Love's not supposed to hurt." Even if I had hours of training under my belt, the only thing kicking or punching her would get me was broken digits.

She dug her claws deeper into my skin, a hot, searing pain tearing through my arms, and I bit down on a scream.

Laurent torqued her head to the side. "Release Miriam or I'll never speak to you again."

Giulia stiffened, her brows drawing together with a shocked, deeply pained look, then she bucked him off and tossed her head. "You can't stay mad at me, amore mio."

I flinched at how hard Laurent's shoulder hit a lamppost.

Her stone eyes darkened to fathomless pits. "I'm going to enjoy killing you," she hissed at me.

Every time I'd faced death, I'd fought back, but there was something so exhausting about this situation. I hadn't reclaimed my power to be murdered over a man, and yet I'd landed myself here nonetheless. A ridiculous, lethal catfight. She wasn't a vampire or a demon, and as much as I wanted to live, I didn't want it to be at the expense of her life.

Laurent woozily stumbled to his feet.

Begging wouldn't sway Giulia. I couldn't overpower her, not even with Delilah, and I wasn't going to depend on Laurent to save me. Yes, I had magic, but why was that my default? I'd lived as a Sapien for most of my life, depending on my intelligence to carry me through. Fighting would solve nothing. We needed to talk.

"He used me, okay?" I infused as much bitterness into my voice as possible.

"What?" Laurent said in a dangerous voice.

"God, just shut up already. Haven't you hurt me enough?" I prayed he clued into my plan. "You think he's capable of returning your love? He's not."

The gargoyle pressed her face so close to mine that the stone swirls of her "fur" pressed into my forehead. "He does love me."

"Wake up, Giulia. He doesn't love anyone or anything except his precious calling."

She swung her heavy stone head to him.

Laurent paused, his eyes flicking to me for a brief second before he laughed cruelly. "Here we go with the theatrics," he said. "Human or gargoyle, you women are alike, believing we're in some fairy tale and that you'll get a happily ever after. We're not."

His voice was so harsh that it was my turn to remember we were playacting.

Still, I sucked in a breath like his words had flayed me. "He used me to scratch an itch and he uses you to help him find dybbuks," I said. "I thought it was more, that we had something special, but when I asked him to go on a date with me, he laughed." It didn't matter that this hadn't really happened. My fear that it could made my voice pinch tight in hurt.

The gargoyle loosened her hold. It wasn't enough for me to get free, but her claws flexed against my skin instead of shredding it. "I'm going to kill *him*."

"No!" I grabbed her forelegs. "He's not worth it. Believe me. Don't waste more time on him. You deserve someone who wants you back."

I struggled to drag in a breath because she was crushing me, but she was also silent and still, processing what I'd said.

Giulia dipped her head close, and I tensed for the bite of her fangs, but her raspy tongue swiped over my wounds, healing them. She pounced off me and I carefully sat up. "Miriam is right. You're incapable of love."

Laurent flinched almost imperceptibly, but he shrugged as if he didn't care. "I don't have time for that bullshit."

"Let me guess," she sneered. "You came tonight because you want help finding a dybbuk. Always with the dybbuks."

"No," Laurent said. "Not a dybbuk. It's—"

"Basta!" She made a slicing motion with a paw. "No more."

She crouched, about to spring back to the rooftop, but at my cry of "Wait" looked at me. This proud, strong gargoyle looked shattered enough that one gust of wind could knock her over. I'd done that. I could justify my actions all I wanted —that I was defending myself, that her obsession with Laurent was entirely unrealistic and one-sided—but I'd destroyed her hope.

For all of Giulia's deadly nature, she had this innocent dream where she and Laurent could find love, and I'd taken that from her. Not to mention that I'd lied to her when I'd last visited, pretending to be an ally when I wanted him for myself. I'd never thought I'd be that woman and I didn't like that side of myself.

I made a lot of big pronouncements about the importance of truth but when push came to shove, I hadn't walked the walk.

I crouched down next to her. "Will you be all right?"

She gazed up at me haughtily. "Certo."

"Still, I'm sorry," I said softly.

She glanced back at Laurent, and when her eyes once more met mine, they were cloudy with the sorrow of stripped innocence—or maybe the heavy burden of knowledge.

I rubbed my arms.

Giulia nudged me gently under the chin with the top of her head. "We both know he's worth it, bella," she said quietly. "But it doesn't make what you said any less true."

With that, she pivoted sharply and in one fluid leap, soared high overhead back to the roof, watching the city.

Laurent and I walked back to the car in silence.

"I'll take you home," I said once I'd strapped in. "I can wait until either Harry or Tatiana get back to ask about the Ascendant."

"Miriam." He paused.

It took me two attempts to fit my key in the ignition. "She really would have killed me."

He didn't deny it. In fact, he didn't say anything. Was he angry? I felt too hollowed out to do more than utter a perfunctory apology. "I'm sorry if I ruined things between you and Giulia."

"She'll come around." He shook his head, clicking in his seat belt. "It's not that."

"Then what?" I checked my side mirror and pulled out of the parking spot, heading back to Hotel Terminus.

Block after block I waited for him to speak up.

"Say something," I said. "You're making me nervous."

"Asking me on a date. You just said that as part of the act, right?"

My stomach twisted because I didn't know how to answer. Should I give him the truth now and expose myself or lie? I mentally slapped myself upside the head. How quickly I was ready to lie again. *Come on, Feldman, have a shred of backbone.*

"You don't want that, do you?" He twisted in his seat so he could lean toward me. There was no hopeful lilt in his voice, more a tense strain. "A date would be—"

I forced a tinkly laugh. "Right? Can you imagine? What would we do, fit in some intimate little restaurant with checkered tablecloths between vampire kills? Go for a long walk on the beach at dawn?" I made a buzzer noise. "Not during the Danger Zone. I've already had one date end with dybbuk possession. I'm good, thanks."

The stoplight turned yellow, and I slowed to a stop.

"Yes." He jabbed a finger at me. "It would all be so..." A streetlight illuminated a ferocious expression on his face.

My breath caught, a thousand possibilities playing out in that pause.

"So..." A frown creased his brow and he slumped against the seat, almost in surrender. "Ridiculous," he said softly. "Good," he said more firmly.

I caught my hand before I rubbed my heart.

The second the light went green, I hit the gas, leaving what could have been behind in a plume of exhaust.

I was an adult capable of having sex without becoming a giddy puddle of feelings. I'd done it before. Admittedly, my deepening friendship with Laurent made it harder for me to separate out those emotions, but if I wanted the sex to continue, and I did, then it was on me to keep those sides separate.

I forced a smile, my hands tightening on the wheel. "Excellent. We're agreed. Though if you tell me that our friends-with-benefits arrangement is over, I might have a thing or two to say about it."

Laurent relaxed. "That's not ending any time soon."

Great. That was great. I mean, I was still fifty-fifty on even wanting a relationship with the guy. Sixty-forty. At least thirty percent in doubt. This way, I kept getting fantastic sex, and who knew? He might get over his issues and realize what we had going was more than friends with benefits. Meantime, I got to take things slow. Very slow.

I pulled up to the curb at his place, not bothering to cut the engine. "Thanks for coming with me to Giulia."

When my bright smile didn't waver under his keen stare, he nodded. "Sure. Tatiana gets back tomorrow."

"That's right."

The awkward silence would normally have made me turn away or dig into my purse with some flimsy excuse, but I just sat there, smiling at him, and he broke our stare first, releasing his seat belt with a click.

"Good night." He leaned in like he was going to kiss me.

I hesitated a second, then did the same.

Except, he'd stopped at my hesitation, so I followed suit, right when he'd moved in again. He hit my cheek with his nose and sighed.

"Good night!" I flashed him a thumbs-up, holding that moronic pose until he'd gotten out and headed down the sidewalk without a look back. Then I dropped my head against the wheel.

So much for my afterglow.

Bright and early Thursday morning, I headed to New York to break the news to Giselle, since there was no point tossing and turning in bed, pretending to sleep. I didn't give her a heads-up that I was coming in case the demon was monitoring either of us now.

When I stepped through the shadows into the Kefitzat Haderech, I begged Pyotr to let me talk to the neon sign. He finally agreed after I promised to bring him BBQ chicken and cornbread to try, just like they ate in the *Fast and Furious* movies.

Once the sign had turned on, I gave it my most charming smile. "Hear me out before you decide, okay?"

It flashed me its skeptical face.

"Great," I said. "I know this is a Banim Shovavim space, but I've got an Ohrist under a demon illusion. This demon may be monitoring her, and I need to discuss breaking his spell. Would it be possible to bring her in here for five—"

I was blown backward through the shadows and into my living room, knocking my potted orchid over, dirt scattering on the floor. Rubbing my shoulder, I returned to the KH.

"You made your point," I said to the sign. "I won't ask again."

Pyotr sighed like he was disappointed and wouldn't let me

take the cute pink baby sock with the lacy ribbon. He stuck me with six dingy stretched-out sports socks that smelled vaguely of mold.

Gross. I rolled them into a giant ball. "Do you know of anywhere in New York that's warded and would be safe from prying demon eyes?"

Pyotr raised his hand, looking to the sign for permission to speak. The sign face nodded. "There is pizza place in Midtown. Entire building was warded by former owners. Now only pizza store is safe but owned by Sapiens." He gave me the address.

"You've earned yourself a double order of cornbread, my friend."

Pyotr beamed.

I emerged outside the ballet company cloaked, remaining hidden while I tracked Giselle down. I finally caught her coming out of class and whispered in her ear, "Psst. It's me, Miri. I need to speak with you, but we can't do it here."

After her initial flustered jump, which she covered by pretending she had a rock in her shoe, she listened to the address and then called out to another dancer. "How long is break, Franny? *Twenty minutes?*" She emphasized the time.

"No, you're not back for two hours," the other dancer replied.

"See you in twenty," I whispered and left.

It took me fifteen minutes to get to the pizza place. I'd expected something more than a hole in the wall with two tables and a large air-conditioning unit that barely stirred the muggy air, but the place smelled delicious. I bought a slice of pepperoni that glistened with beautiful oily cheese and grabbed the table away from the window.

Giselle arrived moments later, looking longingly at the pizza before buying a diet soda. She sat down across from me and popped the tab. "What's with all the cloak and dagger stuff?"

I wiped a string of mozzarella off my mouth. "I found your sister. She's physically unharmed, but she has no idea who she is." I paused to let Giselle take this in because she'd gone pale. Paler than normal.

She nodded for me to continue.

"The thing is," I said, "she's not just a sibling, she's your twin and—"

Giselle jumped up. "What? You have to take me to her."

The employee behind the counter looked up from his phone, but not finding anything interesting, ignored us.

I put my hand on her arm. "Sit. Please. It's not that simple. The demon who cast this illusion has convinced her she's his fiancée, but the illusion isn't seamless and she's plagued with these episodes where she thinks she's supposed to be a dancer."

Giselle gasped. "He's doing this to both of us."

"Yes. Now, if we kill him, the magic will be broken, but that could take a while. The other way is that we undo the illusion one person at a time, starting with you. You'd have to come with me to see some people who specialize in this."

"Of course, anything."

I ate some more pizza to buy time before dropping the biggest bombshell, but there was no easy way to spring it on her. "There's something else that I've verified. She isn't Rory," I said gently. "You are."

Giselle simply stared at me, her mouth opening and closing. Finally, she took a sip of pop and cleared her throat. "Excuse me?"

"You're Aurora." I pulled up the email that I received from the administrator of the twins' dance studio and slid the photo over.

She looked at it without comment then pushed my phone away. "Why does the ballet company think I'm Giselle?"

I twisted my napkin, really wishing she hadn't asked me that question. "Apparently you wanted your sister's life."

"And I got it?" She looked out at the passing traffic, a host of emotions flickering over her face. "When?"

I glanced down at my lap with a sigh. "Right after the real Giselle got into the company."

"Why didn't I as well? Did I fail the audition?"

I hesitated.

"I wasn't invited, was I?" Her face crumpled. "Was I not as good as her? I don't pick up things as easily as some dancers, it's true, but I work really hard."

Just like the woman at the dance school had said. Rory always worked hard where everything came naturally to Giselle, but Rory had been deemed the lesser dancer because of it. I'd seen this in school and work settings too, where effort and tenacity weren't valued as highly as ease. It was a damn shame, especially here.

"According to an old instructor, you were just as good," I said. "Everything you've achieved has been because of you."

"Then why didn't I get my own audition?"

I looked away from the pain in her eyes.

"I wasn't pushed into the same track as my sister, was I?" Laughing bitterly, she shoved her drink away so violently that dark sticky soda sloshed over the rim to splash on the cheap laminate table. "I know how the dance world works. If I didn't have a teacher in my corner in the early days or a mother who—" She let out a soft gasp.

"Your mom was wrong about you," I said. "You can't let the opinion that talent overrides hard work rule your life. You did this on your own."

But maybe I didn't believe in that statement as much as I needed to, and maybe Giselle caught wind of the lie.

She toyed with the "G" pendant on her necklace then closed her fist around it. "Thank you for all your help."

"We're not finished yet."

"Yes, we are." She stood up, but I grabbed her arm.

The employee once more looked over but when I glared at him, he sulkily wandered back into the kitchen.

"You're going to let your sister, the real Giselle, remain in that hell? And what about you? That feeling like your life switched tracks? The itch in your brain?"

Giselle wrenched out of my grasp and leaned forward with a snarl. "I love being a dancer and I'm not giving it up."

"No one is saying you have to."

"You think my sister is going to let me keep dancing with the company in her name? Or that anyone else would want me when word gets out that I'm a fraud?"

My indignation seeped away. I'd held the truth up as some paragon of absoluteness, but truth was a many-layered prism, reflecting different aspects depending on how you viewed it.

Watching this distraught young woman pierced by the truth of her actions and grappling with her world crashing down, I questioned what I'd unearthed. I'd sought the truth in this case for its healing nature, but all I'd done was destroy.

"I know it's not simple," I said, "but the two of you need to return to your real lives."

"Why? According to whom?"

I opened my mouth and then shut it. I didn't get to be the final authority on the twins, but keeping the illusion up wasn't right. "Do you want to live a lie?"

"There's no other way for me to live. Wake up. My sister can't just pick up where she left off. She hasn't danced in three years." She braced her hands on the table, her head bowed, before raising glistening eyes to mine. "Her career is over."

I blinked and sat back slowly. I hadn't considered that. Gigi would return to the death of a dream she'd trained for her entire life, not to mention the mental trauma when she realized what had happened to her.

Giselle shook off her sorrow, her voice hard. "You under-stand now? The only thing to do is keep everything as it is."

"Do you feel any remorse at all?" I said dully. "You ruined her life."

She flinched, then crossed her arms. "What's done is done."

"But—"

"*No.*" There was a wild desperation on her face like a cornered animal. "You did what I asked and I got my answers. It's over." She strode out of the pizza place, her back ramrod straight and her head held high.

I stared vacantly out the window, my faith in humanity destroyed. Giselle had all the facts and yet she was deter-mined to cling to this illusion. No wonder the demon hadn't bothered to hide his work from me. The people he dealt with didn't want these false realities broken.

Where did my responsibility end? Tatiana would say that I'd done what the client wanted and now I should walk away, but how was I supposed to leave Gigi with Edvin? She was a trophy piece for a demon. What happened when he got bored of her? Would she be consigned to some physical torment to go with the mental one she was living?

But would returning Gigi to her "true" life be worse than what she suffered now? She thought being a dancer was a delusion she suffered from. How much harder would it be to know that her own twin had stolen everything from her?

To cap off this awesome meeting, Nav called to find out if the plan was to go for the demon first or the victims?

I lied and said I hadn't met with the client yet and would get back to him shortly.

"Please don't rush to help these poor women on my account. Take your time," he said snidely and hung up.

I dragged myself back to the KH. I wasn't in the mood to watch Pyotr taste his chicken and cornbread, but his excitement at seeing the food broke through my despondency a bit, so I stuck around long enough for him to try his first bites.

He made a face like a cat hacking up a hairball when he tried the chicken, then he fluttered his wings wildly and pounded a fist on the table.

"Do you like it or not?" I said.

"Is terrible! But now I can say 'tastes like chicken'!"

The cornbread was more of a hit so I left him happily munching on that as I marched through the gloomy KH and out the door into my home.

I longed to hide under the covers. I couldn't fix this situation, only figure out what the least shitty option was. What side should take precedence here? Respecting my client's wishes that I leave this alone? Killing Edvin despite the cost to the twins to keep him from doing this to anyone else? Killing Edvin to keep him from coming after Sadie?

If Giselle didn't want me to move forward with this, did I even have that right? And how could I subject Sadie to danger when I was doing it against the wishes of one of the main parties involved?

Would I be better off working for an organization like Carpe Demon if that was an option rather than for Tatiana? People whose morals, for the most part, aligned with mine? At least that bunch was fighting on behalf of humanity. Tatiana was in it for a paycheck, morals be damned.

Would my choices be easier to make if I had a calling like Nav with demons or Laurent with dybbuks?

My turbulent thoughts were interrupted by a notification from Emmett that Tatiana's flight had been delayed until tomorrow.

At least I could put off seeing my employer's smirk when she heard about the outcome of the case. Determined that this day not be a total bust, I called the Bear's Den, relieved that Harry was back.

The gargoyle had never heard of the Ascendant, and his

first suggestion was to ask Tatiana. At this point, I would have, were I not facing a smug "I told you so" from her because of our case. Unfortunately, his second suggestion was to go see Poe. That was out for obvious reasons, and I hung up, feeling dejected.

Then I got to thinking. The danger with raven shifters was in playing games that would give them information they then manifested into reality. Was there some way to engage with Poe to extract facts, neutral information, without any games involved? After all, they owed me for sending me off in the Succubus, knowing I could have been killed.

My determination hardened. Poe was going to pay up—or else.

25

I DIDN'T OVERESTIMATE HOW SCARY I WAS, NOR WAS I a total fool. Since Laurent had offered, I invited him to come with me to find Poe and be my backup. I hoped that having a mission he disapproved of would fill our drive time with sniping and make this first "you don't want to date me" encounter less awkward.

Was him staring impassively at my in-person request before napping for the entire drive less awkward? Hard to say.

I headed into Stanley Park, concentrating on accessing the hidden version under the stone bridge. Once we came through into the Park, I pulled over and shook Laurent awake. "How do you propose to find Poe? This place is massive and if you try to sniff out every raven, we could be here for hours."

He unbuckled his seat belt and rolled down his window. A breeze rolled off Burrard Inlet to whisper through the towering firs. "Bird shifters tend to congregate so there will be a much stronger scent concentrated in one place." He grabbed the hem of his shirt, then paused and opened the door. "I'll shift in the forest and come back."

Awkward status fully engaged.

"I told you that the dating thing was part of the act," I said testily. "So, unless you're having second thoughts about us sleeping together—"

"No."

"Then what's with the sudden modesty?"

Shutting the door partway, he rubbed his thumb over a knuckle. "I haven't gotten close to anyone like I have with you in a long time," he said, slowly feeling his way through the sentence.

I tensed, braced for the "it's not you, it's me" speech.

"Our friendship is easy," Laurent said. I snorted and he gave me a wry smile. "Okay, not easy, but you know what I mean. It's easy to talk to you."

It was on the tip of my tongue to point out that dating didn't mean we'd talk less, but I kept quiet because a tiny frown furrowed between his brows. He was struggling to find his words, and whatever he wanted to say wasn't some glib brush-off speech.

When he looked at me again, there was an almost pointed earnestness to his gaze. "I want to make sure you're not mad and we're okay, because I haven't had anything like this"—he pointed between us—"in a long time."

That's when a couple things hit me. This wasn't the first time in our friendship that he'd mentioned us being okay; it wasn't even the first time since he'd returned from Paris. Also, Laurent was hardly Mr. Chatty, so why this fixation with talking to me?

This wasn't some friendzone move; it was about his parents. About years of them not speaking about the past and a father with whom Laurent didn't even want to converse.

Maybe this was as close as he could get to acknowledging that what we had was special without choking up. What would change other than a label if we did start dating?

Neither of us was sleeping with anyone else, and we could address that bridge if we came to it.

I had my family, good friends, and my magic, in addition to whatever this was with Laurent. All of which made me happy.

"We're okay," I said, infusing every ounce of sincerity into my voice, because it was true. For now. Then I leered at him. "Take off your shirt."

That earned me a very thorough kiss and a striptease reveal of his delectable chest, before he kicked off his shoes and jogged into the forest to shift.

Playtime was over. I had to get my head in the game to face Poe. Jake's drawings were in my purse, but I wasn't handing over even a scrap of information about myself. Not one single fact.

The white wolf returned in no time, hopping deftly into the back seat. I shut the door for him then drove slowly along the dirt lanes that followed old bison hunting trails taken by the Indigenous people centuries before.

Laurent's furry head lolled out the window, but about two-thirds of the way around the Park, he barked softly.

I parked at the side of the road and followed him into the forest.

He stalked silently through the trees, moving slowly so I could keep up over the uneven ground. I wasn't scared of being attacked, thanks to the wolf and my ability to cloak, but if we got separated, I'd never find my way out.

I brushed a hand across a pine tree, my fingers hitting sticky needles. Buzzing mosquitos and the distant sound of lapping water provided a soothing melody for our journey.

A bird called out with a deep, throaty *kraa*.

I looked up at the raven on a branch, watching our progress. "Is Poe around?"

The bird scratched its body with its beak, unresponsive.

Laurent had paused to see what the raven did, but now

resumed his trek.

A few minutes later, we stepped into a bit of a clearing. The sky darkened and the forest turned gloomy. Shivering, I glanced up to gauge how long before the cloud passed.

It wasn't a cloud, but a cloak of black, winging across the sky.

I edged up to the wolf, who was snarling, hanging on to his fur for reassurance as the cloak swept overhead then scattered. Dozens of ravens settled themselves on branches, their beady eyes fixated on us.

My mouth was dry and my heart clattered against my ribs, the sound deafening in the unnaturally still woods.

The wolf growled, his ears flattening.

Despite the hairs on the back of my neck standing on end thanks to all the cold, dead eyes trained our way, I cocked a hand on my hip. "While I appreciate the Hitchcock homage, you're not going to scare us off that easily."

Big words from the woman barely holding her bladder in check.

"I want Poe," I said. "Now."

"You've got me."

I cough-choked, startled by the soft voice from behind.

Poe sat on a stump, their hands in their lap, watching me with a look of mild disinterest.

My partner prowled toward the raven shifter, his canines looking particularly sharp.

I waved a hand at the bird-laden branches. "More games?"

"No, just a little ambience."

"Wonderful. Now that the scene is set, I'm going to ask you a question and you're going to answer honestly. It'll be fun."

"That doesn't sound fun." Poe flapped a ruffled wrist in dismissal.

Laurent lunged and knocked the bird shifter off their perch.

The other ravens shook their wings in agitation.

Poe pecked at the wolf with the razor-sharp beak they had morphed, attempting to beat the animal with one wing, but Laurent dodged the attacks and pinned Poe to the ground.

A sensation of feathers scratched along my back, a sharp threat rather than a velvet caress. The raven shifter had pushed me too far, and this warning only served to harden my resolve to get the answer I'd come for.

"I should have clarified," I said. "The fun part is that if you don't, Laurent will play his own game with you, right now. And I don't like your odds."

The harder Poe fought to get free, the more bored the wolf looked as he added yet more weight to restrain his captive.

Poe cawed in distress, the other ravens answering as one. Their collective call bounced off the trees, making my flesh crawl.

"Enough!" My cry shocked them back into a still silence.

One wrong move and it felt like the air itself might draw blood, but I had shadows in my veins. I was the nightmare relishing her time in the sun.

"You stole my blood to put your augury into motion." Poe blinked in surprise at my growled words. "Yeah, I know all about you ravens. I also know you sent me on the Succubus expecting I'd be killed and sparing you any consequences. But now it's my turn to collect." I held up the token I'd won from the raven shifter, sunlight glinting off the silver disc. "I either trade you this for a question." I flipped the disc up in the air and caught it. "Or, well…"

I nodded at the wolf, who slowly and thoroughly ripped Poe's sleeve with a claw, drawing a thin line of blood along their one still-human arm.

Laurent and I really did have a special relationship.

"Get him off me first," Poe croaked out.

Laurent looked for my agreement before stepping back.

Poe sat up with a wince, brushing dirt off themselves, all

their features now human. "A one-time trade. The token for an answer. No games."

"Give me your promise on that, and that you'll answer honestly," I said. Yoshi had said a promise was a bond. Tatiana treated it like it was, as did the vamps.

"I promise. To all of it." They glared at Laurent. "Happy?"

The wolf sat down docilely beside me and the violent current of energy in the forest ebbed away.

"What's the question?" Poe settled themselves on the stump, their injured arm resting in their lap.

"What's the Ascendant? It likely has some connection to stars."

Poe frowned, looking genuinely intrigued. "I have no idea, but it sounds shiny."

"Which is why I came to you. If a raven can't find out about something shiny, then who can?"

A raven in a high branch cawed.

Poe nodded. "Yes, she must visit the Casino."

The other birds broke into enthusiastic *kraas*, while Poe held up their good arm to placate the wolf, who'd jerked his head up.

"You can't even keep your promise of no games for ten seconds," I said.

Delilah sprung up to stand at my shoulder.

"Untrue. The Casino is where all the information gathered by our kind lives."

"I doubt the Casino is a library. It's the source of that magic, isn't it?" Poe kept an impassive expression on their face, but I pressed on. "Is that why raven shifters perpetuate chaos? To keep the Casino fed? Is it like ohr?"

I didn't take my eyes off the raven and eventually they looked away. I took it as their admission that I was right. "How would this work?"

Laurent thumped his tail against the ground but that was the extent of his disagreement.

"The few outside the flock who know of the Casino's existence must play a game of the Casino's choosing for an answer." Poe's eyes gleamed.

"Let me guess," I said. "The odds tend to be in the house's favor?"

"Yes." They looked amused that I'd gotten it that quickly. "But you have a token and my promise, so you may play without repercussion. I guarantee that if the Casino doesn't have the answer about this shiny-sounding item, then knowledge of the Ascendant has been lost forever."

It all sounded legit, but I'd worked with enough slippery lawyers to know how flowery language could hide loopholes in plain sight.

Laurent caught my sleeve between his teeth and gently tugged me backward with a low growl.

"Your protest is noted," I murmured, disengaging. "Let me think."

If I'd learned anything about the magical community, it was that no one willingly handed over answers. Payment rarely took the form of cash either. These people traded in secrets and information. If I walked away, I'd just have to find someone else with some other hoop to jump through.

Besides, Poe had promised no more games and I was willing to bet that their self-protective instincts overrode any desire to lie to me while the wolf stood by.

I paced around the clearing.

It sounded like the Casino didn't do anything without a price. Why would it help, even with the token? I reviewed everything Poe had said to me, taking the conversation apart word by word, until I figured it out.

"Ah." I wagged a finger at Poe. "You promised you would answer honestly but you never gave me your word that the Casino would. Is that why you agreed to this so easily? I drop in the token, our deal is fulfilled, and the Casino doesn't give a damn fact up?"

The wolf paced in a wide circle around Poe, never taking his eyes off them.

Poe jutted up their chin. "I can't make the Casino comply."

"That may be true." I tilted my head and considered our avian audience. "But how would the Casino fare if all the raven shifters here in Vancouver disappeared?"

"That would be mass murder," Poe said. "You'd never get away with it. Nor would the wolf."

I gave an exaggerated frown. "I didn't say anything about all of you dying."

"You can't make us disappear." Poe twisted around to check where Laurent was. "You're bluffing."

I crouched down in front of them. "I'm all in and I've got an unbeatable hand. Are you willing—is the Casino willing—to take the chance that all I've got is garbage?"

Poe searched my face, their eyes clouded with worry at my unflappability.

I was a terrible poker player, but I wasn't bluffing. Should I throw my cloaking over them all, they'd disappear. Sure, it wasn't in the sense that Poe thought it was, but that wasn't on me. Loopholes and language, I tell ya.

"Now," I said serenely, "could you convince the Casino to participate and then give me your promise on that? And that neither Laurent or I will be harmed in any way."

Poe trained their eyes to the sky for long enough that I was convinced we'd leave without getting a shot to ask the question.

All the while the wolf paced and the ravens silently watched the proceedings.

I forced myself to stand tall and calm, despite my entire body prickling. If I never saw another raven again, I'd be delighted.

Finally Poe stood up and gave a long, high whistle.

Ravens exploded off the branches, swooping down toward us.

I shrieked and threw myself on the wolf, not because I was scared. Fine, I was a little scared, but mostly I was trying to keep the wolf from attacking the birds. He couldn't jump with me practically straddling him, but he still managed to drag me forward several feet.

All those wings beating in unison created a deep *whump* sound that I felt in the marrow of my bones. Dirt, tiny twigs, and pebbles batted against us, stirred up by the ferocity of the birds' descent.

And then, in the flap of a wing, all fell quiet, like a blanket had been thrown over the world. Cautiously I raised my head and gasped.

Poe, Laurent, and I stood inside a small hut made of living, breathing birds. The walls and ceiling rippled like sports fans doing the wave. It was a solid wash of black feathers, their heads tucked and hidden under their wings, the room illuminated by some magic internal glow that mimicked the late afternoon sun outside.

The sight was both beautiful and dreadful.

"Welcome to the Casino," Poe said.

I spun around but they were gone.

A slot machine with the same inky iridescence as a raven's wing stood on an obsidian base. Instead of a button to push, this one had an old-fashioned silver lever to pull situated next to a coin slot.

"You realize this is a game, right?" I said.

"In this instance, it is merely the vessel of the transaction. Nothing more." Poe's words floated on the breeze.

I rubbed the token between my palms for good luck. "Here's hoping."

The wolf shot me a reproachful look.

"Be positive, Huff 'n' Puff."

I dropped the token in, part of me expecting the machine

to remain dark, but it lit up with a bright bing! "See?"

The wolf sat down beside me with a snort.

I took a deep breath and gripped the lever. The metal was cool, its solidity reassuring. "What is the Ascendant?"

I pulled the lever and the machine rumbled.

Aces, hearts, diamonds, even a bunch of grapes spun through the three windows.

A star dropped into the first window, and I let out the breath I'd been holding.

The other two windows continued to cycle symbols.

The middle window stopped. Another star.

"Yes!"

Laurent gave a yip and pulled free.

I brushed off the wolf hair I'd accidentally tugged out and patted his head. "Sorry."

The third window just kept cycling.

"Come to Mama," I crooned.

A heart.

A heart.

A diamond.

The symbols finally started to slow down.

I leaned in.

A crescent of light flared up beside the slot machine and my instincts kicked in.

Of course there would be an ohr flare right when I needed to know something. I needed answers but I also couldn't let these shifters die.

So I did the only thing I could.

There were too many potential targets among the ravens to pick one to protect so I threw my cloaking over the ohr like a firefighter's blanket to smother it. The black mesh swelled up to insane proportions, crowding the wolf and me to one of the raven walls.

Grimacing against the feel of the breathing feathery barrier against my back, I gritted my teeth, dizzily fighting the supernatural life force that powered Ohrist magic, come now to consume one of the unlucky. While Laurent, the birds, and I were outside the cloaking, the ohr's blinding light filled my vision and I tilted forward.

The ohr fought back, seeking to drag me in.

I skidded in the dirt.

The ohr's light hummed around me at a painful frequency. I fell to my knees, bowed double and twisted in the outside of my mesh, struggling like a drowning victim, gasping for breath.

My magic slipped, threatening to let the ohr spill out, but I held on to it by my fingertips until bit by painful bit, the ohr was nothing more than a spark that I crushed.

I couldn't move, blinking hard because I was blinded by the afterimage of that light.

A furry, heavy body flew into me and I fell backward in a tangle of limbs and wolf. The jolt of adrenaline cleared my vision and I stared at the empty woods, the birds now gone. "Did the ohr get them?" I asked in a hoarse voice.

"No." Poe stepped out of the deepening shadows. "You saved us and protected the Casino from this attack."

Laurent jumped in front of me, growling softly, and Poe stopped, their hands held up to show they meant no harm. The wolf fell silent but didn't allow Poe to come closer.

"Attack?" I sat up, checking myself for injury. "Don't Ohrists just draw upon ohr? They can manipulate it to flare up as well?"

"A rare few possess that ability. One of those sought to keep you from inquiring about the Ascendant."

"The new player from the blackjack game?

"I know not."

"Well," I said, slowly getting to my feet, "I didn't want anyone hurt on my behalf, and I had a selfish reason." I glanced at the slot machine, which had gone dark again, its windows blank. "No!" I banged on the top. "You promised."

"The promise is kept." Poe cawed. "The Casino imparted its wisdom."

The wolf turned his head to the sky. After a moment, I saw what had caught his attention.

A half dozen ravens landed on a fat branch above Poe's head. "The Ascendant," they chorused in croaky voices, "is a magic amplifier."

"That's it? It's not a person?" At Poe's head shake, I tamped down my disappointment. My parents had gone after some shark and likely been killed over an amplifier? Not a doomsday device capable of wiping out humanity that Mom and Dad had intended to destroy?

Or sell to the highest bidder.

I scrubbed a hand over my face. If I couldn't ascribe some nobility to them, at least they couldn't be painted as world-ending monsters. Amplifier it was. "What does it look like?"

"A silver rock the size of a fist," the raven shifters chorused.

I squinted at the birds. They *were* shifters, right? Real ravens couldn't talk. I hoped. "Where do I find it?"

"Unknown," the chorus said.

"Awesome." I gestured to the wolf that we were going. "Thanks for the information."

"There is one more thing I gleaned," Poe said.

"If it requires another game," I said tiredly, "count me out."

"Offered freely in thanks. The first game you and I ever played. Do you remember?"

I nodded. "Memory."

"Correct. Darkness gusted across the cards."

"Followed by sunlight," I said testily. "What's your point?"

"It is connected to the Ascendant."

"Which? The darkness or the light?"

Poe shrugged sadly. "I don't know."

26

WAS TRACKING DOWN THE ASCENDANT THE BEST course of action or one that would doom us all? Mom, Dad, McMurtry, how many more would die if I kept poking into the past?

Would I be next?

I was so preoccupied that I didn't register Laurent had led us back to the car until he butted my hip. "Right. Yeah." I unlocked it and he grabbed his shoes in his mouth, trotting back into the forest to shift.

When he returned, I was staring out the window making pro and con lists in my head on what to do.

"Mitzi?" Laurent fastened his seat belt.

"Hmm?" I blinked to attention.

"I'm picking Tatiana up from the airport tomorrow. Do you want to come with me?"

"No, I'll meet you at her place."

Laurent and I didn't talk much on the way back to Hotel Terminus to get his truck, but it was a comfortable silence, and I was relieved when I dropped him off that all awkwardness between us was gone.

It had been a long day and I barely made it into bed before I was asleep.

With Sadie still at Eli's place, the house felt empty and cold on Friday morning, despite it being a hot, sunny day, so I hit up a café. The buzz of caffeine and the energy of the other customers were comforting after that creepy Casino.

Ryann messaged that her Lonestar colleagues in Boston had a solid bead on Learsdon. They were going to apprehend him and then transfer him to Vancouver, where I'd get my shot at him. The trouble was I was no longer as certain of my plan to interrogate him as I had been. Actually, I wasn't certain of anything.

Should I try to find the Ascendant? Should I wait because according to Emmett it was seeking me out? A magic amplifier couldn't track people down, could it? How did this fit into the prophecy?

Those questions were frustrating enough but what about the case? Should I get Tatiana's agreement to kill Edvin and break the illusion on the twins even though my former client had said no?

The truth was that Giselle had struck a deal with a demon to take her sister's life because she wasn't happy with her own and destroyed Gigi's life in the process.

Whether for the rush or dreams of that one big score, my parents weren't happy with what they'd had either. I rubbed a hand over the sting in my chest. Why hadn't I been enough? Had they even thought about consequences or how selfish their actions were? They'd ruined my life every bit as much as Giselle had with her twin.

So where did that leave me?

I took a sip of cold coffee and grimaced. All actions had consequences. I accepted that fact when it came to my job, but this case had been closed. To move forward, especially with Edvin's threat to Sadie, would be selfish and irresponsible.

Still, I couldn't help sending Giselle a final text. *I know it feels impossible but your dancing career doesn't have to be over. I'm sure there's a way out of this, but only if we confront this demon and put things to right. You wouldn't have to feel out of place in something you earned. Think about it, okay?*

She never responded.

Perhaps the past was better staying in the past. If I didn't pursue the Ascendant, then the only loose end was James Learsdon, and provided he hadn't blabbed about me, that would be tied up soon as well.

Could I be happy just living in the present and letting the past go? Letting this case go?

Emmett texted that Tatiana was on her way home from the airport. I grabbed my car keys, pulling up to her place to find Laurent unloading suitcases from his truck. I nodded at the open front door. "How's her mood?"

He placed a blue case next to its match on the curb, but before he could answer, something glass shattered in Tatiana's foyer.

"Raymond, you idiot!" Tatiana's bellow could be heard a block away. "It reeks like a distillery in here."

Laurent grinned. "It's a treat."

"Oy vey." I steeled my shoulders and headed up the front walk. "Wish me luck."

My eyes watered at the stench of vodka. Five intact bottles sat on the bottom stair along with a dozen floral scarves.

Raymond was on his hands and knees wiping up the spill from the bottle he'd broken, repeating names to himself.

"Got yourself a list of enemies?" I said, avoiding the puddle and glass shards.

He looked up blankly.

"You know, *Game of Thrones*? Arya's names that she repeats?"

His face crumpled, like this was a test and he was failing.

"Nothing, huh?" I said. "It was kind of a massive pop culture phenomenon."

"These names are people that I have to deliver the vodka to. I don't like violent shows," he said.

Sparkling conversationalist. "Right. Carry on."

Marjorie sprinted past with a sheaf of receipts in her hand, talking to someone on Bluetooth about a painting that should have been shipped from Moscow. She was obviously the brains of the two assistants, and if Raymond was the muscle, he was lightweight class.

I strolled into the living room, my arms wide. "Welcome home. How was it?"

Tatiana reclined on her loveseat with one arm over her eyes. "Another successful venture. Plus, I got my fill of blini and caviar. That's pancakes and fish eggs."

"I know what caviar is. I've even tasted it. The proletariat is now allowed bourgeoise delights."

"Even with your wardrobe? It's all so inclusive these days," she said with an exaggerated shudder.

"Yes, it was so much better during Louis XIV's reign. Especially that end bit."

Tatiana chuckled. "Touché."

I inspected the small army's worth of matryoshka, the Russian nesting dolls crowding the mantel. "Are you planning to animate these and take over the world?" I said. "Because creepy."

She sat up and looked the dolls over. "They were given to me in thanks by our happy client. Expect to receive one for every possible holiday and your year-end bonus."

"I'd rather get cash."

"Too bad." Wincing, she rubbed her hips. "Oy."

"You all right?"

"I'll be fine as soon as Emmett comes back. Where are you?!" she yelled.

"For the hundredth time, I'm coming!" There was the heavy thump of footsteps and the golem entered wearing purple leggings and a short blond bobbed wig. He held out a glass of water and two white pills.

"You could open a pharmacy with that medicine cabinet of yours, lady. I almost gave you a suppository instead of painkillers."

Tatiana swallowed the pills. "They look nothing alike."

"I didn't say I confused them." He gave her a tight smile.

"Leave her alone," Laurent said, rolling in two suitcases with a carry-on bag slung over his shoulder. "Where do you want these?"

"Put them in the laundry room," Tatiana said. "Except the shoulder bag. I'll take that."

After handing it over, Laurent left with the other luggage.

I sat down on the sofa, shoving Emmett over to make room. "Got a moment for an update?"

"Giselle already phoned me," Tatiana said. "Excellent work, Miriam. You did exactly as the client asked." She unzipped the carry-on and hauled out a huge makeup bag. Removing a tiny bottle, she spritzed it around her face.

Emmett sniffed it. "Can I get some?"

"Lean in," she said and sprayed him.

He wiggled his shoulders. "Refreshing."

"At fifty dollars a bottle, it better be." She waved the bottle at me. "Miriam?"

I shrugged. "Why not?"

After I'd been misted, enjoying the cooling sensation on my skin, I told my boss the details of Giselle's illusion.

She sighed. "Here we go. This is where you tell me that you want to save these women. Then I point out that our client has said case closed, to which you reply, yes but her poor sister blah blah blah. Did I miss anything?"

"I've missed your overwhelming compassion and eloquence," I said.

Tatiana snorted.

"But you're wrong. Sometimes the truth needs to stay buried, so people don't get hurt." I fiddled with the bottle of spritzer that she'd left on the table. "Hurt more than they have been."

Tatiana did a double take and even Emmett blinked in surprise.

"You're just going to leave them stuck in that illusion?" Emmett played some Ella Fitzgerald off his phone. "Are you sick?"

"No, but Sadie isn't worth risking over this."

Tatiana smiled at the golem. "You've been listening to my playlist."

"Yeah, it's not half bad," he said.

"And you, Miriam," she said. "You're showing real growth. I'm proud of you."

"I don't think there's anything to be proud of. Either way, the real Giselle is a victim." I shook my head. "It's not fair."

Tatiana tapped her hips. "Is it fair that I've had chronic pain for decades?"

"Tell me you filmed the guards strip-searching you when you set off the metal detectors," Emmett said.

"Sha, you," she said. "And you"—she wagged a finger at me—"not everyone is as in love with the truth as you've been. After all that our client learned, we should be grateful that all she did was end the assignment and pay in full."

"So grateful," I muttered.

Tatiana speared me with an unimpressed look. "Think about what she did to her twin. How might she come after you if you took her dancing away from her?"

"It's a moot point, since I'm not doing anything." I sighed.

Tatiana stood up, dragging the bag on the floor behind her, and patted my cheek. "Don't frown. You'll get wrinkles."

Emmett watched her go with an admiring look. "Good to have her back."

"Awesome." Though I'd missed her too. There was something comforting about Tatiana's consistency. "What's the deal with her hips? If she'd had replacement surgery, shouldn't that have stopped the pain?"

Emmett shrugged. "Hey, Laurent!"

The shifter entered the room. "What?"

"Did Tatiana have hip replacement surgery?" I said.

"Ask her." He said it kind of cagily.

I raised my eyebrows. "Is it some big secret?"

Laurent glanced up at the ceiling, then shook his head. "I guess not anymore. If she's mentioned the pain, then she probably wouldn't have a problem with you two knowing. She was in a car crash years ago. It was really bad."

"How bad?" Emmett said.

"It was a miracle she survived. She had to learn how to walk again."

Tatiana was so frail. She was tough as nails too, and she'd physically healed, but had the crash caused an irrevocable break somewhere deep inside her? One that never set properly, just like my parents' murders had with me?

"My God," I said. "That's awful."

Laurent perched on the arm of the sofa next to me. "No one outside the immediate family knew. And with my aunt's iron-willed determination, no one ever suspected she'd been hurt, much less that she'd been paralyzed."

"She's quite the actress." Emmett elbowed me. "You should get some tips because you're crap at hiding your feelings."

"And yet you think I like you," I said.

He laughed. "Good one." He grabbed his phone. "I'm going upstairs to hear about the trip. See yourselves out."

As the golem left, the Louis Armstrong song finished up and "Mack the Knife" began.

Laurent smiled. "This is Tatiana's favorite song. Fitting."

My head snapped up, and I shivered, my blood turning to ice.

"Mack the Knife" was about a killer who's compared to a shark.

A shark, of all things.

Dread washed over me in a rush. I grabbed Laurent's arm. "When was Tatiana in that car crash?"

"I was a kid?"

"How old?"

Laurent frowned, pulling his arm out of my grip. "I was ten."

"Are you sure?" My voice rose to a tight squeak.

"Yes. Why?"

I dropped my head into my hands, and screwed my eyes shut, my breath coming faster and deeper.

It wasn't an accident. Jake's message to me hadn't made any sense when I read it because of course my parents' murders weren't an accident.

Except he hadn't been referring to that. It was the car crash that wasn't an accident.

A car crash that Uncle Jake only knew about because someone who was like a brother to him had told him about it.

Are you a baby shark or are you planning to finish what your parents started? That's why James had asked me that question. He wanted to know if I was aligned with Tatiana or if I was planning to finish the job my parents had attempted.

Kill Tatiana.

My parents, the blooming Blums, weren't just the flowers, they too were sharks? Was I the baby shark because killing was in my blood? I placed my hands on the sides of my rib cage like I could force air into my lungs.

The room swam; I couldn't tell which way was up.

Laurent placed his hand on my back. "Miriam? What's wrong?"

Run. I flinched away from him, gripping my purse like a shield as I backed up into the foyer. "I just remembered that I promised Sadie to—" I glanced around, seeking inspiration because my mind was blank. I swallowed. "Shoes. Buy her shoes. I have to go."

He stood up, saying something, but all I heard was the deadly growl of a wolf.

I shrank back into myself, ready to cloak and flee because otherwise he'd scent me out and tear the secret from me.

"Miriam!" Laurent clapped his hands and I snapped out of my trance. "Your heart is racing. What's wrong? What did I say?" He held himself still, his eyebrows drawn together, and his eyes clouded with concern.

Laurent wasn't the actor his aunt was. If he'd known what my parents had done when we first met, he would have told me to fuck off in no uncertain terms.

"Oh," I said softly and rubbed my heart. He couldn't find out. He'd want to tell Tatiana and I wasn't sure I could. How was I supposed to look the woman in the eyes and tell her that my parents had almost killed her?

I didn't think she'd blame me or retaliate against me or my family for what my parents had done, but seeing me would be this constant reminder. I wouldn't want to be around someone like that if our positions were reversed.

And I wanted Tatiana in my life. Not only did I feel alive working these jobs for her, she challenged me. I finally felt like I'd landed somewhere, found my community, and the thought of losing any part of that opened a howling void inside me, threatening to send me to that dark and adrift place that I'd been stuck in for a long time after my parents' deaths.

Call me chickenshit, but I didn't want the reveal of our shared past negating any future we had.

That meant keeping this from Laurent. I wouldn't force him to choose between Tatiana and me, because either way would be horrible for him.

Either way was going to be horrible for me.

"Do you want to come home with me?" he said. "Just to talk?"

I put out my hand to stop his approach. "I can't. Shoes."

"Right." He bit his lower lip, his eyes narrowed, but didn't call out my obvious lie.

I smothered a gasp. Did Tatiana already know? Had she hired me to keep her enemy close? She hadn't killed my parents or McMurtry, I believed her about that, but did she know the truth behind her car accident?

"I have to go." I spun around and sprinted for the door, almost colliding with Tatiana and Emmett, who'd come down the stairs.

My boss grabbed the railing to balance herself. "You're leaving? I haven't even given you the details of the trip. We have a follow-up job if we want it."

"Sadie needs shoes. Did the painkiller kick in? How are your hips?" I searched her face for some key on whether she knew or not, but Tatiana truly was an excellent actor and all I saw was the normal confusion of someone when met with erratic behavior.

She shrugged. "I'd say don't get old, but the alternative is worse."

I gave a weak laugh.

"You look terrible. Go home and we'll speak later." Tatiana brushed past me, Emmett following with a weird look my way.

I'd championed the truth like some miracle cure-all to heal grief and right wrongs. But what was I supposed to do with this great revelation? My loving mother and father were willing to kill someone over a magic amplifier. Had I mourned an illusion of them all these years?

I got into my car, desperately trying to remember how Mom and Dad had acted before the assassin had shown up at our house and murdered them. But I didn't remember anything being wrong. In fact, they'd seemed really happy. They hadn't acted like people being blackmailed or being forced to hurt someone else, so did I want to find out why they'd done it?

I flinched. Was the fact that Tatiana survived the reason they'd been killed or had someone been tying up a loose end?

Even if I dropped my search, how would I convince Tatiana that I no longer had any interest in finding my parents' killer? And how would I continue a friendship with Laurent if I kept this from him?

Time and time again, Tatiana had warned me about leaving things alone and I'd dismissed her as a cynic when the truth was that I'd been a fool.

I didn't have justice and I didn't have closure. All I had was an ugly secret ticking like a bomb in my hands, and for all my soapboxing about the importance of truth, I prayed this never ever came to light.

27

I left a dozen frantic messages for Ryann, hoping that something James said could explain this in a way that made everything all right. But he'd evaded the Lonestars, who believed Dagmar that she didn't have him either.

I hid like a coward for the next two days, texting Tatiana and Laurent that I'd come down with the stomach flu.

The only ones I shared my discovery with were Jude and Eli, both of whom sat in stunned silence as I finished up the story. I'd waited until Sunday after lunch to speak with them when Sadie was out with Caleb.

"No matter what your parents did," Jude said, "your memories of who they were to you are valid."

I buried my head in my hands. "How can I even trust my memories? It's like how Sadie knew I was keeping something from her about my magic. What if on some level my younger self knew they were horrible, and I built them into something else to make myself feel better?"

"You can go all *Blade Runner* with every memory you have and drive yourself crazy wondering if it's real or you can accept it at face value," Eli said.

Jude refilled our glasses from the pitcher of lemonade. "Why did you shut your magic down?"

I frowned. "Because I was terrified my parents' killer would come after me."

"And because you were so angry at them for leaving you that you didn't want to be anything like them." She held up a hand when I started to protest. "You told me that years ago during a very drunk, very late-night talk."

"I really said that?" I didn't need her nod to feel the truth of it in my bones. "So, you think I knew what they were capable of and denied it?"

"No. I think you've been wrapped in grief and anger for so long that it's pointless to speculate. Right here, right now, do you love them?"

"Yes, but—"

"Nope. No qualifications. The way I see it, you either embrace that and let all of this go, embrace it while you keep digging, or just hate them whether or not you do anything."

"Very astute, Rachefsky," Eli said.

She tilted her head. "It's always easier to diagnose someone else. Regardless of what you decide about them, you must tell Tatiana. It's a huge betrayal if you don't."

"Clearly you had no idea about any of this," Eli said, "or you wouldn't have gone to work for her."

I gulped down half my glass, super parched from all my talking. "Fuck. I hadn't even thought about that angle. What if she thinks that's *exactly* why I went to work for her? To get close and finish the job?"

My phone rang but it was Emmett, so I declined the call.

Eli shook his head. "She won't think that if you tell her, because only an idiot would give a heads-up."

"She won't trust me anymore though." I hugged my knees to my chest, wrapping my arms around them. "It's worse if she already knows and hired me to keep an eye on me."

"In which case, she never trusted you," Jude said.

I moved my chair farther back into the shade under the tree in my backyard. "That's you being helpful, is it?"

Jude shrugged. "I've been helpful enough today."

Eli tasted his lemonade then made a face and stood up. "You have to do something beyond faking a stomach flu."

Jude reached for her glass. "Does Laurent know?"

"No. He's not into game playing like Tatiana. If my family had this kind of history with his, he'd never have helped me find you when you were abducted. Not for all the money in the world."

"Do you think he'd go for payback if you told him?" Eli picked mint off a patch that grew wild in the corner of the garden.

I slowly spun my glass around, watching the ice clink together. "No, but for all his bitching about his aunt, the only way he'd stay friends with someone whose parents almost killed her, is if Tatiana knew and was okay with me. His loyalties are too black-and-white."

"I don't think you're giving him enough credit," Jude said softly.

I declined another call from Emmett. I wasn't up to pretending to sound sick enough to get out of going after a potential enthralled.

This horrible past that I'd done nothing to deserve hung over me like an executioner's blade. I felt powerless, a pawn shoved into a game I wanted no part of, except my only way off the board was with the queen's blessing.

Eli dumped some sprigs on the table. Sprawling in his chair, he picked off some small mint leaves and stirred them into his lemonade. "Much as I hate giving Laurent any points, Jude is right. I saw how he stuck his neck out for you. More than once." His head shot up. "Are you sleeping with him?"

"You sweet summer child," Jude drawled.

"I'm slow on the uptake," he said wryly and gave a soft

laugh. "Mir, if you two are in a relationship, then you have to tell him."

"We're not."

"Oh, really? Does he think he's too good for you?" He puffed up his chest and crossed his arms. "Want me to go over there and tell him he's an idiot if he gives you up? I'd know."

"Thanks, but no. It's all good. Well, it was until this." I gnawed on a cuticle.

The night we met Giselle, I'd scoffed at Tatiana's warning that the truth isn't always a good thing. It felt patronizing, like she didn't think I could handle it. A large part of reclaiming my magic had been about facing the truth. I'd hidden an important aspect of myself for too long. It was time to stop being afraid and time to get answers about my past instead of deadbolting it in a closet and hoping it never burst free.

The more I'd investigated Giselle's case, the angrier I'd gotten on her behalf that someone had stolen all memories of her sibling from her. She deserved to know the truth. If I was being honest, some of my drive to solve this was fueled by the test that James Learsdon had sprung on me. He'd killed someone in order to learn the truth of my magic. *My* truth. I felt violated and scared, but I'd been determined to act because I refused to go back to feeling like the helpless child I'd been.

I'd recognized that same fear and vulnerability in Giselle.

Truth had always been personal, but after I connected my parents to Tatiana's car crash, I experienced the ugly conse-quence that in championing my truth, I was violating someone else's right to privacy about theirs.

Was I any better than James?

Or was I worse because I was a hypocrite who when faced with this really hard situation was scared to get through it and grow from those battle scars?

"I'm going to tell Laurent," I said decisively. "Him and Tatiana both. I like my boss. She's shifty and twisty as hell, but she's smart and fierce and she has yet to break a promise to me." I sighed. "As fucked-up as this sounds, it would have been easier if she had killed my parents. I could have hated her and moved on. But I don't want to lose her." I paused. "I really hope I don't."

"Damned if you do, damned if you don't," Jude said, not unkindly.

"Pretty much."

My phone blew up with texts from the golem demanding that I call him.

I wiped my clammy palms off on my shorts. "This isn't about the enthralled hotline," I whispered. "Something's happened."

"Call him back," Jude said. "We've got you."

I hit Emmett's contact button, putting the call on speaker for Jude and Eli to hear. "Hey, buddy. What's up?"

"You need to come over. Now." There was a crash on his end. "Tatiana is in a mood."

Jude and Eli leaned forward.

I gripped the phone. "Wha—why?"

"Giselle told Kadeem that he was right. There was no case. Now he's telling people that Tatiana's a liar."

I sagged back against the chair. "Oh, thank God."

There was another crash.

"Are you kidding me? Get over here!" He hung up.

Eli grimaced. "Maybe keep the news about her crash a secret for another twenty-seven years?"

Jude pointed at Eli. "What he said."

I gathered up the pitcher and my empty glass. "You think I could?"

They nodded but neither of them really sold it.

Five minutes later I was on the road. If Tatiana spent all her anger on Giselle, maybe I could catch her once she'd exhausted that reserve and sort of slip the car crash in. Yeah, right.

However, thinking about what Giselle had done shifted something inside me. She'd slapped this unexpected move on Tatiana, hitting her in a very vulnerable spot.

Sadie was both my biggest vulnerability and my greatest treasure. I couldn't simply sit back and hope for the best. I'd chosen to step away from going after Edvin for Sadie's sake, because if anything happened to me, I'd be no better than my parents. But if the demon remained out there, he could blindside me at any point.

The demon had to die.

New plan. I'd convince Tatiana to bring in Carpe Demon to do the dirty work, and once this case was firmly behind us, I'd sit her down for that important talk.

Marjorie showed me out back where Tatiana and Emmett were seated by the koi pond.

Emmett had his hand on Tatiana's back. With each deep inhale and exhale she took, the reeds in the pond went from shriveled to healthy, causing the fish to dart back and forth in the water.

I sat down beside the golem.

Tatiana straightened up. "I'm fine now, Emmett."

The reeds stayed healthy. Well, most of them. One poor stalk remained bent over, dead.

Before I could launch into my argument to take out the demon, my boss pointed a bony finger at me. "It's your lucky day, bubeleh."

"How's that?" I yanked out the single dead reed, running a finger over the once-pink cluster of tiny blossoms at the top.

"You're going to rescue the twins from their terrible plight." Her eyes glimmered. "The hunters intend to attack Edvin in half an hour."

She was on board with killing Edvin? That was easier than

expected. What a nice change. I was getting exactly what I wanted: the threat to Sadie being removed without any possibility of me getting hurt.

Then I shook my head as the implication hit me. If this was already in motion, Nav had broken his word to me about not doing anything regarding the demon until I gave him my client's go-ahead. Jerk.

"Where are the women now?" I said.

"Edvin will soon take the real Giselle to a physio appointment." Tatiana gave me an address in Manhattan. "Our former client is heading there as well. This ends today."

"Is it the Carpe Demon bunch here leading the charge or is there a New York chapter I need to coordinate with?"

Emmett sent a cagey look at the house but at my questioning glance, shrugged.

"No coordination at all. It's our local group. They claimed the right since Edvin sent that other demon after you here in town," Tatiana said. "Now, enough questions. Take Emmett and go through the Kefitzat Haderech immediately. There's no time to lose."

Was that safe? I wrapped the stalk around my finger. The golem had gone in their once before without triggering Smoky, but Pyotr had sworn to kill Emmett if he ever came back.

Tatiana glared at me, so I nodded. I'd placate the gargoyle.

"You got it," I said. "But before I do, there's just one thing. The twins are going to need each other to get through this. I'd like to spare the real Giselle the knowledge that Aurora got her into this situation."

Tatiana narrowed her eyes. "You're willing to let them live a lie? That's rich."

"It's the kindest way forward for Gigi," I said. "She's lost her lifelong dream and she doesn't need to lose her sister. Promise me that it never goes beyond the three of us that our client sold out her sibling or put the illusion into motion. We'll say the demon did it simply to cause misery."

Tatiana pulled her red shawl tighter around her shoulders. "You wanted to fight the good fight, reveal the truth. Now you get your wish. We owe our *former* client nothing."

She was lashing out because Giselle had pushed the most vulnerable button Tatiana had—her professional reputation, be it as an artist or a macher. Tatiana definitely had a vindictive side that would relish taking Giselle down and putting Kadeem in his place, but at its heart, this was about self-preservation.

I waved away a wasp, my heart heavy because I was partially to blame for this chip in her carefully mortared identity. It was history repeating itself albeit in a less lethal way.

Giselle would still get her comeuppance so why should Gigi be burdened with this knowledge? If this was how Tatiana acted over a simple request that cost her nothing, how would she behave when she learned about my parents?

"Giselle still has to live with her actions and her professional career will be finished. Isn't that punishment enough?"

"I've indulged you over and over again," my employer said. "Now I'm telling you to do your job. I don't give a damn about those women."

A clump of roses on the rosebush exploded, showering us with petals.

Emmett buried his head in his hands with a groan.

"Wait." I shook my head. "Carpe Demon is killing Edvin, which leaves me to get the twins to safety. But if you don't care about the women, then what does my rescue entail?"

"The hunters aren't killing the demon," Tatiana said, exasperated. "You are."

The dead stalk fell from my hand onto the grass. This was exactly what I'd been attempting to avoid. Both times I'd gone up against a demon, I'd had help. Magic help. Emmett wouldn't be of much use.

"You're going to get me killed!" I raked my hands through my hair. "There's a perfectly good organization trained to hunt demons."

"It has to be you." Tatiana gave an annoyed sigh. "You stopped trusting your instincts. You were right about there being something to this case and you kept digging until you hit on the truth. But then you got scared and sentimental. You are a confident, intelligent, and tenacious woman, Miriam. Sentimentality has no place in your life. Neither does underestimating your abilities." She sniffed primly. "It's unbecoming."

Her words landed on me, but where I expected nails and razor wire, I was blanketed in the plushest velvet imaginable. Suddenly, my way forward was clear.

"Tatiana, I have to tell you—"

The golem fidgeted worse than usual, practically dancing in his chair.

I rounded on him. "What is wrong with you?"

He glanced at Tatiana and then started humming like he hadn't heard me, but his gaze darted from me to the house.

"Oh, for crying out loud," she said. "I brought a junior member of Carpe Demon in for a friendly chat. He's enjoying our company here until you return triumphant, having beaten the hunters to their target."

"That's insane. Why would you do that?"

The elderly artist stood up, her spine ramrod straight. "Because when that illusion is broken and our former client loses everything, I want her to know that she has me to thank." She leaned over, her face only inches from mine. "Don't disappoint me."

28

"I KILL PET!" PYOTR LUNGED FOR EMMETT, WHO ducked and dodged behind a stalagmite, but not before sticking out his tongue.

I was on my last nerve. Tatiana had sent me to finish this job to get my instincts and confidence back on track. But she also wanted vengeance on Giselle for her betrayal and the lies she'd told Kadeem. When I thought about how close I'd come to telling her about my parents... What was I going to do?

The bicker twins' arguing snapped me out of my grim thoughts.

"Behave." I smacked both with equally useless results. Damn creatures with hard skin. "Smarten up right this minute." I pointed at Emmett. "Or I'll never work with you again."

The golem gave a tremulous pout. "You wouldn't."

"Try me." I fumed.

Emmett's eyes widened and he swallowed, bobbing his head.

Pyotr put his hands to his ears and wiggled his fingers in a "nyah" move.

I whipped around to the gargoyle. "And you. Be nice to my

friend or you can forget about ever getting another movie or take-out order ever again."

He kicked at a loose rock. "You're mean."

Emmett snorted. "You don't know the half of it."

"Really?"

The golem shook his head wearily. "The stories I could tell."

Lips pursed, the gargoyle lumbered over to his new buddy. "Like what?"

"Like the time—"

"Shut up or else." I selected a sock with multicolored polka dots off the large pile on the rock slab, pulling an ankle sock off my head that had floated down from the vent in the ceiling. "We're not here to bond."

I fixed Edvin's location in Manhattan in my head and the green narrow door appeared in the rock face. Satisfied that at least one thing was going the way it should, I grabbed Emmett by the elbow.

"I don't want to," he whined. "Demons are even worse than vampires."

Pyotr shambled along beside us. "He could stay. Watch movie."

Emmett nodded. "Whaddya say, toots?"

I grabbed him by his shoulders, looking directly into his eyes. "You will come with me and help fight the demon, protecting me to your utmost ability."

Golems' main function was to obey a direct order until it was fulfilled. When Laurent pulled this move on Emmett, he looked like a computer accepting a command. The directive took hold with no pushback.

With me? He grumbled "Whatever" and shook himself loose from my hold.

Pyotr waved us off. "Come back and visit soon."

I stomped out any feelings of guilt for the lonely gargoyle. "If we're still alive, then you got it."

Rain drizzled down on us when Emmett and I stepped out in front of a small physiotherapy office on a quiet side street, both of us cloaked. The front windows faced a small reception area with a selection of exercise bikes, weights, mats, and fitness balls, but a drawn curtain prevented me from seeing the rest of the studio.

I moved us under the broad awning because my mesh didn't prevent us from getting wet.

"If Tatiana's information is right," I said, confident that the traffic noise covered the sound of my voice, "then the hunters will arrive in fifteen minutes." I scanned the neighborhood, but none of the few pedestrians out in this weather were loitering, nor did anyone look out of place.

I was tempted to stall and leave Edvin to Carpe Demon, but Tatiana's wrath wouldn't be pretty. "One of the twins should be accompanying the demon. I'm not sure when the other will arrive. We've got the element of surprise on our side since even the demon can't see through this cloaking, and I won't drop it until I'm in place to take him out."

A jaywalker caught my eye, but it was just a woman with her dog.

I nodded at the receptionist inside. "I didn't count on civilians. Prioritize their safety. If you have to leave me to get them out of harm's way, then do it. That includes keeping the twins safe."

"That's not much of a plan," Emmett groused.

"No shit, but it's the best I've got. I have one shot at Edvin and if I blow it, then it turns into a fight that we're not equipped to have." I paused. "Are you going to be all right?"

"I can handle myself," he said testily.

"I mean... Jude spoke with you, didn't she? Can you control going into prophecy mode?"

He shook his head. "If it happens here, you're on your own."

I hadn't thought about that, but I nodded. "I doubt that'll be the case, but if it does, just take care of yourself."

"Okay, Mom." He scuffed his foot against the ground, but a small smile played on his lips.

I waited until the receptionist disappeared behind the curtain before quietly letting us inside.

With its low light and light blue walls, the space felt more like a spa, complete with soft music involving wind chimes. I wrinkled my nose.

The woman returned holding a stack of charts, but not seeing us, she sat down at the reception desk.

Tugging Emmett with me, and grateful that we'd trained to walk silently together while hidden, we tiptoed closer in time for me to see her fire off a text. *Two minutes to go time.*

She was one of the Carpe Demon people. Whatever plan they had was already in motion and we were walking straight into it. Fuck.

This was about to get a lot more complicated.

The door opened and Gigi and Edvin entered. He shook out an umbrella.

Gigi looked even worse than the last time I'd seen her. Her sunken eyes stood out against her white yoga clothing and runners. "I'm Lotta Krause. I have an appointment with Steve."

The fake receptionist stood up. "He'll be with you in a moment. Why don't you start your warm-up on the exercise bike?"

Edvin helped Gigi take off her coat, hanging it on the coatrack while she headed for the bike. He checked his heavy gold watch. "I have errands to run, my love, so I'll be back in forty-five minutes."

Gigi gave him an absent smile.

The fake receptionist coughed, facing the window.

I summoned my scythe, dropped the cloaking, and swung at the demon's head.

Something knocked hard into my back, and I stumbled sideways, my swing wild.

Gigi screamed and scrambled off the bike.

Another operative charged through the door, joining the psionic receptionist who'd chucked a chair at me and was now closing the blinds.

I was grabbed from behind and lifted off my feet. "Emmett! Put me down!"

"It's not me." He was restraining Gigi from rushing to Edvin.

I kicked backward into the person's shins.

"We can do this the easy way or the hard way," Clea hissed in my ear. "Please pick the hard way."

Her grip was unbreakable, and I swear she weighed less than me. "Let me go, She-Hulk."

"Goody. The hard way. Hold the demon until I get back." Clea clamped an arm around my chest and dragged me backward.

"Will do," the fake receptionist said, shoving Edvin off her partner by firing the desk at him.

My teeth rattled with each step Clea took in her shitkicker boots. I dug my heels in but could gain no purchase on the glossy floor. "We're on the same side!"

We left the main room and headed down a long hallway with smaller treatment rooms on either side.

"I told you once that'll never be true," Clea said. "Your boss kidnapped my operative. Why? So she could have you swan in here first and hit those billable hours?"

"That's not what this is about at all." My struggles didn't slow her down one iota. I'd found one of the few people who wasn't intimidated by Tatiana's protection and who could snap me into fragments and dump my body like puzzle pieces in trash cans around the city. "Listen to me. We both want to help the twins."

The fight up front grew louder, magic flashing, and the sounds of heavy items hitting walls.

"Yeah?" She grabbed my hair, yanking my head back so I was looking at her upside down. "Then how come you didn't do anything until after Tatiana got burned?"

Whimpering, I attempted to keep my scalp from being torn off.

Clea let go of my head because we'd caught up to Emmett, who was dragging Gigi down the same corridor, following my earlier order to him that he prioritize the twins' safety.

"You." Clea grabbed his elbow to haul him along for the ride. "With me."

Opening a door at the end of the hallway, she dumped me unceremoniously on my ass, shoving the golem and Gigi in there with me.

Clea crouched down to eye level. The young woman was once again in full goth glory and I think she'd gotten a new piercing. "Tell your boss that the next time she kidnaps one of my teammates, it'll be an eye for an eye."

She slammed the door behind her.

There was a loud click.

Jumping up, I pounded on it.

"Forget it," Giselle said in a muffled voice, "it's soundproof."

Hail, hail, the gang was all here.

My former client sat morosely on the ground, her legs spread in a wide V and her entire upper body pressed flat between them against the ground in a deep stretch. Her face was hidden from view by the spill of her hair.

That much flexibility was, quite frankly, ridiculous.

"I don't understand." Gigi hovered anxiously beside a massage table. "What are they doing to Edvin? And why are you here? I don't want to listen to more of your crazy stories."

"She's the harbinger of doom," Giselle said, sitting up for the first time.

Gigi looked at Giselle and her eyes went as wide as saucers. My former client refused to make eye contact with her twin, though when Gigi's hand flitted to her neck, Giselle hid her "G" necklace under her shirt.

"Whoa," Emmett said. "Talk about double trouble. You two are spooky identical."

I elbowed him to shut up.

"I hope you're happy," Giselle said to me. "You've ruined both our lives."

"Don't thank me," I said. "If you hadn't lied to Kadeem, we wouldn't be here."

Giselle blanched.

"Now who's the harbinger of doom?" I hopped up on the massage table. "You could have continued to live your dream, but you had to lash out against Tatiana."

"Bad idea," Emmett said, unrolling towels stacked in a cubicle.

"Enjoy your last moments of this reality," I said.

"What are you talking about?" Gigi bobbed her head between her sister and me like a bird.

Giselle opened her mouth like she was going to say something, then she gave a choked moan and dropped her head into her hands in an identical move to her twin.

The women's eyes were closed, their faces contorted in pain, but at the same moment, they reached out for each other and tightly clasped hands.

Time spun out, each strike of the second hand on the wall clock beating deep in my heart.

I was helpless, unable to do anything except watch this illusion fall painfully away. No wait, there was a blanket on one of the shelves. They put blankets on people in shock, didn't they?

Emmett grabbed it from me and wrapped it around

himself. "This is harsh," he muttered.

The real Giselle took a ragged breath, her eyes now open and glistening wetly. "Rory." She hugged her twin, but my former client remained stiff in her embrace.

The real Aurora screwed up her face. "I took your pendant," she said in a voice thick with self-loathing.

I decided to keep calling the real Giselle Gigi, but I'd now call her twin, my ex-client, Rory.

"No, you didn't." Gigi brushed a strand of hair away from her sister's face. "I'm so, so sorry."

Rory looked at her, puzzled. "For what?"

"Pushing you to do this."

At this bombshell, I dropped like a stone back onto the massage table. "Say what?"

"Plot twist." Emmett leaned forward, an avid gleam in his eyes, the blanket now fallen to the floor.

Rory gaped at her sister. "This isn't my fault? I didn't ruin your life?"

Gigi shook her head. "I hated dancing. You knew that. But..." She twisted her fingers until they turned white.

Rory gently pried them apart. "Mom."

I picked up the blanket and refolded it, rapt like my cousin Goldie folding laundry during her soaps.

"Yeah," Gigi said. "She wanted me to dance professionally and she didn't care what toll it took. I was sure that this was the best solution. You could have my place and I could disappear."

"I thought I'd done this." Rory shook her head, bewildered. "And even knowing that, I didn't want to give it up."

"It's okay." Gigi smiled at her. "You always loved dancing more than anything."

"But I shouldn't have loved it more than you." Rory unclasped the pendant and held the necklace out.

"You didn't. This was exactly what I wanted." Gigi took the necklace with a smile. "Though I do want this."

"I remember now," Rory said slowly. "You found the demon and came up with the plan, but I told him I wanted your life. We were in this together."

I'd been largely forgotten, which was fine because my head was reeling. The only bad guy was the demon, not either twin, though I'd never have guessed that in a million years. Was the same thing possible regarding my parents?

I exhaled, drawing the attention of the women.

"Let her remain Giselle," Gigi said to me. "No one has to know otherwise."

"It's not that easy," I said sadly. "The illusion is broken now. Anyone who forgot you, no longer will. And they can tell you apart by your birthmark."

"I'll get it removed and Rory can say she did the same before joining the company. No one will care. We can do this and I can finally figure out what I want to do with my life. No one outside this room ever has to know." She looked so excited.

Rory, on the other hand, was sad. "I don't know if I can continue the ruse."

Gigi slammed her hand down on the massage table. "Yes, you can. I watched you dance for years and you're incredible. You were just robbed of your chance." She poked her sister. "Besides, if you screw this up now, after all we've gone through..." Her gaze went distant and the haunted look she'd worn while with the demon returned, but she shook her head and brushed it away. "You are going to conquer the ballet world, got it, stinky face?"

Rory rolled her eyes, but she also looked hopeful. "Got it. And no more separations."

Gigi nodded. "Never again."

I'd been convinced that this case could only end in doom and gloom and heartbreak, but it wasn't jealousy that had brought this about. It was the desire to escape a role that didn't fit for one that did, haters be damned.

Admittedly, it wasn't the smartest way to go about it, but they were desperate.

I wasn't naïve enough to believe that it would be smooth sailing for them. Even if they were willing participants in all this, being thrust into an illusion and then yanked out of it would take time to heal from.

"Thank you." Rory hugged me. "If you hadn't believed me that something was wrong and taken this case, I wouldn't have gotten Gigi back."

"It was my pleasure." Tatiana always prioritized payments, but my clients' gratitude was richer than any cash.

Shit. My boss was going to be furious when she heard about this happy ending.

"I don't suppose you'll back me up in telling Tatiana that the twins were devastated," I said to Emmett.

He looked aghast. "Lie to a woman who could squash me like a bug? Nooooope."

The fake receptionist finally unlocked us.

I bid the twins goodbye and good luck. I truly hoped that they got everything they wanted this time.

Clea and I exchanged an "until next time" look.

I skipped back to Vancouver through the KH, feeling lighter than I had in days.

Emmett was too dazed to protest going straight back to Tatiana's. "Are you coming in?"

I clapped him on the shoulder. "You can give her the details."

"Coward."

"Self-preservation, my friend." He could take the brunt of her anger on this one. I'd have plenty coming my way once I told her the truth about her car crash.

I got into my car, buoyed by my encounter with the twins, and intending to head over to Hotel Terminus for a much-needed conversation with a certain wolf shifter.

That's when a text came through. *Blood Alley. Now.*

29

I DROVE OVER TO THE VAMP'S HIDDEN TERRITORY with a lump in my gut.

Was the deal I'd struck with Yoshi a breach of Zev's protocol? Yoshi wouldn't do anything that went against his friend and master's wishes, but rules that applied to Yoshi did not apply to me.

It was early enough that Blood Alley hadn't officially opened for business and the only people I came across were human employees pushing cleaning carts, moving furniture, and delivering alcohol.

I hurried past them all to Gargoyle Gardens, picking a path through the statues that kept me in the sunlight.

There was no bouncer on duty at Rome. The front doors slid open silently and I made my way through the club, which was dingy under the bright house lights. Bursts of music played as a group of employees did a sound check, but they ignored me, and I got down to the basement in no time at all.

Zev's red office door was ajar. I knocked and called out to announce my presence.

"Ms. Feldman."

I shrieked, whipping around with my hand on my heart. "Mr. BatKian."

He motioned me into his office. "Take a seat."

I perched on the edge of a chair. "Was there something I could help you with?"

He circled me. "The shark sees the star, the flowers seek the shark, you seek the flowers, and the star seeks you."

My purse hit the ground with a thud, my mouth hanging open. "How—I mean—no—"

The vampire quirked an eyebrow and sat on the edge of the desk. Way too close. I mean, there was that very nice chair on the other side. It was a shame to ignore it.

"Yoshi," I said in a shrill voice. My shoulders were tight and beads of sweat dotted my upper lip.

"You've been on quite the hunt. The golem's divination..." Zev steepled his fingers together. "I'm delighted you've gotten such good use out of him."

His smile did not reach his eyes.

I licked my lips nervously, icily certain that I was about to die. "I—you see—"

"Be quiet." His mild reproach made me nod like one of those bobblehead dolls. "As I was saying, you've been busy. Beyond the golem, you took a trip north for your uncle's letter, and you tangled with that odious shifter."

"Laurent?" I felt my pulse spike at the thought that Zev knew we'd slept together.

"Poe."

I hurried to unscramble my thoughts and follow the conversation. "Were you following me?"

"I keep tabs on those of interest. Now, I take it you've deciphered those words?"

Everything in me screamed to lie, but even if Zev couldn't compel me to tell the truth, I wasn't that good an actor. "Yes."

He went over to a bank of cabinets and pushed on a panel, revealing a fridge. "Water?"

I'd have loved one because my throat was dry, but my hands shook so much that I had to stuff them under my butt. "No, thank you."

"Suit yourself." He uncorked a small dark bottle the size of a personal champagne one, removed one of Jude's mugs from another cabinet, and poured dark red liquid into it.

I watched both transfixed and disgusted.

Zev brought his drink back and sat down once more. "A shark, flowers, and a star." He drank deeply.

"You don't know what it means, do you?" I said. If he didn't, then maybe I could pull a Scheherazade and spin this tale out over a thousand and one nights.

The vampire dabbed his mouth with a linen napkin, then he gave me a pitying smile. "I knew what part of it meant, but thanks to you, I now have the entire puzzle sorted. Tatiana, your parents, and a magic amplifier."

My heart sunk. "What do you mean, thanks to me? I didn't know what it meant when Yoshi..." I faltered at Zev's darkening expression. "When he learned about it."

The vampire sighed. "No, but you left a trail that anyone with half a brain and a limited understanding of events could follow."

I shrank back against the chair. "Did you kill James?"

"Ah, yes. Professor Learsdon." He stood up. "Walk with me."

He led me through an unfamiliar door and down a set of narrow stone stairs. I had my hands on the walls for balance because my legs shook so badly. There was only one thing down here.

The dungeon.

We stopped at a dead end. The single heavy door was lit on either side by electric torches.

"Look." I pressed my legs together, my inner thighs

sweating. "I don't want any trouble and I certainly don't want Tatiana to be hurt—hurt more than she has been."

He laughed mercilessly. "You think that's possible once she finds out what your parents did? Oh, she'll be hurt." He wagged a finger at me. "Tanechka has a legendary temper. I can't wait to see its full extent once more."

I gulped audibly, but if Tatiana got mad, then she didn't already know. My shoulders relaxed. She hadn't hired me because of the accident. Would she fire me for it? Worse? "What if I don't tell her?"

"That won't do. No." He stroked his goatee. "You'll have to set things right."

"How? My parents are dead and I doubt an apology from me is going to cut it."

"Aren't you curious how Noah and Adele Blum, two grifters so minor as to be irrelevant, managed to get the jump on the only female macher in the world? A shark?"

I bit down on my lip so hard to keep from laying into him about shitting on my parents that I tasted blood. "I'm really not," I said in a remarkably even voice.

Zev pressed his hand against a brass panel on the door and it creaked open. "You should be."

"Let me out!" a man cried.

I peered into the gloom. "James?"

"Yes. It's me. Who are you?" He squinted at me through two swollen eyes, leaning forward and rattling the chains attaching his handcuffs to the wall. Dirt matted his hair and his short beard was patchy. He stood with his weight on one foot, his other foot bent upward at a disturbing angle.

"Professor Learsdon," Zev said. "I believe you've met Ms. Feldman." He escorted me into the dungeon, his hand on my back.

I eeped, but the vamp didn't leave me there. No, he stood beside me, immaculately groomed and smelling of a light cologne, where I stank of sweat and James of filth and urine.

"How long have you been here?" I said, attempting to block my memories of my previous visit to this place.

The man shook his head and Zev waved a hand like it was of no importance.

"Ask your questions, Ms. Feldman," Zev said.

"I told you, I don't know any more," the professor cried.

Zev slapped him across the face. The sound cracked off the walls. "I despise whining even more than ignorance."

"Help me," James whispered.

Zev rolled his eyes then winked at me like we were co-conspirators.

I made a noise that was somewhere between a snort, a cough, and a laugh. I was numb, though whether from the cold dungeon or what I was about to hear, I couldn't say.

"Proceed," Zev said.

"Who did you tell about my magic?" I said.

The vampire shook his head and sighed.

A hot rush flared up inside me. *Sorry if I wasn't asking the questions to your liking.*

"No one," James rasped. "I swear. I didn't want anyone else to know about you." He got a dreamy look on his face. "I spent years following whispers about the Ascendant. Finding this treasure and unlocking the mystery of why an amplifier was valuable enough to kill for would have been my greatest achievement." He broke into a coughing fit.

Zev narrowed his eyes and James visibly fought his coughs down.

"What about my parents?" I touched the fingertip that the raven from Poe's cards had bitten, swallowing the question I really wanted to ask. *Is killing in my blood?* "What do you know about them?"

I'd made a choice, picked the side of loving them no matter what I learned. I'd had to hide my complicated emotions around them for so long because of the secrecy surrounding their murders and I felt like a dam had burst. I wanted to hear any scrap, any story, I could. And I wanted to finally talk to Sadie about them.

James looked at me blankly; he had nothing to contribute.

Heels clattered over the stone floor, growing closer. A busty blonde woman in red leather pants and a red blouse sashayed in, dragging an unconscious Rodrigo, who must have been three times her weight. She dropped him like trash at Zev's feet.

Zev glanced down at his minion. "Did you kill him, Dagmar?" His voice was pinched.

I took another step back into the shadows to book it into the KH, but Zev calmly reached behind and clamped onto my wrist, hauling me forward to stand next to him.

The female vamp didn't even glance at me, busy examining her long red nails. "Don't be such a diva." Her accent was pure Boston.

I stifled my laugh like my life depended on it.

Zev's lips tightened, his fingers boring into my flesh.

She trailed one nail along James's jaw. "Did you mess with the elixir formula?"

Even Zev watched the man intently for his answer.

"I didn't. I swear. I told you it was never guaranteed—"

Dagmar lightly slapped his face. "That was your last chance."

Part of me wondered what this was all about, but I was scared that even a hint of curiosity in my expression would draw unwanted attention to me.

"This was a waste of time," she said to Zev. "Let's wrap this up and I'll go home." She ran a hand along her sleek mane. "The moisture in this climate is shit for my hair."

"Please don't give me to her," James begged Zev.

"I promised I wouldn't. And I always keep my promises, don't I, Ms. Feldman?"

"Ye-yes."

Dagmar snorted.

Zev released me and calmly snapped James's neck. The man's head fell forward at such an angle that his lifeless eyes bored into mine.

Dagmar and Zev kissed cheeks, while I hyperventilated, wondering if I'd still be sane when I got out of here.

I inadvertently glanced at James once more.

Or alive.

"Never change, kid," Dagmar said fondly to Zev. Kid? How old was she?

"Really, Dagmar," Zev said with a touch of impatience.

Laughing, the female vamp strutted off, leaving only a hint of rose perfume to show that she was ever there at all.

Well, that and a dead James Learsdon.

Zev prodded Rodrigo with the toe of his highly polished shoe. The man gave a slurred moan but didn't stir. "I told you not to take your eyes off her, Rodrigo." Shaking his head, Zev motioned for me to precede him into the hallway.

"It seems it falls to me to tell you this story," he said.

No more stories, please. I didn't want any more shared confidences with the vampire, especially not one this contentious. But since it wasn't a request, I gave a hesitant nod.

"Thirty years ago, Tatiana was hired to track down a magic amulet by a client who wished to remain anonymous." His tread up the stairs was even and sure-footed, where I jumped at every tiny sound. "She didn't think much of it. The item in question wasn't one she'd ever heard of and as far as she could tell, there was no one else on its trail." He turned suddenly, his eyes gleaming, and I almost had a heart attack. "You think she's something to behold now, she was magnificent back then. And even so, it took her three years to find it. She was on her way to the drop-off with the item when the car accident—sorry." He held up both his hands like he'd made a grievous faux pas. "Attempted murder occurred."

I reached the top stair and turned into the basement proper, my jaw tight.

"Until about a week ago, I too thought it was an accident." From the casual way Zev strolled back to his office, nodding at employees getting ready for the night's clientele, you'd have thought he was telling me a charming anecdote. "Not only did Tatiana have to learn to walk again, she had to rebuild her reputation as a macher because she'd lost the amplifier. It was the biggest blemish of her career."

"That was a worse tragedy in her mind than the paralysis, wasn't it?"

He stroked his goatee, a thoughtful expression on his face. "She said you were perceptive."

I lagged a second behind him. Had Zev just complimented me in a roundabout way?

"What I learned in the past few days, thanks to the good professor, was that two nobodies who weren't on anyone's radar were promised a huge payoff if they stopped her from delivering the Ascendant."

I gritted my teeth against the urge to allow Delilah free rein with the scythe. This was the second time he'd insulted my mom and dad. "I get that my parents weren't in Tatiana's league, but they weren't nobodies, okay?"

They took me to the beach to cool off in the water and poke through tide pools on an overcast day. They read my favorite story books to me over and over, my mom complaining about me begging for just one more, but always giving in. No matter what they'd done, they'd loved me, and I'd loved them.

Maybe this journey wasn't so much about information and facts, but finally getting to properly mourn them.

"They meant something to me," I said.

"Apologies." There was no sincerity behind it.

"And if they had this magic amplifier, it was taken when they were murdered at a later date because I'd never heard of it before or seen anything like what Poe described to me."

"If I thought you did, you wouldn't be walking away

alive." He smiled with a hint of fang. "Should you unleash your shadow, you still may not."

I stuffed my magic deep inside me. "Why would anyone care about this amplifier so much?"

His eyes glittered dangerously for a second before he smoothed out his expression back to his polite mask and ushered me into his office. "Why indeed? That's what I'd like to know."

I didn't believe him. He did know. Something.

The air around me sharpened like a noose and I dug my nails into my palms to keep my heart from racing, because I had the sense that if I questioned him or even hinted that I believed he had more information at his disposal than he was letting on, it would go badly for me.

"That makes two of us," I said as casually as possible, sitting down. "And?"

Zev claimed his seat behind the desk. "That's where you come in."

Dread slithered up my spine at the thought of Zev involving himself in my past. "I'd rather leave well enough alone," I lied. "And besides, won't Tatiana get upset having all this dredged up?"

"Tatiana isn't going to know." He sipped from the now-room-temperature synthetic blood in his cup and I tried not to gag. "Yet. The reason that Professor Learsdon tested you was that the search for the Ascendant has begun again."

I clasped my hands behind my back, digging my nails into my flesh, but keeping my expression calm. "Who's looking for it?"

"Learsdon didn't know, but he intended to blackmail you with that test he arranged into helping him find it. Sadly, he hadn't done his research thoroughly and didn't realize that you could stop an enthralled Ohrist without murdering them."

"Son of a bitch," I muttered.

Zev lifted the still half-full cup from earlier, sniffed it, and set it down again. "As far as I've been able to ascertain, whomever is on the hunt for it does not yet know about you. Or rather, doesn't know you have magic and are therefore a resource. You can either accept your fate and my protection or you can bury your head in the sand and hope for the best. It's a limited-time offer."

I threw up my hands. "What's a limited-time offer? I don't understand what you want."

The vampire leaned forward, his hands folded in front of him. "The Ascendant. Find it and give it to me."

Thank you for reading A SHADE OF MYSELF!

Things heat up in THE SHADE OF THINGS (MAGIC AFTER MIDLIFE #5).

Miriam Feldman's life has become *Running Man* with a side of *Squid Game* when she'd much prefer *The Great British Bake Off*.

When Miri partners up with her detective ex-husband on an off-the-books magical missing persons operation, she expects buddy cop adventures galore. Instead, she gets more than she bargained for, starting with a mouthy golem who's forced onto the team. Their mission? Crash a secret—and deadly—competition targeting non-magic humans to rescue the young woman at the heart of their case.

So, a regular Thursday nowadays.

If that funhouse of horrors wasn't enough, she still must fulfill her oath to a master vamp by locating the artifact bound up with her parents' murders almost thirty years ago. He refuses to say why he wants it, but all signs point to "Danger Danger Will Robinson."

All of that leaves no time in her schedule for sexy times with a certain wolf shifter. Which is probably just as well, seeing as he doesn't know she's been forced to keep secrets from him, too.

Laugh? Cry? Coffee!

Featuring intelligent snark, a slow burn shifter romance, and the perfect dash of steamy sexiness, this complete mystery adventure series will take you on a hilarious wild ride.

Let's get you reading!

Turn the page for an excerpt of *The Shade of Things...*

EXCERPT FROM THE SHADE OF THINGS

The once-elegant gothic manor hulked like a boxer down on his luck. The upper broken window and front door hanging partially off its hinges gave the impression of a bruised eye and a missing tooth while the sagging roof was like a head hunched into its shoulders.

"This can't be where Damien lives," Eli said. "He'd get fried by the sunshine pouring in through all the holes."

"The description of the bloodsucker who lives here matches Damien," I said, hands on my hips.

Eli snorted. "And you trust Tatiana's information on this?"

I squirmed uneasily at the mention of my boss. Not because I doubted her, but because hearing her name reminded me that I wasn't being wholly truthful with her. About a week ago, I'd discovered a bombshell of a secret tying my parents to her.

Not only had I kept Tatiana in the dark, I'd done the same to Laurent, her sexy wolf shifter nephew with whom I'd hooked up. To be fair, he'd been away in the interior of the province stalking a dybbuk, and it wasn't exactly a conversation to have over the phone, but that wasn't the real reason I'd been reluctant to talk about it with him.

Zev BatKian, Vancouver's head vampire, had recently hired me to find the Ascendant for him. I snorted. If by "hired me" you meant "blackmailed me viciously and without remorse," then sure. The new condition of all this protection was that he'd sworn me to secrecy about both this job and the magic amplifier in general until he decreed otherwise. Telling either Tatiana or Laurent was out of the question—for now—despite my wishes.

I was sick and tired of Zev using me to fulfill some unknown agenda and angry that I was left with no real choice but to accede to his demands.

I sighed. Those were problems for future me.

Eli shredded a couple of long grass stalks. "Ian's last known address was a shelter and the residents there are transient. Yes, the employee I interviewed remembered him going off with someone who matched Damien's description, and when you suggested we look into the vamps and got a connection, I was hopeful. But looking at this dump?" He brushed grass off his hands. "I'm second-guessing that employee's memory. That or we were too quick to ascribe the mystery person Ian went off with to a vampire."

"It's the only lead we have. Damien does have a Sapien donor, so that's another point for this being the right place."

We snuck through the unkempt weed-choked grass to the rotted front steps. Really the house was best viewed at a distance. Like from the moon.

The first tread creaked under my foot, and the house seemed to shiver, exuding a gust of stagnant air. A family of mice peeked their heads up through a jagged hole.

Eli tested his weight on the unvarnished stairs, which were slippery with moss, but when the stairs held, he quickly joined me on the porch, once more taking shelter under my invisibility mesh. He pulled out a penlight. "Can anyone see this light if we're cloaked?"

I shrugged, peering inside. "The floorboards are all twisted, and I'd rather not break an ankle, so let's chance it."

Eli cast the light around the entrance hall.

The interior walls were cold to the touch. The tattered remnants of wallpaper were sun-bleached almost colorless save for dark spores of mold that blossomed like a Rorschach test. Rusted wires hung from the ceiling, but any lighting had been stripped.

For all the general decay, the blackout curtains over the windows were nearly new. I jostled Eli's elbow. "Dead give-away." I gave an exaggerated wink. "Or should I say undead giveaway."

My partner groaned.

The stairs leading to the second floor listed dangerously so we headed downstairs first. The stairwell was narrow and twisty but at least the treads were solid. It led to a damp basement, which was just as deserted as the rest of the house.

Most of the space was taken up by an enormous ballroom, where sheets thrown over furniture cast menacing shadows. The warped floorboards with inlaid mother-of-pearl beckoned to be waltzed upon, to be spun, dazed and flushed, by an attractive partner across the room.

Leaving footprints in the thick layer of dust, we wandered through pillars still bearing faint traces of gold gilding. Thanks to a series of warped glass doors, which led out to a wild overgrown garden, there was just enough light to make out the ceiling boasting ornate crown molding.

I could almost hear strains of music over the musty air blowing through the broken panes.

Eli tugged on a crystal knob, but the glass door was stuck fast. "We'll have to check out the top floor, but it looks like this place has been deserted for ages."

I shook my head. "Why hang blackout curtains in a deserted house?"

"Or even just hang them in the entrance hall? Did you see a coffin with a sleeping vamp there? Because I sure as hell didn't." Eli was getting testy, but it wasn't directed at me, and I didn't take it personally. He toed at the dust, erasing a footprint. "We're clearly the only ones who've been down here."

I frowned, teasing out a thought. "Oh! That's it. Come on."

Grabbing his sleeve, I tugged him back up the stairs and into the entrance hall. "Look. The floor is dust-free."

Eli frowned. "So?"

"That means it's been walked on. Damien has been here, which explains the blackout curtains. Hopefully Ian is with him."

"Then where are they now?"

"If I'm right?" I led him outside, turning to examine the rotting door barely holding on to the frame.

Eli prodded me impatiently. "If you're right, what?"

After a moment, a front door zoomed out toward us like a 3D stereogram. The solid modern structure clicked into the frame, almost slyly, as if saying *Little old me? I was here all the time.* Even so its reveal didn't give me the rush of watching a stage magician's showy flourish. It was more a quiet delight that I had access to secrets. Like finding an old book in an archive that you needed or digging up a piece of information at just the right time.

Eli gasped.

"They're still here." Grinning, I pushed on the handle running vertically along the right side and swung the door open.

BECOME A WILDE ONE

If you enjoyed this book and want to be first in the know about bonus content, reveals, and exclusive giveaways, become a Wilde One by joining my newsletter: http://www.deborahwilde.com/subscribe

You'll immediately receive short stories set in my different worlds and available only to my newsletter subscribers. There are mild spoilers so they're best enjoyed in the recommended reading order.

If you just want to know about my new releases, please join my list at: https://deborahwildebooks.com

ACKNOWLEDGMENTS

All the thanks and gratitude to my Deborah's Wilde Ones moderators and world domination co-conspirators Erli and Deb. I am very lucky to have you both in my corner!

Dr. Alex Yuschik, my incredible editor, every book is a joy to work on with you.

To my husband and daughter, thank you for believing in me and coming on this journey with me in ways none of us ever anticipated. Team E.K. for the win!

Finally, I want to thank the many authors who have been so supportive and generous with their advice and friendship. Most of the writers I've gotten to know in the uf, pwf, and romance spheres are women with the belief that a rising tide lifts all boats. Hopefully we will meet IRL soon.

ABOUT THE AUTHOR

Former screenwriter, global wanderer, and total cynic with a broken edit button, Deborah Wilde writes funny, sexy urban fantasy books and paranormal women's fiction.

Smart, sassy women who can solve a mystery, kick supernatural butt, banter with hot men, and still make time for their best female friend are the cornerstones of Deborah's stories. Her books are beloved by readers craving magic adventures, swoon worthy steamy romances, hilarity, and happily ever after.

"Magic, sparks, and snark!"

www.deborahwilde.com